MW01600399

About Rage's Echo

Rage's Echo is not just for horror fans, but for anyone who ever wondered about the implications and manifestations of unforgiveness turned into an obsession. The mystery, intrigue and heart pounding moments illustrate that J.S. Bailey has the ability to pull the reader in and keep their full attention until ALL has been revealed. One woman hunts for ghosts looking for answers about an afterlife, but receives so much more than she expects to find resulting in redemption. Please do not read this book before bedtime, but do be prepared to see the spiritual realm in a whole new way. Rage's Echo is more than just a creepy story; its characters experience fear, friendship and romance as well. J.S. Bailey shows talent equal to Ted Dekker and Dean Koontz; I look forward to reading her books for years to come!

—Kara Grant, A BookLover's Heart

The premise is rather "out there," especially for Christian fiction. Ghosts sort of fly in the face (pun maybe intended) of the orthodox view of the afterlife. But for readers that can appreciate good fiction with a poignant theme, *Rage's Echo* is a solid novel filled with suspense and intrigue... More than a "Christian paranormal suspense" novel, *Rage's Echo* is heavily relational, digging into relevant themes that are a part of all human interaction. None of this takes away from the suspense, which is racheted up in the second half of the novel. And it all boils down to a twist ending that most readers will never see coming.

—Josh Olds, FictionAddict.com

An eerie thriller saturated with suspense and embodying altering twists around every corner. J.S. Bailey possesses a superb writing style that is sure to impress.

—Gavin Pierce, GavinReviews.com

RAGE'S ECHO

To Gloria—

Read...if you dare!

RAGE'S
ECHO

J.S. BAILEY

JS Bailey
3/19/2014

TATE PUBLISHING
AND ENTERPRISES, LLC

Published by Tate Publishing & Enterprises, LLC
127 E. Trade Center Terrace | Mustang, Oklahoma 73064 USA
1.888.361.9473 | www.tatepublishing.com

Tate Publishing is committed to excellence in the publishing industry. The company reflects the philosophy established by the founders, based on Psalm 68:11,
"The Lord gave the word and great was the company of those who published it."

Book design copyright © 2013 by Tate Publishing, LLC. All rights reserved.
Cover design by Allen Jomoc
Interior design by Deborah Toling

Published in the United States of America

ISBN: 978-1-62746-622-6
1. Fiction / Fantasy / Paranormal
2. Fiction / Christian / Suspense
13.06.20

DEDICATION

For Nathan, whose patience, love, and devotion deserve an award.

ACKNOWLEDGMENTS

No author writes a novel alone, and the one you hold in your hands is no different. First and foremost I would like to thank my husband, Nathan, as well as my family, friends, and readers for their undying support in this harebrained endeavor called being an author. I also extend a heaping amount of thanks to Abby Ryan and Kara Grant, who have served as my extra sets of editorial eyeballs on multiple occasions; Janel Schmid, who reigns as my biggest critic; Esther Carlier, who proudly holds the title of biggest fan; Valerie Smith, whose terrifying tale of a haunted dorm room jump-started my imagination; Shawnta Brown, who answered some of my questions about cerebral palsy; and Dante Alighieri, whose *Inferno* provided some of the best inspiration a girl could ever ask for. And last but certainly not least, I have to thank the one who not only blessed me with the ability to tell this story, but held my hand when I needed it the most.

CHAPTER 1

A sound awakened him from a restless slumber.

He stared at the ceiling for a moment. Of course, the sound had been the figment of some fading dream. It was foolish to worry. Even if he hadn't imagined the sound, it was probably nothing more than a vehicle driving by outside or the house settling on its foundation. Children became frightened by these things, not him. The years of lying awake at night and calling for his mother to come save him from the monsters in the dark had long since passed away.

He closed his eyes with the hopes of drifting back to that world where the troubles of the daytime melted into oblivion, but suddenly a floorboard in the room emitted a low creak as if someone were standing upon it.

He lifted his head and peered out into the room. At first he could see nothing, but when his eyes adjusted to the darkness, he saw them.

Five—no, six—silhouettes stood in a semicircle around the foot of his bed. The moonlight filtering through the drapes made them blacker than the surrounding shadows.

Before he could respond to the intrusion, he felt a sharp twinge on the upper part of his left arm. He yelped in surprise and rolled onto his side, only to see that a seventh silhouette stood inches from the edge of his bed. Two pinpricks of reflected light floated in the air. Eyes.

His pulse quickened. "What do you want from me?" he croaked, even though he already knew the answer.

It was so quiet that he swore he heard blood rushing through his veins as anxiety pushed his heart to the limit. Sweat began to run down his forehead. Why wouldn't they just answer him? Perhaps this was some new kind of psychological warfare: standing in the dark and waiting in silence until their victim went mad. It might prove effective.

He tried to sit up and reason with them, but his body felt as though it had turned to rubber. Was he drugged?

The thing next to him jerked its head to the side. Three of the other silhouettes broke away from their group. One joined the first silhouette on the left. The remaining two came up to the right. He was surrounded. No way to escape, unless a guardian angel tucked him under its wings and carried him away to safety.

Everything was still.

But he could hear them breathing.

He didn't dare close his eyes. *God, grant me the serenity…*

Four sets of arms grabbed him suddenly and flipped him over onto his stomach. His own arms were wrenched behind him, and his wrists were crossed and held in place by unseen fingers. He could hear duct tape being torn off a roll. He writhed around to break free from their grasp. It was no use. His hands were bound behind him.

One of the silhouettes at the foot of the bed let out a choked sob.

Cloth was placed over his head (a sack?), and the phantoms wrapped more tape around his ankles and lifted him from the bed. He was limp as a rag doll. Whatever they had drugged him with was working quite well.

The phantoms made no effort to ease his discomfort. They jostled him around as if he were a bag of refuse they were hauling away to a bin. His head banged against the wall as they carried him down the stairs. He cried out to deaf ears.

He heard a squeak. Felt a gust of air. They were taking him outside. Now, crickets. Chirping in the yard. An engine idled close by. A car door opened, and he was shoved onto a sticky leather seat. A radio was playing some Led Zeppelin song, "Dazed and Confused." How fitting.

The phantoms climbed in with him. The one on his right smelled like Old Spice.

Doors slammed closed. Seatbelts clicked. Someone killed the radio.

The car lurched as it moved away from the curb.

Tears stung his eyes. This couldn't be happening. It had to be a dream. A nightmare. His own imagination torturing him while he slept.

But one could not imagine the terror that crippled him or the coarse fabric that scratched against his face with each of his movements or the throbbing in his head where he'd hit it on the wall.

He knew these feelings were real.

He also knew that he would not end this night alive.

CHAPTER 2

Wayne Thompson was sitting at the wrought-iron patio table on his deck and frowning at the spreadsheet he had pulled up on the screen of his computer when his cousin Sidney Miller stepped outside to have a smoke.

He looked up when he heard the soft footsteps of her approach.

Sidney stood in the small realm of light provided by the porch light mounted above the screen door. The single bulb brought out the shine in her red hair, which she had tied back into a bun and adorned with a pair of decorative chopsticks that crisscrossed in an X shape. Wayne's own hair was as dark as black coffee. He and Sidney hardly resembled each other at all.

"Nice out here, isn't it?" she said without enthusiasm. She slid a cigarette from its box and stuck it between her lips. She patted the pockets of her black skinny jeans. "Crap, I left my lighter in the house. Can you toss me that one?"

Wayne had lit a citronella candle to ward off any mosquitoes that might still be hanging around this time of year and left the Bic lighter lying on the table. He picked it up and threw it in Sidney's direction without looking. It hit the wooden planks of the deck with a *thunk*.

"What's the matter?" she asked him, bending to snatch the lighter from the ground.

"You know those things are going to kill you," he said.

She shrugged and lit the cigarette anyway—a Camel Menthol.

Wayne returned his attention to the computer screen, where their unpleasant financial situation was laid bare in a grid of columns and rows. "Would it upset you if I bumped up your rent?"

Sidney was at his side in an instant. Bad news could always perk her up. She leaned in to get a better look at the spreadsheet. Wayne could see its reflection in the lenses of her glasses.

"Oh." She straightened a little. "I thought you said you have a fixed-rate loan."

"I do. The increase is from my homeowner's insurance."

"That stinks."

It didn't stink nearly as much as the smoke she was puffing out into the night air, but he didn't tell her that. At least she had the tact not to do it in his house.

"Would an extra twenty a month be too much?"

"It beats the alternative." She went and leaned against the wooden railing that surrounded most of the deck and gazed vacantly out into the yard. Wayne didn't know what thoughts were running through her mind. He wouldn't ask her.

Oh, well. Sidney could stay out here as long as she wanted, but he was going to go inside before his lungs started filling up with second-hand smoke.

He snapped the lid of his laptop closed and blew out the candle.

"Going in?" Sidney asked. There was a melancholic note in her voice that made him feel guilty for leaving her.

"If I stay out here, I'm going to develop black lung disease."

"Jerk."

He smiled. "Not me." Using the table for support, he pulled himself to his feet. The shift in position made his calves itch beneath his ankle-foot orthotics. It didn't bother him as much as it used to. Some things he'd learned to ignore. Like the unwanted stares.

He tucked the laptop under his arm. It hadn't rained in about two months, and if Sidney tossed the smoldering cigarette butt out into the yellowed grass, it would probably ignite the lot in about two seconds. "Try not to catch the yard on fire."

Sidney made a snorting noise that might have been a laugh. "No promises. But maybe if this place burns to the ground, that homeowner's insurance you've got will let you build a mansion here instead."

"Yes, because a foreclosed mansion is exactly what I need." He limped across the deck. People referred to his way of walking as a "scissors" gait, which he'd always thought was dumb because it made him sound like he was a giant, anthropomorphic pair of shears. Wayne Scissorlegs. The very thought made him shudder.

He paused for a moment in the mudroom to glance back at his cousin as she took a seat at the patio table and drew her knees to her chest. Her face was long, and for a moment she looked much older than her nineteen years. Her shoulders began to quake. She was crying again.

Seeing her like this put a knife through his heart. He was about as adept at offering sympathy as he was at doing the triathlon—and he couldn't do *that* at all.

Sidney's mother had been the one they all turned to when they needed words of encouragement or a shoulder to cry on. But Marjorie Miller was dead. Brain cancer struck her down when she was only forty. That was a year and a half ago. It felt like an eternity.

Marjorie had been a mother to him, too. Even though she had been only twelve years his senior, and even though she knew about the awful thing he'd done, she'd taken him in and loved him just as much as her own children. That had taken guts, he supposed. The two foster families he'd briefly lived with subsequent to the awful thing had feared him so much that he'd only stayed with them for a couple months each. Marjorie had been patient with him, though. She'd taught him that anger and hatred weren't going to fix what had happened.

Sidney began to cheer up when she moved in with him after her mother's death. Since Marjorie and Drew Miller became Wayne's legal guardians when he was fourteen years old, he and Sidney felt more like siblings than cousins, and moving in with her "brother" turned out to be a much-needed change of scenery for her.

Yet Sidney would still sink into a deep depression every month or so. Wayne wished she would find the strength within herself to move on and heal.

After depositing the computer on a clean section of the Formica countertop, Wayne shuffled over to the refrigerator and grabbed a Mike's Hard Lemonade out of one of the crisper drawers. He pried off the cap and took a long, satisfying gulp. Alcohol in moderation was tonic for the soul.

He heard the squeak-click of the back door opening and closing. Sidney walked into the kitchen and threw the remains of her cigarette into the corner wastebasket. Her eyes were rimmed in red.

"I thought Jessica was coming over tonight," she said. "Do you think something could have happened to her?"

"No, she's fine. She's packing." At least he hoped she was.

Sidney frowned. "What do you mean, packing? She's not going on vacation, is she?"

Wayne laughed and took another sip from the bottle. "I wouldn't call it that." Their good friend Jessica Roman-Dell had recently lost her job as a gas station clerk. She'd had enough money in savings to last her two weeks, and those two weeks had come and gone without her finding another source of income. She called Wayne that morning in tears to tell him that she couldn't afford the rent on her apartment anymore. (She had declined his suggestion to go work the street corners downtown for some extra cash.) There was only one thing he could do to help her.

"I hope you don't mind having a roommate," he said.

A look of comprehension appeared on her face. "Oh. *That* kind of packing."

"She told me that if you don't want her in your room, she'd take the basement or junk room instead."

"Yeah, right. She hasn't seen the spiders." She rolled her eyes. "*Packing*. Why is it that I have such a hard time picturing that?"

Wayne finished the Mike's and set the bottle in the sink. "I haven't the slightest idea."

~~~~~

Jessica Roman-Dell was not packing.

Sure, she had *started* packing, but then Ellen Shoushanian called her on the phone and asked Jessica if she wanted to come investigate the woman's house that evening.

Jessica, sitting in a cleared island amid a sea of her scattered belongings, looked from the mound of folded clothing she had been piling into a box to the cat-shaped clock on the wall. It was five-thirty.

"I can be there at six," she said.

Now it was nearing ten o'clock, and Jessica began to pray that something interesting would happen before she died of boredom in Vince and Ellen Shoushanian's moldy basement.

Ellen's words from hours earlier drifted through her thoughts.

Things are constantly moving around by themselves whenever Vince and I've gone out. Would you believe I found the TV remote in the back of the deep freeze one time? Vince swears he had nothing to do with it. But you know, nothing's as odd as the time we came home from church one morning and the spice rack was sitting in the middle of the stairs.

Jessica had considered asking if Alzheimer's might be an explanation for these so-called misplaced objects. The Shoushanians were only in their sixties, but you never knew when someone's mind might start to go.

Misplaced objects weren't the only concerns in the Shoushanian household. Vince claimed to have seen the apparition of a young man two or three times, and both of them swore they had heard lively conversations coming from empty rooms late at night.

Loud radios in passing cars, Jessica had thought, but again she'd remained silent. She had an open mind. If there was a chance she might encounter a ghost, she was willing to take it.

Jessica shivered. She shouldn't have worn flip-flops on this outing. The day had been warm, but the dampness of the basement chilled her. A pipe was leaking somewhere close by. The endless *drip-drip-drip* made her think of Chinese water torture, and she yearned for a ghost to appear to distract her from the sound.

She picked up her thermal imaging camera and panned the room for the umpteenth time, looking for any anomalies in temperature that might indicate the presence of a spirit. The only yellow-orange heat signatures she could see on the tiny screen came from the water heater and some pipes that branched off from it in different directions. She sighed and stared up at the cobwebbed rafters.

"If you're really here," she said, "it would be great if you could come out and say hello."

Silence answered her, as it usually did. Investigations like this were frustrating, especially when you sat and sat and sat for half the night without one blessed thing happening that could be ascribed to the spirits she longed to exist. Sometimes she wondered why she kept at it at all. It was probably the same reason why gambling addicts lost entire paychecks at the craps tables on Saturday nights and kept coming back for more: one night of triumph would overshadow a hundred of failure.

A cricket started chirping off in the corner. Like the leaking pipe, Jessica tried to ignore it.

"Are you just being shy?" she asked. "I can be shy too sometimes. But I am a lot more outgoing than I used to be. Working at the gas station for four years helped a lot with that. Did you used to work somewhere?"

More silence.

She lifted the thermal imaging camera from her lap again and gave the room another sweep. Nada.

This was starting to look like one big waste of time, just like her parents always told her. She could have been at home doing something more productive, like eating microwaveable burritos and watching ancient reruns of *The Carol Burnett Show*—and packing.

It was surprising that her parents cared anything about her hobby, even if in a negative way. The two of them were so caring that they forgot to call her on her last birthday to congratulate her for making it to twenty-one all in one piece. A week later they mailed her a card containing a check for twenty dollars. She used the money to buy more frozen burritos and counted out the remaining change to put in her gasoline fund.

Jessica spoke for a third time. "Can you tell me what your name is?"

If the ghost had a name, she couldn't hear it. She continued. "My name's Jessica Roman-Dell. A lot of people ask me what kind of last name that is, and I just tell them that a million years ago a Roman married a Dell and they got in a huge fight about what last name their kids would have, and neither of them would give in, so in the end they just combined the two. They'd have called the kids Dell-Roman instead, but that sounds stupid. My dad probably knows the real origin of the name, but I never asked him. I don't get along with my parents very well. Did you get along with your parents?"

She waited five more minutes for a response yet heard nothing. With any luck, the digital voice recorder she'd set on the floor would have picked up some kind of ghostly dialogue that had been below her hearing threshold.

Jessica rose from the uncomfortable chair and went upstairs to see if she would have better luck in the kitchen. At least the air would be warmer, and there would be no leaking plumbing or noisy crickets to distract her from her work.

She struggled to see as she ascended the dark stairwell into the living room. A candle had been left burning in the adjoining kitchen, and the light from its feeble flame cast eerie shadows over the walls.

The solitary flame reminded her of the aloneness she felt at being the only living person in the house. Hours before, both Shoushanians had left to go spend the night at their daughter's house so they wouldn't unintentionally interfere with the investigation.

Now Jessica wished that someone could be here to interfere with the absence of companionship. Neither Wayne nor Sidney ever wished to accompany her on these outings. Wayne frequently used the excuse that the sight of him might frighten away any self-respecting spirit, and Sidney—well, her excuses tended to change with the tides on a far-off shore.

Jessica sat down at the butcher-block table in the kitchen. Other people her age were probably sitting at home watching dirty movies and getting drunk. Her parents should have been grateful that she was doing work in the name of faith and science. Just imagine if she found proof that ghosts truly did exist! The afterlife would no longer be viewed as myth but as reality. Hearts could be changed. Maybe it would even make some people start going to church. That would be the coolest thing of all.

She closed her eyes and waited.

The night outside seemed to sigh with the wind that rustled past the house. She heard countless dead leaves blowing over and under each other in their mad dash to the east, where they would no doubt pile up a foot deep along a fence and later serve as a soft playground for the neighborhood kids to jump in.

The candle on the table made a loud *pop*, and Jessica jumped. Maybe it was a good thing that her friends weren't there, because they would have teased her for being such a coward. And a coward was something that Jessica was trying very hard not to be.

Suddenly, a soft, muted squeak echoed down from the second floor of the home. She was on her feet in an instant. She tiptoed over to the staircase. The noise was louder here but still hardly more perceptible than a whisper. She took the stairs one at a time, being careful not to let her footsteps be heard lest she frighten whatever was causing it.

She arrived in a short hallway that had a hardwood floor. A door on the right was ajar, and a thin ribbon of silvery light spilled onto the landing.

She held her ear to the gap between the door and its frame. The squeaking was coming from the room that lay on the other side. This was the moment she had been waiting for all evening. Before she chickened out and went running back downstairs (a sure-fire way to destroy her fearless ghost hunter image), she pushed the door open the rest of the way and stepped inside.

Jessica's emotions made a split-second metamorphosis from anticipation to disgust to embarrassment. In a cage beneath the window, through which shined the light from a streetlamp, a hamster was racing on his exercise wheel, looking like he was having the time of his life.

A sharp cry from the bedroom across the hall gave Sidney a start.

She had spent the last hour rearranging her small quarters to better accommodate Jessica's twin bed. Jessica may have been her friend, but it irked her that Wayne had not given her fair warning about Jessica's impending arrival in their household. She knew she shouldn't complain. It was *his* house, not hers, and besides, Jessica had nowhere else to go. Well, she could have moved in with her parents. Sidney had laughed at that thought. That family had more issues than a magazine.

Sidney had finally finished scooting aside her furniture and floor lamp and settled down on her own bed to begin working on an English assignment (read "Alone" by Edgar Allan Poe, and write six whole pages about what you think it means and how it relates to you, blah blah blah) when Wayne's unmistakable holler derailed her concentration.

She stared through the open doorway at his bedroom door that was shut, as usual. Of course he was just having a nightmare. He often did, which she knew because of the hair-raising screams she had heard on other nights.

She wished he wouldn't talk in his sleep. Wayne had had a very unhappy childhood before he came to live with her family, and though he never spoke of those things during his waking hours, his subconscious mind never ceased to broadcast his memories through the house at night.

She wondered what Jessica would think of their friend's nighttime utterances. Sidney had never told her about Wayne's origins. Wayne probably hadn't either.

Jessica was bound to receive a thorough education by the end of the week.

Sidney refocused her attention and began to read "Alone" out loud for the second time.

> From childhood's hour I have not been
> As others were; I have not seen
> As others saw; I could not bring
> My passions from a common spring...

She broke off. Her drowsiness due to the late hour was causing the words to blur on the page. She blinked a few times to clear her eyes, but she was too tired to concentrate.

Wayne let out another yell. She should probably check on him. She often feared that he might accidentally thrash around so hard in his sleep that he would roll off his bed and give himself a concussion on the nightstand. Even worse, he could fracture his skull and die, further decreasing the number of loved ones she had left in the world.

Wayne was almost eleven years older than she, but Sidney still felt a maternal duty to make sure he wasn't hurt.

She rose from her bed and quietly opened his bedroom door. She could hear him weeping in the dark, muttering unintelligible words too low for her to hear. Suddenly his voice became louder, more plaintive.

"It hurts!" he cried. In the low light she saw him lifting his arm over his face as if deflecting a blow. His skull appeared to be unharmed, thank goodness. "God, make her *stop*! Sweet Jesus, how did you? How did you? How'd..." This changed into a long string of garbled syllables that didn't make any sense.

Wayne was fine; that was good. Time to leave him alone and go to sleep like she should have done hours ago.

She smirked as she backed out of the room and closed the door. Jessica was going to have a blast.

CHAPTER 3

D aybreak.
Jessica staggered out of bed, wincing as she stood up.
Her arms and legs hurt like she had spent the evening climbing a mountain.

She had stayed up much too late. She arrived home from the Shoushanians' place close to midnight and spent the next hour and a half sorting the rest of her things and piling them into boxes. Now, bleary-eyed and exhausted after a night that had been too short, she wished she could brew a pot of coffee—but like everything else, the coffee maker and carafe were boxed up and ready to go to their new home.

She wished that she was as ready as her belongings.

She went into the bathroom and stood at the sink, examining the dark circles that had appeared under her eyes.

Such skin blemishes were a tolerable side effect of the late, uneventful hours that Sidney had despised. Sidney had despised a lot of things about ghost hunting.

"Jessica," she'd say, "I don't know if you've noticed, but *nothing is happening*. Can we please go home now?"

"Just give me one more hour," Jessica would reply. "Something cool might happen."

On one of those rare nights when something cool *had* happened, Sidney begged to go home for a different reason.

They had been sitting in the living room of an ancient house trailer a couple miles north of Eleanor when suddenly they heard a bloodcurdling scream right outside the window.

Sidney's eyes had grown round as saucers. "Holy crap! Someone's being murdered out there!" she cried, digging around in her purse for her cell phone as if planning to call 911.

"It's just a screech owl," Jessica said. She'd often heard them in the woods at her grandmother's house when she was a little kid. "If you call the cops about that, they'll haul you off to prison for being stupid."

Jessica smiled at the memory of her friend's petrified expression. She had taken the unbelieving Sidney outside and shined a flashlight up into a tree to illuminate the feathered culprit, who then took off in flight.

That was the last time they ever went ghost hunting together.

Jessica finished up in the bathroom and went to her room to put on the jeans and navy blue t-shirt she had left out before going to bed.

She put her pajamas into one of the boxes she had marked "clothes." Next, she went from room to room checking closets and cabinets one last time to make sure she hadn't missed anything during her fatigued round of late-night packing, and then, satisfied that every last corner was empty of her belongings, she drifted over to the picture window and stared out at her favorite view for the final time.

Her second-floor apartment in Hilltop Villa may have been cheap, but the view was priceless. Half a mile to the southwest, the Ohio River flowed by in all its brownish-blue glory. Most of the village of Eleanor lay below in the flood plain. The green hills of Kentucky rose up from the other side of the river, where another village—Iron Springs—sprawled out along the riverbank like a mirror image of the Ohio side. Even though she had seen the Kentucky town from afar every day of her life, she had never been there.

She drew back from the window and prepared herself a simple breakfast of a slice of wheat bread and a glass of water. Anything else would have required her to unpack more dishes.

A tear rolled down her cheek while she ate. This past year had been one of freedom. There was no greater feeling in the world than working hard every day to pay your bills and your rent and not having to rely on anyone else to do so. It had all been part of The Plan. She would save enough money to start taking classes part-time at either the University of Cincinnati or Northern Kentucky University (anywhere else was too expensive), and eventually she would earn a degree. In what, she had no clue—she would have figured it out eventually.

It didn't matter now, anyway. The Plan had crumbled when she lost her job, and she had yet to come up with a new one.

Jessica decided to get a head start on emptying the apartment and began to lug some of the heavier boxes out to her Taurus. When the back seat was full, she returned to the kitchen and unscrewed the legs from the table so it would be lighter to carry.

The digital clock on the front of the oven said that it was eight fifteen. If she hadn't lost her job, she would be getting ready for work right now. She would be putting on her blue polo that had her name embroidered in white over the left breast, applying her makeup, maybe even singing a few of her favorite songs in her lousy, off-key alto.

American Dream Truck Stop, with its gas station and 1950s-style diner, had been a great place to work until the local bottling plant closed and cost two hundred people their jobs. Fewer commuters equaled fewer people needing to fill up their gas tanks. American Dream's proprietor, Travis Suleman, had lost so much revenue that he'd had no other choice but to lay her off.

Well, he could have laid off Sidney instead. But no hard feelings.

There came a soft knock on the door. Jessica hopped up from beside the dismantled table and opened it to let Wayne inside.

As usual, Jessica felt an inexplicable lightness at the sight of him in his peach-colored polo and khaki pants. He had put styling gel in his hair again today, and Jessica could detect the faint scent of aftershave.

"You're early," Jessica said to him, giving him a welcoming hug. Yesterday on the phone he'd told her he'd get permission to take the day off so he could help her move. She'd figured he would take advantage of the break and sleep in.

"And you're packed." Wayne's eyes made a quick scan of the room. "To be honest, I expected to walk in here seeing you still cramming things into boxes."

Jessica grinned to mask her feelings. "You underestimate me."

Wayne adjusted his glasses and planted his hands on his hips. "So what are we taking out first?"

"This table's fine. It can lay flat in the bed of the truck."

"Whatever my lady wishes."

Jessica watched with mild trepidation as Wayne bent down and lifted his end of the tabletop off the floor. It hadn't occurred to her that he might not be able to handle this.

"Are you going to be all right?" she asked. He could lose his balance under the weight of the table and stumble down the stairwell into the parking lot. She should have recruited Sidney to help her instead. Sidney wasn't as strong, but at least she didn't have any trouble walking.

Wayne rolled his eyes. He always seemed to know what she was thinking. "What, has Sidney been rubbing off on you? If I didn't think I was going to be all right, I wouldn't have volunteered to do this for you. Now help me lift this thing."

She did as he instructed. There was no use arguing with him. He always won anyway—one of the many things she had learned about him over the years. Like how his first name was actually Robert. When they had first met, he explained to her that for personal reasons he would never go by Robert again and that he was perfectly happy to be "just plain Wayne." With his brown hair, brown eyes, and glasses, he was plain enough to blend into most crowds, except for the facts that he was born with cerebral palsy (spastic diplegia, to be exact) and would only buy clothes from Macy's.

His pickiness for apparel could have been cured by a trip to J.C. Penney or some other store. However, the spastic muscles in his legs that resulted from the cerebral palsy made it difficult for him to walk. Since his balance and gait were poor at best, it would be easy for him to trip on the stairs and get hurt.

She and Wayne made it to the truck without any trouble, though the trip down had been slower than she would have liked. Wayne had backed the truck into a handicapped space (perfectly legal, since he had a handicapped tag hanging from the rear-view mirror) and already let the tailgate down. He'd even been thoughtful enough to lay a tarp down in the truck bed to prevent her furniture from getting scratched. They slid the table top aboard with ease.

Wayne stopped for a moment to catch his breath. "See?" he said. "I made it."

"Of course you made it," Jessica teased, pushing a loose strand of hair out of her eyes. "You're more stubborn than a herd of mules."

They started back toward the open-air staircase. Jessica led the way so she could get the door for Wayne when they got back to her unit. "I wasn't aware that mules traveled in herds," Wayne said.

"Well, they sure don't travel in flocks."

"Swarms, maybe?"

Jessica laughed. "Mule swarms. I think I like it."

Back inside her soon-to-be-former kitchen, Wayne gathered up the detached table legs and held them over his shoulder like a bundle of sticks. Jessica picked up a box of dishes and followed him out the door, staying close to him in case he needed assistance.

"I went on another investigation last night." She panted, feeling the sore muscles in her arms strain against the weight of her cargo. "Ellen Shoushanian called me and asked if I'd drop on by, so I did."

"And you still got all your packing done?" He glanced back at her. "That's an even bigger miracle."

She wasn't going to argue with that. "Hey, in my line of business, you don't pass up a good deal like hers. That house is the oldest one in town."

Wayne snorted. "Line of business? It's not a business when you don't get paid."

"So it's a non-profit," she said. "Big deal."

They deposited their loads into the truck and went back upstairs.

"Once I've compiled all my footage into a documentary and start selling copies, it *can* be a business," Jessica said. It had been one of the many ideas she'd considered while brainstorming a new plan, though she doubted that she'd ever make enough money from that endeavor to amount to anything. "Ellen told me she'd give my phone number to everyone she knows so I can increase my client base."

Wayne tucked Jessica's wastebasket under one arm. "So, was la casa de Shoushanian crawling with restless spirits?"

"If it was, I didn't see them. I thought I heard a ghost upstairs, but it turned out to be a hamster running on one of those metal wheel things."

"Was it see-through?"

"Was what see-through?"

"The hamster."

It was Jessica's turn to snort. "I wish."

She went into the bedroom and looked around to determine which item would be the most logical thing to carry out next. The room was already so empty that it bore little resemblance to the way it had looked only the day before. All of her personal touches—the posters and framed artwork and photographs—had already been packed away. She felt tears brimming in the corners of her eyes.

Quit it, she told herself. This was just a dinky apartment. Not home. Home is where the heart is, and her heart was in her chest.

The tears abated.

She pulled two of the drawers out of her dresser then stacked one on top of the other and headed out of the room.

Wayne was in the kitchen already. His shirt was darkened with sweat. "I heard a joke about a hamster once," he said.

She shifted the drawers to get a better hold on them. "Oh yeah?"

"Yeah. There was a woman who went to see a priest and said, 'Father, you've got to help me. My son has been possessed by the spirit of an evil hamster. You must perform an exorcism right away.' And the priest just looked at her and said, 'Lady, what do you need me for? If you want the hamster exorcised, just buy it a wheel.'"

She resisted the urge to roll her eyes. "Are you sure you didn't come up with that just now?"

"Well…"

"It wasn't funny."

"Don't remind me." He feigned a look of shame.

"But if I keep reminding you, then you won't do something stupid like try to make your own stand-up act." She winked at him.

He sighed. "What would I ever do without you?"

"I'm sure you would weep with loneliness, and the rest of the world would weep with you because of all your awful jokes. Now let's hurry up and get this done before I change my mind and decide to stay here." Not that that was possible—her landlady wasn't about to let her live there for free. Though it would have been nice.

They continued hauling Jessica's things down the stairs and out of the apartment complex, and soon Wayne's truck became too full to load anything else on board. It was an odd feeling, seeing her belongings piled there like pieces of her life about to be hauled away. Tears brimmed again. She banished them, thinking instead of how interesting it was going to be living with her two best friends. Of course it was going to be interesting. It would probably even be fun. Once she was settled in, she could resume the reconstruction of The Plan, and life would be good once more.

"I never realized how much junk you have," Wayne said as Jessica helped him strap the furniture down so none of it would fly out while in transit.

"It's not nearly as much as you've got. I'm not sure how all this is going to fit into your house."

They climbed into the truck. A cardboard tree dangling from the rearview mirror made the cab smell like apples.

Wayne started the engine and let the vehicle coast down the winding hill into town. "What doesn't fit upstairs goes into the junk room or the basement with the spiders. I'm sure they'll look after everything just fine."

"I guess if it takes up too much room, I can try to sell some of it."

"I wouldn't do that just yet. One of these days you might find a job that'll make me look like a pauper."

"Not with my high school education."

"Bill Gates dropped out of college. Look at him."

"He's a geek."

"So are you."

"Am not. Computers bore the heck out of me."

They stopped at a stop sign covered in paintball splatters and turned right onto Buckeye Street.

"How many job applications have you turned in now?" Wayne asked.

"I think about a hundred. It feels like a hundred."

"Hasn't anybody called you back yet?"

She shook her head. Her phone had barely made a peep at all the past few weeks, and when it had, it had only been Sidney calling her about something or another. "Nope. Some days I think I'd be better off on welfare. Mom and Dad would be proud."

They made a left onto Lockwood Street and another right onto Sunset Street before pulling into Wayne's short gravel driveway off to the right. His front yard consisted of two yellow patches of grass on either side of the driveway. Some dead decorative plants in pots lined the edge of the cement-slab porch.

Home.

"Don't mention to Sidney that you'll be living here almost rent free," Wayne said. "She might take it the wrong way."

"Probably. But it's either live with you or live in a box in a back alley somewhere."

"Or with your parents."

Jessica unfastened her seatbelt and hopped out of the truck. Living with her father wouldn't be so bad, but he was married to her mother, so living with him was out of the question. "I think I'd rather live in a coffin."

"Then ask them for money. God knows they've got plenty of it." Wayne opened the driver's side door and eased himself to the ground, hanging onto the handle for support.

"They wouldn't lend me any."

He let down the tailgate. "Did you at least call and let them know you're moving in here?"

"No." She'd considered writing them a letter but hadn't gotten around to it yet. Without meeting his gaze, Jessica carefully undid the straps holding down her furniture and hoisted a freed chair over her shoulder. "Is the house unlocked?"

"Should be."

"Good." Jessica started toward the porch. She could practically feel his gaze boring into her.

"Jessica…"

She turned around. "What?"

Wayne was still standing at the rear of the truck. He opened his mouth as if to continue then closed it and shook his head. "Never mind."

She had known Wayne too long to always be left guessing at his thoughts. "I know what you were going to say."

"Oh, really?"

"You were going to say that at least I have parents and that I should appreciate the crappy ones I've got."

He nodded. "Yeah. That's about right."

CHAPTER 4

Acascade of leaves drifted down from the towering oaks and made landfall around the granite markers that documented the birth and death dates of the residents who moldered six feet below.

Though Jerry Madison had once marveled at the beauty that autumn brought to the world, it no longer interested him. This autumn looked the same as those of his childhood, which in turn were likely duplicates of autumns that existed in the years preceding humanity. It was as if time progressed in a circle, repeating itself over and over again without end.

In truth, this was not so. Time slipped by with an inhuman cruelty, yet despite this, the end of eternity lay further away than the paradise he would never know.

He stood back from the crowd of mourners gathered in the cemetery and watched them with mild interest. Mostly all he could see were the backs of people's heads. The gray haired minister stood next to the casket at the front of the congregation reciting prayers for the newly deceased. The man constantly paused to deliver very un-pious bouts of ragged coughing that made Jerry suspect he was about to keel over into the pit into which the casket would soon be lowered.

About five yards away from Jerry stood a mother and her young son. The woman's head was bowed in prayer, but the kid, who could have been no older than two, was busy staring out at the headstones with a look of curiosity on his face. He was probably too young to know anything about death and would not understand the significance of the burial markers or the funeral that he had been made to attend.

The little guy was facing the opposite direction from the rest of the mourners. His baby-blue eyes twinkled in the sunlight. He caught sight of Jerry and smiled.

Stunned, Jerry lifted a hand and waved in reply.

The boy giggled. "Funny man!"

"Shh!" His mother bent down and scolded her son in a whisper. "What did Mommy say about no talking?"

"But he wave at me!" He giggled again. "Look, somebody color all over his neck."

Oops. Jerry raked his mind for more pleasant matters to contemplate so that what the kid had seen would go away. Fortunately he hadn't been thinking about the other thing, too, because the kid surely would have gone into hysterics. Though it might have been funny.

"Jeremy, be quiet!" The woman scooped up her son and held him on her hip, glancing around in Jerry's direction with suspicion in her eyes. "You crazy kid." She turned back around and lowered her head once more.

Jeremy peeked around her shoulder at Jerry and scrunched up his face as if detecting a terrible smell, but then he made that childish cackle again and turned away.

What a weird kid.

Jerry wondered again what the kid would have done if he'd appeared as he had at the very end. He should try it out on somebody else when the time was right. Anything for a thrill.

An unexpected voice distracted him from his thoughts. "Hello there, good looking!"

The speaker was a young woman who had approached him from the right.

Jerry acknowledged her with a look of skepticism. "Hi," he said. He had no idea who she was. He had never seen her before.

"You sure aren't much of a talker, are you?"

"Not generally."

The woman, whose strawberry-blonde hair was cropped just below her ears, smiled. "You look lonely over here."

"There's nothing I can do about that."

She stared at the inflamed cut on the back of his hand but thankfully did not ask about it. Abigail had once thrown a glass at his head, and he'd held up his hand to protect himself. A good thing, too. The impact split his skin and he had to get stitches. He never forgot about it, which was why the mark could be seen now.

He jerked his head in the direction of the casket. "Is that you?"

The woman grinned. "Used to be. But if you pried the lid off that thing and took a peek inside, what you'd see doesn't look a tenth as good as this." She indicated her slim figure. "This is the best anti-aging treatment I ever tried."

He gaped at her. "Tell me you didn't—"

"Oh, no, no, no." The woman shook her head. "It was lymphoma. That was a joke, see."

He looked away from her, focusing his attention on the ailing minister. "I'm glad to hear it."

His new companion was silent for a moment then asked, "Why are you here?"

"There's nowhere else to go."

"Are you an atheist?"

"Catholic," he corrected. "But God and I haven't been on speaking terms in a long time." And probably never would be again.

"It's never too late to fix that. Say, what happened to *you*, if you don't mind my asking?"

"It's a long story."

"We've got time."

Jerry threw her an irritated glance. He wasn't going to pour out his life story to random strangers who couldn't mind their own business. "Don't you have someplace to be?"

Seemingly hurt, the woman frowned. "Well, of course—but I'd just wanted to stay around for a little while to see how things were going—"

"Isn't that depressing?"

"Not when you know that their sadness is only fleeting." She nodded toward the crowd. "They'll find happiness again. I know it."

Jerry looked up at the expanse of sky populated with thin wisps of cloud. No angels swooped around them with their halos and golden trumpets, nor could he hear any choir of heavenly hosts singing praises to their Creator. "Miss…"

"My name's Janet."

"Once you're there, if you could—will you pray for me?"

She nodded. "I can do that."

"Thank you. And if you run into three little ones who look kind of like me, tell them I'm sorry I can't be there."

He turned away to see if they had started lowering the coffin into the ground, and when he looked back, the woman was gone.

~~~∽∽∾∾∿~~~

The ceremony ended a short while later. In tears, the grieving family and their kin hugged each other and bade their fare-wells. The parking lot soon emptied of vehicles, and in solitude Jerry watched three burly young men shovel dirt back into the grave. The men said little to each other while they worked. They wouldn't have had much to say, anyway. Woman dies, family cries, life goes on. Fill in the hole and go home.

The men completed their job and left. Jerry sat down on one of the cemetery benches and gazed unseeingly at the woods that surrounded the graveyard. He should leave here, find some other place to lurk about in. But where? Everywhere was nowhere, and nowhere was everywhere. Nothing mattered or would ever matter again.

He didn't know if he should be sad or angry or bitter. Sometimes he was all three, and sometimes he was none at all. On occasion he would even think of something pleasant he had forgotten long ago and a spark of joy would light up his whole being for an instant, but then he would remember.

And he would grow depressed.

Then he would become angered by his sadness, because being sad wasn't going to help him get out of this mess. Besides, it only made him feel worse.

Then bitterness would consume him like acid dissolving an old coin. *They* had done this to him. If they hadn't, he wouldn't be here at all.

If he could get back at them…

He couldn't take it anymore. Something had to change. Anything. But what could he, Jerry Madison, do?

Nothing.

Jerry buried his face in his hands and wept, wishing that he could find a way to end his life so the pain of existing would go away forever.

Which, of course, was impossible, because Jerry Madison was already dead.

～∞∞∞～

The busy morning of loading and unloading the Taurus and pickup truck came to an end. After they had labored at putting Jessica's belongings away so as to maintain some sense of order in the house, Wayne suggested that they take a break for lunch.

"Does pizza sound good to you?" he asked, peering into the freezer.

Jessica lowered her gaze to stare at the orange and green gourds Wayne had recently purchased at a local farmer's market to use as a fall centerpiece. Her limbs still hurt as they had when she'd awakened, which was odd, because she hadn't done any-thing to strain them. And now her back hurt, too. "I'm at a bit of a disadvantage to be picky. Are there any pepperonis?"

Wayne pulled out the frozen disk of crust and looked at the label that had been shrink-wrapped over the toppings. "You're in luck. It's got the works."

"If the works include anchovies, you can count me out."

"I'd count myself out." He put the pizza on a tray, set the oven temperature, and slid the tray inside. "Are you all right?"

She massaged one of her forearms to try to ease the pain. "I hurt all over. Too much heavy lifting in one day wears a girl out."

Wayne leaned against the counter and crossed his arms. "I've got Tylenol in the medicine cabinet."

"I should be fine in a while. I'm just not used to this." Massaging herself obviously wasn't going to work, so she folded her hands and placed them in her lap. "This is going to sound dumb, but I have no idea how you do it."

"Do what?"

Wayne wasn't the type to get his feelings hurt, so it was never an issue for her to discuss his disability with him. "You know. You being the way you are and still being ten times more in shape than I am."

"You do know I exercise every morning."

"Yeah." Sidney had mentioned that sometimes Wayne acci-dentally woke her up in the mornings doing jumping jacks in his bedroom.

"When was the last time *you* exercised?"

"I did some pushups a couple months ago." It was true, and it had almost been disastrous.

"It's never too late to start working out. We can even do it together sometime, if you'd like." He winked.

"In your dreams," she said.

"Frequently."

Jessica felt her face turn red.

"You know," he continued, "if you want to get your parents all riled up, just tell them you're shacking up with an older guy who wears pink and gets his nails done every month."

"I'm pretty sure they know you're not gay."

"I know. Steve and I had a little chat about that one time before they moved away."

"You did?" The Roman-Dells had worked with Wayne at Reynolds and Korman, Eleanor, Ohio's one and only public accounting firm. Wayne's often-misperceived sexuality did not seem to be a likely topic of discussion in that place of business, except perhaps behind his back.

"Don't worry. He didn't threaten to kill me if I ever touched you."

Jessica imagined that the color of her cheeks was deepening from red to scarlet. "Should I even ask?"

He laughed. "It's not what you think. We ran into each other at one of the checkouts over at Eleanor Market, and we both saw a tabloid in the display that said something about a celeb coming out of the closet, and your dad asked me when I was going to do that."

Minding his own business was not one of her father's strong points. "What in the blazes did you say to him?"

"I told him I'd never done a man in my life, and then he asked me if I'd ever done any women, and I told him that was need-to-know information. The conversation sort of progressed from there, I guess."

She pictured the scene in her head and couldn't help but grin. "What was Dad doing there, anyway? He never goes shopping."

"I think he was buying a tube of Preparation H."

Jessica clamped her eyes shut. "Thanks for that."

"No, he was getting a bouquet of flowers for your mom. He said it was their thirty-first anniversary."

Jessica nodded. That would have been in 2009, just over a year ago. "It's amazing how they've put up with each other for so long," she said. Her parents, known to most people as Stephen and Maria Roman-Dell and known to her as the dysfunctional couple whose house she had slept in for twenty years, were both an unfortunate combination of workaholic and perfectionist. Her mother had the complete inability to show affection, and her father, who had little personality of his own, tended to go along with everything she did without question.

They had found better-paying work at an accounting firm near Indianapolis last fall, so they sold their house and moved away. Jessica had felt no burning desire to go with them.

"Maybe there's something about their relationship that the rest of us just can't see," Wayne said.

"Not that we'd *want* to see it." Her stomach growled. "That pizza needs to hurry up and cook itself. I'm starved."

"You aren't the only one. I did five times the amount of work you did."

"Then take a nap after lunch."

"Can't. I told Father George I'd come in and get some work done." Aside from his job at the accounting firm, Wayne also volunteered his time at the Holy Trinity church office. "I hope you won't be bored here without me."

"I don't have time to be bored. I've got a bunch of recordings to listen to and watch."

"You'll have plenty of time to do it. Sidney won't be home until three thirty."

Jessica sighed. "Good ol' Sidney. I wonder if she's having fun doing my job."

CHAPTER 5

S idney was busy loading an armful of Mountain Dew bottles into one of the coolers when the bells hung above the glass double-doors jingled softly, signaling the entrance of a customer.

"Be with you in a minute," she said, stuffing the rest of the bottles into place.

"Take your time," said an unfamiliar woman's voice from the direction of the potato chip aisle.

Sidney slid the cooler door closed and walked back behind the counter.

She looked up as the woman plucked a bag of cheese puffs off the shelf.

She did a double take. *No way.*

The woman had wavy red hair tied back with a turquoise barrette in the shape of a butterfly, just as her own mother had always done. The likeness was so uncanny that Sidney half believed that Marjorie Miller's corpse had risen from the grave, brushed off the dirt that she'd climbed through to get out, gotten the munchies, and walked the mile's distance from the Holy Trinity Cemetery to get a pick-me-up.

The woman turned. She wore a simple white blouse and a black skirt that hung to her ankles. Her mother had owned a similar outfit.

Sidney forced herself to regain her composure. Of course this was not her mother. This woman was a little older—maybe forty-five—and had a thinner face and bigger bosom than Marjorie had possessed. She was also wearing Birkenstocks, something that Marjorie would never have been caught dead in. This latter point nullified the zombie theory in its entirety.

The Marjorie lookalike smiled at Sidney and placed the cheese puffs on the counter. "How are you today, sweetie?"

"Fantastic," Sidney lied. She keyed the price into the cash register. "That'll be a dollar ninety-nine."

The woman handed Sidney two dollar bills. "Keep the penny. Are you sure you're all right?"

At first Sidney didn't know what she could be talking about, but then she realized that she'd been unconsciously looking into the woman's eyes. They were brown, not blue like Marjorie's.

"Yeah, I'm good," she said. "Have a nice day."

The woman left. She probably thought Sidney was nuts for gawking at her like that. Sidney's reaction was understandable, though. The brain tended to invent conspiracy theories every time someone died, like *Oh, Mom's not really dead. She witnessed a drug lord blow a snitch's head off in a back alley and had to be put away in witness protection.*

But Sidney had been there when her mother took her final breath. The only thing Marjorie did these days was push dandelions.

Sidney went back to the drink coolers. The Dr. Pepper looked like it could use a few more bottles. The Pepsi did, too. She retreated to the storeroom where cases of extra beverages were kept and gathered up another armload.

Having filled the cooler, Sidney went and sat down on the bar stool behind the counter and stared at the fluorescent light hanging from the ceiling to better pass the time. She'd finished most of her homework. The cigarette case was full. The floor was washed. She was alone and bored as heck.

Then Travis Suleman, her boss, walked in through the doorway that connected the gas station to the diner.

Back in the olden days of her employment, Travis had constantly joked around with customers and employees alike, but lately he'd taken on the demeanor of a burnt-out funeral director.

"Did I just see a customer over here?" he asked, grabbing a Pepsi out of the cooler she had just finished loading. He unscrewed the cap and took a swig.

"Yeah. It gave me something to do for about five seconds."

"Don't look so upset about it."

"I'm not upset," she lied.

He waited for her to elaborate.

She sighed. "Fine. Maybe I am. But it's about something stupid, okay? I just thought she looked like my mom, and for a second I thought it was her. Go ahead. Laugh your head off."

Travis did not laugh but looked at her with pity. "Nobody's going to laugh at you for that. I did the same thing when my dad died. Thought I saw him everywhere I went. Sometimes I wondered if maybe it really was him and he was just dropping by to let me know he was okay."

"Travis, no offense, but I don't believe in those things anymore." Any faith she might have had in a deity had shattered when it became apparent that a loving god didn't give a rat's tush about her or her mom.

He frowned. "You think God takes statements like that lightly?"

Oh, brother. "*What* God? The one whose *will* it was that my mother's brain got eaten up by a tumor? God's just an excuse. Oh, look, he won the lottery. Must be the will of God. Oh, look, their baby died in a car accident. That's the will of God for you!"

Travis's expression was rapidly turning into a scowl.

"Nobody can understand the will of God," he said quietly.

"You've just made my point! People can't just accept that things happen, so they blame them all on a higher power and call it his will. It's stupid."

"So you think I'm stupid?"

"No. Just naïve." She blushed a little since Travis was older than her own father. It didn't matter, though. A person could be naïve at any age.

"Sidney, I pray that your eyes will open one of these days," he said. "It would break Marjorie's heart if you were unable to join her someday."

She could have punched him. *Wanted* to punch him. But then she'd have been fired and stuck in the same sinking boat as Jessica.

"I appreciate your concern," she said, her hands shaking with barely-controlled anger, "but let it go, okay? It's a free country. I can believe whatever I want."

He turned away to go back into the diner with his drink. "Doesn't mean I can't pray for you," he said as he swung open the door with unnecessary force and left her alone once more.

Jessica had been sitting at the kitchen table listening to the audio track from one of her digital voice recorders for about two hours when her cell phone rang.

She paused the track and pulled the phone out of her jeans pocket. The phone recognized the caller from Jessica's short list of contacts and displayed the name of her sister—Rachel Schellenberger—on its tiny screen.

She'd been hoping it was a business calling her about a job interview, but her disappointment ended there. "Rachel!" she exclaimed. "What's up?"

"Hey, Jess!" came the voice of her older sister, who lived hundreds of miles away in one of the suburbs of New York City. Rachel had changed apartments so many times in the past five years that Jessica could never remember where she currently lived. "How's it going?"

"Not too good," she said, "but it could be a whole lot worse. I still haven't found a job, and I had to move out of my apartment today because I couldn't afford it anymore. Other than that, I'm just peachy."

"Aw, you should've told me you were broke! I'd have lent you some money."

"I don't want to be a burden on you guys. I'll manage."

"Whatever. Who're you staying with?"

"Wayne and Sidney. Thank goodness for friends, huh?"

Rachel laughed. "So, are you and Wayne an item now or something?"

Of course that's what Rachel would think. "Ask me that again, and I'll punch you in the face."

"Your arm can't reach that far."

"You want to see me try?" She changed the subject before Rachel could continue her interrogation about her and Wayne. "Anyway, what's up with you? How's Eric doing?" Eric Schellenberger was Rachel's husband, and like Rachel herself, was a displaced Ohioan who had grown up in Eleanor.

"He's doing great. His company laid off about half their office staff this past month, and he was one of the lucky ones who wasn't forced to leave." Jessica could hear a garbled cacophony on Rachel's end of the line as her sister likely switched her phone to the other ear. "Hey, are you coming to the family reunion this Saturday?"

Jessica narrowed her eyes. Nobody had told her anything about such an event, which wasn't too surprising since some of her relatives tended to forget she existed. "What family reunion?"

"The Reyes reunion. Mom and Dad are going. Didn't they tell you about it?"

She snorted. "Do you really need me to answer that?"

"Point taken. But you'd better be there, because Eric and I are coming, and we haven't seen you in ages."

"Where are they having it?"

"The usual place: Campbell Community Park. The invitation says it starts at noon."

So someone had mailed out invitations. They probably just hadn't known her mailing address at the apartment and assumed that her parents would tell her about the event. "That's the one in Cold Spring?"

"Yep."

Cold Spring was a short hop across the river in Kentucky, the state where many members of the Reyes clan still lived. "I can try to make it," Jessica said. She wished she could have used work as an excuse not to go. Maybe later on she could think of a better one.

"If you don't show up," Rachel said, "we're going to hunt you down and drag you out there kicking and screaming." She paused. "Oh, and before I forget, there's something else I wanted to tell you."

"Oh yeah?"

"I'm pregnant."

At first Jessica didn't know what to say. Pregnant? As in, with child? Babies were mysterious creatures that she had only ever viewed from afar. That one would soon be joining their family was almost too strange for her to comprehend.

"You still there?" Rachel asked.

"I'm…yeah. I mean, congrats."

"You don't sound too pleased about it."

Jessica laughed. "It's the last thing I expected you to tell me." Since Rachel and Eric were both young professionals, Jessica had always assumed that the couple would wait to have children when they were older. "When did you find out?"

"Two weeks ago. Both tests were positive."

Jessica realized that she was grinning from ear to ear despite her shock. "So what do *Mamá* and *Papá* have to say about Baby Schellenberger?"

"They don't know yet. I was going to call them next."

"You don't know how honored I am to hear that I got the news before them."

"Don't be too honored. It's just they're probably both at work right now and won't have time to talk. Now I know you're probably tired of hearing good news, but Eric and I decided we want to move back to Ohio."

This was better news than that of Rachel's pregnancy. "I didn't realize you missed me that much."

"Who said I missed you? It's cheaper to live in Cincinnati than out here. So there." Rachel paused, and Jessica could hear a man's voice saying something in the background. "Hey, I've got to hurry up and get off of here before my boss decides to fire me. Eric and I are flying out there on Thursday, and we'll be staying with Uncle Esteban and Aunt Sharon for the weekend. I'll call you when we get in. Okay?"

"Sounds good to me. Love you."

"Love you too, Jess. See you Thursday."

They disconnected, and Jessica leaned back in her chair, feeling elated. She hadn't seen Rachel for nearly two years. Sure, they e-mailed each other all the time and chatted on the phone once or twice a month, but nothing in the world was better than sitting down with your only sister to play board games or cards and gossip for hours about everything under God's blue sky.

She was about to continue listening to her recording when Sidney stormed in through the front door and slung her black leather handbag onto the countertop so hard that it knocked over a couple of pill bottles and an empty cup. One of the bottles fell onto the floor and rolled toward the table.

"I am going to kill Travis," she announced, stooping to retrieve the bottle. Her face was the color of a beet. "And I will enjoy every minute of it."

Surely Sidney hadn't been laid off, too. Then Travis wouldn't have had anyone to work at the gas station but himself. "What did he do?"

Sidney slammed the bottle back onto the counter and righted the other bottle and the cup. "He's a Bible-thumper."

Jessica started to laugh but stopped when Sidney glowered at her. "Since when has that been a problem?"

"Since we stopped seeing eye to eye on certain things. Evidently I'm going to hell."

Jessica tried to keep a straight face. It was true that Travis attended church with regularity, though it wasn't often that he discussed religion at the workplace. She must have been missing out on quite a lot since losing her job. "I'm sorry to hear it. What did he say?"

Sidney headed toward the staircase. "I'm not even going to get into it right now. I've got to finish my English assignment before it kills me." She disappeared up the stairs and slammed the bedroom door closed moments later.

Jessica frowned. What in the world could her problem be? Sidney went to church, too. They usually sat together with Wayne on Sunday mornings. She'd have thought that Sidney and Travis had gotten into a dispute over doctrinal differences if it weren't for the fact that Travis went to the same church they did.

She'd have to ask Sidney about it after she'd blown off some steam.

Jessica's phone started ringing again when she reached to turn her recorder back on. Maybe Rachel was calling her back, or maybe this time it really *was* somebody requesting that she come in for an interview.

The number of the incoming call began with an 859 area code. Northern Kentucky. She had not applied for any out-of-state jobs, so it might have been one of her extended relatives calling her to ask why she hadn't RSVPed to the family reunion she'd known nothing about.

She held the phone to her ear. "Hello?"

"Hi, is this Jessica Roman-Dell?" asked an elderly man who had a stuffy head.

Her brow furrowed. "Yes," she said, "this is she. I'm really sorry, but who is this?"

"My name's Al Tumler. My sister says you know her."

"I do? Who is she?"

"Ellen Shoushanian. Said you wanted to make a documentary about spirit sightings and gave me your number."

Jessica was relieved that she had a connection to this man who knew her name and phone number. "I really appreciate you calling me! Ellen's a nice woman. I don't know her too well, but she always comes into the place where I work—*used* to work—to get her raspberry Snapple tea. I'm going to tell you right now that I'm not much of a pro at this whole ghost-hunting thing. I just thought it would be neat to compile my footage into one big documentary."

"You record a lot of sightings?"

"To tell you the truth, no."

The man's soft chuckle turned into a gut-wracking cough that flooded the phone line for about ten seconds. The poor guy sounded like he was going to hack up a lung.

He cleared his throat. "Sorry about that. Woke up this morning with the granddaddy of all colds. Presided over a funeral earlier today and have been in bed ever since."

"I'm sorry to hear that. I hope you feel better soon."

"You aren't the only one, young lady. But as I was going to say, I'm the pastor at the United Methodist Church just south of Iron Springs. A lot of folks think the church grounds are haunted. Specifically, the graveyard."

"Do *you* think they're haunted?"

"I don't know what to think. Some of the people who claim to have seen spirits out and about are some of the most honest folks you could ever meet. Doesn't mean they weren't just confused about whatever they saw."

"What did they see?"

"It's always different. That's the funny thing. Some saw glowing orbs. Some saw shadows moving around, and nothing was there to cause them. And some say they feel like they're being watched."

His description sounded typical of the many hauntings Jessica had read about. "Is there any particular time of day when these things happen?" she asked.

"No, it seems to happen pretty much any time. Morning. Night. Whenever."

"And you've never seen any of this?"

"Can't say I have. But I've only been pastor there five years. Could be if I'd been there longer, I'd have seen something."

"Has anyone tried to take pictures when they saw these things?"

"Tried? Yes. My oldest daughter saw a shadow shaped like a person standing by the church steps a couple years back and snapped a picture on her cell phone, but the shadow person didn't show up."

Interesting. "So, when do you think is a good time for me to head out there?"

Mr. Tumler coughed. "Any weeknight's fine with me. Tonight's fine, too, but I won't be there to show you around. Got to take care of this cold before it takes care of me, if you know what I mean."

"I don't have any plans for tonight. What's your church's address?"

"It's 876 Hill Road, just south of Iron Springs, like I said. There shouldn't be anyone out there to bother you on a Tuesday night like this. If there is, let me know, and I'll send the wrath of God upon him."

"I don't think that should be necessary. I carry a pepper spray in my purse."

"Sounds like you've got a good head on your shoulders. But still, you've gotta be careful out there."

"Mr. Tumler?"

"Yes?"

"If I do capture footage of ghosts, do you want me to show it to you?"

"Young lady," he said, "if you see a ghost and take a video of it, I couldn't be more amazed than if a meteor fell from the sky and conked me upside the head. And I mean that, too."

~⚬⚬⚬~

Jerry tried to pray, but every time he formed the words in his mind, they scattered like dead leaves caught in a current of wind. He could think of everything imaginable—memories of childhood, old friends, ideas he'd wanted his old English classes to discuss—yet he could not utter one single prayer.

He'd been right when he told Janet that he and God were not on speaking terms. God refused to listen. And for good reason.

Because God doesn't care about people like you, said the Presence that was always with him, lurking on the edge of his awareness like an unwanted guest. It had been with him for years—too many years—and try as he might, he couldn't escape from it.

Sometimes he wondered if it was meant to be with him as part of his punishment. But then again, maybe not. He just wished it would go away.

Jerry's anger swelled at the Presence's words. God was *supposed* to care. Did he care? He must have a little bit, or he wouldn't be here.

Stop kidding yourself, Jerry.

Okay. He would. Maybe. But he had to get out of here. Somehow. He would go mad if he stayed a moment longer. Janet's departure had been a painful reminder of his entrapment. It made leaving here all the more desirable.

Do you really think that leaving is going to help you?

It couldn't hurt.

He tried one last time to put a word in with the Creator. *God, please help…*

His thoughts plowed head-on into a brick wall. Though he could not hear it, he imagined that the Presence was laughing.

Jerry just couldn't do it. It was no use to try anymore. No use at all.

CHAPTER 6

———◇———

A s per custom, Jessica tried to persuade Sidney to come with her when she went up to the bedroom to collect her ghost-hunting equipment.

Sidney, sitting on the bed with a textbook in her lap, only lifted her gaze and gave Jessica a piercing stare over the tops of her purple frames.

"Fine," Jessica said, shouldering her black zippered tote bag. "Be that way."

Sidney rolled her eyes. "Just be careful, okay?"

"Will do."

The muscles in her legs protested as she descended the stairs. Not wanting to spend the rest of the evening in pain, she made a detour into the bathroom and swiped a bottle of Tylenol out of the medicine cabinet. She washed two of the pills down with a glass of water and put the nearly empty bottle in her purse.

In the car she switched on a local classic rock station and backed out of the driveway. Travis Suleman had gotten her hooked on oldies when she started working for him since that's the only music he'd play at the gas station, and now she almost never listened to anything else. The song currently playing was "Carry On Wayward Son" by Kansas. One of her favorites.

The sun gleamed overhead, making the Ohio River sparkle like liquid diamonds off to her left. She had half a mind to pull off the road and start snapping pictures (would have made a nice page in a calendar or even a coffee table book like you'd find in the bargain section at Barnes and Noble), but she'd only be wasting time since daylight hours became so scarce this time of year.

She glanced at the directions she'd printed off the computer. The highway merged with Interstate 275 several miles up ahead. Then once she was in Kentucky she was supposed to get off the highway on the Route 9 exit and follow that until she got to Hill Road.

As the crow flies, Eleanor and Iron Springs were separated by less than a half a mile of river. It took Jessica fifty-five minutes to reach the turnoff for Hill Road, which by her estimation was about two miles northwest of the Kentucky town.

Hill Road headed due south. Like its name promised, the road—marked by a signpost that had been bent to a forty-five degree angle by some unfortunate motorist—ascended a steep incline for a quarter of a mile and then leveled out into meandering curves.

The woods grew so thick on either side of the road that Jessica had the feeling she was driving down a long tunnel. She'd spotted a single ranch-style home nestled among golden-leaved maples shortly after she made the turn, but other than that, there was no indication that anyone had set foot in this part of the tri-state before. *Kentucky, the final frontier*, she thought. *I claim this land in the name of Roman-Dell.* Too bad she didn't have a flag.

A white sign on the right side of the road came into view after a couple of miles. She squinted. "Iron Springs United Methodist Church," read the black script stenciled above the church service schedule. A battered mailbox emblazoned with the number 876 stood sentry by a blacktopped lane that disappeared into the woods.

She swung the car onto the lane while Queen sang "Bohemian Rhapsody"—"Scaramouche, Scaramouche, will you do the fandango?" This had to be the most isolated church on planet earth.

There wasn't even a parsonage in sight. Al Tumler must have been a commuter.

Two-tenths of a mile later, the lane opened out into a vacant parking lot where the faded pavement was interlaced with a web of cracks, some of which had been patched up with squiggly stripes of black sealer. To the left loomed an ancient red brick church that bore a steeple and stained-glass windows (the date on the cornerstone looked like it might have said 1862), and to the right on the other side of the parking lot sat the graveyard Al Tumler had spoken of on the phone. Like Hill Road, all was encircled by a thick expanse of trees that looked as though they might have continued on forever.

She selected a parking space close to the chain-link fence marking the graveyard's front boundary and shut off the engine. Before climbing out of the car, she took a few bites out of a granola bar she'd stowed away in her purse, staring at the head-stones while she chewed. The closest ones jutted from the earth in haphazard angles like they had grown tired over time and slouched to the side to rest. Even from the short distance, she could barely read their epitaphs. She guessed the headstones were about as old as the church.

Having finished her dinner, she wadded up the granola bar wrapper, stuffed it into her jeans pocket, and crammed her purse into her equipment bag. Time to get down to business.

Unexpected stillness echoed in her ears the instant she stepped outside. At home the ambient sound of traffic on U.S. 52 could be heard rumbling by most times of the day, but here the only sounds were those of the wind and a twittering bird sitting on a branch high up in a tree. As eerie as that was, the stillness might be a blessing. She wouldn't have to sort through a hundred uni-dentified noises when she played back her recordings.

But first things first. Photographs.

Leaving her bag on the hood of the car, she held up her cam-era and snapped a few pictures of the front and sides of the old church. Even though no spirits would likely show up in the photographs, she still planned to add the images to her scrapbook. Sidney might even think they were interesting. And if not Sidney, then Rachel. Yes, she would show them all to Rachel when she and Eric arrived on Thursday. Rachel liked to look at pictures just as much as she did.

Next she photographed the parking lot and lane from several different angles. She trudged back out to the end of the lane and took a picture of the church sign just for the heck of it. She even took a picture of a robin that had perched on a fencepost, because he was kind of cute.

Jessica returned to her car to grab her bag off the hood. Time to go check out the cemetery.

No sooner had she slung the tote over her shoulder then suddenly a wave of nausea hit her like a sucker punch to the gut. She doubled over, battling her stomach's overwhelming urge to empty its meager contents onto the pavement. She couldn't puke. Not here, where someone would find it later.

It took all of her strength to keep her granola bar where it belonged. Maybe this was what morning sickness felt like. Or the Ebola virus. Did people with Ebola even puke, or did they just drop dead on the spot? She'd have to look it up when she got home. If she made it home. Because if it *was* Ebola, she might not survive the evening.

She swallowed a mouthful of saliva. As she did, the world around her bathed itself in shades of deep red like she had suddenly put on a pair of crimson-tinted sunglasses.

It might have been the onset of a fainting spell if it weren't for the fact that a distinct feeling of anger came out of nowhere, crashing over her like a tidal wave pummeling a shore. Her hands clenched into fists, and she could feel herself shaking. *She had to kill...*

The bizarre spell passed with the abruptness by which it had begun. The red aura faded away. Her stomach stopped twisting in her abdomen. She rubbed her sweating forehead. In the few years that she had been conducting formal investigations, nothing of this sort had ever happened before.

She had once read that some people believed powerful emotions could be imprinted upon a place where they had been experienced. Maybe someone had once stood in that very spot feeling angrier than they ever had before, and now, weeks or months or years later, Jessica could feel his or her emotion as if it had been her own.

That, or she had finally flipped her lid. She would still add this to her paranormal experiences journal, where she recorded the details of all her investigations regardless of whether or not anything "paranormal" had occurred.

Confident that the nausea was gone for good, she walked down the gravel path that led out among the graves, humming the first few bars of "Bohemian Rhapsody" to keep her spirits up. Her body still ached despite the Tylenol she'd downed earlier. How long was that stuff supposed to take before it started working? She didn't want to take more pills and end up overdosing alone where no one would find her for a day or more.

She kept her eyes peeled, seeking out anything unusual. Shadow figures? Nope. Glowing orbs? Not a one. This evening was going to be a piece of cake.

Up ahead she could see a rectangular heap of dirt that had bouquets of wilting flowers stacked at one end—no doubt from the funeral that Mr. Tumler had mentioned. Uninterested, she glanced to the right.

Her heart skipped a beat or two.

She was not alone.

CHAPTER 7

A solitary male dressed in shades of mourning slouched on a cement bench, seemingly unaware that he had company. He must have stayed behind after the funeral. He was probably one of the deceased's loved ones, too stricken to go home and go on with life in his or her absence.

Jessica knew the feeling. After Marjorie Miller died, Jessica had barely crawled out of bed for a week because it hurt too much to be awake. Marjorie had been a surrogate mother to her much as she had been to Wayne, taking her and Sidney out shopping and to the movies and just doing *girl* stuff that Maria Roman-Dell wouldn't have dreamed of doing. Jessica didn't doubt that Marjorie was rejoicing in heaven, but her absence on earth left a gaping hole in her life that had not yet completely filled itself in. She could only imagine what Sidney had felt.

She shook her head. No sense in making herself depressed when she had work to do.

It might be rude to investigate while the man was still here. But if he had been here long enough, he may have seen some of the shadows and orbs that Mr. Tumler had spoken of. Besides, talking to him might cheer him up. That's the way it was after Marjorie's death. People *talked*. It was better than bottling it all up and having a meltdown later on. That had happened to Sidney's dad about a month after the funeral. Jessica had been dining with them that night, so she witnessed the whole thing, tears, anger, and all. It hadn't been pretty.

She made her way toward the man on the bench, trying to ignore the nagging pains in her muscles.

"Excuse me!" she called out when she was about ten yards away from him.

The man gave no indication of having heard her. She couldn't see his face, so she didn't know if he'd fallen asleep sitting up or if he was stone deaf. But no matter. If the latter were the case, she could easily communicate with him using the pen and notepad she kept in her purse.

She continued toward him. "Hello! You on the bench!"

He still didn't turn around. He didn't even flinch.

Jessica's approach brought her up to his left side, and she immediately sensed that something wasn't quite right. The guy was so still that he might have been a statue.

"Hi," she said, waving to get his attention. It was the only sign language she could remember. "Can you hear me?"

The man turned his head in her direction. His eyes widened. "You were talking to me?" he asked in a soft voice.

Now that she could see his face, Jessica relaxed a little. The man couldn't have been that old, maybe thirty-four at the most. His dark brown hair was disheveled like he'd forgotten to run a comb through it before he came to the funeral, and he wore a black button-up shirt and black slacks. Two prominent dark circles stood out beneath his eyes.

Jessica smiled, grateful that she would not have to resort to writing, because her penmanship stank, and the guy might not have been able to read it. "Yes, who else could I have meant?"

"I don't know." He glanced down at his hands, which lay folded in his lap. A partially healed cut sealed together with medical stitches marred the back of his left hand.

"I'm really sorry for bothering you at a time like this," she blurted, feeling an inexplicable unease at the sight of the wound. "I can leave if you want me to."

A faint smile lit up his face. "You can stay as long as you want. You're not bothering me."

Yeah, right. "Are you sure? I thought you might be visiting someone out here."

He gave her a quizzical look. "Visiting?"

"Well, paying your respects. I heard there was a funeral today."

He nodded. "There was. Some woman named Janet. I didn't know her."

Then why in the world was he here? "So…do you come here often?" she asked, having taken a step in reverse without at first realizing that she'd done so.

"This is my first visit. What are you doing with that bag?"

She unconsciously slid the canvas straps up higher on her shoulder. She hoped he wouldn't try to take it from her. "It's got my equipment in it. I'm hunting for ghosts."

"You mean you're not…?" He shook his head in wonder. "You're kidding, right?"

"Afraid not. I've got a thermal imaging camera, K2 meter, video cameras, voice recorders—you name it, I've probably got it. I'm hoping to find something spooky out here tonight."

"Such as?"

Jessica couldn't help but wonder if the man found her to be an annoyance. "You know, ghostly lights, shadows, apparitions, disembodied voices, that kind of thing."

"You think those are spooky?" His eyes twinkled. "I can think of worse things."

"Like what?"

The man smiled. "Oh, you could come across severed heads, bleeding limbs, human entrails spread across the ground for the scavengers to clean up…"

Jessica took another involuntary step back from him. "I hope to God I don't find anything like that out here."

"Don't worry. Tonight you won't."

"Uh, that's good, I guess." Jessica gulped. Suddenly she felt much too cold inside her sweatshirt even though she was sweating.

"I couldn't agree more." His gaze lingered on her face. "What's your name?"

Jessica briefly considered inventing an alias for the evening in case the guy was a weirdo, but she'd just forget what she told him in the next five minutes if she did. "I'm Jessica Roman-Dell," she said. "And you are?"

"Jerry Madison." He did not offer a handshake. "How are you going to know if you've found a ghost?"

"Easy. If I find a bunch of glowing orbs floating around in the air, I'll know for sure it isn't the birds and squirrels doing it."

"An excellent deduction."

"Are you making fun of me?"

"Why would I do that?"

"Because a lot of people think ghost-hunting is bogus. Including most of the people I know."

He nodded. "That's understandable. I never used to believe in it, either. There's heaven, there's hell, and nothing in between but this lousy lump of rock we call home. That's how I saw things, even though the church claimed different." He gave a short laugh. "And earth might as well be a hell in itself." He paused. "I don't see why you bother looking for ghosts. God knows there's nothing you can do for them. What did you say your name was?"

Jessica hesitated. "I told you already."

"I heard the Jessica part. What's your last name?"

"It's Roman-Dell. Don't ask."

"That's not too common, is it?" he asked anyway.

"Not really. At least I don't think so. The only Roman-Dells I know of are in my immediate family."

"Interesting." Jerry was silent for several moments. "Why do you look for ghosts?"

She shrugged. "It's just one of my hobbies. I used to watch a bunch of TV shows about haunted houses and stuff. I think it's neat that souls can linger behind on earth after death."

A flash of hurt appeared in Jerry's crystal-blue eyes. "You won't think it's neat anymore when it happens to you. You'll pray for someone to come and shoot you to put you out of your misery. Only of course that won't do anything since you won't have a body to get shot."

"I'm pretty sure it's not going to happen to me," she said, somewhat spooked by his sudden change in demeanor. "When I die, I'm taking the first available flight to heaven. First-class, free drinks, and decent movies on those little overhead TV things."

"You can't be that naïve."

Who did he think he was talking to, a kindergartener? "What am I being naïve about? I'm not a murderer or anything. My halo might be a *little* tarnished, but I'm a good person. Generally."

"You're an interesting person, that's for sure." Jerry crossed his arms. "Now go have fun and investigate. I'm not going to stop you."

Well *that* was a relief. Quelling her nervousness when she turned her back to him, she retreated to another cement bench she spotted close to the back part of the cemetery, where gnarled pines grew just yards away from the last row of headstones.

She set her tote bag on the bench and unzipped it. She pulled her cell phone, pepper spray, and keys out of her concealed purse and stuffed them into the pocket of her sweatshirt in case she needed to make a hasty getaway. Jerry still hadn't budged from his seat and looked as if he had no immediate plans to leave. What if he was a rapist? Other than the pepper spray (and maybe the car keys), she had no way to protect herself if he tried to make a move on her. She could kick and shout and maybe hold him off for a minute if he knocked the pepper spray out of her hand, but in the end no one would hear her screams.

Another thing nagging at her thoughts was that her piece-of-junk Taurus was the only vehicle in the entire parking lot. That meant Jerry had walked here, and for what purpose? To sit and stare at cement crosses and angels for hours on end? Or to kidnap unfortunate young women who wandered into his sight?

His voice repeated itself in her mind.

Oh, you could come across severed heads, bleeding limbs, human entrails spread across the ground for the scavengers to clean up... Don't worry. Tonight you won't.

Tonight you won't. And just what in the blazes was that supposed to mean? Would she have found such carnage here on some other night? Was Jerry like that Ted Bundy guy who'd lured a ton of women to their deaths? What a convenient place to hide the bodies.

This line of thought wasn't going to get her investigation started. The best thing she could do was pretend to ignore him and get on with her work.

With the stubborn resolve of a Roman-Dell, Jessica went around setting up her equipment. One voice recorder went on top of a headstone bearing the name of Edna Schultz. Edna wouldn't mind. Next, she placed a camcorder on the ground next to the gravel path and angled it so that anything walking by would be in full view on the recording.

She turned on her second voice recorder. "Today is Tuesday, October 19, 2010," she said, holding the device in front of her mouth like a microphone. "I'm at the United Methodist Church near Iron Springs, Kentucky, investigating some ghost sightings in the cemetery. This place is seriously in the middle of nowhere. The only activity I've seen so far was an angry, red aura-type thing at the edge of the parking lot. Later on I'll check to see if there are any electromagnetic waves present that might have caused me to hallucinate."

Electromagnetic waves could be emitted by power lines or ordinary electronic devices and had been known to instill a creeped-out feeling in people who encountered them. Many hauntings had been attributed to this phenomenon, and for all she knew, it had caused her to imagine the aura.

The setting sun cast long, headstone-shaped shadows that spread over the ground like reaching fingers. Pocketing the recorder, she glanced over at Jerry to make sure he wasn't sneaking up on her.

Her breath caught in her throat.

It may have been a trick of the light, but it looked like a bluish-purple bruise encircled the man's neck like a gruesome collar, and his face appeared to be covered in dark splotches. She squinted to get a better look, and to her relief (though this relief was slim) Jerry appeared unharmed. His gaze drifted in her direction. He gave her a nod of acknowledgment.

As much as she was glad to see that Jerry was all in one piece and she wasn't sharing the graveyard with a very fresh, unburied corpse, unease still squirmed in the pit of her stomach. Why wouldn't he just leave? Night would fall soon, and she had no desire to be alone with him in the dark.

She finished setting up her equipment five minutes later. One last look at the bench told her that Jerry had finally left.

Hopefully that meant he had gone home.

She hung the thermal imaging camera around her neck and made a few laps around the rectangular path while looking at the screen. The sound of her feet crunching in the loose gravel sounded as loud as gunshots in the still air. Fortunately, that meant that if Jerry tried to stalk her, she would hear his approach and have enough time to grab out her pepper spray.

Jessica repeatedly panned the camera back and forth. If the device were going to be her primary indicator of graveyard spirits, she was out of luck. No uncharacteristically cold spots showed up on the screen, and the only major heat signatures the thing picked up were in the shape of two deer grazing near the parking lot. The front of her car glowed orange on the screen, still warm from when the engine was running.

So maybe she was dealing with lukewarm ghosts. No one ever said that spirits had a standard body temperature, seeing as they had no bodies. She got out her voice recorder again. An interview might coax shy spirits out of hiding.

She planted her rear in the gravel and turned the recorder on. "Hello, if there are any spirits out here, could you please make yourselves known? I promise I won't hurt you."

While she waited for a ghost to reply, she looked over at the woods. They seemed so dark. A person might wander in there and never come out again. The place was probably teeming with lost souls who longed to ensnare hapless graveyard visitors and make them their own.

She smiled. The only place she could think of that truly teemed with lost souls was hell itself, and it was unlikely that the entrance to the netherworld would be found in the forests of Northern Kentucky.

"What are your names?" she asked. "When were you—"

Her cell phone chimed. She fumbled around in her pocket. Sidney had sent her a text message.

"Storm coming through around 9:30," it read. "Be careful."

"Crap." It had barely rained in ages, and it had to do it tonight? That hardly seemed fair.

She looked up at the sky. Stars were beginning to appear directly overhead, but off to the west a thick bank of clouds was moving in. Nice.

"Thanks for the heads-up," she replied.

"That's an interesting device you've got there," a voice said right behind her.

Her blood nearly froze.

It was Jerry Madison.

CHAPTER 8

J essica managed to get her feet back under her and whirled around to face the man. He stood barely three feet away on the gravel path, so he must have walked through the grass between the headstones for him to have approached so silently.

She stuck her hand in her pocket and closed her trembling fingers around the pepper spray. "What do you want from me?" she asked, stepping back from him.

His face twisted into a thin-lipped smile. "Are you scared?"

Jessica said nothing. She wondered if she was as terrified as Bundy's victims had been during their final living moments. Then, cursing herself for thinking of something so ghastly, she nodded.

"Why?"

"You're going to hurt me." She sounded like such a wimp. He probably thought so, too.

"Have I given you any reason to think I'd do that?" he asked, drawing closer to her. His feet made no sound in the gravel.

"What else would you be doing out here?"

He folded his arms and frowned. "You wouldn't understand."

"I understand that psychopaths like to nab women when they're alone. Makes their work easier. Right?"

His face darkened. "I couldn't have nabbed you even if I had wanted to. Not really."

Jessica took a small step in reverse. "You look pretty capable to me."

"The only thing I'm capable of is watching the world move on without me. I'm sure you can't imagine what it's like to sit here day after day without companionship, knowing that all the suffering you've endured is payment for what you did and that you've lost all your opportunities for redemption ages ago."

He spread his arms wide. "See all this? This has been my universe for more years than I care to count. I've seen nothing else of the world since I was taken here. Sure, I could have left at any time I chose, but where could I have gone? Heaven?" He laughed. "Don't give me that look. You know exactly what I'm talking about."

Though she longed to flee, Jessica was rooted to the ground. Surely he was just trying to frighten her even more in order to please himself. "Do I?" she croaked, hovering her finger over the button on the pepper spray, which was still concealed in her pocket.

"You can quit playing dumb, Jessica. What did you expect, a dirty sheet with holes cut out for eyes? I'm a human being just like you. Your gadgets disgust me. I'm not going to participate in parlor tricks just to satisfy your whims. My life was hard, and my death was about a hundred times harder than that. Don't try to trivialize it by asking me to speak into a recording device so you can share your evidence with all of your friends."

"I'm not—"

"If you're going to barge your way into my business, then the least you can do is help me."

Jessica swallowed. "*Help* you?"

"Yes. Keep me company. Make my punishment a little more bearable."

"I—I'm not going to be staying here much longer." In fact, she wanted to leave. Right now.

"Then you'll have to take me with you!"

She broke into a run, but he threw himself at her and hooked his arms around her neck the same instant.

He didn't weigh a thing, which was fortunate, because he would have dragged her to the ground if he had. Jessica clawed at him to make him let go. It was like swiping at air. Frigid air. "Get off!" she screamed.

He hung on tight, refusing to heed her request.

Convinced that continuing to fight with him would accomplish nothing, she tore off in the direction of the parking lot, letting out an involuntary moan with each of her footfalls. She arrived next to her car, gasping. A mercury vapor lamp next to the church provided her with enough light for her to see that no weightless man accompanied her. When had he released his grip? Had he even been there at all? Of course he had. A lingering iciness raised gooseflesh on her neck where he had touched her.

She dug her keys from her pocket and succeeded in opening the car door without dropping them from her shaking hands. Once inside, she slapped her fist onto the automatic lock button without thinking. She leaned back in an attempt to calm down.

The foolishness of the situation hit her then. What was cowering in a car going to do? She'd look like a baby. Besides, a person devoid of flesh and blood could pass through metal and glass as easily as she moved through the air.

A voice spoke by the window, nearly sending her through the roof. "Didn't anyone ever tell you it's good to help a stranger in need?" Jerry said, his voice oozing sarcasm.

She didn't reply. Instead, she peered out the window to try to pinpoint his location. All she could see were trees and headstones. No black figure lurked in her field of view.

It was probably a good idea to leave.

She moved to insert the key into the ignition, but suddenly the car dissolved around her. Red. Everything was red. She was sinking into the depths of an ocean comprised of blood. Voices shouted in the distance. It sounded as if she and those speaking stood at opposite rims of a canyon.

Mataste a mi nieta! A man.

Usted es el hijo del diablo! A different man.

Though Jessica knew a miniscule amount of Spanish (her mother was half Mexican), the overwhelming sense of terror that had taken hold of her suppressed her ability to translate the words into English.

The sea of red morphed into one of shadowy faces. They were lit from behind so she couldn't tell what they looked like, but she could sense their emotions. Pain. Grief. Hatred. All directed at her.

She did not want to see them. If she didn't look away, they would get inside her head and nest there like rats, gnawing away her sanity piece by tattered piece.

Make it stop, she prayed. *Make it stop, make it stop, make it—*

Everything around her grew dark. The faces had gone. Something flat lay on top of her body. She tried to straighten herself but found that she could barely move because she was trapped in a small, enclosed space.

Like a casket.

Panicking, she sat up and cracked her head on something solid. The glove box. The thing lying on top of her had to be the floor mat. She must have thrown it over herself for protection, as if a flimsy bit of rubber and carpet could ward off spirits.

A low rumble of thunder sounded in the distance. Sidney had mentioned that the storm would arrive around 9:30, which meant she'd been unconscious for two hours, maybe longer.

She should leave this Godforsaken place before another— vision? hallucination? whatever you wanted to call it—knocked her out. Only problem was all her equipment still sat around in various places outside. She couldn't just leave it all behind. As much as she disliked the idea, she had to retrieve it. She began to sweat.

Chicken, taunted a little voice in the back of her head.

No. She wasn't a chicken. She was just being smart. Smart people didn't traipse out into the dark where weightless things named Jerry lurked. You didn't stick around when faced with danger; you ran like heck so you could live to hunt ghosts another day. Survival mode at its best.

Then again, smart people didn't leave expensive equipment behind to get stolen or destroyed in the rain.

She looked out the driver's side window. From her crouched position on the floor, the only view she had of the outside world was a swatch of indigo sky. It wasn't raining yet.

A scraping sound made her jump. It might have been a raccoon or a dog rooting around for garbage. If it wasn't an animal, then it could have been Jerry, but he shouldn't have been making any sound other than that which bones make when settling in the grave.

"Shouldn't have been" did not mean "couldn't." After all, he'd carried on an intelligent conversation with her. Nothing would stop him from making scraping sounds, too. Right?

Something made a soft thump no more than five feet away from the car.

It was nothing. Had to be nothing. Maybe only the wind.

Jessica picked herself off the floor and climbed back behind the wheel. Wind, she could handle. She stared out at the silhouettes of headstones. Nothing moved.

A drop of rain splattered on the windshield and rolled down the glass in a lazy zigzag. A second and third joined it in quick succession.

She gritted her teeth. If she didn't hurry, water would start seeping into her cameras and drown the sensitive circuitry inside. Driving away without collecting her things just because she might run into Jerry again would be sheer idiocy, survival instinct or not.

"God," she whispered, "it would be really awesome if you could get me out of this mess in one piece."

She made a hasty sign of the cross for good measure and climbed out of the Taurus.

~~∞∞~~

She tripped over something solid the moment she stepped out of the car. A corpse! No, not a corpse. The thing on the ground was her bulging tote bag. It had transported itself here all the way from the back of the graveyard and filled back up with her equipment, too, by the feel of it.

Must have been the source of the scraping noise, if it had been dragged across the ground.

She carried the bag around to the back of the car and set it gently on the trunk so she could see it better in the lamplight. The bag bore definite evidence of having been dragged, because dirt and bits of dead leaves clung to the fabric. She brushed the debris away and undid the zipper.

All of her cameras and recorders were nestled in the bottom of the tote, as were her purse and Maglite. Jerry was quite the gentleman. He'd probably hold doors open for her, too.

"I guess I owe you one," she said quietly, though how to pay back a dead man was beyond her.

CHAPTER 9

His captors drove in silence, and the silence was driving him mad. If they'd turn the radio on again, the music might drown out the imagined sound of seconds ticking down to his final moments. He didn't ask them to do it. They wouldn't have listened.

It briefly crossed his mind that he had no clue where they were taking him. Somehow that seemed immaterial. It didn't matter if they killed him in a warehouse or in a cornfield—he'd still be dead, and they'd still get what they wanted.

As much as he loathed himself for it, he couldn't stop thinking about Abigail. If he hadn't met her, he might be married to someone else. Some nice woman who didn't throw dishes at him. He'd be asleep right now, lying on his side with her warm body snuggled up against his chest, and their children—yes, he was quite sure there would have been two or three of them—would be sound asleep in the next room dreaming of sugarplums or whatever kids dreamed about. If he hadn't met Abigail, he certainly wouldn't be stuffed like a slab of meat in the back of a car with his own executioners.

Regrettably, none of this thinking would change what had happened.

Abigail had been a secretary at the high school where he got his first job. He would never forget the moment when he first saw her standing in the office. Her hair was golden, her skin fair as the snow. Her hips swayed with a youthful seductiveness when she walked. She had seemed friendly at first. She paid attention to him. She listened to his dreams, and he to hers. It was his first real relationship with a woman, so he had no notion that something about her personality was slightly amiss.

Ha—slightly! Abigail was nuts.

When he married her, he'd foreseen none of the marital strife that was to come: the fights, the threats, and the tears; the manic spells and the rock-bottom lows; the brutal name-calling and the shattered dishes that lay like rubble on the kitchen floor. He'd been a young fool in love, and now he'd give anything in the universe to rewind the tape of his life and do it over differently.

The car drove over a bump in the road. His thoughts returned to the present. Escaping into his memories wasn't going to help him escape from the car.

He flexed the muscles in his shoulders. The tape had been bound so tightly around his wrists that his fingers and palms tingled with the onslaught of numbness. For the most part, his limbs still felt like rubber.

To put it quite frankly, he was screwed.

He didn't blame his captors for wanting to kill him. After all, he had done a very bad thing—though what he did brought him more relief than anyone could ever allow themselves to understand. It was funny how something so terrible could feel so good. He would never have to see the faces again. If he'd had the opportunity to continue, he'd have done so without a moment's pause. The world teemed with faces. Grinning faces. Taunting faces. Faces that mocked him in his sorrow and constantly reminded him of what might have been.

He hadn't wanted to do it. But when all was said and done and he had stared down at their dead eyes and stuffed the gun back into his pocket, he knew he had done the right thing.

He wasn't sure how his captors knew it was him. He had made sure that each of the faces lay still, and the dead do not tattle on those who kill them. There was, however, a slight chance that one of them had held on tightly to this world until the police and paramedics arrived on the scene. Perhaps one had uttered his name on their dying breath.

A more likely scenario was that the bullets had been traced to his handgun, but in that case, shouldn't there have been a warrant out for his arrest? Breaking into his house would not have been necessary. They could have just knocked on the door with the warrant in hand, read him his Miranda rights, and hauled him away.

This could only mean that the police had gone above the law and aided in his abduction.

He cursed himself for not having chosen a different weapon. He could have used a golf club or a knife; he owned both. However, those were more suitable for a single killing. The use of those weapons would have given the others the freedom to flee, allowing them to torment him another day—and the thought of that horrified him more than his impending death. The faces, oh, the faces…

The car turned off the road and was now bumping along a gravel lane. The destination couldn't be too much farther ahead now, because gravel lanes tended to dead-end.

The car slowed to a stop. His emotions bordered on the edge of panic. This was it. End of the road, end of the line. He'd be dead within the hour. Maybe within the quarter-hour.

Placing mind over matter in an attempt to wiggle his way out from between his captors, he squirmed around like a dying worm and received a fist in the nose for his effort. Blood trickled from his nostrils and over his lip. The taste of it nearly gagged him.

The car door opened. The captor on the left grabbed him under the armpits and dragged him out onto the ground, which felt solid like a parking lot. The smell of fresh asphalt filled the air.

More car doors slammed. The rest of the intruders who had escorted him from his house must have taken another vehicle, and now all seven of them were regrouping here—wherever "here" was—to take care of him.

He could only hope that whatever they planned on doing wouldn't take very long.

CHAPTER 10

S idney waited at one of the living room windows, anxiously staring out at the downpour. Heavy sheets of rain spattered against the glass with every gust of wind. Being stuck out there must have been terrible. Visibility on the highway would have been almost down to zero. People tended to forget how to drive the right way when it hadn't rained for months, so there were probably accidents all over the place. Fatal ones, too.

A couple of cars turned onto the street, but none of them pulled into the driveway.

She forced herself to step away from the window. Standing there worrying wasn't going to expedite Jessica's return and would in all likelihood make the wait seem longer.

What she really wanted was a smoke. A few draws on a cigarette would calm her down. She'd have to wait until it stopped raining, though. No way was she going to stand outside in this monsoon catching her death, and no way was she going to risk smoking in the house, because she didn't feel like listening to Wayne go on and on about black lung disease or some crap like that.

She sat back down on the couch and gazed at the black-and-white horror flick she'd found on a channel she didn't know they had. She'd muted the television so she wouldn't wake up her cousin. The lack of sound made the movie seem even more boring than it already was.

She yawned. The digital clock on the cable box showed the time as eleven thirty. Jessica should have been home ages ago.

"God, please keep Jessica safe out there," she caught herself whispering. Her face heated in embarrassment even though no one had been around to hear her. Some habits were never going to die. Heck, she still went to church every Sunday morning—not because she believed in any of that stuff, but because it helped pass the time on her least favorite day of the week.

A car door slammed somewhere outside. When a minute went by without anyone coming to the door, she returned to the window to see what was going on. Maybe Jessica needed help carrying something.

Or not. Jessica's car wasn't in the driveway. The sound must have come from another vehicle on another street.

"Don't do this to me, Jessica," she muttered, returning to the couch once more. If her friend had been killed in an accident, she would have no way of knowing until she turned on the news the next day. The only people she would have left would be Wayne, her dad, and her brothers Brian and Kyle. The former two, being older, were likely to die first. And if something happened to Brian or Kyle, she would be completely alone. Then she'd probably end up living to be a hundred and five in some nursing home where the food tasted like crap and they didn't serve Pepsi.

Headlights shining through the window grabbed her attention. She leapt off the couch and ran to the window, fully expecting to see a police cruiser sitting in the driveway even though there was no way an officer would have known Jessica was staying here, but instead her eyes were met with the sight of a forest-green Taurus pulling up close to the house. The headlights blinked out.

One benefit of expecting the worst was that she could never be disappointed. Grinning like a fool, Sidney unlocked the front door and held it open when Jessica came shuffling up onto the porch with her tote bag.

Jessica stepped onto the mat and pulled her hood back. Her hair was a mess, and she was shivering like she'd just gone for a swim in an icy pond. "Thanks," she said, setting down her bag and rubbing her hands together as if to warm them.

"I was starting to think you'd drowned out there," Sidney commented. She closed the door and engaged the deadbolt. There was no need to let her know just how worried she'd really been.

Jessica kicked off her shoes. "It was a close call. The car kept hydroplaning. Took me two hours to get back here." She walked over to the refrigerator and grabbed out a bottle of Mike's. "Do you have a bottle opener?"

"In the drawer under the microwave." Something wasn't right. Yeah, the drive home would have been stressful, but it shouldn't have stressed her out to the point of needing alcohol to soothe her nerves. "Everything okay?" Sidney asked. She pulled a chair out from the table and sat down.

Jessica joined her a moment later and pried the lid off of her drink. She took a sip and grimaced. Her face was chalk-white. "That depends on what you mean by okay. I mean, I'm alive, so I must be okay. Right?"

"You don't look okay. What happened?"

"I think I've made contact."

Sidney blinked. Jessica made it sound like she'd encountered an alien spacecraft. "With?"

"The things I've been trying to make contact with for years."

Of course. "You mean you actually saw a ghost."

"Not just saw. Talked to."

"Really."

Disappointment showed on Jessica's face. "I knew you wouldn't believe me. *I* wouldn't believe me."

"I didn't say I didn't believe you. Just tell me what happened."

Jessica raised the bottle to her mouth and gulped down more of the drink. "You know, this stuff tastes better once you get that first mouthful down."

"You do know that's Wayne's personal stash."

"I can buy him more tomorrow."

Sidney waited. "Well?"

Jessica set the bottle down on the table. "There was a guy hanging out in the graveyard when I got there. Mid-thirties, probably. We got to talking, and he said his name was Jerry Madison. He didn't look dead."

"Then how do you know he was? He could have been some jerk trying to scare you."

"That's what I thought at first, too. But then he jumped on me. And he didn't weigh anything."

Though she was a self-proclaimed teetotaler, Sidney contemplated getting a drink for herself. "What did he do that for?"

"He wanted to come with me, but I was able to ditch him at the last second."

Sidney drew her arms closer to her body. "Were you able to record any of it?"

"I'm not sure. My equipment was on, but I don't know how good the footage is going to be."

Sidney stood up and walked toward the counter, where Jessica had set her tote bag. "Then let's check it and see!"

Jessica shook her head. "I've had enough for one night. I can look at it tomorrow." She finished the alcoholic lemonade and wiped the back of her hand across her mouth. "If I don't wake up and find out this has been some screwy dream, that is. You never know when high EMFs are going to fry my brain."

Sidney didn't know what an EMF was, but she did know one thing: she did not want to wait until morning to look at Jessica's footage. Jessica never got freaked out on ghost hunts, so it was evident that *something* had happened out there.

Half an hour after Jessica went to bed, Sidney turned off the television and lights in the living room. She returned to the kitchen and stared at Jessica's black tote bag. Had Jessica really seen a ghost? The existence of ghosts would suggest some kind of afterlife, which in turn would suggest that there was a higher power in the universe. That was something that just couldn't be. Stories of a supreme being governing all of creation were only fairy tales meant to give comfort to the ignorant.

But Jessica would never lie to her. If she said she had met a spirit, then she had met a spirit, plain and simple.

Of course, Jessica may have been delusional. That was the only possible explanation that she'd be able to accept without having to alter her beliefs.

The tote bag seemed to beckon her. Jessica might be upset if Sidney rummaged through her equipment without permission. Some of it had been quite expensive. She could be careful, though, and put everything back in the bag so it wouldn't appear to have been touched.

She bit her lip. Should she, or shouldn't she? The truth might be terrifying.

The truth might be extraordinary.

She pulled a voice recorder out of the bag.

~~~∞∞∞~~~

That night, despite nearly an hour of tossing and turning, Jessica fell asleep and dreamed that she was a man.

She found herself seated at a round table in a bar with three other men in their early thirties. Even though nobody had mentioned them, she knew their names: Phil Knippenberg, Andy Schlosser, Garret West. The bar was crowded with more men than women. A live band performing on a stage off to one side attempted to play Aerosmith's hit "Dream On."

The smell of liquor and clouds of cigarette smoke hung like fog in the air of the poorly lit room. A waitress whose blouse exposed an ample amount of cleavage brought four foaming glasses of Bud Light to their table, left, and immediately returned with a tray of nachos.

Jessica's comrades dug in like wolves on a fallen doe. She had no appetite and stared down at her man-hands, feeling emptier than the deepest void of space.

"Come on, eat something," Andy urged her.

She shook her head. "I ate before I left the house. And I'm not hungry." A man's voice came out of her mouth. This was one weird dream.

"He's probably thinking 'bout that broad again," Phil said, his mouth full of cheesy tortilla chips that dripped with grease. Jessica could tell from the slur in his speech that this beer was not his first or even his second of the evening. "He's got that funny look in his eyes."

"I can think about whatever I want to," Jessica snapped.

"Get over it, man," Garret said.

"And just how am I supposed to do that?"

Garret gestured over his shoulder toward the bar counter, where a pair of busty women with feathered haircuts were laughing with the female bartender. "I'll give you a dollar if you ask one of those babes out. Doesn't even have to be a date. Just take her home tonight. Heck, let's make it five dollars. I'm feeling generous."

Strangely, the thought of taking an unknown woman to bed was somewhat appealing. And it had been such a long time, much too long...

No. Never again. Relationships of any kind only led to ruin.

Her hesitation must have been too obvious. Andy let out a chuckle. "He'll never do it, because he won't let himself get over dear Abby, that's the problem. Am I right?"

Jessica felt her temper begin to build. "I'm not going to be able to just forget what she did as if it never happened."

Phil lifted his glass into the air. "This might help."

"I'd kill myself before stooping to your level."

Phil grinned. "Then go right ahead."

Jessica gave a hollow laugh. "That's one way to meet the kids, isn't it?"

"Fatherhood isn't all it's cracked up to be," Garret said. "Enjoy your freedom."

Freedom? "Do you understand how much it killed me when she told me? She even made me pay for it, for crying out loud!"

Phil took a swig of his Bud Light. "You act like what she did is some big deal. I made Sherry get two of 'em. You shoulda seen her crying and hanging onto her stomach like it was gonna help. Told her I'd throw her out in the streets if she didn't do it. Gave in like a beat dog."

At first she was too stunned to speak. Surely this Phil creature could not have been that cruel! "But why?"

Phil shrugged. "Didn't want no brats running around. World's too full of 'em anyway."

Bile rose in Jessica's throat, and the next thing she knew, she was on her feet and had her man-hands locked around Phil Knippenberg's throat, fully intent on crushing his esophagus. She heard the chair crash into the floor behind her. "You filthy monster!" she screamed in Phil's reddening face. "How can you even sleep at night knowing what you did?"

Phil tried to speak but couldn't. He reeked like alcohol, and for all Jessica cared he could have drowned in it.

Several sets of hands pried her off of her victim, and Phil drew back, gasping for air. His chest heaved up and down.

"Go to hell," he breathed. Murder shined in his eyes.

"Gladly," Jessica responded as the hands dragged her away from the table out into the night, leaving her alone in the darkness.

The dream changed, and Jessica was that man again. Clad only in boxers, sitting on the edge of a bed. She turned a black pistol over and over in her hands. Six bullets nestled in their proper places. Six shiny passports that would enable her transport from this bleak world to the next.

"God," she rasped in her man-voice, feeling her throat constrict with grief, "if you're really there, if you care about me at all, you'll make this painless."

She put the tip of the gun in her mouth and pulled the trigger.

The weapon clicked like a child's toy gun. She lowered it, dumbfounded. There was no reason for it to have failed to expel the bullet. She pointed the gun at the floor and fired a hole into the rug. The sound of the ensuing blast reverberated throughout the room. Her ears started ringing. Hopefully the neighbors hadn't heard it, too.

So the gun had jammed. It would not happen again.

She returned the gun to her mouth so she could properly execute herself and fired the gun a third time.

The faulty gun emitted another inadequate click. Enraged, she threw the gun to the floor and kicked it across the room.

"Why are you doing this to me?" she shouted. "Can't you let a man end it all in peace?"

Thou shalt not kill, said a voice deep within her mind.

She laughed. "Thou shalt not kill. Thou shalt not kill. Tell that to *them!*"

The dream faded away when Jessica awoke to a dark bedroom. She had the faint sensation of something ominous slithering around in her mind, but the feeling dissipated within minutes. Dreams were dreams. There was nothing sinister about them.

Yet she still lay wide awake in bed for a long time after. Wondering.

CHAPTER 11

W ayne had already left for work when Jessica crawled out of bed aching at nine o'clock. Sleeping in that late was not her usual custom, but after the previous evening's occurrences, she deserved to indulge herself with a little extra sleep—not that she'd gotten much of it. Forget the insomnia. Everything was so *sore*.

In the kitchen Sidney was hurriedly finishing a glass of orange juice and holding a half-eaten piece of toast in one hand.

"Running late?" Jessica popped two slices of bread into the toaster. The breakfast of paupers.

"Forgot to set my alarm." She set her glass in the sink. "I already called Travis to let him know. He said not to worry because hardly anyone's been in this morning anyway."

"What's new?"

Sidney cleared her throat then glanced down at the table. "So, how are you feeling?"

"Awful. You?"

Her cheeks turned pink. "I'm kind of worried."

"What the heck are you worried about? I'm the one who went on some kind of mental trip last night."

"At least we're on the same wavelength. Just don't kill me."

Jessica didn't like the look in Sidney's eyes. It was the kind that puppies on television gave their masters when they'd made a mess somewhere. "What did you do?"

"I kind of peeked at your footage last night after you went to bed."

Oh, boy. "Did you see anything? Like Jerry?"

"No. They're all blank."

"You're kidding." Her heart sank a little. Well, maybe more than a little. There had been photographs and clips from investigations going back six months saved on various memory cards. Even if she had had a mental lapse out in the graveyard and forgot to turn the equipment on, the other tracks should have still been there.

"I'm not. I checked everything. It's like they've never even been used before. You're sure you turned them on?"

"Yes, I'm sure!" Sidney had to have made a mistake, and to prove it Jessica snatched a camcorder from the tote bag. She pressed the power button and swung the screen open, where a tiny menu appeared. Yesterday there had been about fifteen old videos stored on the card. Today there were none. "I don't believe it. All my other videos are gone, too." She flipped the screen closed and set the camera down. "This doesn't make any sense."

"I said they were totally blank. Did you back them up on anything?"

"Yeah, I saved them all on my computer. Except the ones from last night, of course."

"Well, have fun figuring out where all of your files went. I'm heading out." She stuffed the last bit of toast into her mouth, shouldered her purse, and left without another word.

Jessica stared at the toaster. Her slices of bread had popped up a minute or so before. She put them on a plate and slathered them with margarine from the fridge. She'd have to stop at Eleanor Market later on and pick up some waffles or something. Some burritos, too. She had enough money left for a couple packages of those.

She swept the breadcrumbs off the table into her hand and brushed them into the wastebasket when she finished eating.

Now to focus on the mystery surrounding her equipment. Had Sidney really looked at all of them? Yeah, maybe the camcorder malfunctioned and wiped itself clean, but there was no reason for all of her devices to have done the same thing.

Jessica picked up the teal digital camera. She had taken so many pictures with it the night before that she'd lost count of them. They couldn't all be gone.

She turned the camera on, and the lens zoomed out. She hit the review button.

"Oh, crap."

The memory card was empty. The dozens of photographs she'd taken at the church were forever lost in digital oblivion.

"I told you that your gadgets disgust me."

Jessica let out a noise that might have been "Eeep!" and dropped the camera. It hit the linoleum and made a tinkling sound like shattering glass.

Jerry Madison was standing beside the table with his arms folded over his chest. He didn't smile. "Good morning." He looked solid, just like he had last night.

Without thinking, Jessica backed away toward the front door. No way could this be happening. She must have left her mind somewhere between that graveyard and Eleanor, or maybe she was still asleep in bed, though she doubted it.

"I can't look *that* bad," he said. There was a hint of amusement in his eyes.

Jessica's tongue felt like it had been tied into knots. Jerry had to have been in the car with her on the drive home. "You followed me."

"I didn't want to be alone anymore."

"I don't believe this."

"That's an odd thing for a ghost hunter to say."

"Is not. This isn't how it's supposed to be." She felt behind her for the doorknob but couldn't find it.

This time he did smile. "Running away again? Where do you plan on going?"

"Insane?" She gave up on finding the knob without turning around and clasped her hands together in front of her so they wouldn't start shaking again.

He laughed. "You're not insane. I'm here. For real." He glanced around the kitchen and gave it a nod of approval. "Nice place you've got."

"It's not mine. It's Wayne's. I only just moved in yesterday."

"He's the one with the bad legs?"

So Jerry had been spying on them all morning. "Yeah. Besides, he's the only 'he' who lives here."

"What happened to him?"

It was ridiculous standing here talking to someone who might not really exist, but she couldn't help but go on. "He's got cerebral palsy. It's actually a brain damage thing."

"I know what cerebral palsy is," he said. "I'm not from the Stone Age."

An awkward silence arose between them.

Jessica shuffled her feet. There were things she needed to get done today, and they wouldn't *get* done if Jerry planned on staying here watching her. "Are you just going to stand there all day?" she said.

"I can sit, if you'd like."

What a comedian. "How is it that I can see you?" she asked.

"Because I want you to."

"You didn't even know I was there when I first saw you last night. You were facing the other way."

"Do you want an honest answer?"

"Truth's always better than a lie."

He smirked. "If you insist. I don't know why you saw me then. There are a few people who have been able to see me—very few, mind you—but I'd always assumed they had some kind of gift. Are you gifted?"

"You mean with a sixth sense?"

"Whatever you want to call it."

She shook her head. "I don't even believe in that kind of thing."

"You must not believe in much."

"I believe in lots of things," she said, making a mental tally. "God, myself, the healing powers of Mexican food…"

"You're forgetting something," Jerry said.

"I don't like stating the obvious." She felt her cheeks flush. *God, please make him get out of here and leave me alone. Nothing good can come of him being in our house.*

"Look," she said. "I don't want to be mean, but there's nothing for you here."

His face fell. "I told you, I'm lonely. Go ahead, say it. I'm a grown man and should stop sounding like a teenager who's been dumped by his prom date. But you spend a couple of decades by yourself and tell me how *you* feel."

He couldn't really be that dense. "I don't mean here, as in this house. I mean here, as on this planet. You're not supposed to be here anymore. Look for the tunnel of light, or whatever you're supposed to see when you die."

"Some people don't go to heaven."

"You're certainly not in hell, trust me. That's at my parents' house."

"Then when the judgment comes, I'll be spending eternity there with them."

She couldn't help but smile. Maybe his being here wouldn't be so awful after all. "So, what did you do that was so bad? Steal a candy bar?"

He narrowed his eyes. "We don't need to get into that."

"It can't be that terrible, or you'd be in hell already. Are you at least sorry for whatever it was?"

At first, he didn't answer. His face contorted as if he were straining to think. Then his eyes took on a manic glint. "What if I'm not? What if I enjoyed doing it?"

Goosebumps stood up on her arms. "Did you?"

His expression softened. "It doesn't matter. The deed is done, and here I am."

"Right." She stooped to pick her broken camera off the floor. A bunch of tiny somethings rattled around inside. She hoped that the memory card would be salvageable for future use. "I thought I wasn't supposed to be afraid of you."

He laughed softly. "It's entirely up to you how to feel. Yes, I could probably hurt you if I tried hard enough, but I'm not going to. I'm just a bundle of thoughts and memories without much substance, as you can tell."

She set the camera on the counter next to the tote bag. "You managed to pack up my stuff just fine last night."

"It wasn't easy."

"Why did you even bother? I thought that you didn't like my gadgets, and since you're the one who moved them, I'm going to assume you're the reason they're all blank now."

He shrugged and glanced toward the window over the kitchen sink, where a bird had perched on the outside windowsill. "How did you sleep last night?"

"Lousy," she said. "Now about you wiping my equipment like you own it—"

"Lousy?"

Her irritation began to grow. "Yeah. I had a hard time falling asleep, and when I did, I had weird, depressing dreams that woke me back up anyway. Why does it matter?"

He abruptly changed the subject. "Do you want to go for a walk? If you're not too tired, that is."

"Seriously?"

"I can tell you're bored standing here, and it's a nice day."

Boredom wasn't quite what she'd been feeling, but she didn't correct him. "Look." She crossed her arms. "I've got stuff to do. I need to go to the grocery so I don't end up starving to death, I should pick up more job applications since it looks like nobody is planning on hiring me in the foreseeable future, and…well, I'm sure there's something I'm forgetting."

"It's still early. We could go for a walk first."

She sighed. He wasn't going to give up, and she couldn't blame him. How many times had she pestered Sidney about going ghost hunting? Probably a million, and she'd still felt depressed every time Sidney declined her offers. "Would other people be able to see you?"

"Probably not. I don't think so."

"Then they'd think I was talking to myself."

"We could go for a drive instead."

With the amount of gas left in her tank after last night's excursion, they wouldn't be going very far at all, but he didn't need to know that. A short drive might make him happy enough that he would decide to leave her alone once and for all. "Let me get dressed," she said.

In her room, Jessica wadded up her pajamas and set them on the floor at the foot of the bed. Her jeans from last night were too filthy to wear again today. While she was out, she could buy one of those extra-concentrated jugs of laundry detergent in addition to the waffles and burritos. It could be her rent for the month. Wayne would like that.

She threw on a pair of holey blue jeans and a white t-shirt and crept back down the stairs, hoping that Jerry hadn't secretly been watching her while she got dressed. He didn't appear to be in the kitchen anymore. Not good. Maybe he just needed to power down for a while like a computer going into sleep mode. It had to have been a strain maintaining an apparition of himself.

She rounded the corner into the bathroom and latched the door behind her. No Jerry in here either, thank goodness.

She stared at her face in the mirror. Her eyes were bloodshot, her dark circles as pronounced as ever. At least she didn't need to impress anybody today. It would be better to save the makeup she had left for whenever she got a new job.

The kitchen was still vacant when she left the bathroom minutes later. "Hey," she said. "Are you still here?"

If Jerry had replied, she could not hear it. It was unlikely that he had left.

She poked her head out into the living room. "All right, I'm heading out. Just don't scare me when I'm driving, because I don't want to be in an accident." *Or have one*, she thought. She plucked her sweatshirt off the back of one of the kitchen chairs and slipped it on. "Last one to the car's a rotten egg."

Wind buffeted her as she made her way toward her Taurus. The sun was out, and billowy clouds scudded across the sky as though they were fleeing unpleasant weather that pursued them from afar.

The fuel light came on when she started the engine. It was no wonder; the needle on the fuel gauge was grazing the top of the E. Looked like she'd have to pay Sidney a visit at work before going anywhere else.

She pulled up to her favorite island of pumps a few minutes shy of ten o'clock. Intuition told her to check her wallet before filling up. A good thing, too. All she had left was a twenty, a ten, and a handful of change. She dumped her purse out on the passenger seat. Two pennies and a nickel fell out. She checked the coin slot beneath the radio and found three more pennies and one of those gold Sacagawea dollars that nobody ever liked to use. Better than nothing.

Today gas was $2.85 a gallon. If she were going to stop at the grocery store, she couldn't afford to fill the entire tank.

Ask your parents for money, said a little voice in her head. *It won't kill you.*

She didn't want to take her chances with that. She pumped ten bucks of gas and went inside.

"Did you miss me that badly?" Sidney asked. She already wore the glassy-eyed look of boredom.

Jessica handed over her ten-dollar bill. "I was bereft."

"That bad, huh?"

"That, and worse." She glanced out at the empty Taurus. "Do you see anybody in my car?"

Sidney followed her gaze. Her eyebrows knit together. "Do you?"

"Nope."

"Then what was the point of asking?"

"I just wanted to make sure we were both seeing the same thing."

"Are you feeling all right?"

She shrugged. "I ache everywhere. I might go down to the park and walk for a while to stretch things out." It wasn't technically a lie. "And I was thinking of stopping at the store to restock my burrito supply. You need anything while I'm out?"

"That would be a negative. You're going for a walk by yourself?"

"It can't be any worse than doing investigations by myself."

"Watch out for leaping dead guys."

"Ha ha." She moved toward the door. "I guess I'd best be on my way."

"Have fun."

"Yeah," she said, thinking about how awkward it was going to be walking around with a person whom only she could see. "I'll do that."

CHAPTER 12

Smithfield Park sat at the base of Lookout Hill on the eastern end of town, boasting about two miles of wooded trails, a fishing pond that had briefly become a part of the Ohio River during the infamous Flood of 1997, volleyball and tennis courts, a picnic pavilion, and a playground and swings for the kids. Grandma Reyes had taken Jessica and her sister there to play a few times before she died. Jessica's memories of those days had dimmed over the years, though she did remember having fun. Perhaps Jerry would have fun, too.

Only one other vehicle occupied the lot when Jessica arrived. A man stood at the edge of the pond holding a fishing pole with its line cast far out in the water. A tackle box rested on the picnic table beside him.

"I thought we were going for a drive." Jerry was suddenly sitting beside her, looking as glum as a kid whose birthday had just been canceled.

She pointed at the fuel gauge as she tried to still her startled pulse. "See this? I'm running on a quarter tank now, and that's as full as it's going to get until I can find another job. *Comprende?*"

"*Sí. Comprendo.*"

"So you speak Spanglish, too, huh?"

"I studied Spanish for three years in high school. Ancient history."

"That's three more years than I did. I just have the benefit of being a part-Mexican mutt." She undid her seatbelt. "We're in luck. The only person here looks like he's too busy fishing to notice me talking to myself."

She was halfway out the door when Jerry said, "Wait."

She halted. "What?"

He gazed through the windshield at the play area, where the empty swings swayed from side to side in the wind and dead leaves accumulated at the base of a miniature rock-climbing wall. "This was a bad idea," he said.

"What's the matter?" She hoped her voice didn't betray her irritation. After all, the idea had been his, and she wasn't about to waste the trip—not with the price of gas what it was. "You told me you wanted to go for a walk. They have a nice trail here. I think you'll like it."

He gave her a doleful look. "You don't understand."

"You're right. I don't."

"All I see is…" He shook his head.

Nothing about the scene before them struck her as deserving this response. It was a *park*, for crying out loud! "What?"

"Don't worry about it."

"Well, all I see here is a crappy playground. They've had this same set here since I was a kid." She slammed the door and set off toward the trailhead on the far side of the pond. If he was going to pout, he could just stay in the car. Then she wouldn't have to worry about being seen talking to herself if anyone else showed up.

But Jerry fell in step beside her despite his obvious reluctance. When they passed the playground, he made a point of looking the other way at the picnic pavilion, where some trash had blown out of a can and scattered across the cement slab where all the picnic tables sat. So he had a problem with playgrounds? People probably got worked up over even stranger things. Maybe he'd gotten hurt on a playground when he was a kid and developed an aversion to them as a result of the ordeal.

"Feeling better yet?" she asked when they were out of earshot of the man with the fishing pole, not knowing what else to say. What were you supposed to talk about with someone like him, anyway? Politics? Depending on when he'd died, he might not even know who the current president was.

"No."

"Have you even tried feeling better?"

He glared at her. "I hope you never decide to become a psychologist."

"Sorry."

They entered the woods. Signs describing different plants and animals living in the area had been posted along the edge of the trail every so many yards, but Jerry showed no interest in reading them.

"One of my brothers was a psychologist," he said, gazing up at the bit of blue sky visible through the treetops. "But even he wasn't able to do anything for me. That was after I tried to kill myself. Tried to put a bullet through my skull, but someone must have been looking out for me that day, because the gun malfunctioned, and I didn't die after all."

Jessica halted without thinking and stared at him. "Wait a minute. I dreamed about something like that last night. When the gun didn't go off, I shot a hole in the floor."

"Did you?"

"Don't act like you don't know what I'm talking about. You had something to do with it. You were fiddling around in my head!" The very thought appalled her.

"Why would I do that?"

"Heck if I know!" She realized she was shouting, so she lowered her voice so the fisherman wouldn't hear and come running to her aid. "That other thing must have been you, too. The jerks in the bar, I mean." Many of the details of the dream had already grown fainter since she'd risen, but the sense of disgust that the dream had instilled in her remained. "What were you trying to prove to me?"

He continued down the path. "Prove? Nothing. They're only memories. That's all I have and all I am."

She caught up to him. "You said that before."

"Yes. Our whole lives consist of memories, some good, some bad. Mostly bad."

She nodded. "Sounds like my life."

"Humor me."

"You want me to give you my life story?"

"It's better than listening to mine."

"Geez." Where would she even begin? "I guess you could say I've always been a little lonely," she said, stating the first thing that came to mind, lame as it may have sounded.

"So we have something in common."

"Maybe. Did your parents ignore you like you were a Jehovah's Witness loitering on the porch with a briefcase full of *Watchtower* magazines?"

"Quite the opposite. They found the need to pry into my business at every available opportunity."

"Then maybe we don't have much in common at all. My mom and dad never paid much attention to me or my sister. Work was their first love. Still is."

"You have friends to keep you company."

She shrugged. "Not the typical kind. I grew up playing with Rachel and Sidney, so when I started school I just didn't know how to connect with kids my age. I'd usually sit in the back of the classroom daydreaming or reading while other kids did their own stuff. I got picked on a little, but mostly I just ignored that. Except for the one time in the first grade when I finally got tired of Yesenia Solorzano stealing my crayons and I punched her in the stomach."

"What about your friend Wayne?"

She smiled at the sound of his name. "Wayne's been a sweetie since I met him in ninety-four. He's way older than me, though. He and Sidney are actually cousins. Second cousins, I think. I lived next door to them growing up."

"They lived in the same house?"

"Yeah. Wayne got taken away from his family because they treated him like crap, so Sidney's parents took him in."

"Do you like him?"

Her face heated up. "I said he's my friend."

"But you'd like him to be more than a friend."

"Maybe."

He laughed. "Maybe? You should have seen your face when I brought him up."

They passed the turnoff for a secondary trail that looped through the trees for a mile. If Jessica's legs hadn't been hurting, she'd have taken that path in a heartbeat, but instead she kept to the main trail. She didn't want to make herself hurt worse than she already did.

"So what's your story?" she asked. "Where are you from?"

"Originally? Cleveland. I came to Cincinnati for college and settled in Alexandria, Kentucky, when I graduated. Nothing too exciting. I was a high school English teacher. My parents were ashamed—especially my father, who had his own law firm. They thought I wouldn't be able to get by on such a meager salary, but that ended up being the least of my worries."

"Being poor sounds like a pretty big worry to me."

"Death tends to change one's perspective on things."

Up until now it had been easy to pretend that Jerry was some ordinary person strolling around with her, but now the conversation was getting awkward. "I don't doubt that," she said, using an approaching sign covered in facts about the Pileated Woodpecker as an excuse to look away from him.

"It changes everything. We work our whole lives trying to get rich so we can impress the world with our fancy houses and cars,

98

but in the end it doesn't matter how much money we make. What matters most are the choices we make, and unfortunately I made some very bad choices. Do you realize," he continued, his eyes growing livid, "that at any moment Christ might come descending from the clouds, and all souls on earth living and dead will be judged before him? That I have nothing good to say about myself except that I read my Bible from cover to cover half a dozen times and sat in the front pew in church on Sundays? Look where it got me!"

She was about to give him some lame reassurance about him not needing to worry about Judgment Day, but his face contorted as if he were in agony, and he seemed to be speaking to a third person whom she couldn't see. "No, I'm not sorry…it's all God's fault. He should have seen it coming! If he didn't, how can he be God? How can he be anything?"

"Jerry? You okay?"

Though he was still visible as he walked beside her, his mind seemed to have retreated to a place that, like the entity he was conversing with, she could not see. "Can a just God make us suffer so much? He hurts us because he lets others hurt us. If he cared, he'd stop them! I want to hurt them…" He broke off, stopped walking, and looked around wildly. "Jessica? Where did you go?"

She was almost too unnerved to speak. She realized she'd been holding her breath. "I'm right here."

"Where?" He was looking at the air a foot to the left of her head.

"*Here.*"

He shuddered then turned a few degrees to Jessica's right. "Oh." They locked gazes, and his pale face was awash with relief. "For a minute I thought you'd left me. Please don't ever do that."

She wasn't about to make any promises of that nature. "What was all that stuff you just said?"

"What stuff?"

Either he was an excellent liar, or he truly didn't have a clue what he'd just been saying. "I think we should hurry up and get back," she said.

He made no reply. They completed the circular trail in silence. By the time they made it back to the car, the fisherman had left.

"Are we going home?" Jerry asked.

"Not yet." She started the engine. Somehow the thought of lounging around the house for the remainder of the day with only him for company didn't seem all that appealing—not if he was just going to sit and watch her every movement like a disembodied Peeping Tom. "Got to get some groceries first."

"Must be nice."

"If it bothers you, you don't have to go in with me."

"I'll stay in here, then."

She drove back into the main part of town. Traffic had picked up a little, and the police chief—Fred Hargis—was sitting in his cruiser at the edge of the drug store lot aiming a radar gun at the passersby. She slowed the car just in case her speedometer was off. "Jerry?"

"Hmm?"

"How did you die? If you don't mind my asking, that is."

"Do you really want to know?"

"If I didn't want to, I wouldn't have asked."

"Maybe you're better off not knowing."

Why wouldn't he just get to the point? "It's not going to hurt me."

In her peripheral vision, she could see him smirking at her. "Fine. You want to know that badly? I was murdered."

"*What?*"

"I was murdered," he repeated in the offhand manner of one commenting on the weather. "Years ago. Nobody ever found where they buried me."

"Dear God." Unwanted tears blurred her vision. "I had no idea."

"Why should you have? You don't know anything about me."

"I don't know, I just didn't think…" She swallowed. Her mind began to fill with countless questions that she probably had no business asking. She chose what seemed like the safest one. "Why did they do it?"

He shrugged. "Some people just do that kind of thing."

She started to ask him whether or not the perpetrator had been caught, but stopped herself. He wouldn't have any way of knowing that if he'd spent his entire afterlife hanging out at Ye Olde Methodist Church. "I'm sorry," she said. "If there's anything I can do to help…"

"Just don't leave me," he said as she pulled into the Eleanor Market parking lot, which was surprisingly full for it being so early in the day. "I don't think I can handle being alone ever again."

CHAPTER 13

S he hurried through the crowded grocery store aisles as quickly as she could, not wanting to leave Jerry by himself for too long so he wouldn't think she'd ditched him. She had to feel sorry for the man. Dying alone at the hands of a killer had to be one of the worst ways to go. At least Marjorie Miller had been surrounded by a plethora of loved ones when she finally passed. Her husband had even been holding her hand. Jessica's chest grew tighter at the memory. Sweet, laughing Marjorie reduced to a bald skeleton covered in sallow skin from the failed chemotherapy treatments. Yet as the woman died, a faint smile stretched across her face. She was going home.

As Jessica selected her favorite brand of burritos and tossed the package into the cart, she brooded about Jerry's predicament. Did he remain on earth as a result of his own choosing, or was the situation entirely beyond his control? Maybe shame kept him here. Like, *Hi, God, I know you've forgiven me for my sins, but I just feel awful for being a sinner. I'll just stay in this lousy graveyard until kingdom come so I won't have to look you in the eye.* Made sense. A good long talk with Jerry might convince him to pack his bags and move on. He'd certainly be happier in heaven than he was here.

She fully intended to begin that conversation the moment she returned to the car with her groceries and much-lighter wallet, but she was out of luck. Either Jerry had powered down again or he had abandoned ship, and quite frankly she didn't want to strike up a conversation with the empty passenger seat in the event that he really had left.

~~~✻~~~

Jessica sat at the kitchen table with her journal and a ballpoint pen to begin recording all she could remember about the night before.

> 10/19/2010. Graveyard at United Methodist Church south of Iron Springs, Kentucky. I ran into some kind of aura in the parking lot two different times. The second time I had a vision of angry people shouting in Spanish, but I can't remember what they said. Could be a replaying of events that happened there. Note: do research about area. See what kind of history the place has.
>
> Also encountered spirit in graveyard. He appears as a full-body apparition, says his name is Jerry Madison, early to mid-thirties in age. At one point it appeared there were strangulation marks on his neck, but then they went away.

> 10/20/2010. Jerry showed up in the kitchen this morning. All my footage from last night got wiped from my equipment, has to be him who did it. I guess he doesn't want anyone to know what went on between us. We went for a walk at Smithfield Park. Jerry got depressed at the sight of the playground. He got all goofy-acting out on the trail and thought I'd left him even though I was standing right there. He says he'll go to hell if he moves on from here. Probably just being hard on himself.
>
> Oh, and one more thing: apparently someone murdered him.

She lifted the pen from the page and examined what she had written. If anyone were to come across her journal, they would think she had become delusional. Good for them.

Jerry says that his life consists mostly of bad memories, so he and I have something in common. Maybe that's why he's feeling a connection with me and doesn't want to go away—though I have no clue where he is right now. He could be standing over my shoulder invisible and I'd never know.

She would have to ask him about his childhood, though what he'd said made her think that his parents and her own were nothing alike. His parents *hadn't* ignored him. Must have been nice to be noticed. Well, Jessica did have to give her father some credit. He did sometimes read her and Rachel stories before bed even though he usually fell asleep before they did. And he'd taught the two of them to drive. That had been cool. He'd let Jessica drive all the way to Gatlinburg and back one day just to get in the driving hours she needed. She'd bought a souvenir t-shirt at a gift shop, they'd eaten lunch, taken a quick ride up the Space Needle, and went home. It had been a great bonding experience, but Stephen Roman-Dell had barely spoken a word that didn't have to do with work. Heck, he'd barely spoken a word, period. He was a stranger. Just like her mother.

The only things she really knew about her parents were that they had married each other for God knew what reason and eventually produced her and Rachel as proof that they at least shared the same bed. They had never even told Jessica how they'd met each other. Not that she particularly cared.

She got up from the table and stretched. The brief stroll in the woods hadn't helped the pain go away. If anything, the movement of walking had made the pain worse.

The bottle of Tylenol was still in her purse. She took two more pills and prayed for them to work this time.

And now, what to do with the rest of the day? Continuing her job search by car was out of the question since she had about three gallons of gas left in the tank. She'd already hit up all the businesses in Eleanor and even a couple way down the road in

Moscow. Beechmont and Kellogg Avenue weren't too far away, but she didn't want to risk running out of gas while stopped at a light somewhere.

Working out of town might not be that fun anyway. Once a river rat, always a river rat, as the jerks in high school always said. She'd be a fish out of water if she were to go anywhere else.

She still had to do something to keep busy. It wasn't time for lunch yet, and since her ghost-hunting equipment was currently as blank as a new sheet of paper, she couldn't even go over the graveyard footage to see if she'd caught Jerry on film.

She *could* do a little cleaning to prove she was a useful addition to the household.

She went into the bathroom. The tub looked a little dingy, and some specks of toothpaste dotted the mirror on the medicine cabinet. Yes, she could do some work in here. She wouldn't even tell anyone she'd cleaned, just to see if they'd notice.

Wayne kept used plastic grocery bags under the kitchen sink. She grabbed one of those in addition to the roll of paper towels sitting on top of the refrigerator and carried both to the bathroom.

An assortment of cleaners huddled in the cabinet beneath the bathroom sink. Windex and an off-brand soap scum remover would do nicely.

She set to work wiping off the mirror and starting singing "Dream On" in her best Steven Tyler voice. The song had been stuck in her head all morning. "Every time I look in the mirror, all these lines on my face gettin' clearer..."

She tossed the towel into the plastic bag and moved on to the tub. She sprayed the tub surround with the other cleaner. "The past is gone..."

The words died in her throat. Sensing that she was no longer alone, she turned around and saw only the bathroom door, which stood ajar. Hadn't it been open more than that before? A draft might have pulled it part of the way shut.

That, or Jerry did it.

Globs of foam oozed down the tub walls while she waited for the man to show himself. She waited. And waited. The smell of cleaner made her head feel funny.

The bathroom seemed to be staring back at her. More like glaring. Somebody was angry.

"Uh, Jerry?"

Seconds ticked by. The sensation of being watched did not abate.

She returned her attention to the tub and wiped off the cleaner as best she could. "It went by like dusk to dawn…"

Anger permeated the air like smog in an urban metropolis. Suddenly it seemed a very good idea to stop singing.

When she did, the anger lessened but did not dissipate. Perhaps it was all in her head and she was only being paranoid—which, of course, was silly. She was in no danger here. If Jerry had intended to harm her, he'd have done so already.

Something in the air seemed to shift. Now it felt like an unseen entity was examining her under a metaphorical micro-scope. Calculating.

"Look," she said when she finished cleaning the toilet, "if that's you in here, why don't you just say so instead of doing this creepy invisible crap?"

A dark haze started to materialize by the sink then faded away again. Her pulse quickened. "Are you going to say anything?"

She thought she heard a whisper. *Nothing to say.*

"Fine, then," she said. "I don't have anything to say, either."

~~~

Since Sidney spent every Wednesday evening sitting in English class over at the community college, Jessica and Wayne dined alone, which was fine with her. They didn't often get to spend time together like this, and after the events of the morning and previous day, it felt good to hang out with someone who still breathed.

She'd only eaten half her spaghetti before growing too full to finish it. She pushed her plate back and leaned her head on one hand, watching Wayne twirl his own spaghetti around a fork. His eyelids drooped as if he were about to doze off sitting up.

"So how was the graveyard last night?" he asked. He popped the spaghetti into his mouth and chewed. "See any hamsters?"

She hadn't been looking forward to bringing the matter up. If Sidney thought she was crazy, there was no telling what Wayne would think. "It was creepier than I expected it to be," she admitted. "What would you think if I told you I met a spirit out there?"

Wayne nearly choked on a bit of food. If he'd been tired before, he wasn't now. "Met? As in, you introduced yourselves and carried on a conversation?"

Jessica nodded. "Pretty much."

"I would have a hard time believing it."

"But you don't think it would be impossible."

His brown eyes scrutinized her as if he were trying to determine whether or not she had finally lost it.

Before he could get another word in, she told him about her encounters with Jerry, ending with how they had gone for a walk together. She left out the part about Jerry's supposed murder in case the spirit was listening in. He might not want anyone else to know such a personal detail about himself, especially since he'd been reluctant enough to tell *her*.

Wayne's face grew paler while she spoke, though the look in his eyes told her that he still wasn't completely convinced. "Do you think he's still here?"

"I don't see why he wouldn't be. He acts like he can't stand being alone."

Wayne studied her. The clock ticked noisily up on the wall. She could almost hear the wheels turning in his head as his mind processed what she'd just told him.

"You've got to believe me," she said as a tendril of panic nudged its way inside her. If he were to dismiss her claims as imaginary, she would have no one to confide in, and she would be forced to consider the possibility that she really had gone insane.

He nodded after a beat. "I think I have to."

Relief lifted a weight off her chest. "Thank goodness for that. I can't have you sending me off to a padded room when I've only just moved in."

He prodded at his pasta. "This isn't something to joke about. You don't know what kind of person he is. Was." He rubbed his temples with the thumb and middle finger of his left hand. "Don't think I'm mad at you. I just…" He shook his head and stared at his plate. "Did you tell him he needs to leave?" He twirled another forkful of spaghetti and chewed.

"I told him he needs to move on, but he basically said he'll go to hell if he does."

Wayne paused to take a long drink from his glass of ice water. "He's probably just scared. I mean, if *I* died right now, I don't know where I'd go."

She laughed. Wayne thought he was going to hell, too? He and Jerry must have both been cut from the cloth of insecurity. "Why do you people always expect the worst?"

He stabbed at his dinner again, not looking at her. His brow had furrowed. "Isn't there something nicer we could be talking about?"

"Politics?"

"I said nicer." He laid his fork down. "Okay. Let's say I robbed a bank. Where would I be going if I got caught?"

She hoped this wasn't a trick question. "Jail?"

"Exactly. And God knows everything that I've ever done, so no crimes of mine will have gone unnoticed."

"So you'll go to jail when you die."

"Jessica…"

"Sorry. I just think that if you're sorry for what you did, God will forgive you."

"I hope so." His face darkened, and he fell silent.

She sensed it was time to steer the conversation to more pleasant matters. "Yesterday I found out I'm going to be an aunt, and the proud parents are flying in tomorrow for a family reunion nobody bothered to tell me about."

"Only you could manage to make that sound bad," he said, "but tell Rachel I said congrats. It's the Reyes clan having the reunion?"

"Yep. The whole place is going to be swarming with Chicanos."

"Which place?"

"The one over in Campbell County. Rachel and Eric are staying with Uncle Esteban and Aunt Sharon for the weekend."

"You should invite them over for dinner tomorrow if their flight lands in time. They'll make better company than you and Sidney." He grinned.

"And they'll make better company than *you* because they don't have some weird going-to-hell complex."

A quick movement in the corner of her eye caught Jessica's attention. She turned and saw Jerry leaning on the banister at the foot of the stairs, glaring at Wayne with eyes like daggers.

She couldn't even guess what had caused this reaction in him. Was it something they had said? Jerry hadn't looked this enraged any of the times she'd seen him so far, not even when he'd had his fit at Smithfield Park. Jessica gulped. "Uh, Wayne? Does anything in here seem unusual to you?"

"What kind of unusual?"

"You'd know it if you saw it."

"It's him, isn't it?"

She nodded.

"What's he doing?"

"Watching you." *Like he wants to kill you.*

His face paled even more. "Is it okay to talk to him?"

"Sure. Just don't say anything that might be upsetting."

"Where is he?"

"Right there. By the steps." She pointed.

Looking uncertain, Wayne stood up and approached the place she'd indicated with the caution of one stepping up to a land mine. "This good?"

"Uh-huh. You're right in front of him."

"I don't like this." His voice sounded small.

Jerry glanced at Jessica. "Does your friend always act this queer when he gets scared?"

"He's not queer!" she blurted, rising from her chair and stepping up to the unlikely pair like a referee about to break up the weirdest fight in the universe.

Wayne's head snapped around. "Whoa, now. Who isn't queer?"

"Nobody in here is queer," she said. "Right?"

Wayne stepped back a little. "There shouldn't be, unless Jerry is."

This was possibly the worst thing Wayne could have said, even though Jessica knew he was only teasing. Jerry lunged at him, his face apoplectic. Jessica stepped between them without thinking. "Stop!"

Wayne let out a yelp, lost his balance, and fell over backward.

It felt as though ice suddenly flowed through Jessica's veins, and fragments of intruding images filled her mind's eye. Faces of people unknown to her, a yellow house with a For Sale sign posted in the yard, a boy tossing a baseball to another child, a woman hurling dishes out of a cabinet onto the floor...

"What just happened?"

Jessica blinked, feeling disoriented as if the room had turned on its side. A few shakes of her head cleared her of the sensation. "I think he forgot that he isn't solid. You okay?"

Wayne was struggling to his feet. She held out her hand, and he laced his fingers into hers so she could help him up. His hand was freezing. "I'll survive." He paused. "Solid?"

"He tried to attack you," she said, glancing around the kitchen to see if Jerry was still hanging around. "But he's gone now."

Wayne rubbed the small of his back and shook his head. "Why would he attack me?"

"I think it was just a misunderstanding."

"Some misunderstanding." Wayne scowled. "Are you sure he's gone?"

She shook her head, which had started to hurt. "I don't mean he's *gone* gone. I just don't see him anymore."

Wayne straightened his glasses. "I may be stating the obvious, but I think you've gotten us into some serious trouble."

~~~~~

Later, after the red-haired girl came home and she and Jessica went upstairs to bed, Jerry moved into the living room where Wayne was watching television.

The man had changed out of his office clothes into shorts and a purple t-shirt. His black and blue flame-patterned leg braces lay on the floor beside the couch. He stretched his bare legs out on the recliner's footrest, looking as relaxed as a vacationer on a beach. Evidently the man had already recovered from his shock. Resilience. An admirable trait.

He glided over to Wayne's chair and stared coldly down at him. The living man didn't bat an eye. His face was passive except when something on the television amused him and a brief smile flitted across his features.

What he would give to trade places with the man! Wayne must have been in his late twenties or early thirties and seemed to enjoy life just fine despite his handicap. When Jerry was that age, he'd spent most of his evenings contemplating various ways by which he might bring his miserable life to an end—and he had been as able-bodied as the next person. Did having a broken body make a person appreciate life more? Maybe so.

Look at him, Jerry. Look at what you could have had.

Wayne suddenly sat up straighter, no longer paying attention to the television. "Is somebody there?"

"Nobody of importance," Jerry murmured. Wayne wouldn't be able to see or hear him, but something had obviously alerted the man to his presence. A so-called sixth sense? Nah. Wayne knew he was here because Jessica had told him so, and now paranoia was getting the better of him.

Wayne pulled the recliner into its upright position and muted the television. He cocked his head, listening. "If that's you," he said, "I'm sorry that I upset you earlier. But you shouldn't be here. Move on to wherever you need to go. No one's stopping you."

Jerry's temper flared again. He didn't attempt to subdue it. These people were fools to assume that he could magically transport himself to paradise with the snap of his fingers. He suffered here on earth because he was meant to suffer. Their pleas for him to leave weren't going to change that.

"Do you hear me?" Wayne continued. "Heaven awaits you."

You're never going to heaven, Jerry. Tell the fool to stop wasting his breath.

Maybe Wayne would shut his mouth if he could feel the pain.

Jerry reached out and touched the younger man with his mind. *Feel it. Embrace it.*

Wayne made an involuntary jerk, and his face twisted into a grimace. A moan escaped his lips. "Oh, God..." Tears came to his eyes and rolled down his cheeks. His hands curled into fists. "Oh, God..."

Can you tell how much it hurts when you tell me to move on? Jerry thought. *It's like telling a starving beggar to boldly march into a palace to dine at a royal feast he wasn't invited to.*

The man continued to weep.

Satisfied that Wayne had been reduced to a sobbing heap, he withdrew from him. Wayne had had his taste. He'd better have enjoyed it.

~~~∽∾∾∿∽~~~

Wayne didn't stick around for long after that. He dried his tears on his sleeve, glanced warily around the room, and turned out the light.

When he was finally alone again, Jerry wandered over to the bookshelves to see what kind of literature these people liked, if only because he had nothing else to do. He'd been into Shakespeare, himself, even though his students had hated that part of the class. He sort of liked Stephen King's books, too. In fact, *The Shining* was the last book he'd ever read. How long had that been? Twenty years? Had to be more than that. He had stopped keeping track.

One of Wayne's shelves contained several works by Poe and Hemingway. Another held novels written by authors whose works he was unfamiliar with, though by the sound of the titles (*Whispers, Phantoms, Strangers*, etc.) they may have been horror novels or thrillers. A stack of Agatha Christie novels and a large, pink volume lay horizontally across the tops of other books as if they had been stuffed there in haste.

The pink book caught his interest. It was about two inches thick and a foot square. A photo album, no doubt.

He had a sudden, powerful urge to nose around in its pages to learn a bit more about the threesome who lived in this house.

But it isn't any of my business.

The voice spoke in a soothing tone. *Of course it is. You know you want to look.*

He did. He really, really did.

It's rude to spy.

No one will know that you did.

True. One little peek couldn't hurt anything.

He focused all of his energy into lifting the book off the shelf onto the carpet. The act was as exhausting as a vigorous workout would feel to a living person, so it took him several minutes to get a good grip on the binding and lower the book to the floor without dropping it and alerting the rest of the house to his exploits.

He rested for a while then mustered the strength to turn to the first page.

Inside the front cover someone had written, "The Life of Jessica Mary Roman-Dell, 2004-2006." The first page showed pictures of a party. Jessica had written:

> Fifteenth Birthday! January 1, 2004. Wayne and the Millers came over, and we had a blast! Rachel ate too much cake and almost threw up from laughing while we were playing Apples to Apples. She'll probably be mad if she finds out I wrote this, but what she doesn't know won't hurt her, right? Mom actually baked the cake this year. Dad bought me a digital camera so I can finally enter the 21st century like the rest of the planet. I told him that I could use it on ghost hunts, but Mom got mad about that. Oh well, what's new there? Overall, this birthday was awesome!

One photograph showed Jessica blowing out the candles on a cake coated in pink and purple frosting. A handful of others were pictures of Wayne and Sidney and some red-haired people whom he didn't know.

He paused to think. If Jessica was fifteen years old in 2004, then the present year must have been 2009 or 2010. Lord! He'd been gone for nearly a quarter of a century.

Jessica had mounted photographs from school on other pages. Jerry had to smile at some of the clothes the students sported in her candid snapshots. At least the perms and feathered cuts seemed to have become as extinct as the go-go boot.

He grew weaker as he progressed toward the end of the album. The strain of turning the pages with his thoughts was proving to be too much. The pictures were nice, though. Jessica had taken hundreds of pictures of everything from flowers to old houses, and some of them were good enough that she probably could have made a decent living at still-life photography and stopped complaining about not having a job.

A picture on the final page—scenes from Christmas Eve 2006—made him freeze. Was it really? Yes, it had to be. It confirmed the suspicions he'd had since the night before. The odds of this happening had to have been one in a million, unless fate had had a hand in it all.

Funny, how fate could simultaneously curse and bless a man.

Thank you for this.

Anytime, Jerry. Anytime.

He smiled and replaced the album on the shelf, expending every last bit of energy he could muster. Now all he needed to do was determine how to use the situation fate had dealt him to his advantage.

CHAPTER 14

"Hail Mary, full of grace, the Lord is with thee..." Wayne sat on the edge of his bed, pinching the black beads of his rosary between his fingers. He had a hard time preventing his hands from shaking.

It had been a year or two since he had last prayed the rosary. He'd had to get out a prayer book to remember the words of the Apostle's Creed and the mysteries he was to reflect on during each decade of prayers to the Blessed Mother. For Wednesdays it was customary to use the glorious mysteries of faith—the resurrection, the ascension, the descent of the Holy Spirit, the assumption, and the coronation.

It was difficult to focus on both praying and reflecting on the resurrection, especially considering what had just happened down in the living room.

He shuddered, remembering the sensation that had gripped him. Like being buried in a pit with his own filth. Only it hadn't really been his, had it? Jerry had shared something with him either for some kind of bizarre bonding experience or to make a point—but whatever it was, its meaning was lost on Wayne.

He cursed himself for allowing his mind to wander and resumed his prayers. "Blessed art thou among women, and blessed is the fruit of thy womb, Jesus. Holy Mary, mother of God, pray for us sinners now and at the hour of our death. Amen."

He reflected briefly on the resurrection. Jesus had sacrificed himself and risen again so that all the sinners of the world might find eternal life. That included Wayne, who would never deserve the reward even if he devoted the remainder of his days to serving the Maker.

It also included Jerry.

"Hail Mary, full of grace, the Lord is—" A tap on the door startled him.

Had Jerry come to assault him a third time?

He waited, and when the tapping sounded again, he said, "Who's there?"

"It's me," Jessica said. "Can I come in?"

He let out a relieved breath of air. "Just a minute." He slipped his t-shirt back on so she wouldn't see the marks on his back and hobbled over to the door. "What's up?"

Jessica's hair was tousled, and her eyelids were heavy. She wore only a pair of old shorts and a baggy Class of 2007 t-shirt. Her toenails were painted red.

The room suddenly felt much warmer than it had just a few minutes ago.

"I can't sleep," she said.

"Must be contagious." His heart rate sped up.

She looked past him as she scanned his bedroom. "You know, I've never actually been in here before. What's with the rosary?"

He shrugged. "Just the usual, praying for the dearly departed so they may find everlasting joy that isn't in my house."

She cast her gaze to the floor. "I hope you're not mad at me."

"I told you I'm not mad at you." Maybe a little frustrated, though she didn't need to know that.

"It's my fault he's here."

"Did you tell him to come with you?"

She smirked a little. "I'm not *that* stupid. I just feel bad for him. It can't be any fun for him to be here when he can't interact with us like a normal person." To his surprise, she went over and sat on the end of the bed and rested her chin on her hand, staring glumly at the floor. Now that she wasn't wearing her usual sweatshirt and blue jeans, he realized she had lost some weight. He'd guessed her at about 140 pounds before. Now her arms and legs were like sticks. Wasn't she eating anymore?

"Did you really just come over here to tell me you couldn't sleep?" he asked, resisting the urge to go join her.

She shook her head. "I just want someone to talk to. I tried to tell Sidney what's going on, but she got kind of nasty with me."

He sat down beside her anyway. So much for resisting urges. "She's just been depressed again this week," he said. "Don't be too hard on her."

Jessica looked more surprised than he'd expected. "I thought she was doing a lot better than she had been."

"She's not." A blind person could have seen that.

She sighed. "She just acts mad whenever I'm around her. And worried. I don't get it."

"Don't you talk to each other anymore?"

"Not like we used to. She's so distant lately."

Had Jessica recently taken a look in a mirror? "She's not the one who's constantly shutting herself in people's houses all by herself."

Hurt shined in her eyes. "I always invite her to go with me."

"Has it occurred to you that maybe she has good reasons for not wanting to go?"

"Well, yeah."

"So why don't you let her be?"

"Because I'm lonely! You don't know what it's like." Her voice became strained, and she turned from him, probably hiding her tears. As if tears could bother him.

"Look at me," he said.

She did, but only after swiping a hand over her eyes first. "What?"

"I have a suggestion."

She scooted a few inches away from him. "What kind?"

He suppressed a smile. What did she think he was thinking? "The kind involving my cousin," he said. "She's off tomorrow. Go hang out with her somewhere. Someplace that might cheer her up."

"Oh." She gave him a sheepish grin. "It'll take me all night to think of one."

"Then you'd better get started."

"Yeah, maybe so." She stood up so fast that Wayne jumped in surprise. "I should let you get some sleep. Good night. Or morning, whatever it is."

With that, she ducked back out into the hallway and into the other bedroom without a sound. Her door made a soft click as it latched into place.

Wayne stared dumbly at the other door for several moments before closing his own. Why in the world was she acting so skittish all of a sudden? She had to know how he felt about her; she wasn't stupid. If she had that much of a problem with it, she wouldn't have accepted his invitation to move in.

He pulled off his shirt and draped it over his desk chair. He should just ask her. They had known each other for sixteen years. But what if she didn't love him that way? She acted like she did, but that could have been wishful thinking on his part. Besides, there were lots of things he hadn't told her if only because he had told so few others. Her feelings might be hurt if and when she learned that he had kept certain things from her.

And she might run.

He returned to the bed. He could think about Jessica later. He picked up the rosary with full intent to continue praying for Jerry but hesitated and lay it down on the nightstand. The hour had just changed over into the single-digits. If he stayed up any later he'd end up falling asleep at his desk at work.

He could continue praying in the morning. Hopefully waiting until then wouldn't be a mistake.

Jessica was running through a dark cemetery into a forest even darker than the surrounding night. A sense of hostility hung in the air like invisible smog. She had to get away from them—*had to*—but no, they were without doubt gaining on her. She could feel them at her heels!

"Wake up," said a voice far away from her, far beyond the forest she had entered.

"I'm…not…sleeping!" she gasped through clenched teeth as she ran.

"Earth to Jessica and Sidney! Do you read me?"

"Loud and clear," said a second voice. What gives?"

"Good lord, Jessica, did you die in here? Get up!"

Jessica jolted fully awake. Sidney was groaning and sitting up in bed on the other side of the room. Wayne stood in the doorway.

"I'm alive," Jessica said, swinging her legs off the side of the bed and standing up. The final shadows of the dream faded into reality. It must have been early if Wayne hadn't left for work yet, and the fact that he had awakened them like this bothered her. "What's going on?"

Wayne was wearing a white t-shirt under his peach-colored work shirt, which he had left unbuttoned. He also wore a pair of boxer shorts and seemed to have overlooked the fact that he had not yet put on pants. Jessica pretended not to notice, but her face heated anyway.

"A slight inconvenience," he said. "I can't find my braces."

"What makes you think we did something with them?" Sidney yawned and wiped a hand across her face. "Eww, I must have been drooling in my sleep."

"*Did* you do something with them?" he asked.

Sidney crossed her arms, insulted. "Why would you think I'd do something as low as that? I haven't touched the things." Her attention turned to Jessica. "You didn't, did you?"

Jessica shook her head. "Nope." Taking Wayne's leg braces would have been almost as mean as stealing a wheelchair from a paraplegic, the key difference being that Wayne didn't always need the braces in order to walk—they just locked in the range of motion of his feet and ankles so he would have better balance. "Where had you put them?"

"I took them off in the living room last night." Something like fear flashed through his eyes. "Only now I don't see them anywhere."

"Do you think you could have been sleepwalking and stashed them somewhere?" Sidney asked.

"If I had sleepwalked," Wayne said, "I probably would have fallen down the stairs and broken my neck."

"I guess we should get looking before you're late for work," Jessica said. Wayne's boss might not be very understanding if he showed up late for having lost two items that he almost always kept with him.

Wayne led the way down the stairs and stepped into the living room with unnecessary caution, leaning into the wall for support. "I know I set them right here," he said, gesturing at the floor beside the couch.

"You sure you didn't move them anywhere else?" Jessica asked, sensing there might be more to this situation than Wayne was letting on. He acted like he was about to jump out of his skin.

"Positive," he said.

Sidney got down on her hands and knees and peered under the couch. "Hey, I found a penny." She reached her hand in and withdrew a dusty coin, which she placed on the coffee table.

Wayne kneaded his forehead. "This is great."

"Well, they've got to be here somewhere," Jessica said. She checked behind the couch while Sidney looked under the recliner. Old cough drop wrappers and crumbs resided between the back of the couch and the baseboard. No leg braces.

Wayne left the room, muttering something under his breath. Moments later, cabinets started banging open and closed in the kitchen.

Sidney straightened. "Am I the only one around here who hasn't been acting like a basket case these last few days?"

"What, you think he stuffed them somewhere and doesn't remember doing it?"

"They certainly didn't walk out of here on their own."

Jessica suddenly had the feeling that Jerry was watching them. Her heart skipped a beat. Jerry! Surely this couldn't be some sick game that the man had chosen to play. Sure, his moods were as unstable as a two-legged stool, but this? This was juvenile.

Wayne returned to the living room and sank onto the couch. "I don't believe it. I'm going to be late for work. Charlie's going to kill me."

Charlie Korman was one of the partners at the accounting firm. Jessica had met him a few times when her parents had worked for him. He seemed like the kind of guy who'd expect his employees to show up even if they lay on their deathbeds, which was probably the reason her parents had been hired in the first place. They and Charlie were kindred souls.

"I could drive you there," Sidney said. "If they turn up, we can take them to you."

"Come on, I'm still able to *drive*."

"And what if you step on the wrong pedal? I don't want to have to scrape you off a phone pole with a spatula."

Wayne glanced at the clock on the wall. "Fine, if it makes you happy. Just don't forget to pick me up this evening, because there's no way I'm walking home without braces on."

"Don't forget to put on some pants before we leave."

He glanced down at himself. "But I can walk home without those." He stomped back upstairs.

"You want me to stay here and keep looking?" Jessica asked Sidney, eager to interrogate a certain someone about the whereabouts of the braces.

Sidney eyed her with suspicion. "Yeah. You do that."

~~~

"Jerry, are you still in here?" Jessica called out as soon as Sidney's Camry left the driveway. "If you're the one who hid Wayne's braces, that isn't very nice."

Their unintended guest failed to make an appearance.

Having nothing else to do, she gave the living room and kitchen another cursory inspection then checked the first-floor bathroom to see if Wayne might have left his braces in there. He hadn't.

Where did that leave? Wayne wouldn't have gone into the mudroom or junk room at the back of the house last night, though that didn't mean his braces hadn't been hidden there. They also could have been in the basement, however unlikely that was. The more logical thing to do was to first search the places where she knew Wayne had been.

Like his bedroom.

She ascended the stairs and pushed open his bedroom door. Unlike the man's wardrobe, most of the décor in the room was done in shades of cream. Cream walls. Cream carpet. Cream pillows and bedspread. The place was as spotless as an operating theater, though it smelled like vanilla instead of disinfectant.

She didn't remember seeing the braces last night when she had been in the room. And why had she gone in in the first place? *Lead us not into temptation*, the prayer said, and she marched right into it anyway. She could tell Wayne hadn't wanted her to leave, so she did the intelligent thing and got out before anything improper happened between them. Jessica: 1, Temptation: 0. She could only hope she hadn't hurt his feelings.

But anyway—the braces. Maybe they had been kicked under the bed.

The bed was centered in the room with its headboard pushed against the right-hand wall. A nightstand to the left of the headboard held a lamp, a worn Bible with a bookmark sticking out of the middle, and the prayer book and rosary that lay on the bed the night before.

She lifted the edge of the bedspread and only saw an assortment of Rubbermaid containers filled with old papers. No braces.

A wooden writing desk sat in the left corner closest to the door. Wayne had neatly stacked up a bunch of old issues of *People* and *Better Homes and Gardens* on top of it next to a cup of pens that was shaped like a miniature watering can. A cork bulletin board covered in Post-It notes and newspaper clippings hung on the wall above the desk.

A wallet-sized copy of her senior picture was tacked to the edge of the board. Awkward, seeing her face pinned there like an idol in a shrine.

She moved into Wayne's private bathroom, which connected to the bedroom along the left-hand wall. Dirty clothes had been piled into a hamper. A toothbrush, tube of toothpaste, and a comb lay in a perfect row on the vanity. A Glade plug-in beside the sink puffed the vanilla smell into the room.

Still, no braces.

Nobody could misplace two objects that were over a foot long each and made of plastic and metal. They were too large to get squashed somewhere out of sight like missing socks or to be accidentally thrown out like an unwanted electric bill.

The only explanation for their disappearance was that Jerry had taken them, which still made no sense, because he had nothing to gain from it.

She left the bathroom and made one final inspection of the bedroom. Where else was there to look? The closet, of course. Wayne could have been so tired while getting ready for work that he might have carried the braces there while he was getting his clothes and shut them inside without thinking.

She slid the door aside with a bit too much force, and the vibration from it hitting the frame sent a precariously placed shoebox tumbling off a shelf onto the floor. The lid fell off on impact, sending a confetti of newspaper clippings across the carpet.

There were no leg braces in the closet. She had made a mess in vain.

Hoping that the clippings hadn't been arranged in any certain order, Jessica stooped down and started stuffing them back into the box, not paying attention to what any of them said until one headline caught her eye.

"Police: Boy Killed Own Mother in Self-Defense," it read.

Startled, she brought the yellowing paper closer to her face so she could read the tinier print.

Georgetown—Most people facing assault will not hesitate to harm the assailant in order to save themselves. For one local teenager, that meant ending his own mother's life.

The woman, whose name has not yet been released, reportedly beat her thirteen-year-old son with a fireplace poker when he refused to bring her a glass of vodka and instead emptied the bottle of alcohol down the drain. The boy managed to wrestle the poker away from her and bashed her over the head with it, instantly knocking her unconscious. He called 911, but the woman was pronounced dead when emergency personnel arrived at the scene.

"Evidence indicates that the teen has been subject to extreme abuse multiple times in the past," said Officer Harry Watson, who was present at the scene. "He's lucky to be alive."

When asked why the boy was limping as police escorted him out of the house, he told them that he suffered from cerebral palsy and that the ankle-foot orthotics he was required to wear were several sizes too small—

his mother had apparently refused to get him fitted for a larger pair.

"As grim as this case is," Watson said, "the child is fortunate to have been removed from this terrible situation. We can only pray he'll have a brighter future ahead of him."

The boy has been temporarily placed in foster care. It is unclear if charges will be pressed against him.

"Oh no." She covered her mouth with one hand. "Oh no, oh no, oh no…"

She was vaguely aware of the sound of a key turning in a lock down below. The front door opened, and light footsteps crossed the entryway floor into the living room.

"Jessica?" Sidney's voice carried up the stairwell.

Jessica crammed all the clippings back into the box and shoved it back onto the closet shelf. She walked out onto the landing and forced herself to speak. "What?"

Sidney returned to the foot of the stairs, holding a familiar blue and black flame-patterned leg brace in each hand.

"Where did you find them?" Jessica asked. Her mind was still too numb to fully process the fact that Sidney must have seen the braces as soon as she set foot inside the house.

Sidney's voice was strained. "They were sitting on the floor. Right next to the couch."

CHAPTER 15

"How did they get there?" she asked dumbly.

Sidney's eyes narrowed. It was becoming her most common expression. "You tell me. You're the only one who could have put them there."

"But I didn't." At least she could use the reappearance of the braces as an excuse for her shock at finding the article.

"Don't try to tell me the ghost did it."

"What else could it be?" She descended the stairs into the entryway and crossed her arms.

Sidney transferred the one brace from her right hand into her left and pushed her glasses further up on her nose. "I don't believe in fairy tales anymore."

"Wayne believes me. Just ask him."

"That's because he's infatuated with you! Of course he's going to believe whatever you tell him."

Jessica's temper began to rise. "I'm not lying."

Sidney's gaze bored two holes into her. "You wouldn't lie to save your own life."

"Then what makes you think I'm lying now?"

"I don't think you're lying. I think you're nuts. Now excuse me while I return these to their rightful owner."

Sidney strode out the door and slammed it behind her, leaving Jessica standing speechless at the bottom of the staircase.

"You have an interesting way with your friends."

Jerry was sitting on the end of the banister, looking bored.

Jessica planted her hands on her hips and tried to stifle her anger so he wouldn't get mad at her, too. "And *you* have an awful lot of nerve doing that to Wayne."

"What did I do?"

"Do I have to be specific? You tell me."

He frowned. *Frowned*, for crying out loud! As if he really hadn't a clue.

"I'm starting to wish I'd never gone to that cemetery," she said. "Then maybe my best friend wouldn't think I've flipped my lid."

"Maybe you have."

"You're avoiding the issue."

He studied her. "Which is?"

"You barged into our house like you own the place, and now you keep messing with us like you think it's funny. Why are you trying to ruin our lives?"

"How am I ruining anyone's life by being here?"

"First off, you tried to hurt Wayne last night, and second, you took his stuff. Not to mention Sidney's acting like a jerk with me."

He was silent for a moment. "If you think that arguing with a friend about spiritual matters constitutes ruining a life," he said, "you've got a lot of growing up to do. Did you already forget that I said I was murdered?"

"No." Her face flushed.

"So don't you think that saying that I'm ruining your life by being here is a little melodramatic?"

"Hmm. Maybe." Now that they were on the subject, she had to ask him one of the questions that had buzzed around in her head since the day before. "How did that end up happening to you?"

"It's a very long story."

"The longer the better, right?"

"Not in my case." His stare drifted away from her, and he seemed to be gazing at a point far beyond the confines of the room. "But since you absolutely must know, I was taken from my house in the middle of the night. Kidnapped, if you will. They drove me from Alexandria to that graveyard at the Methodist church. There's a clearing way off in the woods. They made me walk there all the way from the parking lot even though I was still half sedated from whatever they stuck in my arm. Shall I go on?"

Jessica nodded.

"They bound me to a chair and took the bag off of my head so I could look at them face to face. Someone came up behind me with some rope and pulled it tight around my neck." He grimaced. "Do you have any idea what that feels like? It's awful. You can feel the fibers cutting into your skin, and your esophagus starts to collapse, so it's like something huge is stuck in your throat and you can't get any air around it. I thought it would be all over within seconds, but before I could pass out, he let go." He broke off. "I'm not sure how to put this in a way that won't offend you."

Jessica waited. She could let him take his time.

"Well," he said, distressed at the memory, "I guess you could say they disemboweled me."

"*Disemboweled?*" Even though she hadn't yet eaten breakfast, her stomach protested at the sound of the word.

"Sorry, I thought it sounded better than gutted."

That much was true.

"When it finally happened," he continued slowly, "it was… relief. All the physical pain was gone, and suddenly I was looking at myself from above. I was like a sad, discarded thing bleeding out in the chair."

For a split second, she had the urge to give him a consoling hug. Then she remembered what he did to Wayne.

"When it happened," she said, "you didn't see a tunnel of light?"

"No."

"But that's what we're supposed to see."

"Maybe for some, but for me it happened just the way I said." He paused. "I know what you're thinking, and I hope it won't make you doubt your belief in a holier afterlife. Just because I saw nothing of the sort doesn't mean that others haven't."

A car door slammed outside. Sidney was back.

"You never doubted your faith because of that?"

Footsteps came up the walk.

He shook his head. "Not even once."

He disappeared.

Jessica pulled the door open for Sidney as soon as her friend set foot on the porch. Sidney threw her an annoyed glance and walked past her into the kitchen.

"What's the matter with you?" Sidney asked. "You look like you've seen a...never mind."

Jessica coughed a few times. "So, what did you say to Wayne? About the braces, that is."

Sidney poured herself a glass of orange juice and sat down at the table. "I told him exactly what happened."

"And?"

"He said that something here must not like him very much." She sighed. "I can't believe he's bought into this."

"Well, maybe he's right." Jessica's stomach growled. "Did you have any plans for today?" she asked, grabbing the box of waffles out of the freezer. She stuffed two of them into the toaster and found some margarine in the door of the fridge.

Sidney swirled the juice around in her glass. "Not in particular. I was going to finish up my English homework, maybe get a head start on next week's assignments. Why?"

"I thought you might want to go do something. Like we used to."

"Like what? You couldn't pay me to go on another ghost hunt."

"I don't mean that. I'm talking something fun. Something *you* think is fun."

Sidney's brows knit together as if she had forgotten what the word fun meant. She remained silent.

"By the way, where's the syrup?"

"Cabinet above the microwave. You can't miss it."

Jessica retrieved the bottle and set it on the table. "You want some waffles, too?"

"Nah, I've got some NutriGrain bars."

Jessica had spotted them on the same shelf as the syrup, so she brought Sidney the box and set it down beside her.

Sidney made no move to take it.

"What's the matter?"

"This is going to sound awful, but I can't remember the stuff we did together."

The waffles popped up. Jessica set them on a plate and carried them to the table, where she slathered them with the margarine and syrup. "You can't remember those stupid skits we did in drama club?"

Sidney pulled a NutriGrain bar out of the box and peeled back the wrapper. "I remember *those*."

"Good, because if you didn't, I'd have to take you to the doctor to get your head examined."

"You're one to talk." She bit off the end of the bar and chewed.

"I think one of my favorite skits was the one where Toby Mitchell played the robber who broke into a house where there was a slumber party, and we all beat him up with pillows and bottles of nail polish," Jessica said.

"Yeah, and I accidentally smashed the one bottle on his head, and purple nail polish went everywhere." She smiled. "But that was all stuff in school."

"We had real sleepovers, too."

"Uh huh. We did Mad-Libs and laughed so much we almost puked. I think I saved some of them. I'll have to dig around later and see if they're still in my desk."

Evidently, Sidney could remember more than she admitted. "And remember how we'd get out our old Barbie dolls and dress them up in Ken's clothes?"

Sidney nodded. "I guess we did used to have fun. Probably wouldn't be much fun anymore, though. I don't even know what happened to my dolls."

"Who cares about dolls? We should just hang out."

"Looks like we already are."

"True."

"Not to change the subject," Jessica said, "but can we please talk about my so-called insanity?"

"Do we have to?"

"I want to know why you don't believe in ghosts."

"That's like asking me why I don't believe in Santa Claus."

"Ghosts won't bring you coal if you've been naughty."

Sidney made an exaggerated eye roll. "Can't you see where I'm coming from? If there really are ghosts, why hasn't anyone come up with solid proof of their existence? The answer is because they're not real."

"But souls…"

"That's another thing! There's no proof anyone's got one. I don't see how *this*"—she jabbed Jessica in the arm with her finger—"can have some immortal essence that we can't see."

The source of Sidney's depression was becoming clearer. "So now you're telling me that you don't believe in God, either?"

To her surprise, tears welled up in Sidney's eyes. "How can I? When Mom first got diagnosed, I prayed practically every waking moment. I said the rosary. I posted bulletins on MySpace asking my friends to pray with me. You've got to remember that. I prayed my little heart out. And guess what! She died anyway." She took off her glasses and rubbed the tears from her eyes.

Jessica's own eyes grew misty. Talking about Marjorie's death even after this length of time was like peeling off an unhealed scab and letting it bleed. "I'm sorry."

"Now do you understand where I'm coming from?"

"Yeah, but people are supposed to die. It's going to happen to everyone sooner or later."

"She was only forty years old!" Sidney's face was red. "She could have lived another forty. Or fifty." She fell silent again as she finished her NutriGrain bar. "I'm sorry if it seems like I've been mean to you. You just don't know what it's been like. Mom was closer to me than anyone else. I told her things I'd never tell you guys. She was my confidante. When she died, it felt like my soul went with her. So maybe you're right saying that people have souls, 'cause it sure feels like I'm just an empty shell."

Jessica felt an unwanted pang of jealousy at the mention of the bond that Sidney and Marjorie had shared. "This probably sounds awful, but I'd give anything to have a loving, dead mother than the one I've got."

Sidney's jaw dropped. "At least you still have the chance to get to know your mother and make up for all the years you've despised each other!"

"Who said she despises me? She'd just be happier if I'd never been born."

"Did she ever say that?"

"No. But she barely even looked at me unless she was complaining about something."

If Sidney had had the ability to set people on fire with her gaze, Jessica was sure that she would have gone up in flames. "Grow up, Jessica. It's not like she beat you. Think of the kids who have to live with *that*."

Jessica's pulse quickened. The newspaper clipping! Did Sidney know about it? She had to. She had lived with Wayne for years. Then again, the boy in the article wasn't necessarily Wayne at all. He may have saved the clipping just because it interested him.

Jessica's cell phone began to ring, breaking the awkward silence that had hung in the room for the past several seconds. *Thank you, God.* She nearly dove out of her chair reaching for her purse. She held the phone to her ear.

"Hey, Rachel!" she said, her mood making a marginal improvement. "Where are you?"

"We're standing at the baggage claim," Rachel said. "We'll be heading over to Uncle Esteban's if and when our suitcase appears, but we were wondering if you'd want to come to lunch with us before we head out there."

That was the best thing she'd heard all morning. "That would be great! Where did you want to go?"

"I thought we could all go to Tim's Taco Barn if it's still open. Sound good to you?"

Tim's Taco Barn was one of Eleanor's few surviving restaurants. Jessica had applied for a job there after Travis Suleman laid her off, but they never called her in for an interview. "You bet! What time?"

"Be there at a quarter to twelve. If we're not there yet, get us a table. Hang on a second—Eric, our bag has the blue stripe along the edge. No, not that one!" She groaned. "Sorry, I've got to go before we end up stealing someone else's suitcase. See you in a bit!"

She laughed. Eric was probably just messing with her. "Bye, sis." She ended the call and looked at Sidney.

"What was that about?"

"Lunch with Rachel and Eric," she said. "Now you'll have time to get your homework done. If Jerry bothers you, give him a time-out."

Sidney rolled her eyes for what was possibly the hundredth time. Big surprise.

CHAPTER 16

Sidney went up to her bedroom to retrieve her English textbook and CD player as soon as Jessica left to go meet her sister for their lunchtime rendezvous.

Jessica could be so aggravating sometimes. Everything always had to be about *her* and *her* problems. Could Sidney be upset about her mother dying? No, because Jessica's mother was a jerk, and having a dead mom is better than having a jerk mom. Perfect logic.

She plugged in her CD player next to the couch in the same place where Wayne's ankle-foot orthotics had made their miraculous reappearing act. *Miraculous.* Yeah, right. That was about as miraculous as pulling a rabbit out of a top hat.

She popped in her Chopin CD and turned the player on. Forget about Jessica. She'd fess up to the deed sooner or later.

In the kitchen she fixed herself a plate of nachos. Homework food, she liked to call it. She carried the plate out to the couch and started reading a passage while she ate.

After several minutes it became clear that she would not be able to concentrate, because all she could think about was Jessica and her outrageous ghost story. The realization that Jessica's claims were getting to her that much made her blood boil. What was her problem? None of it was real. She should just disregard the whole thing like she would with tales of alien abductions and Bigfoot sightings.

Thing was, Jessica didn't seem like she was crazy. But true crazies might not give any outward sign of their craziness, so how in the world was she supposed to know whether or not Jessica had really gone off the deep end with this whole ghost thing? And heck, Sidney herself had sort of believed in ghosts before, right? Just not the walking, talking kind. She was almost surprised Jessica hadn't said that Jerry wore a sheet.

She set her book aside, deciding she needed to smoke. Badly.

Her purse lay on the kitchen counter. She unzipped it and pulled out the pack of Camel Menthols and her lighter. She would take a quick smoke break on the deck and come back inside when she felt better.

As she started toward the mudroom behind the kitchen, the half-empty pack of cigarettes flew out of her hand and landed on the floor six feet away.

She stared at it for a long moment before picking it up. Had she been so jittery from arguing with Jessica that she had unintentionally flung it? Weird. Maybe a single smoke wouldn't be enough.

Suddenly something cold raised hairs on her neck. She slapped her skin, thinking that some kind of bug had crawled onto her, but nothing was there.

Your mother died of cancer, and you would willingly increase your own risk of getting it by smoking? a voice said in the back of her mind.

Nice try, conscience. Smoking a few cigarettes a day might eventually lead her to develop lung cancer, which, as far as she knew, could be cured far easier than brain cancer.

A strong breeze whipped her hair around when she stepped out onto the deck. Some of the trees were already bare of leaves. The thunderstorm from the other night had helped with that. Now that the area had finally received rain, she no longer had to worry about accidentally torching the yard with a smoldering cigarette butt.

She slid one cigarette from the box, lit it, and plopped down at the patio table. She wondered if Jessica was having fun hanging out with her sister. Rachel had always seemed like a nice girl. Unlike Sidney and Jessica, Rachel had never taken a big interest in acting and instead devoted her teenage and college years to the study of calculus, statistics, accounting, and finance—subjects that Sidney wouldn't study even if she were paid to do so. Though since her current plans were to become a doctor, there would probably be a million other horrible classes she'd be required to take.

Her mind continued to wander as she stared at the surrounding houses and yards. Some children in the yard directly behind theirs were playing on a swing set, and they squealed with laughter each time their mother gave them a push to make them swing higher. The drone of a lawnmower several houses down, combined with the balmy warmth of the day, made her eyelids grow heavy. She could rest for a little while. No need to get all of her homework finished today when it wasn't due until next week...

Suddenly her head shot up. The cigarette had gone out and slipped through her fingers and now lay several feet to the right of her chair, as if it tried to roll away from her when it hit the deck.

The children in the other yard were still swinging. The lawnmower that had lulled her into semi-consciousness still hummed as its owner made circuits around his yard. The wind blew as strong as ever.

So why did it seem as if something was wrong?

Sidney stood and turned in a complete circle to try to pinpoint the source of her unease. She half-expected to see a person peering around the corner of the house at her, but nobody was there.

Maybe someone in another yard was watching her, and she had somehow picked up on their gaze. However, the yards to the immediate left and right of the property were vacant of anyone she could see. The mother and children weren't looking at her, either, because they were facing the other way.

This was ridiculous. Jessica's delusions must have been getting to her head. Why else would she feel like the gaze of two invisible eyeballs was piercing the back of her skull?

No matter how hard she tried to quash the feeling with logic and common sense—*there are no such things as invisible eyeballs!* she told herself—it became so unnerving that she had no other choice but to go back inside.

An unnatural quietness filled the house, which was odd since she hadn't turned off her CD player before going outside, and she hadn't been out there long enough for the Chopin CD to play in its entirety.

Her feet rooted themselves to the mudroom floor. What if someone had snuck into the house? They could have been staring at her through the window when she was on the deck, hence her sudden paranoia.

She grabbed a Swiffer mop that had been propped against the wall and held the handle in front of her like a spear. She stepped into the kitchen.

"Hello?"

Nobody was there.

She tiptoed to the right into the entryway and ascended the stairs then proceeded into the bedrooms and Wayne's bathroom. Not a soul in sight.

She relaxed and went to the living room to see what had happened to the music.

The screen had gone dark on the CD player. She pushed the power button to see if the player had somehow learned to turn itself off, but nothing happened.

"Huh." Maybe something was wrong with the electric outlet.

She carried the CD player to the other side of the room and plugged it into the outlet next to the television. She hit the power button again. The CD player came on.

This was too weird.

As she pondered all the possible reasons for a single outlet to lose power, a book sitting on the couch caught her eye.

The feeling of dread returned full-force. The only book she had left on the couch was her English book; only now it had been joined by another. One she had not read in a very long time.

She picked it up with one shaking hand. It was the Bible her mother gave her for her First Communion, and it lay open to the page where Moses received the commandments from God.

Someone had used her highlighter to circle two verses: *I am the Lord thy God, which have brought thee out of the land of Egypt, out of the house of bondage. Thou shalt have no other gods before me.*

Was this some kind of joke? She'd have said yes if she hadn't been the only one home.

There had to be an explanation for this. Everything had an explanation. Problem was, she couldn't think of one.

For the first time, she wondered if Jessica's delusions weren't delusions at all.

She shook her head. That was no way to be thinking. She would solve this mystery, one way or another.

She closed the Bible and returned it to its proper place in the bookshelf. Time to get back to work.

She finished the last few nachos and resumed reading the passage for her next assignment. She was to compare two poems— "Annabel Lee," another Poe work; and "Thanatopsis" by William Cullen Bryant. The subject of both was death. Some comparison. She hadn't a clue as to how she could write an entire paper about them. *Well, you see, the narrator of Poe's work lost his true love in death, and Bryant's work says we're all going to die anyway, so Poe's narrator should just put on a happy face 'cause he'll be joining his lady love in no time.*

The track changed on the CD, and Chopin's "Tristesse" began to play. Though the nineteenth-century etude had to be one of the most beautiful pieces of music ever written and was one of

Sidney's favorites to listen to, its name literally meant "sadness." She let out a ragged breath. Death. Sadness. Lingering spirits. Magically-appearing Bibles and leg braces. It was all too much.

She slammed the English book closed and drew her knees to her chest. Was this going to be how she spent the rest of her life, turning into an emotional wreck at the slightest provocation? Her heart felt like it was gripped in an iron fist, and the pain of grief burned through her like fire.

Part of her mind wanted to end it all. There would be no more pain. No more days of trying to come to terms with the fact that her best friend was gone for good. Death couldn't be that terrible. It would be like going to bed for a long nap and never waking again. Nighty-night, world, it was nice knowing you.

A calm presence filled her like warm honey. Startled, she lifted her head and blinked away the tears. Again, she felt as though she were being watched, but this time the sensation aroused her curiosity more than her fear.

"Mom?" she whispered then cursed herself for being so silly. This felt more like the presence of a friendly stranger than that of the woman who had carried Sidney in her womb.

Which was just as absurd.

Please don't cry, a voice said in her mind. Her conscience again, most likely.

The presence felt even closer to her now, like somebody was sitting next to her on the couch. Watching.

Goosebumps spread across her skin. Before, where she had sensed the unusual calmness, she now felt something akin to pity.

Jessica would be having a field day if she were here. She'd have gotten out her cameras and recorders and whatnot and would be performing an all-out investigation.

The thought that Jessica might be right crossed her mind again. This time the notion seemed less silly.

She forced herself to rise from the couch. She needed to find Jessica's bag of equipment. Where had she last seen it? Probably in the bedroom amid all of Jessica's other crap.

The feeling of being watched disappeared when she ascended the stairs.

I'm losing it, she thought. *Really, really losing it.*

Jessica had stashed her equipment bag at the foot of her bed. A silver voice recorder lay at the top as if it had been waiting for her.

Sidney picked it up. She had never used the thing, though it shouldn't be too hard to figure out. And since it had been wiped clean, she bore no risk of accidentally erasing any of the other tracks Jessica had stored in it before.

In the living room, she switched off the CD player and sat down at the end of the couch. She turned the recorder on.

"Is anyone here?" she asked, staring at the place where she had sensed the presence. "If so, can you tell me what your name is and what you're doing here?"

Jessica had once mentioned that it was better to use open-ended questions during these interrogations instead of leading ones like, "Is your name Jerry Madison?" or "Did you hitch a ride in Jessica's car the other night?" Of course, the whole thing was utter baloney. Most likely the only responses she would hear during playback were those of complete silence.

She waited for about a minute before continuing. "If you're here, can you make yourself known to me? Can you turn my CD player back on?"

A sudden wave of anger took her by surprise. "Sorry," she whispered.

The anger ebbed slightly.

"If…if you could show yourself to Jessica, can you do it for me?" Surely seeing a spirit wouldn't be so bad if she were expecting the sight of it. "I just want to know that you're here."

Silence.

Her pulse increased with her frustration. She was making herself look like an idiot. "This is ridiculous! I can't believe I would be so stupid as to believe this ghost crap. I'm *done*." She switched the recorder off and marched it back to its original place in Jessica's tote bag in the bedroom.

"I'm never going to get my homework done going at this rate," she muttered, zipping the bag closed.

She turned. Her eyes widened at the sight of the thing standing in the doorway that she had only just walked through.

Before she could convince herself that it would be in her best interest to run or hide or do anything to get away from it, her surroundings faded away into a black world where the only sensation was the sound of her own screams.

CHAPTER 17

Jessica didn't have to wait very long for Rachel and Eric to arrive at the restaurant. She'd barely had a chance to take a look at the menu when a gray Nissan Altima pulled into a space right outside the window. Rachel climbed out of the passenger side and shouldered a purse that was either Vera Bradley or a convincing fake.

The couple strolled around the side of the building to the entrance. Eric said something to the hostess when they walked in. Jessica stood up and waved at them. "Over here!" she said.

"Jessica!" Rachel hurried over to the table, leaving Eric in her wake.

They hugged. Then Jessica stepped back to take a good look at her sister. Rachel's light-brown hair was cut a lot shorter than it had been the last time they'd been together—it was currently about the same length as Wayne's—and she had put on a bit of weight, which was probably good for her and the baby since she'd always been so skinny.

"Never be gone for this long again," Jessica said. "Two years is ridiculous."

Rachel laughed. "Come on, you know it's only been a year and ten months. Big difference."

Jessica turned to Eric. "And how has the new father been?"

"As good as ever," Eric said. His dishwater-blond hair was cropped in a buzz cut, and he wore an Izod polo and a pair of khaki pants, making him somewhat overdressed for the occasion. He and Rachel slid into one side of the booth. "For the most part."

Jessica returned to her side of the table, noticing for the first time that she had unintentionally sat in a bunch of tortilla chip crumbs no one had bothered to clean off the seat. She brushed them onto the floor before sitting down. "Why? What's up?"

He closed his eyes for a moment. "I can't stand airplanes. Rachel nearly had to sedate me so I didn't fly into a blind panic during takeoff."

Rachel smirked. "He almost cut off my circulation gripping my arm. You'd think he'd never been on a plane before."

"I didn't like it any of the other times, either."

"What did you do when you flew to Florida last year for that trade show? Don't tell me you held your boss's hand during the whole flight."

Eric wore a deadpan expression. "What happens at thirty thousand feet stays at thirty thousand feet. That's all I'm saying."

Jessica smiled. Listening to their banter was a pleasant contrast to the week's more unusual events. "Rachel told me you guys are moving back to Cincinnati."

Eric nodded. "That really depends on if I can find other work. A few places around here are hiring—I sent in my resume to four or five—but have any of them called me back for an interview? Nope."

"Sounds like the story of my life," Jessica said. "I applied for a job here a couple weeks ago."

"I see that's worked out well for you."

"Yeah. Judging from the condition of this booth I'd say they need to hire someone who knows how to clean, but I guess that's not part of the job description."

"Go home and grab a bottle of Lysol. Maybe they'll catch on and hire you on the spot."

If only it were that easy. "I just hope you have better luck in your job search than me." Eric helped manage a company that distributed cigarettes, candy, and other products to convenience stores all over New York City. His prospects for finding a similar job in Cincinnati were slim at best.

"Yeah," he said. "Me too."

Rachel was scanning the menu. "Aw, they don't have the burrito grande anymore. Guess they didn't want to turn the locals into a giant pod of whales."

"The burrito supreme is good," Jessica said. "It comes with rice and refried beans on the side."

Rachel patted her stomach, which was still reasonably flat since she couldn't have been more than five or six weeks along in her pregnancy. "This poor kid is going to weigh half a ton at birth if I keep eating like this."

A waitress named Angela whom Jessica had been loosely acquainted with in high school finally noticed them and came to the table. "Can I get you guys anything to drink?" she asked in a bored tone.

"Actually, I think we're ready to order everything now," Rachel said to her. "Eric?"

"Hmm?" He glanced up from the menu. "Yeah, I'll take a tea and the burrito supreme. With beef."

"I'll have the same," said Rachel.

Jessica grinned. "Make that three of them, only I want Coke."

Angela jotted down their order with the enthusiasm of a limp rag and left them.

"So other than being jobless and broke," Rachel said, "how have things been?"

Hectic? "I don't even know where to begin."

"Living with Sidney and your boy toy can't be that bad."

Her face heated up. "He's not my boy toy. And Sidney and I haven't exactly been getting along these past few days, so yeah, it can be that bad."

Rachel made a *tut-tut* sound. "That's what you get when you move into another woman's turf. All-out war."

"Poor Wayne," Eric said. "How has he been taking all that estrogen flying around in his house?"

"He hasn't thrown either of us out yet, so it can't bother him that much."

"He still works at Reynolds and Korman?"

"Yep. He's as crazy as Mom and Dad, crunching those numbers all day. I don't know how he stands it."

"Hey, you do whatever pays the bills," Rachel said.

Eric snickered. "Sounds like how I got through college."

A glass of Coke appeared on the table in front of Jessica. "Here are your drinks," Angela said as she set the other glasses down. "Is there anything else I can get for you?"

"No, I'm good," Jessica said. "You?"

"We're fine," said Rachel. "But thanks."

The waitress gave a halfhearted nod and drifted over to the next table, repeating her question to the couple seated there.

Jessica cleared her throat. "So, did you ever talk to Mom and Dad about Baby Schellenberger?"

Rachel's face darkened, and Eric shifted uncomfortably in his seat. "I did."

If their reactions were any indication, that conversation had gone about as well as a morning stroll through an army trench. "What happened?"

Her sister took a deep breath. "Mom asked me if I thought bringing a child into the world was wise. Wise! You like that?"

Jessica blinked. "What's her problem? She brought us into the world."

"I'm not going to waste time trying to analyze our mother's warped philosophy. All I know is when she said it, she sounded more sad than angry. I kind of got the idea that she thinks the world today is too terrible for a child to be raised in."

None of this came as a great surprise, though it still annoyed her that Maria Roman-Dell would be that cold about the announcement of her first grandchild. "What did you tell her?"

"I said that God will give us as many children as we're meant to have. Then I asked her to put Dad on the phone."

"What did *he* say?"

A faint smile pulled at her lips. "He was thrilled. Said he was happy for us and to keep him posted about Baby's progress."

Again, not very surprising. "At least there's one semi-normal person in the family."

Rachel lifted an eyebrow. "Normal? He married Mom."

"I said *semi*-normal. But maybe she bewitched him."

"Very possible."

"Love potion?"

"I wouldn't put it past her."

"You know," Jessica said, "they never told me how they met. Maybe she stalked him and captured him when he wasn't looking and then dragged him to the altar by his hair."

"You two are depressing," Eric said as he flipped through the alcoholic beverage menu without really looking at it.

Jessica grinned at him. "*We* aren't depressing. Our family is."

"And you were the dummy who married into it," Rachel added. "You'll like the Reyes clan, though. Mom's cousin Marco portrays a female magician on the weekends at a bar downtown, and his sister Elena performs in plays in some of the local dinner theaters. I've heard she's pretty good."

Eric perked up a little. "Do we get a family discount if we go?"

"To where, the bar or the theaters?"

"Either one's fine. It beats sitting here listening to you two lamenting about Maria."

"*You* didn't have to live with her for twenty years," Jessica said.

"Eighteen years was bad enough," said Rachel. "But that's all in the past, right? I'm going to be as civil as possible with Mom when I see her on Saturday."

"Do you care if I order a margarita?" Eric asked.

"What? No!" Rachel snatched the menu away from him. "Quit being so melodramatic."

Jessica and Eric locked gazes for a moment, and he winked. "Isn't that why you fell in love with me in the first place?"

"No, I think that the reason I fell in love with you is because I had some kind of mental lapse and I didn't know what I was doing, and now I'm stuck with you until one of us croaks. Ooh! Here comes our food."

Not much was said over the next few minutes as each of them dug into their respective burrito supreme. As she started on her mound of refried beans, it occurred to Jessica that she had almost zero cash in her wallet. She might have to borrow a few bucks from Rachel, come to think of it. At least her sister would understand. She hoped.

Rachel took a long sip of her iced tea. "So, how has Sidney been doing? I haven't seen her in ages."

Jessica had to finish chewing before speaking. "Not so good. I thought she'd be doing a lot better at this point."

"What did you expect? The poor girl's been through hell. I can't even imagine..." Her voice trailed off, and she gazed unhappily at her plate for a few moments. "I felt really bad when we couldn't make it to the funeral. Marjorie would have wanted us to be there."

"I'm sure she understood that you couldn't get off school to come out here." At that time Rachel had been in her final semester of college.

"I know, but that doesn't make me feel any less guilty." She stabbed a hunk of burrito onto her fork and chewed it slowly. "Wayne's been doing good, you said?"

"Yeah." Jessica drank some more of her Coke. "Did I tell you he's letting me stay at the house for free?"

Rachel and Eric exchanged glances. "Free, huh?"

"Well, he can hardly expect me to pay rent when I don't have any money." She stared out the window at the Nissan Altima they had arrived in to avoid looking them in the eye. She knew what they were thinking. It was the same thing the entire village would think once word began to spread that Wayne had taken her in—one downside to living in a small town. You could pick your nose and the whole place would be buzzing about it in under an hour. "Do you want me to show you the place when we're done eating? Sidney's home right now. She'll be glad to see you again."

"We're going over to Eric's parents' house for dinner this evening," Rachel said, the knowing glint still in her eye, "but I guess we can drop on by for a little while. Do you have any more ghostly footage to show off from your investigations?"

Jessica hesitated. Would Rachel believe her, too? Probably. "I saw a full-body apparition at a graveyard near Iron Springs," she said.

Rachel's eyebrows rose. "Really? Did you take a picture?"

She shook her head. "The only evidence I have is in here." She tapped a finger on her temple. "Sorry."

"But that's amazing!" Eric said, suddenly more excited than he had been since arriving at the restaurant. "Did I ever tell you the apartment I stayed in my first year at NYU was haunted?"

"No, seeing as this is probably only the third time I've actually talked to you." Though they had attended the same public school, Eric had been two grades ahead of Rachel and four ahead of Jessica, so their paths had not often crossed prior to his engagement and marriage to Rachel.

He laughed. "Right. Sometimes I forget who I've told and who I haven't."

"That's because he's told just about everyone who'll listen," Rachel said.

"Hey, you'd tell people too if it happened to you." He looked at Jessica. "None of the guys believed me. Stuff was constantly moving around, doors would open and close for no reason, I would hear whispering in the corners whenever I was alone…" He shivered. "I did some research and found out that a student had overdosed on heroin and died in there about ten years before. I barely slept for the rest of the semester."

"Did you ever see an apparition?" Jessica asked.

"No, but I swear I heard someone calling my name when I was alone at night. And I wasn't drunk when it happened, either."

"So he says." Rachel winked. "Jess, did I ever tell you about the creepy thing you did when you were about three?"

Creepy thing? "No, unless you're talking about the time I wiped boogers all over the wall because I didn't want to clean my room."

Rachel laughed. "I'd forgotten about that! No, this was seriously creepy stuff. I got up to pee in the middle of the night, and I walked past your bedroom door, and you were carrying on a conversation with somebody I couldn't see."

"What's so creepy about that? I was probably talking in my sleep."

"That's what I thought at first, too. I stood in the doorway listening, because it was the funniest thing I'd ever heard in my life, but then you started getting really weird. 'Who's Jesus?' you asked. 'Why do you live with him? Will I live with him too, someday?' You kept pausing like you were listening to somebody. I can't remember everything you said. It was too long ago. But I do remember watching you give the invisible person a bear hug and saying, 'I'll try to be good so I can live with you and Jesus. I'll really try.' Then you lay back down and went back to sleep."

Jessica didn't know what to think. She had no memory of this, and Rachel had never mentioned it before. "You're kidding me."

"I'm dead serious. You scared me so badly I almost told Dad."

"Why didn't you?"

Rachel snorted. "There isn't anything he could have done about it."

"I was probably just dreaming about something I learned in Sunday school."

"That's the thing. Grandma Reyes had started taking me to church around that time, so I had a fairly basic understanding of Jesus and God and all that, but she thought you were too little and didn't start taking you until you turned four. You couldn't have heard of Jesus before that point."

"You never talked about church stuff with me?"

"I was five years old, for crying out loud! I talked about cartoons and Barbies, not theology. What made you want to become a ghost hunter in the first place?"

"You know why. I saw some shows about it on television, and I thought it was so cool that I decided to give it a try on my own. That's all there is to it."

"That may be," Rachel said, "but if you ask me, I'd say that the seed of that idea was planted years before on that night I just told you about."

"I wouldn't have known it was a ghost."

"Well, maybe deep down you did."

"I wish I could remember."

"Me too. Then you could tell me who you were talking to."

Jessica frowned. Not once during the years she lived with her parents had she seen or heard anything that could have been categorized as paranormal. She had even done a few practice investigations there when she bought her first voice recorder. Nothing odd ever turned up, which led her to believe that the house was about as haunted as she was dead.

Then again, Wayne's house hadn't been haunted either until Jerry decided to show up.

"I guess it could have been some lonely spirit passing through on the way to wherever," she said.

"Now *that's* creepy." Rachel dabbed at her lip with a napkin. "Though I guess that's not as creepy as seeing a full-body apparition, right?"

"If only you knew," Jessica said.

CHAPTER 18

"Y ou know, I don't think I've ever been inside here,"
Rachel said when she and Eric joined Jessica on the
porch at Wayne's house. "Looks cute."

"Don't tell that to Wayne. He'd probably sucker-punch you."
Jessica pushed the door open. "Hey, Sidney, guess who's here!"

There was no reply.

"Sidney?"

Jessica glanced out at the driveway to see if she had overlooked a missing vehicle, but Sidney's Camry was still in its usual
spot, and since her friend wasn't the type to take solitary walks
around the neighborhood, that meant she had to be somewhere
in the house.

"Go ahead and sit down," she said. "I'll figure out where she is."

Rachel shrugged and sank into one of the kitchen chairs. Eric
clasped his hands behind his back and remained standing. "I've
been sitting too much already today," he explained.

Jessica went into the living room. "Where are you hiding?" A
Swiffer mop lay on the carpet between the couch and coffee table.
What her friend had been using it for, she had no idea.

She went upstairs. "Sidney?"

She halted in the entrance to the bedroom and brought
her hand to her mouth. Sidney lay spread-eagled on the floor.

Motionless. Her glasses had been knocked askew, and a tiny bead of blood glistened on her lip.

She knelt down beside her and put two fingers on Sidney's neck. A faint pulse throbbed in her veins, and now that her own heart had slowed to a more reasonable pace, Jessica could see that Sidney's chest lifted and fell with nearly imperceptible breaths.

"Guys, can you come up here for a minute?" she called. Her voice cracked. "Sidney's hurt."

Two sets of footsteps pounded up the carpeted stairs. "What's the—" Rachel gasped as she came through the doorway.

"What happened?" Eric bent over Sidney's still form with concern in his eyes.

"I don't know. It looks like she knocked herself out."

"Well, she's breathing. That's always a good sign." Eric shoved his hand behind Sidney's head and lifted it. "Help me sit her up," he said.

Jessica slid her hand under Sidney's right shoulder blade, and together she and Eric got her into a sitting position.

Sidney groaned. "What's your name?" she mumbled. "If you're here, give me some sign…" She opened her eyes and blinked a few times. "Jessica?"

Jessica let out a pent-up sigh of relief. "Don't you ever scare me like that again. What in the world did you do to yourself?"

Sidney's entire body began to tremble. "Oh, geez, I must have… I mean, it was standing right there." She lifted a finger and pointed at Rachel, who frowned and stepped aside as if to make room for whatever Sidney had seen.

"What was it?" Jessica asked, fearing she knew the answer. Her heart resumed its frantic pace.

Her friend's eyes welled up with tears. "It was horrible! I—I turned around to walk out of here, and it was blocking the way, and—and…" She began to hyperventilate. "Geez, I feel so dizzy…"

"Talk to me, Sid. What did you see?"

"It was bleeding everywhere!" She clamped her eyes shut. "I could see stuff coming out of its stomach! I thought it was going to spill out all over the floor. And its face…there were dark splotches everywhere. Like broken blood vessels. All over its neck, too. It was wearing smiley face boxers. Nothing else." She let out a nervous giggle; then her mood abruptly changed, and her face contorted with anger. "What kind of monster did you let in here?" she demanded.

"I didn't—"

Sidney wasn't finished. "Did you tell *them* about what you did?" She jerked her head toward Eric and Rachel. "About how you had to nose around out in that graveyard and invite that thing home with you?"

How remarkable that Sidney's opinion of ghosts had done a complete reversal in the span of an hour. "I didn't invite him! He came along on his own."

Rachel and Eric stared at Jessica, uncomprehending. "Is there something we missed?" Rachel asked in a small voice.

Jessica wet her lips with her tongue. "I guess I kind of left out the bit about the full-body apparition following me back here."

Rachel's face turned white. "You saw something that looked like *that*?"

"He didn't look that way to me," Jessica said. "He was just an ordinary guy who *wasn't* wearing smiley face boxers."

"You mean he was naked?" A muscle twitched at the corner of her sister's mouth.

"No! He was wearing a button-up shirt and slacks. And he wasn't bleeding."

"Too bad you didn't get any pictures," Eric said.

Sidney stood up and rubbed her lip, smearing the droplet of blood on her fingers. "Great. Now *I'm* bleeding. Excuse me while I wash." She strode past them and went downstairs.

"Jessica, is this all true?" Rachel asked.

"I'd swear it on all the Bibles in the world."

"But this is insane! Why would something like that follow you home?"

"He told me he was lonely. His name is Jerry Madison."

"Oh, boy." She lowered her voice to a whisper. "Are you sure he's a ghost?"

Jessica scowled at her. "As opposed to a figment of my imagination?"

"No, not that. What I mean is, what if it's a demon pretending to be a ghost? I've read about cases like that before. They trick you into thinking they're harmless, but then they possess your mind when you least expect it, and the next thing you know, you're killing people in the name of Satan."

There wasn't a hint of humor in Rachel's eyes.

"I think you read too much," Jessica said.

"I'm serious."

"It sounds like a History Channel special."

"It's not."

"There aren't any demons in this house."

"That's what they'd want you to think!"

Jerry suddenly appeared two feet to the left of Eric. The spirit appeared troubled. "Jessica, I—" he started to say, but silenced himself, frowning.

Rachel must have sensed a subtle shift in the atmosphere from Jerry's arrival. "I'm going back downstairs," she said, and left the room.

Jessica followed her and Eric back to the kitchen. Jerry was already standing by the sink, still wearing a perplexed frown. His brown hair looked messier than usual. Nobody else seemed to notice him.

"But seriously," Rachel continued, "you really do need to start being more careful. Doesn't it say something in the Bible about how we're not supposed to communicate with spirits or something?"

Jessica shrugged. She had never read the entire Bible to know one way or the other. "God's a spirit," she said. "Right?"

"You know that's not the kind I'm talking about."

"What's the big deal, anyway? You've never had a problem with me going on investigations before."

"You've obviously never had this kind of trouble before, either."

Sidney came out of the bathroom, sparing Jessica from having to come up with a fitting retort. "I must have bit my lip when I passed out," she said then froze mid-step. "Uh, Jessica? Can I talk to you alone for a minute?"

"Sure."

Rachel and Eric looked at each other and shrugged. Jerry remained silent and eyed the pair with curiosity.

They went to the living room. "Is that him?" Sidney whispered. Her eyes were open so wide they practically bulged from their sockets.

"So he's letting you see him now, too?" Maybe he felt bad for indirectly causing their argument and sought to amend things by appearing to her.

"He did while you were stuffing your face down at Tim's Taco Barn. Remember?"

Oh. Right. "What does he look like to you now?"

Sidney glanced into the kitchen again. "The way you described. Black clothes. No gore. He just waved at me. Doesn't look very happy, though."

At least they were both seeing the same thing. "Now that you know I haven't gone *loca* on you, can we stop arguing about ghosts?"

Sidney's shoulders slumped in defeat. "Sure, but that doesn't mean I want him here. Make him leave."

"I think you'll have to take that up with him."

"Guys?" Rachel called. "You all right?"

"We're fine!" Jessica said. Then to Sidney she said, "Pretend he isn't there. I don't want to freak them out."

Sidney gave a silent nod.

"Sorry about all of this," she said to Rachel and Eric when they returned to the kitchen. "Things aren't generally quite this hectic around here."

"Hey, no problem," Eric said. "You had a scare and passed out. I'd have done the same thing."

Nobody said anything for several moments. Jerry leaned his nonexistent weight into the counter, studying them.

"Well," Rachel said, reaching for her purse, "it's been great seeing you again, Sidney, even if the circumstances have been a little...odd."

"Same here. How long are you going to be in town?"

"Just for the weekend," Eric said, "but if we're able to find jobs and a house around here, you'll be seeing us a lot more often."

"That's great." Sidney forced a smile that looked more like a grimace. "Good luck."

"Thanks. We'll need it." Rachel gave Jessica and Sidney each a hug. "See you Saturday, sis. And..." She closed her mouth and shook her head. "Just be careful. Okay?"

"I'll be as careful as I always am."

Rachel gave a short laugh. "Why don't I find that very reassuring?"

"Beats me."

Jessica and Sidney showed them to the door. Though it would have been nice for them to hang around for a few more hours, part of her was relieved to see them go. Rachel didn't need to start stressing out worrying about Jerry and demons and crap. Wasn't stress supposed to be bad for pregnant women? It might hurt the baby.

They both turned to Jerry when Rachel and Eric's rental car backed out onto the street. "Now what in the world do you think you're—" Jessica swore. Jerry was gone as well.

Wayne spent the entire morning struggling to keep his thoughts on the tasks at hand. Cindy, the firm's secretary, asked him if he was feeling okay at least three times, and he only heard half of what was said during the staff meeting at nine thirty.

Charlie Korman rapped his fist on the doorframe of Wayne's corner office at eleven. "Care if I come in?"

Wayne jumped and swiveled his chair around to face his boss. Today Charlie wore a black tie with a pumpkin pattern printed on it. Wayne straightened. "No, not at all. What is it?"

The older man took a few steps into the room and sat in a spare seat Wayne had pushed up against the wall. "I should be the one asking *you* that. What's going on?"

Wayne tried to prevent his expression from betraying him. "Nothing. Why?"

Charlie gave him a pitying stare. "Nothing, my foot. Something's eating at you."

"And if it is?"

"Then I'd like to know if there's anything we can do to help. You've been sitting around in a daze all day."

"Sorry." Wayne smiled, hoping the look appeared authentic. "It's just one of those days. I didn't get a lot of sleep last night."

"Are you sure that's it?"

"I'm positive. I was there."

They stared at each other for a few long moments. Wayne began to sweat beneath his work shirt. Finally Charlie rose. "Well, I guess I'd best get back to work. But really, Wayne. If something's wrong, don't hesitate to tell me about it."

Wayne gave a solemn nod but said nothing else. Charlie disappeared through the door.

Good riddance. Charlie meant well, but Wayne was not about to go to the man with stories of restless spirits playing havoc with him in his own home.

The office emptied out around lunchtime. Instead of joining the majority of his coworkers at the café across the street, he ordered a chicken wrap to go and took it back to the office with him, claiming he needed to go over a client's financial statements one final time.

He sank into his swivel chair with the chicken wrap in hand and gazed at the icons on the computer screen, thinking.

Fact: Jerry had attacked him, sent his emotions reeling, and stolen his ankle-foot orthotics for no apparent reason.

Conclusion: Jerry wasn't a very nice guy.

Jessica said that the spirit was lonely. Yeah, Wayne could understand that. But why had he taken such a liking to her? The cemetery at that church had to receive lots of visitors, and Jerry had obviously not chosen to follow any of *them* home.

A pang of jealousy flared briefly inside of him. *Don't be stupid*, he told himself. It was unlikely that Jerry would be seeking a romantic relationship with a living person since finding love would have to be the least of his worries. Then why was Jerry there? What was his motive for leaving his haunting grounds? The loneliness theory just didn't hold up.

Taking a bite of the chicken wrap, he opened up the Internet and typed "Jerry Madison" into the search bar on Google's home page. The search returned numerous links to social media sites like Facebook and LinkedIn, neither of which was likely to help him determine the identity of his house's newest resident if he had passed away before the dawn of the twenty-first century.

He checked the profiles anyway. Most of the ones on Facebook were private, so all he could see were their default photographs, which didn't help him much, because he didn't know what Jerry was supposed to look like.

He redid the search, adding the word "obituary" to the end of the keywords. More results came up, but none of the deceased Mr. Madisons were from Kentucky or anywhere else in the tri-state.

Jessica had to have known more about the man—the spirit—than she was admitting. But if he asked her anything unflattering about him in his presence, would he be subject to another attack? That was something he preferred not to risk.

Several minutes ticked by as he finished the wrap and washed it down with a bottle of Dasani. Maybe he could talk to Father George the next time he was at the church office and ask for his opinion on the matter. He could imagine the priest's voice: *You mean you don't know what to do? Pray for the man, Wayne! Pray for the repose of his soul!*

He returned his attention to the screen, his fingers hovering over the keyboard. There were billions of Web pages floating around in cyberspace. At least one of them had to mention Jerry in some way or another.

A search for "Gerald Madison obituary" revealed nothing standing out in importance. He deleted "Gerald" and typed "Jeremiah" and then "Gerard." Still nothing. He banged his hand on the desk in frustration. When had Jerry died? If he could find that out, his search would have been a hundred times easier.

He did another search for plain old "Jerry Madison." He probably just hadn't looked through enough pages to find the information he was looking for.

The clock read twelve fifty. Lunch hour ended at one. He would have to look quickly if he were to find anything useful before then.

Wayne clicked through page after page of results, none of which looked promising. Then at precisely twelve fifty-eight, the title of one link caught his eye. "Campbell County Missing Persons 1980-1989," it read.

Hmm.

He clicked on it and was taken to a page listing unsolved missing persons cases from the county across the river. One caught his interest right away.

He read.

Apparently a thirty-three year old Alexandria man named Jerry Madison had been last seen buying a bottle of Benadryl at a Walgreens on June 30, 1986. When he had not responded to phone calls for three days, his mother and father drove down from Cleveland to see if anything had happened to him. Mr. Madison's car was still in the driveway, and none of his belongings seemed to be missing, not even his wallet and driver's license. Mr. Madison's parents hired a private investigator to locate their son, but there were no leads as to his whereabouts, and nobody had seen him since his trip to Walgreens. He was declared dead in 1993. A grainy photograph of Mr. Madison taken in 1983 only told Wayne that the man was Caucasian and had brown hair.

His heart broke a little. The man in the picture was smiling, but his eyes told another story. Black emotions lay just beneath the surface; Wayne was quite sure of that. He knew the feeling well.

Nothing in the article indicated that this was indeed the Jerry Madison that Wayne was looking for. He printed a copy of it anyway and stuffed the papers into his pocket before Charlie or anyone else came back from lunch and asked him why he was squandering their office supplies on something as irrelevant as a twenty-four-year-old missing persons case.

He would have to show Jessica the article when he got home, assuming that she or Sidney would remember to pick him up. Then, if she agreed it was the right man, they would have to work together to try to figure out just what Jerry wanted with them. And, God willing, they could convince him to depart to a more peaceful eternity before one of them got hurt.

"I have something to show you," Wayne said that evening. He unfolded the paper and spread the two-page article out on the table.

Jessica and Sidney came around to his side of the table and leaned over to read the article. Both of them wore a haggard look as if they had experienced some ordeal while he was at work, though neither mentioned what it might have been. Further piquing his suspicion was the fact that they had acted uncharacteristically cheerful during dinner. Something had to be up.

He carefully watched Jessica's face while she read. At first she looked mildly curious, but then she stiffened. "Where did you get this?" she asked, keeping her eyes fixed on the page.

"From this newfangled thing called the Internet. Have you heard of it?

"You know that's not what I meant. How did you know this was him?"

Bingo, he thought. Luck was with him today. "Call it a hunch. Alexandria isn't too far from where you found him. And think about it. A mysterious disappearance? That could be part of the reason why his soul isn't at rest."

Jessica slowly turned her head and stared at the foot of the staircase before refocusing her attention on the article. "He told me he was murdered," she whispered.

It grew so quiet that Wayne swore he heard a radio playing a Nirvana song in a passing car. "Murdered?" Brilliant. No telling what bitter feelings a *murdered* soul might harbor toward the living.

Now Sidney was the one to turn and look at the stairs. "I'd believe that," she said.

Their behavior was giving him the creeps. He decided to choose his words with care. "Did he say how?"

"I don't think we should be talking about this," Jessica said.

"You're the one who brought it up. Who did it?"

"He didn't say."

"Did he know the person?"

Jessica shook her head. "I don't know. I think he probably did. And he made it sound like it was a bunch of people."

"I saw him!" Sidney blurted. "He was cut to ribbons."

Jessica threw her a fearful look.

"You mean he was stabbed?" Wayne asked.

"No. Gutted. Like a dead animal on the road that has its innards leaking out all over the place." Sidney's face flushed. "Sorry. That's what it looked like."

Wayne rested his chin on his hand. This new insight into Jerry's background was more disturbing than he'd anticipated. To Jessica, he said, "Do you think it was a ritualized killing?"

Her brow creased. "What the heck does that mean?"

"I'm saying that if it was a group of people performing the murder, it could have been some kind of cult sacrifice."

Jessica snorted. "You think this is Indiana Jones? People don't do that stuff anymore."

"I know it sounds farfetched, but you'd be surprised at what some people do. Where's the body?"

Another glance at the stairs. "Jerry's body?"

Wayne couldn't resist the urge to roll his eyes. "No, Jimmy Hoffa's body. What do you keep looking at?"

"Nothing!" Jessica and Sidney chorused.

A sudden chill made the hair stand up on his arms. "He's here listening, isn't he?"

Sidney shook her head. "Not Jimmy Hoffa. No way."

"He told me his body is somewhere in the woods behind the graveyard," Jessica said.

No one spoke for a few beats. Sidney tapped her foot on the floor and kept eyeing the stairs with trepidation.

"Do you realize that if somebody finds his body," Wayne said, "it's going to open up a decades-old case? His family could finally have closure, and maybe he would, too."

"So, who's going to go dig him up?" Sidney asked. "People would wonder what they were doing out there with a shovel in the first place."

She had a point. "But if the case gets cleared up, he might be able to move on from here."

"That isn't why he's here," Jessica said. "I told you, he'll go to hell if he moves on."

"Oh." That little fact had slipped his mind during his excitement at the discovery of the article. "Then again, he doesn't have any proof that's going to happen since he's obviously never been there. I mean, if that's where he was supposed to go, wouldn't he already be there?"

"Not if hell isn't real," Sidney said.

Wayne and Jessica both stared at her.

She shrugged. "Just saying."

"Let's not get into that again," Jessica said.

Sidney glanced at the stairs for the thousandth time and stood up abruptly. "Hey look, he's gone. I can go upstairs now." She hurried away from the table and took the steps two at a time. Her bedroom door slammed shut above them seconds later.

It was amazing what a person could miss out on while sitting in an office full of bean counters all day. "What was that about?"

"You know, Sidney's just being Sidney. Apparently she doesn't believe in God or heaven or any of that stuff anymore." Jessica turned from him and started toward the living room.

"Wait."

Jessica halted. Her expression was strangely blank. "Yeah?"

"Other than the obvious, what's on your mind?"

Her cheeks turned pink. "Articles. I've had enough of them for one day."

"What was so bad about what I just showed you?"

"That's not the bad one. The one I read earlier was a real eye-opener."

He wished she would get to the point. "And?"

"It was disturbing."

It looked like she wasn't going to elaborate unless he started badgering her. "Look, Jess. If something's bothering you, tell me about it." Now where had he heard that before? Charlie! God help him, he was turning into his boss.

"Well," she began, "I was hunting for someone's leg braces in his bedroom this morning and opened the closet to see if they were in there, and a shoebox full of newspaper clippings sort of jumped out at me and spilled everywhere, and when I was picking them up I sort of read one that caught my eye."

It took a few moments for her words to register. Shoebox? What had she…?

Oh, no.

Panic seized him. She hadn't. *Couldn't* have. Not that. "Tell me you didn't."

She looked him straight in the eye with a boldness she didn't generally exhibit. "Well, I did. Was that article about you? The one about the kid, and the mom…"

He took in a ragged breath and uttered a silent prayer for guidance. This was the moment he'd been dreading for years. Either Jessica would take into account the situation he'd faced and understand that he had been left with few options, or she would think he was a freak and leave him. "Who else could it have been about?"

Her lower lip quivered. "You mean you really…" She blinked. "I mean…why?"

God, please make her understand. He was sweating so much now that he was starting to smell like a barn in midsummer. "Why what?"

"Why did you keep that article?"

Good question. "It's…" He shook his head, suddenly at a loss for words. "How could you understand?"

"I don't. That's why I'm asking." Her eyes were moist.

He shrugged. "I guess it's just a reminder."

"Some reminder *that* is. Anyone else would have thought you were keeping it as a memento."

Now that he really thought about it, it did seem kind of crazy to keep such memorabilia lying around. "I don't want to screw up again," he explained.

She crossed her arms. "Well *that's* good to hear."

The sarcastic tone in her voice hit a raw nerve inside of him. "Would it make you feel better if I told you that it's been eating at my conscience for seventeen years? That for years I was sure *I* would be going to hell?"

"You can't go to hell for that. It was self-defense."

"Doesn't matter. I could have run away and called the authorities. I chose violence instead."

She sniffled. "What was it like? I mean…how did you feel? Doing it?"

"Mortified?" It was best to steer the conversation somewhere else before she tried to dig any deeper. He stood up and smoothed his slacks. "Hey, I think there's a *Carol Burnett Show* marathon on TV Land tonight. I'll go turn it on." He walked past her and stopped when it became clear she had no plans to follow him to the living room.

"Wayne?"

He turned. She looked so small and frightened standing there in her baggy clothes that he longed to go back and hold her, reassuring her that the thirteen-year-old monster he had been would never rear its ugly head again.

"Does Sidney know about this?" she asked.

"Yeah. And so does Drew. They had to know. Everyone in the family did."

She dabbed at her eye. "Why didn't you ever tell me? I wouldn't have told anyone."

"That isn't why I never told you."

"Then why?"

He sighed. The proverbial cat was out of its bag and well on its way to getting cornered up in a tree. "I was afraid it would change the way you feel about me. As a person," he added.

At first she didn't say anything. Her mind seemed to be churning with unspoken thoughts.

He waited, not daring to speak lest he say the wrong thing.

"Wayne," she said, "you've been my friend for as long as I can remember, and nothing is going to change that."

Thank you, God. "So you don't think I'm a freak who needs to be locked up?"

A smile peeked through her grim demeanor. "You'll always be a freak to me as long as you keep getting manicures all the time."

"Don't tell me you want me to start acting like a barbarian."

"I think the proper term is acting like a man."

"I can act like one of those anytime you want me to. Just say the word." There. He said it. It had only taken him a million years.

But she acted as if she hadn't even heard him. "What were you saying about Carol Burnett?" she asked.

"It's on," he said, moving into the living room and silently cursing himself for what he'd just said. Jessica had become denser than a brick wall. "Just thought you might want to watch it, that's all."

She followed him and plopped down on the couch. He switched on the television and set it to the appropriate channel. The image of Carol Burnett and Vicki Lawrence in their "Went with the Wind" skit filled the screen.

Jessica curled up on her side and gripped a throw pillow to her chest. He may have misread her expression, but it looked like she was wincing. "What are we going to do about Jerry?" she asked.

"Shouldn't I be the one asking you that?" he said as he removed his ankle-foot orthotics and set them on the floor. God willing, they'd still be there when he got up the next morning.

"I'm at a loss."

"Sorry."

On the screen, Carol Burnett strode out in her curtain dress, complete with a giant curtain rod that stuck out past her shoulders on each side.

"I have an idea," he said. It was a lousy idea but better than none at all.

"What's that?"

"Well, he's been acting angry. Right?"

She lifted her head. "Only to you, and maybe Sidney. And I sort of sensed this angry feeling when I was singing in the bathroom, but that might just mean he doesn't like Aerosmith."

He'd suspected as much, though those last bits surprised him. "So we should be nicer to him. Show him that we really do want to help him out."

"That'll just make him *want* to stay."

The thought had crossed his mind. "True, but I was thinking that if he knows we care, he might listen to us and move on."

"No offense, but your idea stinks."

"I never said it was a good one."

The skit ended minutes later and went to a commercial break.

"There is another thing you can do," he said.

"What?"

"Try to find out more about who he is and where he came from. Maybe we'll be able to come up with a way to help him out based on that."

"What if he doesn't want to talk?"

"Then ask politely. But try to hurry, because quite frankly, my dear, I don't want to spend the rest of my life looking over my shoulder for a dead guy who hates me."

CHAPTER 19

S idney stared at the dark ceiling of the bedroom. Her heart was pounding too hard for her to relax and fall asleep, plus every time she closed her eyes all she could see was the phantom bloody corpse thing that had dropped by her room for a visit.

The bedroom walls creaked. She drew her comforter tighter around her body. The sound was probably caused by the temperature change outside, because ghosts didn't make noises when they walked around. Or did they even walk around at all? More likely they just glided from place to place and made it look like they were walking because that's how they had moved around in life.

Something clicked beside her head, and she nearly screamed because her nerves were wound so taut. It sounded like somebody rapped a fingernail on the bedside table where her alarm clock sat. The lighting in the room was too dim for her to see if Jerry was standing there trying to frighten her. It didn't make sense for him to be such a jerk. All she'd done was get out Jessica's blasted recorder and ask him a few questions.

The tapping sound came again. This time it was directly overhead, up on the ceiling.

Mice. It had to be mice. Cute, stinky, smelly mice.

Tap. Now it was on the wall by her headboard.

Tap. Back to the bedside table.

Tap. The middle of the air between her bed and Jessica's.

Sidney pulled the blanket over her head. *God, please make it go away and never come back here ever, ever again.*

At that moment she didn't care that she was agnostic and probably wouldn't get her prayers answered by a deity or any other unseen power. She just didn't know what else to do. Sleeping out in her car would be stupid. Running away would be even dumber than that.

Jessica rolled over in her sleep. "Make them stop looking at me," she said in a garbled voice. "Don't like their eyes…monsters…"

As if on cue, Wayne let out one of his customary dream-yelps from his bedroom.

Tap. Tap. Tap.

"Gotta kill them, make 'em go away…" Jessica mumbled.

Tap. Tap-tap.

"Why did you do it? Why did you do it?"

Tap.

Sidney could take no more of it. Dumb or not, she had to leave the room or she would go insane.

When she sat up, she looked over at Jessica's sleeping form. It may have been her imagination, but the room seemed even blacker where Jessica lay, as if the scant light from streetlamps and the alarm clock had been sucked into a void.

A single sentence intruded upon Sidney's thoughts. *We don't want you.*

The shadows over Jessica's bed grew even darker.

Hoping that all of this was her imagination getting the better of her, Sidney slipped on her glasses, wadded up her blanket, and tucked it under her arm. The living room couch would be vacant tonight. But not for long.

~∞∞∞~

Jessica was viewing the world once again through a man's eyes.

She—he—was sitting at a table in an unfamiliar kitchen, staring out the window at a bright-green lawn. No fence separated the yard from the one behind it. A woman at the neighboring house was hanging out her laundry on the line. Her baby sat in a stroller parked beneath a broad maple tree. An older child of six or seven rode her bicycle in circles through the grass, making *vrooming* noises as she went.

He couldn't stand to look at them, so he turned away. Abigail had just called. Said she had just gotten back from the women's clinic. He'd had no idea she planned on going—how could he, when he hadn't seen or spoken to her for months? But the deal was done, she said. There wasn't any going back. She'd written the check from their joint account. Served him right, she said. He'd helped make the thing.

But why? he had asked. *I would have taken custody.*

She'd laughed.

He demanded to know where she was. The line went dead.

A pain greater than any he had ever known filled him then. He rose and staggered to the bathroom and started retching over the toilet like a hung-over teenager. Nothing would come up but acid that made his throat burn.

He had to do something. Go somewhere. Anything to get his mind off of what had just happened. Remaining idle would only make him go insane.

He threw open the front door and ran. Down the sidewalk. Out onto Main, past the churches, then down Alexandria Pike. His calves and lungs began to burn like his throat. Spots swam before his eyes. He felt like he was going to die out here in the heat of mid-spring. The thought didn't bother him. What did it matter if he lived or died? The only thing he had been living for was putrefying in a dumpster behind a clinic.

His legs carried him all the way down to the community park. Since it was a Saturday, many young couples were there playing with their children, tossing horseshoes, swinging, and the like. Many heads turned as he ran down the nature trail that encircled a pond coated in patches of lily pads. He did not want anyone to look at him. He wished he could just disappear and never be seen again.

He sank into the grass by the pond's northern bank and wept.

A female mallard paddled by on the pond's glassy surface between the lily pads. Four ducklings swam in her wake. Why was it that animals as simple as ducks could have a family when he could not?

Two children were playing a game of tag a short distance away. One of them stopped and said something to the other, and they both looked in his direction. He locked his gaze with theirs. They seemed so innocent and content with life, just as his own child undoubtedly would have been under his care.

Suddenly his sadness was replaced by an inexplicable anger at the children who watched him. What was so special about them that they had deserved to be born?

He thought about the other two children he and Abigail had lost—the ones who had died of natural causes before birth. He had been heartbroken then, but neither of those instances compared with this. *This* child was well on his or her way to being born. How Abigail could have been so cruel as to do this was beyond him.

Suddenly the world was filled with the aberrant sound of creaking footsteps, and Jessica jerked awake, her heart hammering. Jerry had been showing her something again! Something about what had happened—

Wayne's voice carried across the hall from his bedroom. "Stop it! Stop, please don't…"

Jessica was out of bed and running before she had time to contemplate what she was doing. She threw open his door and flipped on the light, fully expecting to see Jerry attacking him, but the only soul visible was Wayne, tossing and turning as if fending off a phantom from a dream.

He grew still, blinked, and sat up. He wasn't wearing a shirt.

He pulled his blanket around his chest like an embarrassed woman caught in bed with her lover. "What's going on?"

Her heart rate slowed a few beats. "You were shouting."

He rubbed his eyes. "It happens. Lord, what time is it?"

"Uh…" She glanced at his alarm clock. "Looks like it's about one. I—I thought someone was hurting you."

He flopped back down on his back. "I'm fine. I talk in my sleep sometimes, if you're to believe my cousin."

Footsteps ascended the stairs, and Sidney appeared in the doorway. "Is something wrong?"

"She thought I was dying," Wayne said. He yawned.

"Did not!" Then to Sidney she said, "What were you doing down there, anyway?" The footsteps that had awakened her must have been Sidney leaving the bedroom in the first place.

"Relocating." For the first time, Jessica detected fear in her friend's eyes. "To the couch."

"What for?"

Wayne pulled the blanket over his head. "Can you please let me get some sleep? I've got work in the morning."

"Sorry." Jessica turned off the light and closed the door. She and Sidney faced each other in the hall. "What for?" she repeated in a whisper.

"Between you two talking in your sleep and a bunch of weird tapping noises—"

"I was talking in *my* sleep?"

"Yeah. Something about killing people."

She strained to remember the dream she'd awakened from. There had been a woman hanging out clothes, and a park, and ducks. "I don't remember dreaming anything like that."

"Well, you did, 'cause I had to hear all about it."

"What were you saying about tapping noises?"

"It was probably nothing." The look on her face said otherwise.

"So you're just going to leave me alone up here?"

"I wouldn't say you're alone," she said, moving back down the stairs. "You have plenty of company. Trust me."

Shrugging, Jessica returned to bed. The room was much too quiet without the sound of Sidney breathing. What so-called tapping had Sidney been talking about? The bedroom was as silent as the grave.

CHAPTER 20

Jessica got out her journal and laptop computer and went to the deck so she could enjoy what was bound to be the last warm day of the season. If she could change one thing about the town of Eleanor, it would be the erratic weather. Temperatures could soar into the nineties in July and plunge below twenty or even ten in January, and there never seemed to be a comfortable temperature in between.

Except for today, of course.

She kicked off her flip-flops and propped her bare feet up onto one of the metal chairs. Time to do some research.

She logged into Wayne's wireless network. The signal wasn't very strong—only three out of five bars—but it would have to do.

It didn't take her long to find the website for the Iron Springs United Methodist Church. She was almost surprised they had one. The page hadn't been updated in three or four years, so there were listings for "upcoming" church events like bake sales and youth group meetings that had occurred while Jessica was still in high school.

The "about" tab told her that the congregation had begun meeting in churchgoers' homes in 1860 while the church was built. Construction concluded in 1862. Pastor Albert Tumler's face was pictured at the bottom of the screen. He had silvery hair and a beaming smile and looked like he was about sixty-five years old.

She could call and ask him who the pastor had been in 1986. Then, if that man were still alive, she could try to contact him and ask if he or anyone else had noticed a group of people dragging a man to his death one summer night all those years ago.

Though if there *had* been witnesses, surely one of them would have phoned the police. You just didn't see that kind of thing and not say anything about it, unless you had a couple of screws loose somewhere in your head.

She turned to a new page in her journal and began to write.

> 10/22/2010. More things to ponder: Jerry Madison went missing in 1986. Jerry admitted that he was kidnapped and practically butchered by more than one person. They took him to the woods behind the cemetery to do the deed. They must have been familiar with the area to know how secluded it was. Were they churchgoers? Is some kindly old Methodist really a perverted killer?

Going back to the graveyard and having a peek in the woods didn't sound like such a bad idea. What could it hurt? If she came across Jerry's remains, nobody would need to know about it.

She would, however, need an excuse to be there in case she was seen. A plan was already forming in her mind. It had to be better than Wayne's be-nice-to-Jerry-and-he-will-leave plan.

Jessica went back into the house and located Al Tumler's number in the list of received calls on her cell phone.

She dialed, praying that the man would buy her story.

"Hello?" The man's much-clearer voice came on the line. He must have recovered from his illness since Tuesday.

"Hi, Mr. Tumler? This is Jessica Roman-Dell. I'm the one who did the investigation in the graveyard the other night."

"Of course! How did it go?"

"Let's just say you've got one creepy place out there. I saw a full-body apparition, and no, I didn't get a picture. Unfortunately."

"Wow." He paused. "You've got a lot of courage, young lady."

She didn't bother to tell him that she had nearly wet herself when Jerry had jumped on her. "Thanks. I do have some questions, though."

"Fire away."

"Well, I was wondering if the church owned the woods surrounding the graveyard, and if so, how far the property extends."

"You bet they own it. It was all part of a farm a hundred and fifty years ago, and when the farmer died, his property was willed to the local Methodist community. They sold off a lot of the acreage to raise enough money to build the church, but there's still a good twenty acres left of the original lot. Fifteen of that is wooded. Why do you ask?"

Here goes nothing. "You'll probably think this is silly, but a friend of mine has a metal detector, and we were wondering if it would be okay to use it in the woods there." Part of that was true. Wayne did own a metal detector that was currently collecting dust in a closet. "If we find anything valuable, we could give it to you."

He laughed. "What are you looking for, buried treasure? You won't find much, I can tell you that. Hardly anyone goes out there."

"Yeah, but there could be a lot of older stuff. Indian head pennies, stuff like that. If you don't want us digging around so close to the graveyard, I can understand, though."

"No, no, I don't have a problem with it. Only problem is you'll run into roots if you try to dig for anything in the woods. All the good stuff you're thinking of is going to be close to a foot deep or more, so the roots may have even grown over top of them by now. You'll probably come home empty-handed."

"Hey, I'm sure we'll find *something*." If she did dig up a few coins, it could provide her with an alibi if anyone saw her and asked what she was doing. And if she were fortunate enough to locate Jerry's resting place, she could claim she had stumbled upon it purely by chance.

"Well, good luck," he said. "Just whatever you do, don't dig anywhere near the graves."

She smiled. "I won't do that. I promise."

When she ended the call, a slight feeling of guilt edged its way inside of her.

She, Jessica Roman-Dell, had lied.

~⁓∞∞⁓~

Wayne only worked until noon on Fridays, so Jessica spotted him limping up to the house shortly thereafter.

"How would you like to go metal detecting with me today?" she asked when he stepped into the entryway.

His eyes were bloodshot, and he blinked, not understanding. "Metal detecting?"

"Yeah. I figured we could go check out those woods where Jerry says he died."

"Ah." He moved toward the refrigerator, frowning. "Any particular reason?"

"I'm curious." Extremely curious. "And it's not like I have anything better to do."

He pulled a container of leftovers off the top shelf of the refrigerator and sighed. "You know what they say about curiosity." He dumped cold spaghetti onto a plate and stuck it in the microwave.

"I'm not a cat, and besides, it was your idea." She sat down. She'd been thinking about Wayne's theory that Jerry wasn't at rest since his body hadn't been found. It was doubtful that it was the real reason Jerry was still hanging around, but she supposed it could have been a contributing factor.

"I didn't say that *we* should do it," he said. "You hungry?"

"No, I'm good. I had some pizza rolls right before you got here."

The microwave beeped half a minute later. Wayne joined her at the table and twirled a clump of pasta around his fork. "All right. Let's say we dig him up. Then what do we do?"

She hadn't thought ahead quite that far. Chances were good that they wouldn't find him, anyway. "We might understand him a little better."

"You were supposed to do that by talking to him today."

"Yeah, and I haven't seen him since yesterday evening. For all I know, he's spending the weekend in Newport-on-the-Levee looking at the fish."

"Did you call out to see if he was hiding somewhere?"

"I did a couple of times." She'd done that as soon as she got off the phone with Mr. Tumler. "He wouldn't answer me."

"Maybe he really did leave."

"I doubt it." She watched him eat in silence for a few moments. "Sorry about waking you up last night. I had no clue you talked in your sleep."

"It's all right. Lack of sleep isn't going to kill me."

"It could."

"But not today." He paused while he took a drink of water. "I'm just glad that these"—he rapped on one of his leg braces through his slacks—"didn't do another disappearing act during the night. Though I sort of sprinkled holy water over them before I went to bed. You know, just in case somebody tried to mess with them again."

"You have holy water?"

"I got a bottle of it from church a couple years ago. I keep it in my dresser."

She couldn't help but smile as she pictured Wayne blessing his leg braces. "If you want to keep all the creepy things out, you can flood the house with it."

"Nah, that would ruin the drywall, and then I'd be more destitute than ever after paying for repairs."

She laughed. "You're not destitute. You make what, forty grand a year?"

Wayne scratched at his temple. "That forty grand goes pretty fast these days with all the bills I've got. I'm lucky if I can save a hundred dollars a month."

She stared at him. "I had no idea."

He shrugged. "If it weren't for the muscle relaxant and doctor visits, it wouldn't be so bad. I can't exactly cut back on those, though." He was right. The muscle relaxant helped loosen up the stiffness in his legs so he could walk easier.

"Why did you let me move in here if you're having that much trouble paying the bills?"

"Why?" He smiled. "Some things are worth more than money."

"Thanks. You could teach Mom and Dad a thing or two."

"Not likely." He swallowed his last bite of spaghetti and took his plate to the sink. "I guess I'd better change out of these clothes if we're going on a metal-detecting expedition."

"Then you do want to go with me?"

"Not really. But are you going to give me a choice?"

~∾∾∾∾∾~

"This is one creepy place you found."

They were heading down Hill Road, coming up on the entrance to the church. Jessica was filled with an unnerving sense of déjà vu, and she felt almost as jittery as she had the first time she went on stage in front of the whole high school.

"Doesn't it look like something out of a horror film?" she said, spotting the church sign up ahead.

"I don't see any axe murderers, so we're probably in good shape." Despite his cheerful banter, a grim pallor settled over Wayne's face. He knew as well as she the morbid implication of what they were about to do.

"Turn here," she said.

He swung the pickup truck onto the lane. "Seems like an odd place to build a church."

"Tell me about it. A Gothic mansion would be perfect out here."

Wayne parked the truck in a space close to where she had parked the other night. Like before, no other vehicles were present in the lot.

Neither of them spoke for several moments. Jessica stared at the countless headstones that stood before them like a petrified army. She spotted the bench where she first met Jerry, half-expecting to see him there again.

The dull pain that had been throbbing in her body for days sharpened.

"You ready?" Wayne said.

Jessica unbuckled her seatbelt. Suddenly it almost hurt too much to move. "No."

She climbed out of the truck and went around to the bed, where they had stashed the metal detector, a shovel, and a five-gallon bucket. She had the crazy urge to laugh. What good could they possibly do by being out here? Jerry was dead. Digging him up wasn't going to fix that.

She handed the metal detector to Wayne and picked up the shovel and bucket. "Are *you* ready?"

"Sure. Lead the way."

Jessica nodded. They needed to get this over with.

She set off down the gravel path. "See that bench?"

"Uh-huh."

"That's where he was when I first saw him."

"Sitting right there?"

"Yep." The path curved to the left, but Jessica kept walking straight on toward the trees. Most of the headstones in this part of the graveyard seemed to be from the nineties and early two thousands.

A dismal thought struck her. What would her own headstone look like someday? Who would come to her funeral? What bitter end was she not suspecting? Cancer, like Marjorie? Murder? An accident?

How blessed people were to not know.

Her footsteps crunched in the detritus on the forest floor. The leaves were dead. The sticks were dead. The soil that the trees grew in was dead.

Her limbs burned. Maybe it was a sign that she would soon be dead as well.

"It's going to be a pain trying to dig for anything in all this," Wayne said behind her.

"We'll find the spot. He said it was a clearing."

"Yeah, in 1986. Could be so overgrown with new trees that we won't be able to find it."

She hadn't thought about that. "Then we won't find anything, we go home, and we figure out how to put up with you-know-who for the rest of our lives." She stopped to scan the woods for thinning trees. It looked the same in all directions.

"Is that a building?" Wayne asked.

She turned. "Where?"

"There. That little thing." He pointed.

Sure enough, some kind of structure mostly concealed by undergrowth and vines sat about fifty yards in front of them. "Looks like a cabin. You want to take a look?"

Wayne was already walking past her. His awkward gait made it easy for her to catch up.

Jessica made it to the cabin first. It didn't look very old, even though the forest had already tried to reclaim it with Virginia creeper. She found the door on the narrow side of the building. She swiped away some of the burgundy vines and tried the knob. The door swung inward. "Hey, it's unlocked!"

"And probably full of mice," he said, coming around the side to join her.

Light from a grimy side window illuminated most of the single-room structure. Two benches sat on each side of the room, creating a narrow aisle down the center. Everything was covered in dust and spider webs. She stepped inside. Someone might have left behind a coin that she could say she found with the metal detector.

She scanned the floor, noting that a giant black five-pointed star had been painted on the boards. Its tip pointed toward the opposite end of the structure, where a long table that looked kind of like an altar sat. An inverted cross hung on the wall above it.

Her skin began to crawl as she looked back down at the painted star. Her feet were planted in the center of the pentagon formed by the crisscrossing lines. "Uh, Wayne?"

"Hmm?" He walked up beside her.

She pointed at the floor and then the wall. "What do you make of this?"

"Oh. That's unusual." He fell silent for several moments. "Do you think that the pastor you talked to knows about this?"

She shook her head. If Al Tumler had known, he wouldn't have permitted her to come out here. "Maybe it's some kid's idea of a joke. They could have found the cabin and put up the cross and star just to be funny." The sense of foreboding in her gut told her otherwise.

Wayne leaned into the doorframe. "In any case, it doesn't look like anyone has been here for a while. I don't think we have anything to worry about."

He was right. As unsettling as the occult symbols were, they weren't about to hurt anybody.

She walked toward the door and stopped. It felt wrong to leave the cross hanging like that. "I want to fix it. You know, make it a little holier in here."

"Whatever floats your boat. I'll wait outside."

He left her alone. Suddenly the small room felt overly confining like a prison cell.

She crossed the room. The boards creaked beneath her feet, indicating a hollow space under the floor. What if there were bodies of sacrificial victims down there? She pushed the thought from her mind. People might murder each other left and right, but this was the twenty-first century, and people didn't make sacrifices anymore, regardless of what Wayne had said earlier.

She reached the inverted cross, which was about two feet long and made of wood that had been painted dark brown or black. She lifted it from its hook, flipped it the right direction, and leaned it against the wall. Much better.

She started toward the door again when the red aura she had experienced the other night slammed into her without warning. The walls and benches turned crimson. *Not again.*

"Wayne!" she cried as the sense of anger permeated her. She could see nothing but red, red, red.

For a moment she thought she was sinking like a victim of a shipwreck. The distant shouts she had heard before echoed through her head.

Mataste a mi nieta!

Usted es el hijo del diablo!

Her vision cleared faster this time. She came to, lying on the ground outside of the cabin. Wayne's concerned face loomed over her.

"What happened?" he asked.

She sat up. The pain in her limbs had subsided for the time being. "The same thing that happened in the parking lot when I was here the other night. Some kind of replaying of emotions. Really, really angry ones. Couldn't you feel it?"

"It did feel a little odd in there," he admitted. "The air got heavy all the sudden. You say it happened before?"

She explained the previous incidents in great detail. "And this time," she said, "I remember the words I heard. 'Mataste a mi nieta. Usted es el hijo del diablo.'"

"Something about the devil?"

"The son of the devil. That's what hijo del diablo means."

"And the rest?"

"Heck if I know. I didn't bring my Spanish-to-English dictionary with me."

"Your Grandpa Reyes was a full-blooded Mexican."

"So? I'm part German, Irish, and Cherokee, too, and I hope you don't expect me to know anything about *those* languages."

He picked up the metal detector. "You win. Now come on. I don't want to end up being out here after dark."

"Yeah, that isn't very fun."

"I can't imagine why."

Jessica retrieved the bucket and shovel. The pain was returning bit by bit. "I say we walk…this way." She turned in a direction that might have been west. Then, if they still didn't find the place where Jerry died, they could just head south back into the graveyard and go home.

The trees thinned to their right a minute or so later, indicating a clearing. But was it *the* clearing? They would soon find out.

She took a deep breath to calm her frantic heart. Coins. They were only looking for coins.

A minute later they stood motionless at the edge of the clearing, which wasn't technically clear since a few stunted saplings devoid of leaves grew among the long-dead weeds. One larger tree with a trunk the width of her thigh grew in the center.

"Let's do this," Wayne said.

Jessica nodded. "I guess we should start right here and work our way across."

The metal detector emitted a series of beeps when Wayne turned it on. He swept it over the ground in a four-foot arc. Surprisingly, it beeped again. "Iron," he said. "Just a few inches down."

Jessica stabbed the shovel into the dirt where he indicated. The dirt seemed to consist mostly of half-decayed sticks and leaves. She picked up a clump and held it out for Wayne to sweep again with the detector.

Another beep. "Break it apart," he said.

She split the clump in half and held a piece in each hand. He held the head of the metal detector over her left hand. *Beep.*

Jessica started to divide that clump of dirt yet again when something poked her finger. A brownish-orange bit of metal protruded from the dirt. It was a nail.

She tossed it into their bucket and brushed the dirt off of her hands. "It looks like metal detecting is just about as productive as ghost hunting," she said.

Wayne was already sweeping the ground again. "Why do you think I haven't gotten this thing out for so long? The most valuable thing I ever found was a quarter from 1960. I spent at least ten times that on this thing's batteries."

"I bet I spent more on my equipment than you spent on your batteries."

"I don't doubt that. Are you even going to do any more investigations now that all this has been going on?"

She didn't see how she could. "I don't know. I want to. It's all I've got. All the other plans I've made have failed miserably. I can't let this fail, too."

Beep. "What plans?" Wayne placed his foot on the ground where the detector had located the new bit of metal. He moved his foot aside for her to start digging.

"You know. Go to college. Do something important. Something that'll pay me enough to support myself." She held up the new chunk of dirt. "Something that people might actually care about."

"Since when have you cared about what other people think?" *Beep.*

She divided the dirt in half. "Don't mix up other people with my parents. I couldn't care less about what they think of me. But society tends to frown on twenty-one-year-olds who have no job and no education. I can't just spend the rest of my life sitting around like a lump on your couch trying to figure out what a manic-depressive spirit wants and how to make him stop acting like a little kid whenever he gets angry." She sighed. The inactivity of the last few weeks was catching up to her. "I feel so useless."

This time her right hand was the one holding the piece of metal. She picked through the dirt and pulled out a greenish circle the size of her thumbnail. She handed it to Wayne.

He flaked off some of the dirt and held it up between his thumb and index finger. "A 1978 penny. Nice."

Jessica scooted most of the dirt back into the hole and stomped it flat. Wayne seemed to be ignoring her jobless woes. "Well?" she said.

He moved away from her, sweeping the metal detector from right to left as he made his way toward the larger tree. "Well what?"

"I was expecting you to say something wise and profound."

"I'm not really in a wise and profound mood. Besides, what do you expect me to say? Yes, you're a useless loser? Yes, you need to find something important to do for the rest of your life? You're the one who has to figure out what to do. Nobody else is going to do it for you."

Though his words were true, they still hurt. "That sounds pretty wise and profound to me. The only problem is I don't know *what* to do."

"Do whatever you want. You like ghost hunting. Figure out how to turn that into a career. You said that Ellen Shoushanian gave your number out to umpteen people."

"Yeah, including her brother, which is how I got into this crazy situation in the first place."

"Do you regret coming here?"

"I haven't made up my mind about that yet." If she had never come to the graveyard and met Jerry, she would probably be sitting at Wayne's house right now either reading or pigging out on junk food. "Okay, maybe I don't regret it. At least it's given me something to do."

Over the next half hour, they uncovered two more pennies, another nail, a silver dime from 1962, and a warped piece of metal that appeared to have melted in a fire. Nothing indicated that a murder had ever occurred there.

"It looks like Mr. Madison may have been lying to you," Wayne said. He sat down on the ground and handed her the metal detector. "You're going to have to take over for a while. My legs are wearing out."

Jerry wouldn't have lied to her, because there would have been no point in doing it. "Bones aren't made of metal," she said. "Remember?" She switched off the power and laid the metal detector on the ground beside him.

"Finished already?" he asked.

"Far from it. We've got our cover story now that we've found assorted crap, so now we get down to business." She scanned the ground. Now she could no longer pretend they were only looking for coins. The uneasiness returned.

"What, are you going to excavate the whole place?"

"No. I'm going to try to think like a killer."

Wayne blanched. "You make it sound like all killers are alike."

"Oh. Yeah." She gulped. "I'm going to try to think like Jerry's killers."

"Much better."

"Hmm." If Jerry's body had been left to rot aboveground, the smell would have attracted scavengers. Nothing would be left of him by now. However, the killers wouldn't have wanted to risk anyone stumbling across a decomposing corpse that had obviously not died of natural causes. They would have either driven his body to the river and dumped it, or they would have buried him. Jerry's claim that his body was in the woods ruled out the first theory. Now the question was whether or not they had dug him a grave ahead of time. If they hadn't, and had instead dug a grave in haste, then it probably wouldn't be very deep because that would have taken more time to do.

"How deep would someone have to be buried to prevent animals from smelling them and digging them up?" she asked.

"I think the standard is six feet."

"Yeah, for people who are buried the normal way. Do you really think whoever did him in would have taken the time to do that much digging? I mean, if I had done it, I would have wanted to hide the evidence as quickly as possible before I got caught."

"In that case, I'd say he'd have to be at least a couple feet down. Too bad he isn't here to tell us."

Now there was a thought. Jerry could have hitched a ride with them and could be watching them at that very moment. "Jerry, are you here?"

"Do you see him?"

"No."

"Good."

They needed to stop stalling. For all she knew, this might not even be the right location, and the more they talked, the less time they would have to search elsewhere. "I guess I'm just going to have to pick a spot and start digging."

She plunged the shovel into the earth and went to work. She paused several times to catch her breath. Wayne was right. She should start exercising more often, especially if she were to take up grave digging as her newest hobby. Sweat ran down her back and forehead in rivulets. This was ridiculous. Do this much longer and she'd pass out.

Jessica finally leaned against the shovel, panting. The hole was three feet in diameter and only about eight inches deep. "We should have borrowed a backhoe," she said.

Wayne rose. Bits of dirt and leaves clung to his pants. "It wouldn't have fit through the trees." He turned the metal detector back on and swept it across the dirt she had uncovered. "Not a thing," he said when he finished the sweep.

"Did you already forget that his body isn't going to make that thing beep?"

"There could be a bit of metal in whatever he was wearing. Maybe a zipper or something in his shoes."

"He said he was kidnapped from his own bed. They wouldn't have let him put on shoes." Plus, hadn't Sidney said he was wearing boxers when she had seen his apparition? "And I don't think anything he was wearing had a zipper."

"He could have had on a ring or a necklace. Glasses, even."

"I never saw him in glasses."

"That's because if he had any, they would be in here, not with his spirit."

She snorted. *He* had never seen Jerry except for in the missing persons photo he'd found online, so he wouldn't have understood. "In that case, he should have been stark naked every time I saw him. He looks like how he remembers himself, so if he had worn glasses, he'd have been wearing them all the times I saw him."

She straightened and continued with her grim task. The hole would not get dug by itself.

Shadows lengthened over the next two hours as the sun journeyed further west. She and Wayne took turns digging—their hole was now twelve feet across and two feet deep—and they stopped every once in a while to see if any more metal would turn up. All they found was some more nails and a pull tab from an ancient pop can.

"It's getting late," Wayne said after a while. "You sure you don't want to head home?"

Yes, she wanted to say. *I'm tired and sweaty and exhausted, and everything hurts.* "Not until we get this pit filled in. I don't want Mr. Tumler to send the wrath of God upon me for ruining church property."

"Well, let me do one more sweep." This time Wayne walked at a sloth's pace to make sure that every inch of ground was covered.

"Are you sure that—"

The metal detector emitted a high-pitched beep.

Wayne looked at her. "What's that you were saying?"

Her stomach churned. "You want to take a guess what it is?"

"I say it's something silver. Maybe another old dime."

"I'll go with another pull tab."

Wayne gestured at the shovel. "Then let's find out."

CHAPTER 21

———— ❈ ————

I t turned out to be neither.

Jessica pulled up a chunk of dirt, bringing with it a shred of thin black plastic that looked like a piece of a Hefty garbage bag.

A bead of sweat trickled down her scalp. She tossed the dirt aside and dug in again. This had to be it.

More plastic came away with the next scoop. She set the shovel aside and began to scrape the dirt away with her hands. Wayne knelt beside her and worked at the dirt in a different spot, most likely ruining his manicure in the act.

Within five minutes a two-by-two-foot section of the ancient bag had been uncovered. Jessica looked up at Wayne. Her pale face was reflected in the lenses of his glasses. "I still say it's a pull tab," she said. She tried to give him a reassuring smile, but for some reason the muscles in her face refused to change expressions.

She returned her attention to the bag. The shovel had torn a hole in the end closest to her. She gripped the edges of the shredded plastic and ripped it open even further.

A yellowed skull stared back at her with empty eye sockets. The mouth was open slightly, as if it were uttering a silent plea that had never been answered.

She struggled to hold in the tears. She couldn't just start crying. It wasn't going to help anything.

She reached down to touch the bone but hesitated. "What do you think set that thing off?"

Wayne grabbed the metal detector and held it over the skull. *Beep.* "See if you can open his mouth wider than that."

Gingerly, she placed her hand on the jawbone and tugged it downward to reveal more teeth. Dark spots marred three different molars.

"Dental fillings," Wayne said.

Jessica nodded, silently thanking Jerry for having bad teeth. "I'm going to uncover more of him."

The bag ripped easily since it was so old. Loose dirt sifted through the bones of the collapsed ribcage. Some of the ribs were chipped over the place where the heart would have been.

The arms, somewhat visible through the ribs, were pinned beneath the body. The bony hands were clenched tightly into fists that had never been given the chance to relax. The wrists were tied together with strips of a grayish, fraying substance that looked an awful lot like old duct tape.

The body ended at the pelvis, which was draped with scraps of yellow fabric. "His legs are gone," she said as a new wave of nausea assaulted her. No wonder Jerry had mentioned that bit about the bleeding limbs when she'd been out here before. He had been talking about himself.

"Maybe…" Wayne swallowed. "Maybe they wouldn't fit in the bag." He abruptly walked away from the grave, covering his mouth with his hand.

She stared at his back for a moment or two then glanced back down at the skeleton. If she guessed correctly, Jerry's lower half was in a second bag close by. His killers would have been reluctant to throw his remains into the river, because it was so easy for stuff like that to wash up on the banks. They had still taken an enormous risk in leaving him here.

A chiming sound made her jump. She'd forgotten that she had put her phone in her pocket.

"Did you two elope?" read the white words on the screen.

"You know it," Jessica replied. She put the phone back in her pocket. It chimed again. She didn't bother getting it back out to see Sidney's reply.

She had difficulty grasping that the pile of bones at her feet had once been part of a living, breathing person. Jerry's face had been painted in flesh over this very skull. A heart had once beaten inside the now-broken chest, and two blue eyes had looked out onto the world from those gaping sockets.

Wayne's silent sobs turned audible.

"It makes you think, doesn't it?" she said. Her own voice was strained. "Knowing that we'll all end up looking kind of like this in the end."

He took off his glasses and lifted a hand to his eye. "I guess. It's just…I can't stop thinking about what I went through as a kid. The crazy mood swings my mom had, acting sweet one moment and whipping me until I bled the next."

The warm air suddenly felt icy on her skin. "You mean it wasn't just a fireplace poker?"

He turned. His eyes were more bloodshot than ever. "Here, take a look." He pulled off his shirt. His skin was the color of milk, like a plant that grew stunted in the dark. He limped toward her and turned again.

Countless thin scars crisscrossed his back like a roadmap. Most were concentrated at the top between his shoulders, though a few snaked down and disappeared under the waistline of his pants.

"I'm sorry," she said. If he'd been hiding these scars for most of his life, what other scars lay hidden in his memories? He might be more broken on the inside than out—yet still, Wayne always found something to smile or laugh about.

Suddenly she had the urge to kiss him, to hold him and tell him that all was okay and that she didn't care that he had killed someone, because she loved him anyway.

But doing that next to a corpse hardly seemed proper.

He put his shirt back on after a beat or two. "I think about the torment she put me through, and then I look at this and realize that none of what happened to me even compares to what they did to him."

"But he only went through one night of it."

"So? I thank God every day for letting me live. Jerry certainly can't thank him for that."

Jessica would have personally preferred death over repeated abuse, but it wouldn't have been wise to mention that. "Should we call the police about this?" she asked.

Wayne gestured at the huge area they had dug up. "They won't believe we were only looking for coins if they took a look at this archaeological dig we made. They'll think we knew about the body ahead of time."

"We did."

"And you think they'll believe that a ghost told you where to find it?"

"Some cops might."

"But probably not."

This stank. "Well, we learned two things by coming out here," she said.

"What's that?"

She held up a finger. "One, Jerry was telling me the truth, and two, somebody used to meet in that cabin for a Satanic Mass or something."

"You think whoever used the cabin had something to do with Jerry's death?"

"My guess is yes. If people came out here all the time for their freaky church services, they'd know about this being a convenient spot to hide a body."

"So you think it *could* have been a sacrificial murder."

She shook her head. Something didn't sit right with that theory. "There's too much anger permeating the air around here.

If someone were making a sacrifice, wouldn't they be happy about it?"

His lips formed a faint smile. "I guess so."

"Exactly! And if those emotions do have a connection to Jerry's murder, I'd say that whoever killed him did it out of anger."

"Was Jerry a Satanist? They could have killed him if he'd tried to leave their coven."

"He can't be." Jerry had mentioned going to church and reading his Bible and fearing God's judgment. A Satanist would mock those things, kind of like the way someone had mocked the cross in the cabin by hanging it upside down. "I'm pretty sure he's just a fallen-away Christian."

"All right," Wayne said. "Then what in the world did he do to make them decide to butcher him?"

Before she could answer, the phone in her pocket chimed a third time. "Oh, Sidney, what do you want now?"

The first message Jessica had ignored made her smile. "You should have invited me. I could have been the flower girl," it said. Then, "Please come home. I'm scared."

She frowned. Sidney would be by herself with Jerry, and while Jessica was sure that their altercation in the bedroom the day before had been a simple misunderstanding, she didn't blame Sidney for being worried. She typed, "We'll be there soon," and hit send.

"What was that about?" Wayne asked.

"Sidney. I think we should hurry up and get this covered back up before something bad happens between those two again."

~⌇⌇⌇~

Sidney's car was not in the driveway when Jessica and Wayne made it home shortly before seven.

Jessica was relieved that Sidney wasn't there to see that they were covered in sweat and grime. She'd undoubtedly ask what they had been up to and have a heart attack when they told her, though they would have to tell her sooner or later. It would only be fair.

The house was eerily quiet. Jessica turned on the kitchen light to dispel the gloom.

"You think I should call her?" she asked.

"Go ahead. I'll be in the shower." Wayne pulled off his muddy gym shoes and went upstairs.

Jessica dialed Sidney's number. The phone barely finished its first ring when Sidney came on the line. "Where have you been?" she said in a frantic voice. "I thought you'd be home hours ago."

Since there was no telling where Sidney had scampered off to, Jessica thought it best not to mention the grave digging over the phone in case somebody else overheard. "We were metal detecting at the Iron Springs United Methodist Church. We found some coins."

"You mean you were doing something as dumb as that when I was at home fearing for my life?"

Surely Sidney was exaggerating. "What happened? And where in the world are you?"

"Dad's house. I figured it would be safe here."

"Safe?"

"Jessica, I don't think you're dumb enough to have already forgotten about *him*."

"What did he do?"

Sidney lowered her voice. "Hang on, let me go to a different room before Brian and Kyle start giving me funny looks and tell Dad to have me committed. Okay." Jessica heard a click as a door latched into place. "He's nuts, Jessica. Looney. Not right in the head."

"You're talking about Jerry?"

"Of course that's who I'm talking about! When I came home from work, I couldn't get the front door open. Somebody jammed the kitchen table up against it and stacked all the chairs on top of it so no one could get into the house. And those chairs are heavy!

Fortunately he must have forgotten that we have a back door, so I went around and came in that way. Then when I tried to turn on the lights, they wouldn't work, so I went to the basement and found out that half the breakers in the house had been tripped. Must be why my CD player stopped working yesterday. It's like he overloaded the circuits drawing enough energy off of them to move stuff around."

As bizarre as that was, Jessica couldn't see why Sidney had been so frightened. "Why didn't you just stay here?"

"Duh! If he can move stuff as heavy as that, what's going to stop him from getting mad at me again and chucking me through a window?"

Jerry must have done the furniture stacking not long after she and Wayne had left. Which meant… "I don't think he was mad at you." Jerry had probably heard them talking about digging up his remains and become upset. That would be kind of distressing, knowing that someone was going to mess around with your bones just to be nosy.

"You think he did it for fun?"

"Come home, and I'll tell you all about it. And I promise there isn't anything to be afraid of. Wayne's got holy water."

She snorted. "Fine. I'll be there in a bit." The line went dead.

Jessica and Wayne had picked up burgers and fries from a Wendy's in Iron Springs for dinner, so she went right upstairs to get clean clothes to put on after her shower. If Sidney hadn't eaten yet, she was on her own.

The water was already running in Wayne's bathroom when she made it to the landing. She would have to wait to shower until he finished so she wouldn't steal all of his hot water.

She paused outside her bedroom door. Was Jerry hiding in there? It would be nice to speak with him alone and try to talk some sense into him.

She swung the door open and flipped on the light switch. "Is anybody in here?"

Nothing looked like it had been disturbed since she and Wayne left. She closed the door and sat down on the floor between the mismatched twin beds. "I'd like to talk to you. Is that okay?"

"You found it, didn't you?" Jerry was suddenly sitting Indian-style on her bed. His face was long.

Jessica nodded. She would have to speak carefully so as not to incite one of his bursts of anger.

"What did you expect that to accomplish?"

"I don't know. I was hoping it would give us some answers."

"You don't need answers. Nothing you find is going to help me *or* you."

"We found something else out there, too."

An eyebrow lifted. "What's that?"

"A cabin. With an altar and inverted cross and pentagram inside."

At first he said nothing. He only stared at her.

"You know about it, don't you?" she said.

The minute changed on Sidney's alarm clock. Jessica waited.

At last he nodded. "I didn't know about it at first," he said slowly. "I only came across it later, after I saw some people traipsing through the cemetery into the woods one night. I recognized some of their voices, so I followed them. They had a prisoner with them. A girl. She might have been ten years old."

Jessica's vocal cords tightened. "What were they doing with her?"

"They took her to that cabin and raped her. All of them, even the women. I could have tried to step in to scare them away, but I didn't. Because I know what it's like. To do something so horrible yet enjoy every moment of it. It's like consuming the forbidden fruit. Have you ever done anything like that?"

"Well…" She had to think. "I used to do really dumb things when I was a kid to make my parents mad, because then they'd pay attention to me."

"Do you regret it?"

"Yeah. I was being immature." She didn't elaborate by telling him about the broken vase and the flooded bathroom. She'd just been a stupid kid. "What happened when those people were done? With the girl, I mean."

"They killed her." His voice held a slight tone of remorse. "Tore her throat open with a knife. I saw her spirit leave her body. She seemed confused at first, but then her face brightened with a look of pure joy, and she disappeared. I was happy for her, but at the same time…jealous. That she would go home to her Maker while I was left alone and hopeless in a cabin full of scum."

Sweet Jesus. To think she had stood in the very place where that had happened! "Do those people still meet there? We thought the cabin was abandoned."

He shook his head. "As much as I understood them, I couldn't allow myself to let them hurt anyone else. The next time they arrived with a victim, I drove them out. And the next time, and the next time. Eventually they stopped showing up. I assume they meet elsewhere now, if they meet at all."

"Who were they?"

"People." He smiled. "You and your friend are wasting your time on this whole solving-the-mystery-of-my-death business. You think that I'm still here because of the way I died? That I'm restless because I never had a funeral? I told you why I'm here. It's because of what *I* did. Not what they did. And please take my advice. Quit prying."

~~~

Jerry stayed behind in the bedroom when Jessica went to take her shower, struggling against the temptation that had seized him like a snare.

Jessica should have suspected him. She did not come across as being stupid, but any person with multiple brain cells would have figured it out days ago.

That meant one thing. She didn't know.

The thought both amused and sickened him.

In truth, he shouldn't involve himself with her anymore. He could go away somewhere to silently wait for the final judgment while the world fell apart around him. Jessica would go on with her life, and she would die blissfully ignorant of the things that transpired during that summer when the world still reeled from the Chernobyl disaster and glam metal had been all the rage.

The Presence nudged at his conscience like a bratty kid prodding a dying animal with a stick. It had been doing that a lot these past few days. *Where's the beauty in that?*

It made a good point. Justice had never been served. He could have forgiven those awful people for killing him, but did they deserve it? No! They deserved to be torn from limb to limb and left out for the buzzards to consume.

The thing was they wouldn't have killed him if he hadn't done something very, very bad first.

Don't think that way. They didn't have to kill you over it.

True.

They could have forgiven you. *And you know they never did.*

Should they have?

It's the proper thing to do, isn't it? Good Christians say so.

But they weren't good Christians! And neither was he, for that matter.

Doesn't matter. They killed you, they've walked free for far too long, and they should pay for what they did, shouldn't they?

He didn't even know where any of them lived anymore. Some of them might have even died during the last couple of decades.

Then use what knowledge you already have.

Yes…he could do that.

Suddenly all the faces swam in his mind's eye. The laughing, giggling faces that mocked him with every glance.

We're more special than your baby 'cause our mommies wanted *us,* their eyes seemed to say. Countless phantom voices filled his head in an echoing playground chant.

More special than your *kid,* we're *more special than* your *kid,* we're *more special than* your *kid…*

Echoing, echoing…

He could see himself lifting the revolver. Drawing back the trigger. Delight filled him at the sight of the stunned look that appeared on the first one's face as the bullet tore a hole through its skull. The others were in too much shock to move, like a trio of fawns caught in a high-wattage beam of light. He cut them down in rapid succession.

He could remember the lightness in his chest. The immense feeling of relief knowing that he would never have to see their faces again.

It felt good, didn't it?

Yeah. It had. Better than he had felt in his entire life, in fact.

They took that feeling away from you, Jerry. They tortured you. Do you remember how it felt when they cut you open? Do you remember how frightened you were?

Yes. All too well.

People say that the punishment should fit the crime. Did yours?

Of course it hadn't. They did something far worse than he'd ever done.

So you see? Justice, Jerry. Serve it well.

CHAPTER 22

W ayne fixed a giant bowl of popcorn, and he, Jessica, and Sidney ate sitting on the couch while an *Everybody Loves Raymond* marathon played on the television. Wayne kept the volume low so they would be able to hear each other with clarity.

Jessica and Wayne took turns telling Sidney what they had been up to all afternoon. Jessica felt a little guilty adding even more items to her friend's list of concerns, but what else were they going to do? Lie to her?

"I can't believe you did that," Sidney said when they were finished. She looked even more agitated than she had sounded when Jessica talked to her on the phone.

Jessica couldn't believe it either. Purposefully digging up an unmarked grave was one of the brashest things she had ever done, and that was saying something for the girl whose main hobby was gallivanting around the county alone looking for ghosts. "I know it's crazy. I just had to see it for myself," she said, rubbing her aching calf. "Proof, I guess. It makes everything seem more real."

Sidney gave a short laugh. "It seemed real enough to me when he showed up in our room." She glanced down at her hands. "I'm really sorry about not believing you. I was just being a big dummy. When you said you'd recorded a bunch of stuff and all your equipment turned out to be blank… I mean, if the situation were reversed, you'd have thought I was nuts, too, right? Don't answer that," she added with a blush.

"It's okay," Jessica said. "I've been a big dummy about some things, too." It was nice that the animosity between them had successfully been eliminated. If something were to permanently damage their at-times shaky relationship, Jessica didn't know what she would do. "I hope you forgive me."

Sidney rolled her eyes. "What, are we all going to join hands and start singing kumbaya? Of course I forgive you. As long as you forgive me for being a turd."

Jessica grinned. "You're forgiven." Now maybe things around here would seem a little more normal—with obvious exceptions. "So," she continued, changing the subject, "do either of you want to come to the family reunion tomorrow?"

"You mean I could be an honorary Reyes for a day?" Sidney said. "I'm…well, honored. But I've got work, and I promised Dad and the boys I'd spend the rest of the day with them, so I'm going to be a no-show."

"I'll go," said Wayne. His half-closed eyes and lined face made him look unimaginably tired.

"Great," Jessica teased. "Everyone will think you're my lover."

"I see nothing wrong with that." He smiled weakly and yawned. "I can't wait to see the looks on your parents' faces when we show up hand in hand."

Sidney began to make retching noises. Jessica kicked her in the shin.

"You can look at my parents all you want," Jessica said, "but I'm going to keep my distance. I wouldn't want to upset them by reminding them I exist." She changed her tone when Wayne gave a derisive eye roll. "To be honest, I really don't know what I'm going to say to them. It's been so long."

"Say whatever you want," Sidney said. "As long as it's nice. Tell your mom you like her outfit or something."

Jessica sighed. Suddenly the prospect of seeing her mother and father was more unpleasant than that of digging up Jerry's remains. They had nothing in common, and most likely if they did strike up a conversation they would end up berating her for losing her job and wasting time with ghosts and whatnot.

"I'll just stick with Rachel and Eric as much as I can," she said. Spending additional time with her sister was bound to be more fun than making awkward small talk with Stephen and Maria.

"Are we supposed to bring something to eat?" Wayne asked.

"Probably. I was thinking maybe potato salad."

"Who's going to make it?"

She cleared her throat. Preparing food that didn't involve a microwave required rocket science that she wasn't quite familiar with. "We can get store-bought potato salad. They have all kinds at Eleanor Market."

"Way to make an impression on your family," Sidney said with a smirk.

"It would be a better impression than if I brought crappy, homemade potato salad."

"If it's going to be this much of an issue," Wayne said, "I can make it myself."

"How about this—we can collaborate on it," Jessica said. "We could bring some drinks, too. Like more of that Mike's Hard Lemonade."

"Do I look like I'm made of money?"

"I can buy one six-pack. I've got a few dollars left in my bank account." Very few.

"What, did you drain it all paying the rent here?"

Oh, crap. So much for the end of animosity. Jessica quickly looked to Wayne, who was giving his head a slight shake.

It took Sidney a split second to pick up on their thoughts. "Please tell me you really aren't living here for free."

"I have to," Jessica said, praying that they wouldn't end up fighting all over again. "At least until I can find another job."

"You can't be that broke. Where did all your money go?"

"I bought stuff with it."

She blinked. "What kind of stuff? Wait. You blew your savings on your equipment, didn't you?"

It was an effort to prevent a defensive tone from entering her voice. Her equipment was some of her most prized possessions, and the way Sidney talked she made it sound like Jessica had spent all of her savings on lottery tickets or some other thing like that. "Some of it I used on that. My thermal imaging camera was about seventeen hundred, and my voice recorders and K2 meter were about sixty bucks a piece." She didn't bother mentioning the assorted memory cards and blank CDs and DVDs, which probably totaled up to somewhere around a hundred or so dollars. Or the photo albums, or the photo developing, or the massive quantities of Coke and junk food…

Sidney curled her lip in disgust. "I can't believe you blew it all on that junk."

Jessica counted to five before speaking. "I had my apartment rent, too. Pretty much all the same expenses you have, except for the tuition."

"And to think I don't even get a family discount." Sidney folded her arms and glared at Wayne.

"How about we avoid getting into another argument?" Wayne said as he sat up straighter in the chair. "Sidney, if you were in the same position as Jessica, I'd let you stay here for free, too. Can you accept that?"

Sidney sighed, but her spiteful expression remained. "I guess."

"Good. You're going to give me ulcers if you two keep bickering like this."

"We're not bickering," Jessica said.

"You could have fooled me." He stood up and wobbled a little. "I know it's early, but I'm going to bed. With all that digging we did, I'll be surprised if I can get up without the aid of a forklift in the morning."

He left them. Jessica had the sneaking suspicion that he really just wanted to leave her and Sidney to sort out their dispute by themselves.

"Are you just going to mooch off of people for the rest of your life?" Sidney asked when Wayne's bedroom door closed overhead.

"I'm not mooching!" If her blood had been simmering before, it was now reaching full boil. "You think I like things being this way? I'd move out of here in a heartbeat if I had the money!"

"Have you even been looking for a job?"

"Yes, but nobody's hiring."

"That's when you look for work somewhere else. That's what your parents did."

"Yeah, but they didn't lose their jobs. They just wanted one that paid more. And trust me, I'm not moving to Indianapolis to get a job that pays minimum wage."

"You could start taking classes—"

"I'm broke, remember? *No tengo dinero.* I probably don't even have enough to buy a textbook."

"Take out a loan."

"And what kind of bank is going to lend out money to someone who barely has two cents to her name?" A slight headache began to throb behind her eyes. *Keep it friendly,* she told herself. "Sidney, I really have been trying. Honestly. Now is there anything else you're going to complain about?"

"You haven't done your laundry yet, and it's cluttering up my room."

Jessica couldn't help but laugh. Maybe Sidney wasn't as upset as she'd thought. "I'll get to it. Anything else?"

"I don't like you talking in your sleep."

"And I don't like you being negative all the time. You're giving me a migraine."

"I don't like your car taking up all the space in the driveway."

"And I don't like how you've turned all atheist on me."

Sidney squared her shoulders and gave her a penetrating stare. "It's agnostic, dork. And I can believe whatever I want to, so save your breath and leave me alone."

"Ha!" Maybe there was hope for her friend after all. "If you're agnostic, then there's that little piece of doubt floating around in there, isn't there? Part of you still wants to believe, because if you didn't believe *anything*, you wouldn't have anything to live for. Right?"

A muscle twitched in Sidney's cheek. "Do I have to live for anything?"

"You've got to live for *something*."

Her eyebrow arched. "Oh yeah? What do you live for?"

"Lots of things! Spending time with you two dorks, the promise of a more interesting tomorrow…and I guess what I really want to do is make some epic contribution to society that'll help people out somehow."

"Like what?"

"I haven't figured that out yet." She glanced down at her hands and noticed that some of her fingernails were still caked with dirt from earlier. "I wanted to help people by proving to them there's an afterlife, but now I don't see how that's going to work." It obviously hadn't helped Sidney.

"Okay." Sidney nodded. "What does God have to do with that?"

"It's his will."

"It sounds like your will to me."

"No, my will would be to become ghost hunter extraordinaire and gorge myself on burritos until I weigh three hundred pounds. God's will is different than that."

"Now that we're on the subject," Sidney said, "do you think it's God's will that people die of starvation every day in third-world countries?"

The throbs of pain behind Jessica's eyes worsened. "I don't think so. If more people helped out, those poor people wouldn't have to die at all."

"Then your God sure stinks. If he cared that much about poor people, he'd send them manna like he did with those people in the desert a million years ago."

It didn't look like this discussion was going to go anywhere but in endless circles. "I think," Jessica said, "that God works mostly through other people. A person is sick, they pray that they'll get better, and God sends them a doctor."

"Makes me think of Don Corleone having other people do his crap for him."

"A bolt of lightning might strike you down for talking like that."

"It isn't storming. And besides, what do I have to worry about?" Sidney flashed a grin and picked herself off the couch. "I'll be in the shower. If I get struck by lightning, I'll be sure to let you know."

<hr />

Pain wracked most of Jessica's body as she lay in bed that night, and the stiffness in her cramping limbs made it impossible for her to relax enough to fall asleep.

Worry gnawed at her. Unexplained pain like this could very well be the onset of something horrible like fibromyalgia, in which case she would have to suffer through unceasing agony for the rest of her life. The Tylenol she took before bed might as well have been sugar pills for all the effect they'd had on her.

Sidney coughed in her sleep and rolled over. God had evidently decided to spare her after she had spoken so nastily of him, because no lightning struck her down while she showered.

A short time before, Jessica had heard Wayne get up and adjust the thermostat down in the entryway, so now the room felt as sweltering as a sauna. Jessica kicked off her covers so she wouldn't melt in her pajamas and run all over the floor like spilled wax, but at least then she might not hurt anymore.

"Jessica." Jerry's voice spoke beside her head. She could not see him.

"What is it?" she asked in a whisper.

"Can we talk somewhere?"

"It's the middle of the night."

"You aren't asleep. What does it matter?"

She sighed. "It doesn't, I guess." She got up and slipped her bare feet into a pair of Sidney's fuzzy pink slippers that lay beside the bed. They were about a size and a half too small, so her heels stuck out the backs. "I hope you don't mind chatting outside. If I stay in here another minute, I'll die of heatstroke."

Jerry made no reply. Jessica tiptoed from the room and out to the deck. The porch light clicked on as soon as she stepped through the doorway. No one visible followed her.

The outside temperature was cooler than she had anticipated, or perhaps the contrast with the temperature in the house made the air seem colder than it actually was. Her breath formed fleeting clouds of mist every time she exhaled.

"Where are you?" she asked, hugging her arms close to her chest to warm them.

A vague haze materialized between her and the door and slowly came into focus. "Sorry…" Jerry said. He faded away for a moment and appeared again as he usually had. Black clothes. No blood. That funny scar with the stitches on the back of his hand. "Sometimes this is difficult." He wringed his hands together and kept glancing around him as if keeping an eye out for someone or something that he didn't want to see. "I'm so sorry."

His evident agitation unnerved her. What in all of God's creation could frighten someone who was already dead? "What are you sorry about?"

He seemed to struggle for words. "Have you ever…wanted something so badly…you know it's wrong, but you have to do it, because if you don't you know you'll die?"

Jessica took a step backward. Did he forget that he couldn't die again? "I'm not sure what you're talking about." She wasn't sure she wanted to know either.

The light above the back door shined through him, as if the image of himself he projected was not complete. He looked her right in the eye. "Do you know anyone named Sarah?"

"Sarah?" What kind of question was that? "Not personally. Why?"

The light made his eyes seem to glow. "Are you sure?"

"Pretty darn."

He smiled. "I want to kill my wife."

Jessica's heart beat faster. "Your wife is Sarah?"

He shook his head. "No. Abigail."

She didn't know anyone named Abigail, either. "Why do you want to kill her?"

"Because I'd still be alive if she and I had never met."

"*She's* the one who did this to you?"

"Not physically, no. If you can imagine the chaos of my final years as a line of dominoes, you could say she pushed the first one that made all the others fall."

"What good is killing her going to do?"

"It will make me very happy." His smile broadened as if to emphasize that fact. "Don't you want me to be happy? I know you do, because if you didn't, you wouldn't hound me about moving on."

"But you've got to be reasonable!"

"What does it matter to you if I hurt her? She killed my child. She knew it would hurt me, because it was painful enough when she miscarried our first two. She found out she was pregnant with the third right after we separated, and it was my understanding that we would have joint custody of the child. I was wrong." His face darkened. "I pray you will never learn how it feels to have all your hopes and dreams ground into dust."

The bits of dreams Jessica remembered began to make more sense. "Why did she dislike you so much?"

"Too many reasons. I didn't make enough money. Our house wasn't big enough, and I wouldn't sell it and buy a larger one. I read stupid books. I snored. I didn't like her friends. I was too religious. And according to her, I was a control freak."

Abigail sounded even nastier than Jessica's mother, if that was possible. "Why did you marry her in the first place?" She had often thought to ask her father that same question.

"You're probably thinking I was a fool, don't you?" He laughed. "And you'd be right. Abigail was beautiful. I was an awestruck twenty-two-year-old who thought he'd found God's gift to mankind. But let me tell you something. If there's one thing I learned from our relationship, it's this: people can have the body of a monster and the soul of an angel, or they can have the body of an angel and the soul of a monster. There are few who lie in between."

Jessica fell silent to process her thoughts. If Jerry had three deceased children, she could use that information to repress his desire to hurt his wife. "Do you think that your kids are going to be happy seeing their daddy down here plotting murder?" she asked.

"It wouldn't surprise them." He winced. "Nothing new..." The manic expression she had seen on his face before returned. "I can't kill anyone, anyway. It's not right. Stooping to her level again like a blind idiot...do unto others...but she *deserves* it... Oh, God, I want to put my hands around her neck and snap her bones one by one by one."

He started to fade away again and came back into focus. "I don't want to hurt you," he said. Genuine sadness shined in his eyes. "You've been too kind."

She realized her teeth were chattering, only partly from the cold. "How so?"

"You don't hate me."

"Yeah, but you're scaring the crap out of me right now."

"Can't help that. Being scared is your own choice." He tilted his head upward. "Look at all those stars."

She followed his gaze. Clouds were rolling in from the west, but overhead several twinkling constellations were still visible in the blackness. "What about them?"

"It's so easy to forget and start thinking we're only after-thoughts in the mind of God. It's so huge out there. We're smaller than dust. No meaning to our lives. I lied. I doubted, once. My cousin died. So young. A car accident on a snowy high-way. I wrote a poem about it for one of my assignments. I named it 'Christopher,' after him. I never forgot the words." He began to recite:

> In those days I knew no sorrow.
> Sun did shine in endless day.
> Only now, and no tomorrow,
> Not a thought of life's decay.
> Death came like a thief at nighttime.
> Sly, unwanted phantoms took
> Your hand and led you far away
> To places where we cannot look.
> Eyes stare from a frame that sits in
> Silence on a dusty shelf.
> Your frozen smile cannot deceive
> That force which seeks to claim myself.
> From the picture frame you grin in
> Blissful innocence of youth.
> But in those days, did you know sorrow?
> Or could you see the grimmer truth?

He was silent for a time. Jessica thought of Marjorie Miller, gone from the world far too soon. Jerry had died even younger than she, his children far younger than that. And what had any of them left behind? Memories as frail as smoke. Nothing more.

Yes, it was easy to doubt.

"I got an A on that assignment," he said at last. "My English teacher told me that I had the makings of a true poet, but I never wrote another. I couldn't bring myself to do it." He looked at the sky again. "I miss him so much. I miss all of them. It hurts. I can't stand it. I love them, and they don't even know where I am."

"I could look them up and call them."

"And tell them what wonderful shape I'm in? 'Sorry, Mrs. Madison, but your son isn't at peace and never will be again.' You don't tell people those things. It would crush their hopes."

Since he was acting a bit more coherent and less disturbed than he had been only minutes before, Jessica decided to ignore his warning not to pry and continue to glean more information from him. "Who were the Satanists you got mixed up with?"

His wistful expression morphed into a glare. "You never give up, do you?"

"Not generally."

"Why is it so necessary that you know?"

"It gives me a better understanding of the situation."

"You don't need to understand it better. Mind your own business for once and let me be."

"If you tell me, I'll stop pestering you about it." She shivered. The temperature had already dropped a few degrees since she had come outside, and her thin pajama top didn't do much to protect against the cold.

"Do you promise?"

"Cross my heart and hope to live."

His shoulders slumped. "Very well. But I only knew a couple of them. As to the other ones, your guess is as good as mine."

She waited. "Well?"

"Two were named Rich and Joanna Zimmerman. They were neighbors of mine."

The names meant nothing to her.

"See?" he said, reading her thoughts. "I knew you wouldn't know them. They seemed like a nice enough couple. I had no idea what they were until…well, never mind about that. It's amazing what people can hide."

"What did you do to them?"

He smiled. "Absolutely nothing."

"I don't believe you."

"Then don't."

"Do you want to kill them, too?"

He didn't answer. He suddenly looked distracted. "I've got to find Abigail. And then I've got to find…but I *can't*! For the love of God, why can't you leave me alone?" His voice rose to an angry shout, and Jessica hoped that she was the only one who could hear him. He covered his face with his hands. "I'm slipping away. Don't let it take me!"

"Nobody's taking you anywhere." Not that she could see, at least. Was something else here with them that she didn't know about?

He uncovered his face and began to fade. "I can't make it stop…"

He disappeared.

For the first time, she noticed that the night was alive with sound. The hum of distant motors, the rustle of leaves, the metallic pinging of a rope banging against a flag pole… These things were real. Far less dreamlike than the last several minutes seemed now that Jerry was gone.

It crossed her mind that she, too, might be slipping away. Nobody could ever be wholly certain as to what was real and what was not. She could be totally wrong about Jerry. Maybe he existed only in her head. She could have imagined that Sidney saw him so she wouldn't feel as alone in her delusions.

Heck, she could be wrong about everything. God. Life in general. Herself. Who was she to say that Sidney was wrong in her beliefs? Everyone with a differing opinion had to be wrong somehow; otherwise, everyone would have the same opinion. The fact that every human held different beliefs meant that every human was wrong.

What a sobering thought.

She yawned. Despite the pain, she really did need to get some sleep so she wouldn't feel more miserable at the family reunion than she already expected to be.

She waited for another minute to see if Jerry would reappear. He didn't.

She tried to be as quiet as possible when she went back into the house and latched the door. She poured herself a glass of water in the kitchen. Who was she kidding? Jerry had to be real. That nonsense about him being a figment of her imagination was just a tired brain talking.

She returned to the bedroom.

"What're you doing?" Sidney mumbled.

Jessica kicked off the slippers and lay on top of her blankets. "I just went outside to get some fresh air. Everything's fine."

But everything wasn't fine, was it? She had just lied. Again.

Sometimes it's best to bend the truth for one's own gain, murmured a voice inside her head. *And sometimes it's best to get even.*

~∽∾∽~

Something murky slithered into Jessica's dreams once again. The pathetic child was too stupid to even realize what was going on. This amused the Presence, whose name was Vindictam, to no end. Her ignorance and spite would be her downfall, much as Jerry's weaknesses had led to his—but at least he'd been intelligent enough to realize what was happening, even if that realization hadn't come until it was too late.

The Presence spoke to Jessica's mind in tones sweeter than honey. *Kill them,* it said. *Kill them...*

And in the silence of the night, it could hear Jerry repeat the words like echoes in a void.

The young woman giggled softly in her sleep. Her friend in the other bed sat up and stared their direction with wide eyes. This also amused Vindictam. Sidney Miller was the most emotionally volatile person it had ever encountered other than Jerry Madison. An easy mark.

It picked up the same tiny pebble it had been using the other night and sent it careening into the wall beside Sidney's head. *Tap.*

We don't want you, it said to her as it had before.

Tap. Tap.

But this time Sidney did not flee to the ground floor. She muttered something—a prayer?—and suddenly Vindictam felt a fraction of its strength leave. *The little witch.* Her attempt the other night had done nothing. What had changed?

It couldn't keep wasting its time on the redhead. It devoted all of its attention to Jessica because it needed her the most. *Remember what they did to you. Remember how they made you hurt.*

Her lips moved to form words. "I remember…"

CHAPTER 23

"The high today is only going to be fifty-five," Wayne said, switching off the television in the living room. "I hope your relatives were smart enough to rent a place that has heat."

"There's a lodge at Campbell Community Park," Jessica said. She was still wearing her pajamas and stood at the kitchen counter peeling potatoes. Her hands were already tired, and more bits of peel were landing on the floor than on the plate she had intended to pile them on. "I'm sure we'll all be inside. They have a rec room with skee ball and some arcades with Pac Man and Space Invaders. At least they did the last time we were all there."

He joined her in the kitchen. "Whose idea was it to have a family reunion in October?"

"My guess is Uncle Esteban, since he's the one who organizes the thing. *El Día de los Muertos* is in a couple of weeks, though. It probably had something to do with that." The Mexican holiday coincided with the Catholic feasts of All Saints and All Souls and involved the gathering of family to remember and honor their deceased loved ones. Even though almost all of her living relatives had been born in the United States and hadn't so much as placed a toe on Mexican soil, various members of the Reyes family sought to keep some of the old traditions alive so they wouldn't lose sight of their non-European roots.

Wayne plucked a piece of potato peel off of the counter and flicked it onto the plate. "Do you think they'll be serving candy skulls?"

"I'd say there's a strong possibility of that."

"Neat. I've never had one before."

"They're more for decoration than anything else. You can eat them if you want, but they're pure sugar, so you might get diabetes or something if you eat too many of them." She set aside a peeled potato and picked up another. "Hey, I've got some news for you. I learned something else about Jerry last night."

"Oh yeah?"

She nodded. "It's kind of sad, actually. His wife had an abortion, and he didn't want her to, and he says he wants to kill her to get back at her for it."

Wayne's eyebrows rose. "This many years later? Seems kind of obsessive. You'd think if he wanted to kill her that badly, he'd have done it when he was still alive." He got a giant pot out of the cabinet next to the oven, filled it with water, and placed it on the stove. He did the same with a saucepan and placed a few eggs in it to boil.

"Yeah," Jessica continued, nearly peeling her finger instead of the potato, "it's not like he could hurt her now, anyway. I just hope he doesn't try to find her and do something stupid like levitate a table and chuck it at her head."

He picked up the handful of potatoes that were already peeled and set them on a cutting board. "Did he say who the lucky lady is?"

She paused to think. Sarah? No, he had never told her who Sarah was or why he'd even asked if she knew her. His wife's name had started with an A. "I think he said her name is Abigail. I thought about looking her up in the phone book, but I was afraid Jerry would see what I was doing and figure out where to find her."

"What's going to stop him from looking in the phone book himself?"

"Hopefully a little self-control." She bent down to grab another stray peel she'd dropped on the floor. "Or I could just burn the phone book we've got so he doesn't start flipping through it when we have our backs turned."

Wayne began slicing the potatoes into cubes. "Nah, don't do that. Did I ever tell you that I used to study name meanings as a sort of pointless hobby?"

Now *that* was a change of subject if she'd ever seen one. "I don't think so. Why?"

"I was just going to say that if I remember right, Abigail comes from ancient Hebrew and means source of joy."

Jessica flexed her tired fingers and picked up the next potato. "What's your point?"

"It sounds like Mrs. Madison is the anti-Abigail."

"Based on what he told me, I'd have called her something a little less friendly than that. Do you know what my name means?"

"It means God is watching. I think that one is Hebrew, too."

That had a nice ring to it. "And what about Wayne?"

"You're going to laugh at that one. It means wagon maker in old English."

She smiled. "I think you've got to be wrong about the meaning of my name. Jessica *has* to mean 'woman who cannot stand to cook and wants the wagon maker to do it instead.'"

"You'll make a terrible housewife."

"And you'll make a terrible husband, because you still act like a woman half the time, hence the cooking."

He pretended to look insulted. "There's nothing wrong with being in touch with one's feminine side."

"Just don't start wearing dresses. Okay?"

"Not even for Halloween?"

"I could make that exception."

"We could dress as each other and pass out candy to the kids."

"Too bad I don't wear dresses then, huh?" She finished peeling the final potato, rinsed it, and handed it over for him to cut. "Now what do you want me to do?"

"Find a bowl that we can put this all in when it's done."

"Sure." She carried one of the chairs over to the counter and stood on it so she could reach the top shelf of the cabinet where Wayne kept all of his Tupperware containers. A green bowl with a matching lid looked like it would be about the right size, so she grabbed it down and set it on the counter. "Is this good?"

"Perfect. You might make a good housewife yet."

"That sounds so old-fashioned. Can't I just be a regular wife?"

"Only if you don't make me cook all the time."

"That sounds like a marriage proposal."

"It does, doesn't it?" He gave her a sidelong look.

"You just don't want me to leave here if I get another job."

"I'd be all alone."

"You'd have Sidney."

"She's family. That doesn't count."

"She'd kill you if she heard you talking like that."

"I know." He scooped up all of the little potato cubes and dumped them into the pot. He turned the temperature on the burner up all the way. "But she isn't here right now, so what does it matter? Besides, it's not her house."

"You mean to say that if we got married in some hypothetical universe, you'd send her packing?"

"What, would you *want* her to stay here? She'd have to either move back to Drew's house or find her own place. I told her when she first moved in not to expect to live here forever."

It was apparent that Wayne had thought this scenario through at some point prior to this conversation. That thought made Jessica's heart flutter. "What other things might there be in this hypothetical universe?"

He placed his forefinger on his chin. "Kids. Lots of little brown-haired brats who like to shop at Macy's."

"How many is lots?"

"Seventeen."

She gave him a dubious look.

"Okay," he said, "more than one."

"My hair is going to turn gray awfully fast in this hypothetical universe."

"It can't be that bad. Just give them a box of crayons and some paper, and we wouldn't hear another peep out of them."

"Why do I get the feeling that the Wagon Maker doesn't want this to be hypothetical at all?"

"I shouldn't have told you what my name meant."

"Stop dodging the question."

"Never."

She brandished the potato peeler at him. "I can force it out of you."

He picked up the knife and waved it slowly back and forth. "I can protect myself."

"You wouldn't stab me, would you?"

"Only if you started peeling me first."

Suddenly, something heavy fell over in another part of the house with a loud *thump*. They both lowered their culinary weapons and stared at the open doorway between the entryway and living room. "I'll check it out," Jessica said, setting the peeler on the counter. Hopefully nothing out there had been broken.

The source of the noise became apparent as soon as she entered the living room. Several books had fallen out of the shelf and now lay in a haphazard pile on the floor. No sooner had she stooped to pick them up when a bunch of Wayne's Dean Koontz novels flew off a shelf right in front of her, narrowly missing her feet as they hit the carpet.

No need to wonder who the culprit was.

"Stop it!" she shouted. "What's gotten into you?"

Books fell from a third shelf and lay still. She waited. Nothing more happened.

"Is it something we said?" Wayne shuffled up behind her. He was still holding the paring knife in one hand.

She began shoving books back onto the shelves, not particularly caring what order they went in. "It's always something we said."

"Well," Wayne said, "either we start censoring everything we say, or we force you-know-who out of here before he starts causing some serious damage. My homeowner's insurance doesn't cover angry ghosts."

Jessica nodded and returned to the kitchen. As much as Jerry's plight aroused her pity, she couldn't have agreed more.

~~~

At eleven thirty they departed for Campbell Community Park in Cold Spring, Kentucky. Jessica balanced the bowl of potato salad on her lap and buckled her seatbelt.

"We got everything?"

"I think so," she said.

"Good." Wayne climbed behind the wheel and slammed the door shut. "Hang on one second." He pulled a white plastic bottle emblazoned with a gold cross out of his pocket and stuffed it into the cup holder. Holy water.

"Expecting trouble?" she asked.

"No. I'm expecting the unexpected." He backed the truck out of the driveway.

"My mother isn't a demon, you know. Holy water isn't going to have any effect on her."

"Sorry, I was all out of sharpened stakes."

Jessica started to laugh, but the emotion suddenly died within her. She would see her mother and father within the hour. She should just ignore them. They never had anything good to say. They would disapprove of her living arrangements even though she and Wayne weren't doing anything objectionable. They would call her a failure for having lost her job.

Then again, they might not speak a single word to her. Somehow, that would be the most hurtful thing of all.

"What do you look so glum about?" he asked when they turned onto U.S. 52 and headed toward the interstate.

"Nothing." Now that she'd had some practice, lying wasn't so hard. Sometimes it was best to bend the truth a little, especially if the lie wasn't going to hurt anyone.

"Do you care if I turn on some music?"

"It's your truck. Do whatever you want."

He prodded the power button on the radio and tuned it to a pop station that Jessica had never cared to listen to. Lady Gaga was singing "Bad Romance," which had a catchy tune that always got stuck in her head and drove her half mad. "I retract my statement."

"Too late now. It's my truck, remember?"

"If you weren't driving, I'd punch you."

"Lucky for me, then."

Jessica closed her eyes. At least their trip would be short.

They arrived in Cold Spring less than thirty minutes after they left the house. Traffic on U.S. 27 was already backed up, Justin Bieber was singing his little heart out, and Jessica could have sworn that her ears were about to start bleeding.

"You're going to have to direct me now," Wayne said.

"Get into this lane and turn at the next light." She pointed at the lane to their right, where a long string of vehicles idled bumper to bumper as they waited for the light to change.

Wayne stopped and flipped on the turn signal. "You could have told me that while there was still room to get over."

"Sorry, your music is killing off my brain cells."

He smiled and bumped up the volume. She punched him lightly on the arm.

Fortunately, a kind soul in a Buick allowed them to merge in front of them, saving them from having to miss their street and turn around. They made a right at the traffic light.

"Now it's just ahead on the left."

"I see it."

Wayne slowed the truck and waited for a line of cars to pass by before making the turn into the park entrance.

Campbell Community Park consisted of a ball field, a large play area for children, two picnic pavilions, and the three-story Kemper House, which had formerly been a home but was now rented out for family gatherings like the one today. Jessica had often wondered if the place was haunted since it was so old, though nothing odd had ever happened to her during the various reunions she'd attended there. She'd have to call the park office sometime and see if she could get permission to investigate there anyway.

Wayne pulled into a parking space next to a familiar gold Lexus that bore dark-blue Indiana license plates.

She gulped. Her parents were already here.

Remember what they did to you. Remember how they made you hurt.

"I think I'll just stay in the truck while you have fun hanging out with the kinfolk," she said, staring out the window at the white brick building where Maria and Stephen lay in wait.

Wayne killed the engine. "You're too old to be acting like that."

He was probably right. "God grant me the serenity," she muttered, and climbed out of the truck into the shade of the massive maple trees that swayed in the breeze between the house and the faded pavement.

Wayne led the way up a handicapped ramp onto a white, wooden porch where Esteban Reyes and one of his cousins whose name Jessica couldn't remember were having a smoke and laughing about something or another that, knowing her uncle, probably wasn't all that funny.

"Jessica!" the former exclaimed when he saw her. "Long time no see! And who is this?"

Jessica gave her uncle a one-armed hug since she was hanging on to the potato salad with the other. Esteban was her mother's only sibling, and sometimes she wondered how such vastly different people could have been born from the same womb. "It's good to see you, too. Haven't you met Wayne before?"

Uncle Esteban squinted, and Jessica could tell that he was attempting to figure out why Wayne walked with such an unusual gait. "I don't think so." His jovial smile returned, and he held out his hand. "It's nice to meet you, young man. Don't let any of these Reyes folk pick on you too much."

Wayne shook his hand. "I've known Stephen and Maria for years," he said. "Nothing can scare me."

Uncle Esteban and his cousin burst into laughter again. "Better not let my sister hear you!" Esteban said with a twinkle in his eye. "Now, Wayne, this here is Ernesto. His dad and mine were brothers."

He proceeded to give Wayne the family history, which Jessica had heard about a thousand times over the years. Her grandfather, Andrés Reyes Pizano, came to the United States as a small child along with his parents and five siblings. Instead of giving their children two surnames as per tradition, Andrés and his wife Karen only gave their son and daughter the name from the paternal side of the family since it was the American thing to do. Jessica was glad that the tradition had been dropped, because if it hadn't, her name would be Jessica Mary Roman-Dell Reyes, and that just sounded terrible.

"—it on the table inside."

"Sorry, what?" Jessica looked up. Wayne, Uncle Esteban, and Ernesto were all staring at her, no longer smiling.

"That bowl you're carrying," her uncle said. "You can set it on the table with all the other food inside."

"Oh. Okay." She took a deep breath and walked past them into the big room where numerous round tables had been set up and covered in orange and brown plastic tablecloths as befitting the season. Food covered a long buffet table off to the left. There were deviled eggs, veggie and meat trays, scalloped potatoes, dinner rolls, at least eight giant bags of potato and corn chips, salsa, cheese dip, and homemade churros, to name a few of the items that had already begun to make her mouth water. Two big trays of decorated candy skulls sat at the far end of the table. Wayne was in for a treat.

She set the potato salad between the deviled eggs and a veggie tray. She took off the lid and pulled out the spoon she had stashed inside.

Wayne remained outside talking to the other men, and Rachel and Eric hadn't shown up yet, so she had nobody else to talk to. Some older Reyes women whom she didn't know very well were sitting at a table at the other end of the room talking in rapid voices and showing each other photo albums.

Suddenly a peal of laughter echoed in from the adjoining room. She recognized it as belonging to Marco, the cousin who dressed as a woman and did magic tricks on the weekends.

"Oh, Maria," she heard him say, "you remember that one time when..."

He and Maria walked into the banquet room, still chatting. Neither of them looked at her.

Since he wasn't at work, Marco Reyes—the brother of Ernesto, Jessica was fairly certain—was dressed in a rather ordinary outfit of jeans and a gray turtleneck sweater. Maria wore a dark-gray skirt with a matching blazer, a cream-colored top, and black pumps. Her black hair was piled on top of her head and pinned in place with a silver clip shaped like a flower blossom.

Maria was fifty-two years old and didn't look a day over forty. Her ability to age gracefully was the only thing Jessica had ever desired to inherit from her.

Though she had intended to be a pacifist today by not engaging in any arguments with her mother, Jessica's temper began to rise at the sight of her. Maria's outfit had probably cost more than Jessica's last rent payment at the apartment complex, and here Jessica was wearing jeans that had a hole in one knee, a hooded sweatshirt with fraying cuffs, and sneakers that had been old three years ago.

Maria must have sensed Jessica's gaze, for she turned suddenly. "Oh. Hi, Jessica." She smiled, but the look in her eyes was distant.

Hi, Jessica. No "I've missed you." No warm embrace. No sign that she cared.

"Where's Dad?" Jessica asked in a weak voice. Her pulse pounded in her ears.

"He went down to the grocery store with David to get napkins." David was another of her cousins. "They left just a few minutes ago."

"Does it usually take two people to buy one thing?"

Maria's eyes narrowed. "Does it matter?"

"I guess not." If Jessica guessed correctly, the men were picking up cases of beer, too, which was all right since she and Wayne had opted not to bring any drinks after all.

"I'll leave you two alone," Marco said. "Esteban might need help with something." He slipped away, throwing one last glance over his shoulder as he departed.

"Rachel told me you're living with Wayne," Maria said. The distant look returned.

"Yeah." *Don't say anything stupid,* she told herself. *Please don't say anything stupid.*

"Is that a permanent arrangement?"

"I don't know."

"You're not sharing a room, are you?"

Her face heated. "No."

Maria gave her a knowing look. "He's thirty years old, Jessica. Don't assume he's letting you live there for purely benevolent reasons."

Jessica's temper refused to be held at bay. "So what about that?" she blurted. "You're probably just afraid of me getting pregnant and bringing another child into this cruel world, or something stupid like that. But I'm still a virgin, for your information, so you don't have anything to worry about for a *long* time."

The room grew as quiet as a tomb. The women with the photo albums gaped like beached fish. Maria's eyes blazed. For some reason, Jessica no longer cared.

"Do you *want* to humiliate me in front of my relatives?" her mother hissed.

Did she? "I—"

"I think I came in on the wrong end of that conversation," Wayne said, coming up beside them holding a can of Pepsi. He gave Jessica a warning glance.

The women at the back of the room resumed their conversation but still threw Jessica and her mother snooping looks every few seconds.

Maria's gaze flicked from Jessica to Wayne. "Hello, Wayne," she said in a politer tone. "You've been well?"

He bowed his head. "Most of the time. I still put up with Charlie five days a week. He says he misses you two. Your replacements are so clueless we don't know how they managed to pass the CPA exam."

Maria smiled. "It's nice to hear we made an impression on him. Tell everyone we said hi." Then to Jessica, she said, "If you see your sister, could you tell her to come talk to me? I have a present for her."

"What, is it for the baby you don't want her to have?"

Her mother opened her mouth as if in shock. "What in the world has gotten into you?"

Jessica felt a tug on her arm.

"Sorry, she's had a stressful week," Wayne said, leading her away from Maria. "Don't take it personally."

They went back out to the porch. Uncle Esteban and Ernesto were talking to some of the new arrivals out in the parking lot.

"What do you think you're doing?" Wayne whispered.

Tears brimmed in her eyes. The brief encounter with her mother made her feel like curling up into a ball and crying until the sun shined no more. "I don't know! Every time I look at her I just want to make her hurt like she made me hurt all those years."

Wayne put his hands on her shoulders. She didn't bother pushing him away. "You've got to put all that behind you! You can't hate someone forever. Do you think I still make myself sick over what my mother did to me? It took me years, but I finally did learn to get over it—and if I can, you can, too."

She looked into his coffee-brown eyes, which were giving her the hardest stare she had ever seen Wayne use. "Well, I can't just quit calling myself Jessica and get over it. That's why you don't go by Robert anymore, isn't it? You couldn't stand for people to call you what she did."

He dropped his hands. "Jessica…"

She brushed him off. She had made a mistake in coming here, and not even the promise of a free meal was going to convince her to stay. "Let's just go home," she said.

He shook his head. "Nope. You need to start acting like an adult, and in order to do that you have to get along with people you don't like. Is that so hard to do?"

Yes! Why couldn't Wayne understand? "She deserves to be hurt. She needs to know what it's like."

He gave her a cold look. "Has our friend been giving you ideas? Revenge isn't the way to solve things."

"It's an awfully tempting one."

The new arrivals, who happened to be Elena the dinner theater actress and her husband and young children, gave them both warm smiles but didn't say anything as they walked past Jessica and Wayne into the house. They probably didn't even remember who she was. Not surprising.

Uncle Esteban and Ernesto made their way back up the walk.

"Hey, Wayne," Uncle Esteban said when they reached the porch, "you ever had a candy skull?"

Wayne shook his head. "That would be a negative."

"You ought to try one and see if it makes you go into a coma. My wife made them."

"I'll think about it."

Cousin Ernesto laughed. "Don't chip a tooth."

The two men went inside, leaving her and Wayne alone again on the porch. More cars pulled into the parking lot, including one gray Nissan Altima.

"You don't know what it's like," Jessica said to him. She felt as if a carefully built dam inside of her had suddenly sprung a leak, and a vast lake of buried emotions was gushing out through the hole, drowning everything else in its wake. "Never giving me hugs or kisses or a shoulder to cry on…"

"Rachel and Eric are here," Wayne said, scanning the parking lot. His face was grave. "I suggest you act happy to see them."

CHAPTER 24

"You never responded to the text I sent you earlier," Rachel said while they ate. She, Eric, Jessica, and Wayne had selected a table close to the rear of the room by the women with the photo albums, because Maria and Stephen were sitting toward the front. The arrangement had given Jessica's mood a minimal boost.

"I didn't know you sent one." Jessica picked up her purse and slid her phone out of its compartment. "Oh, that's why. My battery's dead. What did you want?"

"Nothing important." Rachel stabbed a piece of broccoli onto her fork and dipped it into a glob of ranch dressing. "I've been craving jalapeno sauce like crazy today, and I wanted to know if you had any you could bring for me."

Jessica wrinkled her nose. "That spicy stuff? You'll burn the kid."

"No, I'm just toughening him up. Or her. Whatever it is." She popped the broccoli into her mouth and chewed. "Ranch is still pretty darn good, though."

Wayne and Eric started telling each other stories about their respective places of employment. While they talked, Jessica's gaze drifted over to her parents' table. She had been right about the beer. Stephen and David returned from the store with a package of napkins as well as two cases of Corona and two of Bud Light. Now her father was sipping a can of the latter, saying something to Marco and emphasizing a point with his free hand like he usually did. Maria sat between them, smiling and looking like a retired runway model in that fancy outfit.

Why did you ever have kids when you clearly have more fun without them? Jessica wondered. *There's lots of ways you could have prevented us from being born.*

She returned her attention to their own table. "What did Mom give you?" she asked Rachel. She had seen the two talking by the buffet table shortly after Rachel and Eric arrived. Maria had passed Rachel a tiny gift bag. A peace offering, Jessica thought. There was no other reason for the woman to give her daughter a gift.

"Oh!" Rachel's face brightened. She reached into her purse and pulled out a pink-and-blue baby rattle that had a white bow tied around the handle. "She told me she knows it's probably too early to give me anything like this, but she didn't know when else she'd be seeing me. And she told me she's sorry about the way she reacted when I told her about the baby. She said it was the last thing she'd been expecting me to say. Sound familiar?"

"She could be lying."

"Why would she do that?"

"To make you like her."

"Well, I do feel a little more warmly toward her now that she doesn't think I'm an idiot for letting this weirdo knock me up." She ruffled Eric's hair, and he swatted at her without pausing in his conversation with Wayne. "Look, he acts like he doesn't even hear me."

Jessica didn't believe that their mother would have changed her mind on the matter in the span of only a few days. Maria was too stubborn for that.

"Are you okay?" Rachel asked.

She looked at their parents' table again. Maria was spooning a glob of their potato salad into her mouth. "Did Mom ever tell you that she loved you?"

Rachel paused. "I don't think so. I don't really remember."

"Why do you think she doesn't love us?"

"She does love us. She just doesn't know how to express it."

Jessica smirked. Way to go for rationalizing Maria's short-comings. "How hard can it be to say I love you?"

"I don't know, Jess. But can't we just leave it in the past where it belongs?"

Why did everyone have to keep going on like that? With Wayne it was understandable since he hadn't grown up in their house, but Rachel had been there. She harbored the same negative feelings that Jessica did, so it was dumb for her to act like Maria's lack of parenting was excusable. "Today isn't in the past," Jessica said.

"Didn't I tell you to start acting like an adult?" Wayne butted in.

She gave a snort. "Now you're sounding like somebody's dad."

"I'm practicing."

"I thought that was all in a hypothetical universe."

"Did I miss something?" Rachel asked.

"Nothing you need to know about," Jessica said, not quite in the mood to let her sister in on hers and Wayne's personal jokes. She wished Wayne hadn't brought it up.

"Now I'm curious."

"Don't be."

"We were just talking about future things," Wayne said. "Purely hypothetical, though."

Rachel laid down her fork. "Like what?"

He didn't miss a beat. "Hover boards. If we're to believe *Back to the Future*, kids should be using them about now."

"Don't forget the flying cars," Eric said.

"Those, too."

"What in the world do hover boards and flying cars have to do with being a father?" Rachel asked him, looking skeptical.

Wayne shrugged. "When you figure it out, be sure to tell me, because I haven't the slightest idea."

Jessica forced herself to continue eating. Why was everyone acting so cheerful when a witch was sitting only a few tables away from them? She wanted to stand up on her chair and shout, "Look at her! She may have the body of an angel, but inside she's a monster!" Someone had told her that another person was like that, too. Had it been Wayne? No, he wouldn't say that kind of thing, because he was too nice for his own good, except for the fact that he'd bludgeoned Mother dearest to death with a fireplace poker. Strangely, that thought amused her. Maria could have used the same treatment. *When there's something deranged in the neighborhood, who you gonna call? Mom Busters!*

She swayed a little in her chair. It grew difficult to think clearly. She hadn't slept well, had she? Her brain felt as though it were lost in a fog bank. *Who you gonna call...*

All sound in the room grew fainter and eventually ceased. Her mind drifted like an anchorless ship lost at sea. Where was she? Not at home, though home was where the heart was, and her heart was in her chest, and her chest was attached to the rest of her, so she *must* have been home, because home was anywhere...

Her vision cleared. She saw her mother. Sitting in a recliner, reading a book. Turning the pages, one by one.

"Mommy, read me a story!"

Ignored. Another page turning.

"Please, Mommy?"

A glance. "They'll teach you to read when you're in school. Then you can read stories whenever you like."

"But I want you to read me a story. Mommy, please! The little girl next door says her mommy reads her stories all the time..."

Her mother. Scrubbing a counter in the kitchen.

"Mommy! I cut my finger!" Blood. Pain.

A pause. "What did you cut your finger on?"

"There—there was a piece of glass in the yard, and I picked it up and—and—"

Leading her into the bathroom. Washing the cut, wrapping it in a bandage.

No kisses. No more blood, but pain…

Her mother. Doing paperwork by the window in the living room.

"Mom, do you care if I go hang out at Sidney's?"

A distracted glance. "Hmm?"

"Sidney's house. Do you care if I go over there?"

"No, go ahead. Why would I care about that kind of thing? Why would I care? Why would I care? Why would I—"

Laughter. Jessica twitched. She was sitting at a round, covered table in the Kemper house at the park in Cold Spring, and Eric was laughing at something Wayne had said. "Good one!"

Jessica rubbed her eyes and blinked. She must have dozed off for a moment or two. Fortunately she hadn't slumped over and fallen out of her seat. Her mother would have died of embarrassment, though her demise wouldn't have greatly concerned her. *Who you gonna call…*

A Reyes walked past the table carrying a bottle of Corona. Rachel nudged her husband in the side. "Hey, look. I told you they'd have alcohol here."

Eric wrinkled his nose. "Corona? That stuff smells like a skunk."

Rachel pointed across the room. "I see someone with a can of Bud Light. Go knock yourself out."

"Might as well." He rose from his seat and ambled over to the coolers beside the buffet table.

"Jess, you look tired," Rachel said.

"Do I?" She blinked. "I cut my finger."

Rachel frowned. "On what?"

She wobbled in the chair again and gripped the edge of the table to steady herself. "There was a piece of glass in the yard. It cut me when I picked it up. She never kissed it to make it better."

"What are you talking about?"

Why didn't she understand? "No kisses. She never let herself get too close, to make things simple if something happened. Just a pretense of motherhood, like doing it out of duty because you know you have to."

"Are you feeling all right?"

A hand placed itself on her forehead. "She feels a little warm. She might be running a fever."

"And that's going to make her start acting drunk? What's in her glass?"

The cup she'd poured rose into the air. "Looks like Pepsi or Coke."

Her vision doubled. She blinked again to bring everything back into focus. Two people were sitting at the table with her. A man and a woman. Other people were in the room, too, talking and eating.

"Jessica, can you hear me?" The man was speaking. He had glasses and gelled hair.

Of course she could hear; she wasn't deaf! Who did these people think she was?

"I think she's having a seizure," the woman said.

"Then why is she still sitting up?"

"Not all seizures are like that. Sometimes they only cause an altered state of consciousness. She might not even remember it when it's over. Jessica, honey, snap out of this!"

She shivered. Someone must have left a door open, because the air in the room was turning to ice.

Another man came and sat at the table. He was holding a blue can of beer that had beads of condensation built up on the sides. "What's going on?"

Eric! His name was Eric. And with him were Rachel and Wayne, and she was Jessica, and they were at a miserable family reunion at a park in Cold Spring, Kentucky.

Jessica shook her head. She'd zoned out again. Half of her food remained on her plate. "Sorry. What did you say?"

"Are you coherent now?" Rachel asked.

"Am I ever?"

Rachel didn't seem to be in the mood for humor. "What was that all about?"

"What was what about?" A few tendrils of fog wove in and out of her thoughts, derailing any line of thinking before it could come to fruition in her head.

"Do you want me to take you home?" Wayne asked. She realized that he was gripping her hand so hard that her fingertips were starting to turn purple. She returned to full alertness in an instant.

"No, I think I'm fine now." Jessica forced a smile. "Did somebody say something about a seizure?"

"You were having one."

How odd. "It must not have lasted very long."

"If it had lasted any longer, I'd have hauled you off to the nearest hospital to get your head scanned," Rachel said. "You haven't had one of those before, have you?"

"Not that I'm aware of." She had fainted a couple of times running around in the heat when she was a kid, but that was it. "Maybe it's from stress."

"Stress doesn't do that to people. Wayne thinks you're running a fever."

She touched her forehead. It felt sort of warm, but that might have just been because her hand was cold. "It must not be much of one."

"Just take it easy, okay?"

"I haven't not been taking it easy. I'll be fine. I swear."

Rachel didn't seem convinced. She picked up her fork and stabbed a piece of cauliflower. "If you insist."

Wayne released his grip on her hand. "I'll keep an eye on her."

"I can keep an eye on myself," Jessica said, not liking how everyone was suddenly treating her like an invalid. One weird spell didn't mean anything was the matter.

She bit into a baby carrot and glanced over at her parents' table again. Her father, having finished his beer, yawned and checked his watch. He said something to her mother, who shook her head. She couldn't hear what they were saying over the hubbub.

"So," Jessica said, "are Mom and Dad driving straight back to Indy after this?"

Rachel shook her head. "No, they're staying with us tonight at Uncle Esteban's. Aunt Sharon's giving them the guest bedroom down the hall from us. Why?"

Who you gonna call? "Just wondered." She stood up. Her drink had gone to her bladder awfully fast. "I'm going to the bathroom. Be right back."

She wove her way around tables full of chattering Reyeses who barely even glanced at her and strode through the doorway she'd seen her mother and Marco come through earlier. The women's restroom was on the left. She felt fine. No doubt her strange spell would not be repeated.

She pushed open the door of the first stall and latched it behind her. Fine, fine, fine; oh, yes, she felt fine. Even the pain had taken a break, and she felt—

Fog overtook her unexpectedly, and before it could occur to her that she might not be as fine as she'd thought, she was gone.

⚬⚬⚬

Sidney had taken her laptop to work so she could kill time and post some online discussion questions for her English class. She couldn't see why she had to do that in addition to attending her Wednesday night lecture, but you didn't argue with that kind of thing when you were the dimwit who'd signed up for that particular class in the first place. At least the semester ended in December. And at least she was only taking the one class.

The console on the counter beeped, signaling that somebody was using their credit card to pay at the pump. Chances were they wouldn't even come in to say hi, much less buy anything.

She took a swig of Pepsi and popped a handful of Cheetos into her mouth. Even though Travis may have been a Bible-thumping pain in the behind, he was still cool enough to let her stuff her face on the job as long as she paid for her indulgences first.

It only took her a few minutes to complete her required discussion posts, most of which had to do with the Poe and Bryant poems she'd had to compare for the week's assignment. Then she logged into her e-mail account and saw she had five new messages, all of them spam.

The customer outside hung up the nozzle, got back into their car, and left.

She sighed. Having customers come inside and keep her busy for a minute or two was too much to ask for these days.

She wiped the orange powder off of her fingers onto her pants leg. Since her homework was done for the time being and she had no other pressing matters to attend to, she decided to try to find out more about Jerry. Somebody had to have suspected that he'd been murdered. A person vanishes without taking their wallet or car along with them; they have to be either in witness protection or dead.

No customers lurked in the parking lot. She glanced through the glass door connecting the gas station and diner. Travis stood beside a booth chatting with some of the regular restaurant patrons who were probably the only reason that the diner hadn't gone out of business ages ago. Hopefully he'd stay put while she conducted her online investigation. No telling what he'd think if he saw what she was looking up.

She ate another Cheeto and typed "Campbell County Kentucky murder 1986" into Google's search bar. Some crumbs fell between the keys. She could clean them up later.

One of the first links that the search returned bore the headline, "No Suspects Linked to Alexandria Shooting."

Interesting. The missing persons article Wayne had found specifically stated that Jerry had lived in Alexandria.

Pulse quickening, she clicked on the link, which took her to a reprinted article from a library archive. The article had been taken from a July edition of a newspaper she had never heard of. She popped another Cheeto into her mouth and began to read.

Her eyes widened as she scrolled down the page, and she accidentally inhaled part of a Cheeto when the second to last paragraph caused her to make an involuntary gasp. *Holy crap.*

She managed to cough a few times. Her eyes watered, causing the revelatory words to blur on the screen. They couldn't be true. But they had to be. No one else had that name.

She sat there dumbly, not knowing what to do. This information was going to alter everything that Jessica had ever known, because she *couldn't* have known before. And why in the blazes hadn't she been told?

This news could not wait. Sidney fumbled for her cell phone and dialed Jessica's number. It went immediately to voicemail.

Crap.

She tried it again. Jessica's recorded voice came on the line a second time. "Hi, this is Jessica. I can't come to the phone right now, so please leave your name and number after the tone."

She closed her phone and took a deep breath. Wayne didn't own a cell phone, so she wouldn't be able to reach Jessica through him, either.

The clock on the wall said it was two. She didn't get off work until four. She could feign illness and convince Travis to let her leave, and she could drive out to Cold Spring to tell Jessica the news to her face and possibly prevent something very bad from happening, if she were correct in her assumptions.

Come to think of it, her stomach wasn't feeling all that great anyway—not now that she knew what happened. To help it feel even worse, she chugged down the remainder of her Pepsi in a single gulp and jumped up and down a few times for good measure. Her innards lurched in protest. Perfect.

She snapped her laptop closed and stuffed it back into its carrying case. She stuck her head through the doorway into the diner. "Hey, Travis?' she said in a weak voice that surprisingly didn't need to be faked.

Her sandy-haired boss turned from the couple he was talking to. He'd been acting kind of cold toward her since their little argument the other day, so he didn't smile when he saw her. "What is it?"

"Stomach," she said. "I think I'm catching one of those bugs that's been going around."

He frowned, his eyes full of concern that made her feel guilty for lying. "Are you sure?"

She gave a fierce nod. "I feel like I'm going to puke my guts out."

The couple in the booth wrinkled their noses and scooted up against the wall to be as far away from her as possible.

Travis took an unconscious step back from her. "If you're feeling that bad, leave. Helen should be fine over here by herself for a while."

Thank you, God. "Could I? I can make up the last two hours on Monday if I'm feeling better then."

He untied his grease-speckled apron and draped it over his arm. "We can talk about that later. Now scram before you contaminate the whole restaurant and get me in trouble with the health inspector."

At least some of his old humor was returning. Sidney thanked him, raced back into the gas station, and swiped her things up from behind the counter.

God, she prayed, figuring that a quick prayer was worth a shot, *please let me be making mountains out of molehills. Please don't let me be too late.*

CHAPTER 25

L ike Christ on his way to Calvary, they forced him along to his place of execution, though fortunately they hadn't required him to carry anything, because he would have crumpled to his knees under the weight. The effects of the drug slowly wore off, but he hadn't regained enough strength to resist them and run. All he could do was stagger where they dragged him, and pray.

They were clearly in a forest now. Tree frogs chirped up above, and the earthy smell of decaying leaf matter filled the air. Soft voices murmured close by. Something crackled. He caught a whiff of smoke. Maybe they were going to burn him at the stake.

"We got him," a man said so close to his ear that he jumped.

A hush fell over the forest. Hands forced him into sitting position and lashed him to what felt like a lawn chair. Any moment now and they'd douse him with gasoline and ignite him with the strike of a match.

His clock was rapidly winding down to zero. He knew that just as he knew the sun rose in the east, and it occurred to him then that he would never see daybreak again—nor the blue of the sky, nor the white orb of the full moon traversing the heavens on a summer night.

Tears streamed down his cheeks. A sudden dizziness made him sway like a drunk in a prison cell. He couldn't die like this, blind to the world. "Please let me see!"

The bag was torn from his head. He blinked. Dozens of people stood before him in an unfamiliar forest clearing. A crackling bonfire raged behind them, turning each figure into a silhouette not unlike the ones who had kidnapped him.

A woman among them began to weep with a bitterness he knew all too well.

He licked some of the blood from his lips and struggled against his bindings. "Untie me!"

Another woman approached him and spat at his feet. "Why should we?"

He recognized her voice. Though he had suspected her to be a part of this, it still shocked him to know she was here. He decided not to answer her question. "How did you know it was me?" he asked instead.

"Don't play us for fools. You're the only one it could have been." Her seething voice could have frozen an ocean. His skin prickled.

"How is that?"

Though he couldn't quite make out her face, he had the idea she was smiling. Odd, since he'd put a bullet through her only child's brain just two days before. "Joanna saw you do it."

Joanna Zimmerman? The woman who lived next door whose husband was a cop? "Then why didn't she tell the police?"

"Who said she didn't?" came the voice of said policeman. He stood right behind him, meaning that he had been one of the faceless phantoms who had brought him here.

The implications of this repulsed him. "But—but why all this? Why didn't you arrest me?"

"Maybe we should be asking you why you did it!" shrieked another familiar voice. Meredith Scott. Another childless mother, thanks to him.

"I had to do it!" he roared, suddenly a hundred times more furious than frightened. "Don't you get it? They wouldn't stop looking at me! They knew what she did to me! And they mocked me about it everywhere I went! I didn't want to kill them, but it was the only way I could make them stop!"

Angry shouts in both English and Spanish arose from the crowd, but he barely heard them. He could understand their anger, yes, but his deed had been for the greater good—his own.

"I don't have the slightest idea what you're talking about," the woman in front of him said as she took a step in reverse.

"Ready?" Rich Zimmerman asked directly behind the chair.

She gave a curt nod.

For one panicked moment he looked into her dark eyes, searching for a glimpse of mercy. "Maria, please…"

His words were cut short as a rope pulled tight around his neck. He tried to rise by taking the chair with him, but the pain was too great for him to do much more than wriggle.

Please God let this be fast, oh please, oh please, oh please—

"That's enough!" Maria exclaimed after only a handful of seconds. Then he could breathe again, but only with difficulty. She had had a change of heart! He nearly wept with joy, but instead he shook like an overwrought leaf. Thank you, Jesus.

Maria leaned over him. A faint trace of vanilla-scented shampoo lingered in the air around her. Here was the moment of forgiveness. She would untie him and apologize profusely, and all would be good in the world.

"This is for Sarah and the others," she hissed. Something gleamed in her hand. She gripped the collar of his t-shirt in a bony fist and tore it and his flesh open with a knife in a broad swoop.

Pain blossomed across his chest. What did she think she was doing? This was not forgiveness. The blade sank into him.

Dragged across his abdomen. The sound of his own tearing flesh was as unbearable as the pain. He started to black out but held onto his consciousness with all his might, because if he fainted he knew he would never reawaken.

Jeers filled the night air. He had no idea what they were saying. Warmth ran down into his lap. Something vital had been severed. Oh, God! This had all been a mistake. He shouldn't have killed them. It solved nothing. Now he would die, too, and be sentenced to an eternity in a part of hell he had carved out for himself.

God, please forgive me!

The blade slid between his ribs with a moist sound like separating pieces of meat. The point met his pulsating heart, which shuddered and fell still.

He closed his eyes.

Thy will be done, he thought, and died.

CHAPTER 26

S idney drove past the house first just in case Jessica and Wayne had returned home. The empty place in the driveway next to the Taurus told her that they hadn't.

She sped out to the highway, zipping around slow-moving vehicles that were probably speeding, too. Hopefully all the state highway patrolmen had taken the afternoon off, because any delay in delivering the news to Jessica might spell certain disaster for those involved in what had happened all those years ago.

The article had begun tragically enough. Four girls were shot dead in the backyard of an Alexandria home in the early afternoon of June 28, 1986. A thirteen-year-old had been watching her six-year-old sister and two of her sister's friends while their mother made a quick trip to the grocery store to pick up a package of Popsicles for the girls to enjoy on the warm day. The four had reportedly been sitting at a picnic table playing Candy Land when the mother, Amy Walsh, had left. When she returned no more than fifteen minutes later, all four children lay dead on the ground with gunshot wounds to their heads.

The victims' names—Megan, Josie, Lauren, and Sarah—were listed along with those of their parents. Sidney had never heard of the girls. She had, however, heard of the latter victim's parents, because she'd lived next door to them for close to eighteen years.

As Sidney barreled across the bridge into Kentucky, it dawned on her that she had never been to Cold Spring. Jessica mentioned

248

that it was on U.S. 27. Following the signs, she took the first exit ramp on the left and merged into a line of slowing cars driving south out of Cincinnati.

She got stopped at a traffic light by the main entrance of Northern Kentucky University. Traffic crept forward. A few lights up, she spotted a green sign emblazoned with the name of the park and a pointing arrow. She turned right. Her heart pounded as if she had just jogged all the way from work. There. On the left. The park entrance.

She whipped her car into the lot so fast the tires squealed.

She put the car in park and looked around. She recognized the Roman-Dells' gold Lexus sitting a few spaces down from hers, but Wayne's pickup truck was nowhere to be seen. They had left already? She might have passed them on the highway. The fact that they were gone did not necessarily mean they had returned home.

Some of Jessica's relatives milled about smoking on the porch of a giant white building that proclaimed to be "The Kemper House," judging from the fancy sign posted on the lawn. Jessica's father leaned against the porch railing, holding a can of Bud Light in one hand while he talked to a bronze-skinned man who looked a little bit like Jessica's Uncle Esteban but was somewhat fatter and had less hair. A cousin, she supposed. Jessica had about a million of them.

She got out of the car and ran up to them. "Stephen!" she said, panting. "How long ago did Jessica and Wayne leave?"

Stephen Roman-Dell stood about six-two, and his blondish hair grayed at the temples. Neatly trimmed sideburns stretched down to his jaw line. He didn't appear to be a liar like the article made him out to be, but she knew that he and Maria had lied to Jessica for her entire life. Sidney wanted to ask them why but didn't dare bring the matter up for fear of what she might learn.

Stephen's eyebrows knit together when he saw her. "About twenty minutes ago. Why?"

The Hispanic man he had been talking to gave Sidney a skeptical look that made her feel more out of place than she already was. "I need to talk to them," she said. "It's really important."

Stephen frowned and set his beer on the porch railing, swatting away a fly that had attempted to perch on the rim of the can. "Have you tried calling her?"

"Her phone keeps going to voicemail. Did they say where they were going?"

Sadness filled his eyes as he shook his head. "Jess didn't even say hi to me today." He turned to his comrade. "She say anything to you, David?"

"Not a word." Like all of the Reyeses Sidney had met, David lacked even the slightest Mexican accent. He brushed his hand absently through his sparse hair. "I thought she looked mad the whole time she was here."

Sidney felt a flash of annoyance at her friend for being such a jerk to her own family, even if they *were* a bunch of liars. "Is Rachel at least still here?" Maybe she could talk to her instead. Rachel needed to know the truth, too.

Stephen shook his head again. "She and Eric left around the same time Jess and Wayne did." He started to lift his can of Bud Light to his lips but set it down again. "I noticed your cousin barely left Jess's side the whole afternoon. Are they more than friends now?"

Like *she* knew. "I'm sure at least one of them wants it to be that way."

"I knew it!" David exclaimed.

Stephen made a sort of half-smile. "Tell Jess we're happy for her. And tell Wayne I didn't mean to embarrass him like I did in the store one time. He'll know what I mean." His smile broadened. "Boy, will he."

"I'll do that," she said, not having a clue what that last bit was about. "Sorry, but I've got to go now. I'm kind of in a hurry."

Some of the cheer left his face. "If I hear from any of them, I'll let them know you were here."

"Thanks. Bye, guys." She retreated to the car. When she had buckled herself in, she looked through the windshield at the porch one last time. Stephen and David had their eyes fixed on her like she was E.T. going home. They probably thought that the majority of her marbles had rolled out of her head and into the river. Maybe they had.

She made it back to Eleanor before four o'clock. The red pickup truck had returned to the driveway. She could hear its engine still ticking when she got out of the car.

"Jessica!" she exclaimed when she burst into the house, deciding not to waste time getting to the point. "I've got awful news!"

"She's not here," Wayne said, coming down the stairs. His leg braces lay beside the table in the kitchen, so he must have been exercising by walking up and down the steps without them. "She and Rachel decided to have a girls' day out. What happened?" He stopped on the bottom step. His eyes bore a haunted look that put her senses on red alert.

She wanted to ask him the same thing. "I've been trying to track you guys down for over an hour and a half. Do you know where they went?"

"I have no clue." He sank into one of the kitchen chairs and stretched his legs out in front of him as best as he could. "Why aren't you at work?"

Her mind had become so overwhelmed in her quest to locate her friend that at first she didn't know what he was talking about. "Work?"

"Yes, that place where you've supposedly been employed for three years."

"Oh. Work." She gave him a sheepish smile. "I developed a sudden illness that mysteriously cured itself as soon as I left the station. Wayne, I have some really bad news."

"It can't be as bad as my news," he said.

His tone made her gut squirm. "Why, what's your news?"

"You tell me yours, first."

"Fine." She got out her laptop with shaking hands and set it on the kitchen table. She found the archived article again in less than a minute. She slid the computer across the table to him. "Read it."

He turned the laptop around so he could see the screen. His forehead creased, and she thought his face might have paled a few shades. "Wow." He leaned back in the chair and rubbed at the slight stubble on his chin, seemingly lost in thought.

"What do you think?" she asked.

He stared dolefully at the screen. "Those murders happened two days before Jerry's disappearance."

"You saw that, too."

"It's kind of hard to miss." He fell silent, but she could tell that behind his eyes his mind was churning. "Jessica told me that Jerry did something terrible, but he wouldn't say what it was. I guess this is it."

She'd come to the same conclusion the moment she'd read the thing. "Can you really blame him for not wanting to tell anyone?"

He didn't answer, still lost in his own thoughts. "Someone found him out. That's got to be why he was killed."

"Exactly! If Jerry really did do this," she said, gesturing at her computer, "and if Jessica told him her name when she met him in the graveyard, he'd have made the connection that she's related to Stephen and Maria. That's why he followed her here!"

"You think Jessica's parents are responsible for his death?"

She shrugged. Two boring accountants, cold-blooded murderers? She almost laughed at the thought. "Maybe they didn't do the actual deed, but they have to have played a part in it. Otherwise this would be too big of a coincidence. I think he wants Jessica to lead him to her parents so he can hurt them."

The muscles hardened in Wayne's face, and tears brimmed in his eyes. "Jessica zoned out and started talking nonsense at the reunion. She acted like she didn't know who any of us were for a minute, and she kept talking about how she wanted to hurt Maria just like Maria hurt her when she was a kid."

She swallowed. "Do you think it was Jerry talking?"

"I hope not. That would mean he's already been in contact with her parents."

Sidney didn't want to think about what that might mean for the Roman-Dells. "Why did you let her go out with Rachel if she was acting like that?"

"I think it was Rachel's way of keeping an eye on her for the rest of the afternoon. And I can't just stop her from hanging out with her own sister."

"Do you have Rachel's cell phone number?"

"I wish I did."

"And you don't know where they went."

He shook his head. "I don't know if *they* knew where they were going."

"Ugh." This was frustrating. "This really has been a day for bad news, hasn't it?"

Wayne leaned back in his chair and kneaded his reddening eyelids. "I haven't even told you mine yet."

He hadn't? "What could be worse news than all this?"

He told her.

When he finished, he folded his arms and gazed at her with something like deep remorse shining in his eyes.

She had felt the blood drain out of her face while he spoke. "And you didn't tell Jessica?"

"Not much to tell, is there?"

"Could be a coincidence."

He sighed. "Maybe." But he didn't look convinced, and now that the facts he'd laid out sank in, she wasn't so sure *she* was convinced, either.

"All right," she said, clasping her hands together and trying not to think about what he'd just said. "We can ponder that some other time when we're all relaxing on a beach somewhere. But right now we've got to find Jessica!"

"She'll turn up soon enough if we stay here. They won't be gone all day."

Why couldn't Wayne understand how much danger their friend was in? "Don't you get it? Somebody's going to be hurt. That's the whole point of this. Jerry's killers were never caught, and now he's going to make them pay."

"How is finding Jessica going to stop him from doing that when she's already seen her parents today?"

She moved to grab up her purse. "Because if we find or get a hold of Jessica, maybe she can try to convince him to be nice and move on without hurting anybody."

Wayne lifted an eyebrow. "Move on to where, Sidney?"

"Hades," she said without missing a beat. "I've heard the weather's great."

CHAPTER 27

"Where do you propose we go?" Wayne asked as he fastened the braces around his legs.

Sidney couldn't stop tapping her foot on the floor. Her nerves were stretched so thin that the slightest touch would have made them snap. "I think Rachel's staying with their Uncle Esteban. Maybe they're hanging out there catching up on old times."

Wayne rose and dug a phone book out of the cupboard. "There's no sense in driving out there unless we know for certain that's where they are." He plopped the book onto the table and thumbed through it. "Raleigh, Raymond, Remington, here we go. Reyes." He leaned closer to the page. "Esteban isn't listed."

"Are you sure that's the right phone book? I think he lives near that park in Cold Spring."

"Yeah, it's the Cincinnati edition." His eyes scanned the page. "Hmm. Marco Reyes is listed. I wonder if he's still at the reunion."

"Marco?"

"He's Maria and Esteban's cousin who does some weird tranny magic show. Hand me the phone."

She passed the cordless phone over to him, and he dialed the number printed in the phonebook. He swore. "Nobody's home." He glanced at the book again. "Ernesto's listed, too." He punched in Ernesto's number. His face lit up. "Hi, Ernesto? This is Wayne Thompson. I met you earlier at the reunion. I was with Jessica.

Uh-huh. I was wondering if you might have Esteban's phone number. I really need to get a hold of Jessica, and I think she and Rachel might have gone back to his house." He held the phone away from his mouth for a moment. "Get me a pen."

She leapt up and swiped a pencil off of the counter. It would have to do. "Okay, go ahead," he continued. He jotted down a ten-digit number in the white margin to the left of the names. "Thanks. Yes, I'd say it's very possible that we'll be meeting again. Same here. Uh-huh. Bye."

He ended the call and immediately dialed Esteban's number. "Keep your fingers crossed," he said.

She crossed all of her fingers. Nothing wrong with a healthy dose of superstition.

"Hello, Esteban? This is Wayne Thompson. Is Jessica there right now?" He swore again. "Did she say where she and Rachel were going? Wait. I thought this was your home phone number. I really need to talk to her, and her cell phone's dead. Thanks." He scribbled down another number. "Do you have Rachel or Eric's cell phone numbers, by chance? Oh. Thanks anyway."

He hung up and took an exasperated breath. "This is starting to get ridiculous."

She held her own breath while he dialed the next number. *Please be there, Jessica. Please, somebody answer the phone.*

Wayne set the phone down after several seconds. "Nada. If they're there, nobody's picking up."

"Not even Eric?"

"For all I know, he's their chauffeur."

"You think we should drive out there anyway, just in case?"

"I don't really see the point."

Sidney gritted her teeth. "We can't just sit around here waiting for something to happen!"

"Yes, we can. Besides, I don't even know the guy's address. He's going to think I'm some kind of overprotective nut going after his niece if I call him back and ask him where he lives."

"You could call that Ernesto guy back and ask him."

"No. Listen." His face was stern. "You know Rachel is going to drop Jessica off here before going back to Esteban's place. If we drive back to Cold Spring or wherever, we might miss them. And I think we should talk to the two of them at the same time, for obvious reasons."

Sidney nodded. "You'd think someone would have mentioned it," she said. "You know, that Sarah existed."

"You'd think."

"Or even if they hadn't wanted to mention it, there would have been pictures. Old craft projects. Drawings. Stuff kids make. It's like they buried her memories right along with her."

He shrugged. "Maybe it was less painful that way."

The phone's shrill ring cut through the air, nearly sending Sidney's heart into orbit. Wayne snatched up the phone and thumbed the button. "Hello?" A pause. "It's Esteban again," he mouthed. "They went to Kenwood? Geez. Okay. Just out of curiosity, does the name Sarah Roman-Dell mean anything to you?" Another pause. "Hello? Esteban?"

He removed the phone from his ear. "I don't believe it. He hung up on me."

⁓⁓⁐∞⌀∞⁐⁓⁓

Eric had dropped Jessica and Rachel off at the Kenwood Towne Center on the northeast side of Cincinnati and then left to browse the Barnes and Noble across the street for more reading material that he could look at on the flight home. In reality, Jessica knew he'd left so he wouldn't have to suffer looking at women's clothing with them all afternoon.

She wished she could have gone with him, because walking around with Rachel here in the high-end mall in her crappy clothes made Jessica feel as out of place as a hobo in the White House. She'd only been to the mall one other time when she'd accompanied Wayne on one of his excursions to Macy's. It hadn't been enjoyable then, and it wasn't now, but Rachel had insisted that she come with her. Jessica figured spending time together here was better than not spending time together at all.

"How can anyone afford this stuff?" she said as they wandered through Dillard's. She caught sight of a black, spaghetti-strap dress that bore a $300 price tag and winced. That was as much as she made in an entire week at American Dream.

"Credit cards and eternal debt, baby," Rachel said. "Ooh, isn't this one cute?" She pulled a glittery red dress off of another rack and held it up to the front of her, striking what was probably supposed to be a seductive pose. "How do I look?"

Jessica pretended to give it great thought. "Like a tramp."

"Thought so."

She put the dress back and wandered off to another part of the women's section. Jessica fell in step behind her, barely glancing at the other clothes. It felt like railroad spikes were being hammered into her skull. She had taken some Tylenol on the ride over, and it hadn't kicked in yet. If she could just take a nap and sleep it off she would be fine, but she'd have to wait until Rachel had had her fill of window-shopping before she could find a nice, comfy bed to lie down in.

Rachel was saying something. "What was that?" Jessica asked, coming up beside her.

Rachel turned. "Oh, I thought you were right behind me. I wanted to know if you felt like zoning out again."

"No, but I'm not feeling so great anymore." She massaged her temples. This headache was starting to make the week's bizarre pains feel like tickles in comparison.

"I saw you popping pills in the car. Headache?"

She nodded. "It's about a twelve on the Richter Scale."

"The Richter Scale only goes to ten."

"I know."

Rachel hoisted her purse straps farther up on her shoulder. "You don't think this has anything to do with that weird spell you had earlier, do you?"

The thought had crossed Jessica's mind, but she had dismissed it immediately. More likely the headache had been birthed from her confrontation with Maria. "Only if they're both from stress."

"The way you've been talking, you probably think cancer is caused from stress, too."

She glared at her sister, feeling angry at herself for the wave of irritation that suddenly coursed through her. "Look. I've been through a lot this week. Maybe it all upset some sort of balance in my head and made me a little loopy for a few minutes." She hadn't told Rachel that she'd zoned out again in the bathroom at the Kemper House. One minute she'd been walking into the stall, and the next minute she was standing at the sink washing her hands with no memory of what happened in between.

"You haven't been through *that* much," Rachel said.

Her head pounded like a bass drum. "I've been through plenty! Losing my apartment—"

"You moved out on your own."

"—arguing with Sidney about stupid things—"

"That can't be that stressful."

"—putting up with—" She broke off. Putting up with what? The mind-fog rolled in for another visit, and for a split second she couldn't remember where she was. *Who you gonna call?*

"Ghosts?" Rachel suggested.

Jessica stifled a giggle. Sounded like her sister was the only one losing her mind around here. "What ghosts?"

"Very funny."

"How am I being funny? You're the one talking about ghosts all of a sudden."

Rachel's bluish eyes flared wider for a moment. "You mean you have no idea what I'm talking about? Your little graveyard excursion and the bloody spirit that Sidney saw?"

Jessica shook her head, which only made it hurt worse. "Sidney doesn't believe in ghosts. Why would she say she saw one?"

"That's it." The last traces of humor abandoned Rachel's face. "I'm taking you to the hospital." She did an about-face and strode toward the nearest exit.

Jessica jogged after her, nearly colliding with a display of silk ties. "Why? I've just got a headache."

"And you had a seizure, and now you're having either selective memory loss or a heck of a lot of fun at my expense, which isn't like you. *Something* is clearly wrong in there."

They stepped out into the crowded parking lot, where sunlight glinted off thousands of vehicles. Rachel cursed and retreated to the cement just outside the store. "Great. I forgot Eric has the car." She got out her phone and dialed. "Eric, come back over here. We need to take Jessica to the emergency room."

"I do *not* need to go to the hospital!" Jessica shouted, not caring that people walking into the store were giving her and Rachel a wide berth. "What're they going to do, take out my brain and soak it in a bowl of Efferdent to get the plaque out?"

Rachel ignored her. "Please hurry." She shoved her phone back into her purse with unnecessary force. "When is your birthday?"

Evidently Rachel thought she had developed amnesia. "January first, nineteen eighty-nine."

"And when is my birthday?"

"February twentieth, nineteen eighty-seven."

"And Wayne and Sidney's?"

Jessica rolled her eyes. This was some test. "May eleventh, nineteen eighty and December third, nineteen ninety. Do I get an A?"

"I'm not finished yet. When was the last time you went ghost hunting?"

"I don't remember. Monday night, maybe." Suddenly the image of a merry hamster danced in her head, and she smiled. "Yeah. At Vince and Ellen Shoushanians' house."

"So you don't remember anyone named Jerry."

She shook her head. "Only Jerry Springer. But I don't think he's dead."

"Stop acting like this is a joke!" Rachel sounded like she was on the verge of tears. She needed to stop getting worked up over nothing; it was bad for the baby.

"Then you stop acting like I'm going to drop dead!" Jessica crossed her arms. "I can't go to the hospital. I don't have any health insurance. Or money."

"Yes, you've been rather emphatic about that last point. Oh, *where* is Eric?" Rachel craned her neck to look out over the sea of vehicles. "Wait. I think I see him."

Jessica's heart fluttered. They couldn't do this to her. She needed rest, not a physician! "Please don't take me to the hospital. I'm just tired. Let me go home and sleep this headache off, and I'll be fine."

Rachel didn't answer. The Nissan Altima pulled up to the curb outside the department store, and they climbed in.

"Don't take me to a hospital!" she blurted to Eric before either of them had a chance to speak. "I'm not sick!"

Eric cocked his head and looked into the rear-view mirror. "You look okay to me."

"That's because I am! Rachel thinks I've lost my mind because I can't remember something that she thinks I should."

Rachel was kneading her eyelids with her fingertips. "God help me," she said.

Eric cast his bewildered gaze back and forth between them. Jessica almost felt bad that he'd gotten caught in the middle of this. "What am I supposed to do?"

"Take me home! I just want to go to bed."

Silence. His eyes studied her. He glanced back to Rachel, who must have already given up, because she wasn't nagging anymore.

"If you don't do it," Jessica said, coming up with the best threat she could think of, "I'll disown you as a brother-in-law. Forever."

"Now that's just brutal." Eric stepped on the accelerator and eased the car away from the curb. "What is it you don't remember?" he asked when they were back on the main road minutes later.

"She seems to have forgotten about Sidney seeing an apparition," Rachel butted in. "And about her own experiences with it."

There she was, talking about that again. When could she or Sidney have possibly seen a ghost? Maybe this was some elaborate practical joke that Rachel had concocted to mess with her aching head. Smile, you're on Candid Camera, and now the whole world knows your sister tried to make you doubt your sanity.

"Memory wipe," Eric said. "It happens all the time in the movies."

"She could have a tumor, for crying out loud!"

Jessica sat forward. She needed to convince Rachel that nothing was wrong, or she would never leave her alone. She put on a cheery face. "I'm fine! Really. I was just messing with you about not remembering. I guess it wasn't very funny, huh?"

"You make a horrible liar."

"When have I ever lied to you?"

Rachel sighed.

Silence settled over them. Jessica leaned her head against the window and watched the mile marker signs flash by along the highway. The Tylenol must have finally begun to work, because the pain behind her eyes had dulled to a more bearable throb. Even the unexplainable aches and pains that continued to afflict her had begun to fade.

She closed her eyes. Rachel and Eric were gabbing about something—her, most likely—but she paid them no attention. She could just pretend that she was already asleep if they asked her anything. Funny, how simple lying turned out to be once you'd tried it a few times.

Her consciousness wavered, and a face swam before her in her mind's eye. A woman. Blonde, with dark brown eyes. Abigail. The one who had to die, though she would not be the first to perish at her hand. Abigail could be spared until the very end, her death being the grand finale of it all. It might take months to track her down. The wait would be worth it. Everything that had happened was worth it.

A tear of joy rolled down the curve of her cheek, and through the ebbing pain of her headache, she smiled.

CHAPTER 28

W ayne was more distraught than he would let on to his cousin. Now that his initial shock had worn off, an almost paralyzing anxiety set in, tightening his chest so much that he could scarcely breathe. He wanted to leave but knew he shouldn't. If only he could be in two places at once!

"I am not going to drive to Kenwood," he said, even though it took every ounce of his resolve not to hop in the truck and exceed every speed limit known to mankind so he could get to Jessica at the mall before something terrible happened, if it hadn't already. He laced his fingers together in a gesture of prayer. *Father, please guide us.*

Sidney paced back and forth across the kitchen and entryway. She threw a glance out the window every five seconds, which began to grate on Wayne's already frazzled nerves. "We've got to do *something*." She'd said that at least a thousand times already. She'd end up saying it a thousand more, too, if Jessica didn't turn up soon. Wayne didn't know which was worse, that or the pacing.

"Pray," he said, craning his neck to see out the window, too. "It's got to be more useful than wearing a rut into my floor."

Her eyes flashed. "I'll do what I want." She paced onward.

The clock on the wall ticked the seconds away like a bomb counting down to detonation. It was now after four o'clock. If Jessica were to have dinner with Rachel and Eric, she might not be home until after dark. Then again, if she did stay with them, she might be safe. Who knew? He wished he did, because not knowing was killing him.

"Are you cancelling your plans tonight?" he asked Sidney in an effort to distract his reeling thoughts.

She halted. "What plans?"

"You were going to hang out with the guys. Remember?"

"Crap! I totally forgot! I guess I can come down with a stomach virus again." She grabbed her phone off of the table and started pecking away with her thumbs. "There. I told him I don't feel good and won't be coming over."

The unexpected sound of gravel crunching beneath tires outside lifted some of the apprehension that squeezed Wayne's chest, and he took a welcoming breath of relief. Jessica was home. He had allowed himself to get worked up over nothing.

Babbling voices moved up onto the porch. Sidney threw the door open so hard that it bounced off the wall and smacked her in the side on its rebound. "Come in!"

A yawning Jessica walked in first, followed by Rachel, whose short hair stood out in odd little tufts that made it look like she had run her hands through it a hundred times. Eric brought up the rear, wearing an uneasy look that made all the worry come crashing back down on Wayne like a tsunami.

"She's lost it again," Rachel said to him as she glanced at Jessica, who hadn't so much as looked at him since entering the house. "I take no responsibility in the matter."

Jessica stood next to the refrigerator, bearing the confused look of one who'd just awakened from a day-long nap. Was Jerry really the reason why she had acted so oddly at the reunion and why she looked like this now?

Wayne cleared his throat. It was best to speak with caution, just in case the beast could hear him. "Why didn't you take her to the ER?"

Eric put his hands in his pockets and started examining the tiles on the kitchen floor. "She didn't want me to."

For a second Wayne thought Jessica's eyes flared wider. "That's because I'm fine," she said in a faint voice. She shivered and hugged her arms close to her body.

Wayne continued to scrutinize her. Something was off, and not just in her tone of voice. He stepped closer to her. "Look at me," he said.

She lifted her chin and gazed at him blankly. The pupils in her eyes were far too dilated for the amount of light in the room, turning her blue-gray irises into rings barely the width of threads.

"What?"

"There's something really bad we need to tell you guys," Sidney said before Wayne could ask her how she felt. "You might want to sit down."

Jessica suddenly became more alert, as if she only just realized she was standing in his kitchen. "Wait a minute, I think I left my purse out in the car. I'll be right back." She hurried past them and slammed the door shut behind her.

"Could somebody please tell me what's going on?" Rachel asked. "The way today is going, I feel like I've fallen down a rabbit hole."

"Just wait," Sidney said. "It's going to get worse."

Wayne silently cursed her for being so blunt, but he supposed that was better than sugarcoating news as serious as this.

Seconds passed by like eons. What was taking Jessica so long?

He was about to go outside and check on her when a car engine roared to life.

The situation had worsened already.

The three able-bodied persons in the room dashed to the window ahead of him. "Jessica's driving away!" Sidney exclaimed.

Wayne made it to the door and stared out through the pane of glass just in time to see the green Taurus back out of the driveway. Tires squealed as the car lurched forward and disappeared down the street.

Rachel swore. "What in the blazes is she doing?"

"Isn't it obvious? She's running away." Wayne started to turn the doorknob but stopped himself. What could he do, chase her down in the truck? Not likely.

Sidney gaped at him. "And we're just going to let her go?"

"I can try to follow her," Eric said, still staring out the window. "If she's out on fifty-two, she should be easy to spot."

"But we don't know which way she's going!" Rachel exclaimed.

He and Sidney couldn't put this off any longer. "We need to talk before any of us go anywhere," Wayne said, turning from the door to face the three of them.

"But Jessica—"

"I have an idea she won't be heading too far."

Rachel eyed him with suspicion. "How would you know that?"

He didn't answer. "How about we all sit down? Sidney, show them what you found on the Internet."

Rachel sank into a chair. Eric sat down beside her and put his hand over hers. "Lord, my nerves are shot." Rachel sniffled.

"It's okay," Sidney said softly. "So, you want to see what we found?"

Wayne held up his hand. It was shaking. "Wait." He looked at Rachel and Eric. "How much do you know about Jerry Madison?"

"Nothing," Rachel said.

"Isn't he the spirit who followed Jessica home?" Eric asked, glancing cautiously around him as if fearing that Jerry might come after him just for mentioning his name.

Rachel nodded. "You think *he* has something to do with the way she's been acting today?"

"It's possible." Wayne took a seat across from her and Eric. "But before we go talking about Jessica, you need to understand some things first. Yes, she met Jerry at a graveyard the other night. She said he was lonely and refused to move on from this plane of existence because he would go to hell for something terrible he'd done."

They stared at him, wide-eyed and pale. He could only imagine what wild thoughts ran through their heads.

Wayne continued. "Jerry also told Jessica that he'd been murdered and that his body lay somewhere in the woods behind the graveyard. I did some research online and found out that a guy named Jerry Madison went missing from his house in Alexandria in 1986, and nobody ever saw him again. Are you both with me so far?"

The couple nodded. "So Jerry did something that got him killed is what you're saying?" Eric asked.

Wayne took a deep breath. *Here we go.* "Yes. Now take a look at what Sidney found earlier today."

Sidney passed the laptop over to them. "Don't shoot the messenger," she said, and began to bite her nails.

Rachel's brow creased while she read. Suddenly every last bit of color drained from her cheeks, and she put her hand over her mouth.

Eric leaned back, shaken. "Who's *Sarah* Roman-Dell?"

"Can't you read?" Rachel snapped. She read from the screen. "The four victims were identified as Megan and Josie Walsh, daughters of Patrick and Amy; Sarah Roman-Dell, daughter of Stephen and Maria; and Lauren Scott, daughter of Meredith. All three families are residents of Alexandria." She shook her head. "What the heck?"

"Evidently," Wayne said as calmly as he could, "you aren't Stephen and Maria's first child."

"But that's impossible!" Two spots of color returned to her cheeks. "I mean, I know that Mom and Dad lived in Kentucky before they bought the house here in Eleanor, but how..."

"Did you ever wonder why they moved?"

"They said it was because of work! You move to where the jobs are. That's what they always told us."

"But if they'd just lost their only child, they wouldn't have wanted to stay there. Right?"

Rachel continued to shake her head. "This makes no sense. I have tons of relatives. Why didn't anyone ever mention her? If she really did exist, they can't have just forgotten about her. There would be photographs and things." She gasped. "Photographs! Oh my gosh. I never realized it."

"What?" Eric asked.

"Pictures," she said, sounding strangely excited. "Years ago I was digging around in some boxes in the basement looking for some old drawings I'd made when I was in kindergarten because I wanted to show them off to my friends, and I found a bundle of pictures tied together with a rubber band—stuff from birthday parties and whatnot. I thought they were pictures of Jessica, because the kid had dark-brown hair like her, but it was weird because I didn't remember seeing anything like them before, and because I wasn't in any of them." She gave a hollow laugh. "Mom and Dad hardly ever took pictures of us. There had to have been at least a hundred in that stack."

"And you never suspected anything?" Sidney asked.

"What was I supposed to think? That my mother and father had another kid they conveniently forgot to tell me and Jessica about? One who had obviously received far more of their attention than we ever got?" She paused. "Oh, God. If they were that close to Sarah, her death would've ruined them."

Eric tore his gaze away from the computer. "What does all of this have to do with this Jerry guy?"

"Everything, I think," Wayne said. "These murders happened two days before Jerry's disappearance, and it was in the same town."

"You think..." Rachel swallowed. "That Jerry is the one who shot them all?"

Wayne shrugged. "That's what it looks like."

"Why would he have done that?"

"I'm not sure." That was a lie—God knew he'd spent the last half hour mulling over all the different reasons why a man would suddenly blow away four innocent kids playing outside, and he could only come up with one that made any sense. "It seems like he just snapped." Wayne could understand that, because he had been down that road, seventeen years before.

He remembered that moment well. He, Robert Wayne Thompson, had been sitting in the filthy home of his childhood, trying to do his homework on a section of the sofa that wasn't buried under unwashed laundry and empty liquor bottles. His legs and feet were killing him as the too-small ankle-foot orthotics constricted his movements. He'd have taken them off and risked immobility to end the pain, but his mother would have flown into one of her typical rages and started hurting him again. Better to endure the pain of the leg braces than the pain of her whip.

"Robert," she called from the bedroom. He stiffened. He had thought she was asleep. She called again. "Robert?"

He tried to calm his frantic heart with deep breaths. "What?" he asked in a cracking voice that had only begun its adolescent deepening the week before.

"Bring me my bottle."

He didn't need to ask what bottle she was talking about. She always kept a pint of vodka on the counter beside the coffee maker.

"Kay." He went to the kitchen and picked up the hateful drink. He started toward her room but halted. The stuff was killing her, and while he cared little whether she lived or died, he knew that if she drank more, she would only grow more volatile. The woman rarely beat him while sober. Sometimes she actually seemed friendly and begged for forgiveness for hurting him. But after four or five glasses of the stuff...

He unscrewed the cap and poured the contents of the bottle down the drain.

He heard movement at the other end of the house. "What's taking so long?"

She appeared in the archway connecting the kitchen and living room. Her bloodshot eyes widened as she looked from the empty bottle in his hand to the sink, and then to his face. Her mouth opened in a wordless snarl of rage. She dashed into the living room, and before he could lock himself in his bedroom to hide from her, she returned with a sooty fireplace poker and swung it at him.

He ducked. The poker clipped him on the shoulder. Pain blossomed from the point of impact like shock waves, and he staggered. She struck him again. And again. He could hardly breathe. He had to get the poker away from her before she killed him.

He caught her off guard by lunging toward her instead of running away, and the moment of surprise allowed him to jerk the poker out of her hands before she could do any serious damage. The altercation should have ended there, but something broke loose inside of him, and the next thing he knew, *he* was beating *her*. The poker smashed into the side of her head, and she crumpled to the floor, screaming. But he couldn't stop. All the years of abuse seemed to concentrate into a physical energy that he channeled into the weapon. He pounded her face until the screams stopped and her visage was unrecognizable, but even then he was unable to regain control of his senses.

He didn't know how long he beat her. He felt something wet on his face and noticed that his hands and much of his front were coated in red. He blinked a few times, dropped the poker to the floor, and gaped at what he had done.

All because he had finally snapped.

In the present, Wayne took a deep breath. He couldn't keep everything from them. "Okay," he said. "Let me tell you my theory. According to Jerry, his wife had an abortion against his will. Let's say he developed a complex about children since his own kid was dead. Maybe he couldn't stand the fact that other people's children were still alive, and he flipped out when he saw those four girls playing in the yard. Bang bang, no more girls, no more worries." *Until the next batch of kids came along,* he thought. If Jerry's life had not ended, there was no telling how many other children would have died at his hands.

Rachel frowned. "That's the most ridiculous excuse for murder I've ever heard."

He shrugged. "Most excuses for murder are, which brings me to the next point: Jerry's own disappearance and murder. Only I don't think his murderers' excuse was ridiculous."

"Whoa. Wait just one minute." Rachel glared at him. One of her eyes was twitching. "You think his murder was in retaliation for the other murders?"

"Yes, otherwise the timing of his disappearance would be too big of a coincidence. He specifically told Jessica he'd committed some terrible deed. This has to be it. The parents or somebody found him out and killed him."

"My mother and father are not murderers," Rachel said in a cold tone.

He had to make her believe him, or she would never fully grasp the danger that her sister and parents were in. "What does a killer look like to you?"

"Not like them."

"What about me?"

"Wayne…" Sidney warned.

"What *about* you?" Rachel asked.

He sighed. Now wasn't the time. "Nothing."

Rachel was quiet for several moments while her mind processed everything he'd told her. "Okay. Let's set all that aside for one minute. Why has Jessica flipped her lid?"

"I don't think she's just Jessica right now."

Rachel blinked. "What?"

He rose. "Call your parents. Tell them that if Jessica shows up wherever they are, to stay away from her because they might end up hurt. Or worse."

CHAPTER 29

Maria Roman-Dell was helping her sister-in-law clean up the Kemper House banquet room after most of the other Reyes descendants had gone home. Thank goodness the day was drawing to a close—as much as she had enjoyed seeing her brother again, all the socializing had worn her out. Returning to the silence of her office on Monday couldn't come soon enough.

"Hey, congrats on the grandbaby," Sharon said as she wadded up one of the disposable tablecloths and tossed it into a giant garbage can they had been lugging around the room. "I meant to tell you earlier."

"Oh!" Maria hadn't been aware that anyone outside of her immediate family had heard the news. Rachel or somebody must have let it slip. She forced a smile. "Thank you."

Sharon laughed. "Don't sound so grim about it." She dragged the garbage can to the next table and set to work clearing that one as well.

Maria's job was to salvage as much plastic silverware as possible for Sharon to reuse at the next family gathering. She paused to gather up a gummy fork and knife off of the table and stuffed them both into a used Kroger bag. "I'm just worried. I mean, they're so young. Maybe too young." She moved to another table and gathered up more utensils. Sharon likely thought she was a hypocrite. After all, Maria had gotten pregnant for the first time when she was twenty-two, and Rachel and Eric were already older than that, though not by much.

"I'm sure everything will be fine," Sharon said.

Maria doubted it. Nothing was ever fine. "They told me they're thinking about moving back here early next year."

"You should follow their example. Some of us have missed you."

"We would, if we could. Stephen's been complaining about Indianapolis practically since we closed on the house there. Says he'd like it better if they had Skyline Chili and the Reds, and he can't stand the Colts. I told him to get over it, but you know men and their sports."

Sharon rolled the trashcan to the next table. "What's stopping you from coming back?"

"We each make seventy grand a year and get two weeks' vacation on top of that." Maria smiled. She and Stephen had spent half of July at a lake house in the Catskills. The scenery and weather had been so perfect that for perhaps the first time in her adult life she had dreaded returning to work.

"I guess that would be a good reason to stay put."

In Maria's opinion, it was an excellent reason. "There's not much left for us in Cincinnati, anyway. Not really."

Sharon paused in what she was doing and planted her hands on her hips, scowling. "And just what are we?"

"It's not *you* who's the problem." Maria hurried to the next table before Sharon could see her face. "You've seen how some of them look at me and start whispering when my back is turned. Not to mention Rachel and Jess not wanting to have anything to do with us!"

Her sister-in-law frowned. "You can't just run away from what you created. You say the girls don't want anything to do with you, but did you ever act like you wanted anything to do with them?"

Maria felt blood rise into her face. "Don't you start on that, too."

"I'm only stating the truth. If you can't handle that, then maybe you deserve all the flak you're getting."

Maria was about to come up with a defensive retort when Esteban walked into the room reeking of cigarette smoke. "Maria, can I talk to you alone for a minute?" The typical cheery gleam had gone out of his eyes. A sense of foreboding knotted up Maria's stomach. Esteban had only looked this dour on a few other occasions, and none of them had been pleasant.

"What can she hear that I can't?" Sharon asked.

His jaw was firm. "Fine, you can hear, too. Jessica's boyfriend called me a while ago trying to track Jessica down. Apparently her phone is turned off."

Maria couldn't see what was so secretive about this statement, yet the feeling of unease did not lessen. "He doesn't have Rachel's cell number?"

"I guess not. But anyway, someone told me that she and Rachel went to Kenwood, so I called him back to let him know, and all the sudden he asked me if the name Sarah Roman-Dell meant anything to me."

Wayne had...what?

She stood in stunned silence for what seemed like an eternity but was probably only a second or two. She forced herself to speak. "What did you say?"

"Nothing. I hung up."

"You didn't."

He turned his palms upward in an exasperated shrug. "What was I supposed to say?"

"You could have told him that the name meant nothing to you at all! Now he'll think you're hiding something!"

"I could blame the dropped call on poor reception if anyone asks."

"Yes, because calls drop all the time in the middle of Suburban America."

As if in response to their argument, a cell phone began playing a high-pitched version of Rondo Alla Turca, the ring tone Maria had assigned to Rachel's incoming calls.

Praying for the first time in years that her carefully crafted illusion of reality wouldn't come crashing down like a flimsy house of cards, she made her way toward the purse and accepted the call. "Rachel, what is it?" she asked, trying her best to sound as though nothing were amiss.

Her daughter's words came out in a rush. "Mom! Wayne says you've got to stay away from Jessica, she's not right in the head, and she might hurt you and Dad, and she just drove off, and we don't know where she is. Wayne thinks she's looking for you, and we *know* about Sarah being killed so don't try to deny it—"

The house of cards had been reduced to rubble. It was all Maria could do not to drop the phone from her shaking hands. "Honey, slow down. What is all this?"

She could hear her daughter take a deep breath. "Sidney Miller found an old article about a quadruple homicide that took place in eighty-six. One of the victims was Sarah Roman-Dell, daughter of Stephen and Maria. Care to explain?"

Maria squeezed her eyes shut. She had to come up with a reply but was at a complete loss for words.

"Mom?"

There was no use for continued denial. "Yes," she said quietly. "That happened."

"No crap, Mom! Would the gunman possibly have been named Jerry Madison? A *neighbor*, perhaps?"

A mixture of anger and disbelief flared inside her. "How would you possibly know about him? He went missing before you were even born!"

"Yeah, 'cause he's *dead*. Only not really. I mean, he is, but—" There was a scuffling noise, and Wayne Thompson's voice came on the line. "Maria?"

"Yes?" Her voice shook as much as her hands.

"If you see Jessica, let us know immediately, and we'll come get her. But *do not* let her anywhere near you."

"I don't understand. What's the matter with her?"

"We can talk about that later." There was an edge to his voice she had never heard him use before, and she had known him since he was a boy of fourteen. "But promise me you'll call either me or Rachel if she turns up."

"I don't know your number."

He gave it to her. She had nothing to write it on, so she could only hope she would remember it later if needed. "Promise me," he repeated.

"I—I promise."

"Good. And *please* be careful." The line went dead.

She stared vacantly at the wall for a moment. She started to return the phone to her purse, but put it in her jacket pocket instead.

"What happened?" Sharon asked.

"I don't know," Maria said, and burst into tears.

~~~

Wayne handed the phone back to Rachel.

"Now what?" asked Sidney. She was wringing her hands together so tightly that her knuckles were turning white.

He had been trying to figure out just that. He was a public accountant, not a detective. "Eric, you take Rachel back to Esteban's house. She's had enough stress for one day."

Eric nodded. "And if Jessica shows up?"

"Tie her up, and don't let her leave."

Rachel's face took on a greenish hue. "Then we should call you?"

"That would be the plan. Actually, let's all get each other's numbers, just in case."

They each took turns reciting their cell phone numbers—and home number, in Wayne's case—while the others programmed them into their phones. Wayne scribbled down the numbers on a scrap of paper.

"Okay," Wayne said, regretting his lack of a mobile phone for the first time in his life. "I'm going to head out and start looking for her at her usual haunts. Sidney, you should stay here in case she comes back."

"I am *not* staying here!" she retorted, crossing her arms. "You know she's not coming back until she finishes whatever she's up to. Besides, you won't have a phone with you."

"I can borrow yours."

"Then *I* won't have a phone."

"You'll have one if you stay here."

Sidney swore. "This is stupid."

"It's not. If she realizes she's forgotten something, she might come back to pick it up."

"Like what? A butcher knife?"

"Eric, let's go," Rachel said, moving toward the door in an eager rush to get away from them. Wayne didn't blame her.

Eric nodded. "Good luck, guys."

Wayne gave them a solemn wave of farewell. "Same to you."

They left, and Sidney turned to him. "You seriously want me to sit here on my behind even longer than I already have been?"

"You haven't been sitting at all. You've been pacing around like a nervous wreck."

"That's because I am a nervous wreck!" Tears welled in her eyes. "I hate feeling so helpless!"

Wayne put his hands on her shoulders in an attempt to calm her down. "I feel exactly the same as you, and I'm not letting myself get so worked up about it." Though he was tottering dangerously on the edge of losing self-control. "Now, please. Give me your phone."

With great reluctance, Sidney retrieved her cell phone and handed it to him. Wayne pocketed it, feeling its weight fall against his leg. "Thank you. And if she shows up, call me."

"Will do."

Wayne went outside and got into the truck. He decided that first he should cruise around town to watch for Jessica's car, and if he didn't see it or its driver anywhere, he would go to Cold Spring for the second time that day. They were the only two logical places to look.

He killed the radio so he would be able to focus better on his surroundings. Many people owned Ford Tauruses, and though Jessica's was an older model not seen as frequently these days, it still might be hard to spot in a parking lot full of other vehicles.

Keeping his eyes on the vehicles sharing the road with him, Wayne couldn't help but feel that this situation was a test that God had assigned to him without his consent. Wayne had once killed someone who was supposed to protect him, and now someone he had silently vowed to protect was in great danger of being killed— because, if Jessica's mind were truly not her own anymore, what damage might that do to her body? To her brain? To her soul?

Saving Jessica might be atonement for what he had done. Failure to save her would prove to God that Wayne was not worthy to even breathe the air that the Lord had provided.

The main street of Eleanor boasted a number of businesses: American Dream Truck Stop, some restaurants, a grocery store and Family Dollar, a hair salon, some banks, and a dying video rental. Jessica's car was not present in any of their lots. Wayne turned onto Ash Street and slowed down as he passed the library. Only two cars were parked out front. No Jessica.

Not a single car sat in the lot at the abandoned hulk of the bottling plant. There was one Taurus in the parking lot at Smithfield Park, but it was a deep-burgundy color, not dark green like the one he sought.

Wayne drove down Water Street, past his and Jessica's childhood homes. His cousins Brian and Kyle were busy playing with a Frisbee in the Millers' front yard. Neither of them saw him pass by.

The parking lot at Holy Trinity was already filling up for the evening Mass. One circuit of the lot was enough to tell him Jessica wasn't there.

"God, a little help here would be great," he said. If he were permitted only a single prayer for the rest of his days, he would pray for Jessica and her family to be safe. To heck with Jerry. Yes, it was a pity that the man had lost his child, but that was no excuse for tearing three other families apart.

If only someone could talk Jerry into being reasonable. How hard could it be? He refused to leave the earth behind, which was understandable considering the obvious alternative that Jerry would have to face.

Someone would have to convince him that staying here was more painful than hell, which was, of course, a lie.

All Wayne had to do was figure out what he was going to say.

~∞≈∞~

Sidney waited for fifteen minutes before she couldn't take it any-more. Staying in this house would help no one—not the Roman-Dells and definitely not Jessica or Jerry.

Since driving around the tri-state searching for Jessica was going to be about as easy as finding a particular drop of water in a pond, her efforts might not help anyone, either. But at least Sidney would have something to do.

She would have to take some precautions, however. If Jessica's brain had indeed turned into some kind of duplex that housed Jerry's mind as well as her own, she may become violent.

Taking a deadly weapon with her would seem desperate and hostile. Something less threatening might work better.

She stood in the doorway of the junk room. Something in here would have to work.

A souvenir Reds baseball bat leaning against a storage cabi-net caught her eye. She picked it up and tested its weight in her hands. It was solid but not too heavy. Perfect.

Suddenly bile rose in her throat. Jessica was her best friend. Heck, if she didn't count her cousin, she was her *only* friend. Jessica could be annoying and overly religious and somewhat insensitive, but she had always meant well. And now Sidney was considering bludgeoning her.

She took the bat with her to the car. Maybe she wouldn't even find Jessica. Maybe she wouldn't have to use the bat for protection after all.

~~~

It was dark.

Jessica was sitting in her car eating a burrito. The wrapper it came in told her that it had been purchased from Taco Bell. When in the world had she stopped there? Maybe a kind stranger had picked up dinner for her, which was nice of them, if not a little creepy.

She paused in her chewing and peered outside. She was in a large parking lot, parked beneath a street lamp. A group of drab cement buildings loomed off to the left. Almost all of the windows in the buildings were dark. A few young people laughing about something walked by on a sidewalk running perpendicular to her parking spot. The glass muffled their voices so she couldn't make out what they said. None of them paid her any notice.

She set the burrito down on the seat beside her when it dawned on her that she had no idea how she'd arrived in this place. She was not in Eleanor, that was for certain. They didn't have a Taco Bell in town.

"How are you feeling?" asked a voice close by.

Jerry Madison sat in the passenger seat, looking as calm as a man relaxing on a beach. Apparently she had set the burrito in his left leg. He showed no displeasure at the intrusion.

His question was unimportant. "Where am I, and how did I get here?" she demanded. This was almost like the time she'd had her tonsils out back in high school. She remembered everything prior to the surgery, and *boom*! She was in the recovery room with no recollection of the surgery itself. At least that incident had an explanation.

She had been with Rachel at a mall. Eric was somewhere else. A bookstore, maybe. She and Rachel had been arguing about something, but the topic of their disagreement eluded her.

And now she was here, in her own car. Several hours must have passed, since the sun no longer hung in the sky. Neither Rachel, Eric, nor their rental car was in sight.

Jerry gave her a pitiful smile. "Use your eyes and tell me."

No direct answers. Not surprising. Direct answers would make things too easy.

A police cruiser drove by. The side of it was emblazoned with the Northern Kentucky University name and logo.

"We're in Highland Heights," she said. "That's just down the street from Cold Spring."

"Yes," he said. "You drove here. Don't you remember?"

The glint in his eyes made her uneasy. Yes, she should have remembered, but she didn't. She held up her unfinished burrito. "And I guess I went through the drive-thru, too?"

"You have the receipt." He gestured at her purse.

Not taking her eyes off of him, she stuck her hand into the main pocket and grasped a slip of paper that had not been there before. She switched on the overhead light. The date and time were printed on the receipt. Apparently she had visited the Taco Bell at 6:52 p.m. The burrito was still marginally warm, so her stop at the restaurant couldn't have been very long ago.

She turned the key in the ignition to turn on the dashboard lights. It was 7:02.

"I have a confession to make," Jerry said.

Her pulse quickened. "Oh yeah?"

"I knew your parents."

Now *that* was news. "How?"

"They lived two houses down from me, and we attended the same church. I knew them for years."

She caught onto his error right away. He couldn't have been well acquainted with her parents if he had this one basic fact wrong about them. "Nice try. They don't go to church and never have."

"Then why are you so faithful?"

"My grandma started taking me to church when I was little. She had me baptized when I was nine." She shook her head. "You've got to have my parents mixed up with somebody else."

Jerry shrugged. "Just because they don't go to church now doesn't mean they didn't years ago. You don't believe me? Fine. I'll tell you everything I know about them. Their names are Stephen and Maria. Maria's father came from Mexico, her mother from Norwood. Stephen's family lived in the Cincinnati area for decades. He was one of three children. Maria has only the one brother. Your parents were both accountants and met each other as freshmen in college. Do you believe me yet?"

Though she hated to admit it, everything he said was correct. Even the circumstances of her parents' meeting made sense. "What's Mom's brother's name?"

"That's easy. Esteban Reyes."

"You could have just heard about him at the family reunion."

"True. But I met him long ago at a church festival. Maria introduced us to each other."

He still could have been lying, though she couldn't guess what the point would be. She had to think of something that he wouldn't know from being at the family reunion or from eavesdropping on her conversations with Wayne, Sidney, and Rachel. "Do you know Mom's parents' names?" she asked.

"Andrés and Karen. I never had the chance to meet Stephen's parents, but I think his father's name might have been Zachary or Zachariah or something like that."

Again, all true. Her long-dead Grandpa Roman-Dell *was* named Zachary. "Okay. I know that you lived in Alexandria. But if you lived on the same street as Mom and Dad, that means they would have lived in Alexandria, too, and they never told me that."

"Sorry about your luck."

As odd as this news was, she decided he was telling the truth. "So, what did you think of them? You can be honest."

"Haven't I been honest with you so far?" A smile tugged at his mouth. "Maria was more talkative than Stephen. Your father always struck me as being dull. Sorry."

He still could have picked up on those traits at the family reunion if he'd followed her there, but she nodded anyway. "That's okay. Were you friends with them?"

"More like friendly acquaintances. We got along well. For a time, at least. Stephen hooked me up with some of his old college drinking buddies thinking it would cheer me up to be out in public with people, but I don't think he realized what scum some of them really were."

Phil Knippenberg, she thought. The dirt bag from her dream had known her dad?

Jerry continued. "Maria even made me dinner one time when I came down with the flu." He cast his gaze downward, probably mourning the fact that he had been unable to partake in the pleasure of eating for nearly a quarter of a century.

"Why didn't you tell me all of this before?"

He gave a noncommittal shrug. "Do you love your mother?"

"I'm supposed to."

"But do you?"

"Maybe." She sighed. She didn't want to go into this again. "Sometimes people hurt you so much that you can't love them. I wanted to love her. She's just never given me a decent reason to do it."

"So you think love should be conditional? That you can only love someone if they treat you the right way?"

She took a bite of the now-cold burrito, chewed, and swallowed. "You're one to talk. You hate Abigail, right?"

Her words must have ignited a spark of anger inside of him, because he glared at her. "We aren't talking about her right now. We're talking about Maria."

"What about her?" She set her dinner down again. "No, I don't like her very much. Nothing's ever going to be right between us. She lives in her world, and I live in mine, and it makes life a whole heck of a lot easier that way." She flicked a tiny piece of lettuce off of her jeans onto the floor. "I don't want to talk about her anymore."

"But I do."

"Why? Did you have a crush on her or something for bringing you dinner?"

He glowered at her. "I never had a crush on the woman. Not even for a minute."

"Then why are you fixating on her all of a sudden?"

"Because," he said, "Maria Roman-Dell, accountant extraordinaire and devout churchwoman, is the one who slaughtered me like a pig in the woods behind that Methodist church."

At first she stared at him, speechless. Then she smiled. Her mother, a killer? The idea was laughable. Maria hated to get dirty. Disemboweling another human being was bound to be...messy. She swallowed and tried to block the image from her mind. It would have been worse than messy. Maria would have been covered in—

"You don't believe me," he said.

"Mom can't stand the sight of blood."

"She didn't seem to mind so much then."

"You said it was a group of people who did it. And the Satanists!"

"Maria orchestrated the whole thing. I think the original plan was just to strangle me—hence the few moments someone jerked a rope around my neck—but Maria made whoever it was stop so she could finish the job herself."

They were both quiet for a few beats.

Oh, you could come across severed heads, bleeding limbs, human entrails spread across the ground for the scavengers to clean up...

Mommy, read me a story!

Suddenly Jessica wanted to run. She would run and run, off the campus, out to the highway, and she would run back across the bridge into Ohio, and she would keep on running, past Eleanor, running until she collapsed from exhaustion and died.

She remained glued to the seat. "Why? Why did she do it?"

The manic look contorted his features, and he began talking faster. "You don't know what it's like. My baby gone and suddenly babies everywhere. They looked at me, and they'd smile and coo like they knew what had happened and didn't want me to forget it even for a minute.

"Faces were everywhere. I saw them in church. I saw them at the park and in the neighboring yards. I tried to ignore them, but it only got worse. They grew older, and I knew my baby would be the same age as them, and it killed me, because I'd missed out on so much. No birthday parties. No little-league champs or first-place ballerinas. No scraped knees needing kisses. You don't know what it's like. Being like that. Everything crashing down. I wanted to die. I tried to die. I prayed for death every single day, and it didn't happen.

"Then one day I heard laughter outside. There were children. Four of them. Playing a game in the yard behind mine. So innocent and full of the life my child never got to know."

Jessica didn't like where this was going.

He went on. "I didn't want to do it. But I had to. It tortured me. If I let them live, it would never end.

"I shot the older Walsh girl first. Then her sister. The Scott girl started to scream, and I took her down before she could run away. Stephen and Maria's girl watched it all happen. She was so numb that she didn't even cry. I put a bullet through her forehead. Killed her instantly."

Jessica felt cold. "Stephen and Maria's…girl?"

"Yes. Sarah. She looked a lot like you do. Dark-brown hair, blue-gray eyes just like yours. They never told you about her? What a shame. They doted on that child like she was the heiress to an empire. Nearly made me sick. She was smart, too. Was reading first-grade level books by the time she turned three and spoke perfect Spanish."

"So you're saying…" Her head swam. "You're saying that I had another sister. And the only reason I don't anymore is because of you."

"Yes."

"You killed four children!"

"I didn't want to. I really didn't." His voice held a note of remorse, but he was still grinning like a man who had just won a million dollars.

Tears made her vision blur. "Then why didn't you stop yourself?"

"I *had* to do it! If I didn't, I would have died!"

"I hate to break it to you," she said, realizing that she'd edged so far away from him that her back pressed against the door, "but I think that happened anyway."

He said nothing.

"Didn't anyone hear the gunshots?"

"How should I know? Two sets of neighbors were out of town. It was the week before the Fourth of July, so a lot of kids had been setting off bottle rockets and M-80s and Roman candles. What was the significance of some more loud bangs?"

She only heard half of what he said. "You killed four kids who never did one blessed thing to you! And I thought I could convince you to go to heaven?" She had been an idiot.

"I said I didn't want to do it!" he roared.

"It's your fault that my entire childhood was hell! If my parents really did have a little girl named Sarah who you murdered…" She blinked away tears. "You ruined them. They might have been bad already, but you made them worse. You made it so they couldn't get close to a child again."

"*They* made themselves that way. It was their choice."

"You killed their kid!"

"And in turn, they killed me. Are you happy?"

"No! You're a monster!"

He shook his head. "Abigail was the monster. She pushed the first domino."

"Stop blaming other people for what *you* did!"

"If Abigail hadn't—"

"I felt sorry for you! I wanted to help you! I—get out of my car. Now." She didn't want to listen to him anymore. She had to ditch him. Curse her stupid ghost-hunting hobby. If she were to listen to her own advice, she only had herself to blame for getting into this mess.

Jerry didn't move. "I'd like to see you try to make me."

"In the name of Jesus, get out and leave me alone and never talk to me again."

He actually snorted with laughter. "I think you've forgotten your holy water and blessed crucifix. What else do you have?"

"Please leave."

"We have too many things to get done. We only let you take a break so we wouldn't cause you permanent damage, not that that really bothers us. If we kill you, you'll get to meet your sweet big sister, and won't that be a nicer family reunion than the one we visited earlier?"

Alarm bells went off in her head. We? Was the invisible person she'd heard him talking to before with them this very moment? "What are you talking about?"

"Nothing important. Nothing to worry about."

And the fog rolled into her mind once more. The drab campus melted away, and it was just the three of them alone together: Jessica, Jerry, and a murky presence she couldn't quite identify. The latter seemed to think something was incredibly funny; she could sense its laughter. Maybe it had been something one of them said. No matter. She was relaxed, and she was at peace. There was no pain.

As if watching from afar, she saw herself starting the car and leaving the nearly empty parking lot behind. She didn't know where they were going. Somehow, it didn't matter very much. She would just sit back and enjoy the ride.

CHAPTER 30

Sidney spent the next hour patrolling every single street in Eleanor. Every time she saw a dark-green car her heart skipped a beat, and then she would curse herself for getting her hopes up over nothing.

Her stomach growled. She hadn't eaten anything since the Cheetos at work. Oh well. She wasn't going to allow herself to stop anywhere for a pick-me-up. She'd only be wasting time.

Sidney pulled into a bank parking lot to think. Where could she go next? Cold Spring? Alexandria? Iron Springs? She didn't know Esteban Reyes's address, and she had no phone with her that she could use to call up Rachel or Eric to ask them where the man lived.

Hmm. Maybe there was still a payphone at Eleanor Market. She could drive back to the house and use the phone there, but the store was just a block down the street from her current position. Much closer than home.

She zipped back out into traffic and turned into the grocery store lot, selecting a space right along the edge of the building. She was in luck; there *was* a payphone here. She fished some quarters and the slip of paper containing Rachel's and Eric's numbers out of the bottom of her purse and went outside.

Fifty cents and ten seconds later, she was on the phone with Rachel.

"Hey," Sidney said. "Did you two make it back to Esteban's yet?"

"Just got in the door." Garbled voices were conversing in the background, and Rachel's voice lowered. "My parents are here now."

"Okay. Um, just out of curiosity, what's the address there?"

"Hang on a sec." More distorted sounds. "I'm outside now. Let me see…looks like the house number is 223. 223 Martin Court. Why?"

"Muchas gracias," she said, deciding that an explanation was not in order. "Gotta go now."

She replaced the receiver and dashed back to the car, repeating the address over and over in her head. She could be in Cold Spring in twenty minutes if the traffic wasn't too bad. But what the heck would she do there? Jessica obviously hadn't shown up at her uncle's house yet.

So where in the blazes was she?

<hr/>

"We are going to have a talk," Maria said, giving her daughter and son-in-law the most businesslike stare she could conjure. The couple had taken a seat on Esteban's couch and were squeezing each other's hands like they thought this evening would be their last.

Esteban and Sharon had brought in chairs from the kitchen. Stephen sat in a swivel office chair to Maria's left, tapping his foot on the floor. His face was as solemn as stone, and he stared down at his loafers with the air of a criminal receiving the death penalty before an accusing jury.

"What would you like to talk about?" Rachel asked, smiling sweetly. Eric made a similar grin but glanced away as soon as he and Maria locked gazes. He acted like he was afraid of her.

It was best to get straight to the point. "You mentioned a certain name to me on the phone." She had to force herself to say it. "Jerry Madison."

"Yeah. I did, didn't I?"

"What makes you think he had anything to do with... with Sarah?"

Rachel and Eric exchanged glances. Rachel chewed on her lip, hesitating. "Are you sure you want to know about that?"

"Yes," she said. "I do."

Rachel let out a breath. "Okay. Earlier this week, Jessica went on an investigation at a Methodist church near Iron Springs. Well, the graveyard, not the building. Apparently she had a successful evening."

Maria tried not to let her expression betray her. Nobody was supposed to know about that graveyard or what lay behind it. "Successful?"

Stephen started coughing. "Sorry," he said, rising. He went off to the kitchen. Maria could hear him filling a glass at the sink. He returned to his chair with a half-empty cup and lifted an eyebrow as if to say, *Well, aren't you going to say something?*

"Do you believe in ghosts?" Eric asked.

"Me?" Maria gave a nervous laugh. "Show me one, and I might."

"Jessica met one," Rachel said. "He followed her home."

"And you're going to believe something like that?"

"She isn't the only one who saw him. Sidney did, too."

Levelheaded Sidney Miller? Unlikely. "And this has to do with Mr. Madison because...?"

"Don't act dumb, Mom. You know that's who she met."

"I doubt that a ghost would have the ability to introduce himself to anyone," she said, trying but failing to picture the scenario.

"Well, he did. Sidney said he was bleeding all over his chest, and he had ligature marks around his neck."

"Don't forget his shorts," Eric said.

"Oh yeah. She said he was wearing smiley face boxers."

The memory of Rich and Joanna and the others dragging the sorry soul out into the woods rose like a corpse from her grave of buried memories. He had looked so frightened when they uncovered his head—so *ridiculous*—that she had almost laughed at the sight of him. Rachel was right. He had indeed worn boxer shorts like those she described, and there was no way she could have known unless someone present at his execution had told her.

She became aware that everyone was staring at her, waiting. Her face grew warm.

"Well?" Rachel said.

It was an effort to keep her voice at an even tone. "Well, what?"

Her daughter shrugged. "You're the one who wanted to know how we knew about him. So, what do you have to say? Does any of this sound familiar to you?"

"Rachel," Stephen said in a warning voice. "Let it go."

"I'm not going to let it go. Apparently Jerry is still a bit upset about what happened to him, and—"

"Upset?" Maria blurted, automatically rising from her seat as she did so. "He's *upset*? Do you even realize what he *did*?"

"You be quiet." Stephen said. He looked at Rachel and Eric. "Take my advice and stop right now. Nothing good's going to come about if you dig deeper into this."

Rachel pursed her lips. "What, are you afraid we'll turn you in for what you did to the guy?"

Just how much did Rachel know? "You wouldn't do that to your own parents," Maria said, sitting back down when the room began to lurch like a funhouse ride. Nightmares of going to prison had plagued her ever since that terrible night. Incarceration was, in her opinion, a worse fate than death.

"That's not our decision to make. You could turn yourselves in, plead guilty, and get a lesser sentence or something. But that's not what we're worried about."

"We think Jerry's going to try to hurt you for what you did to him," Eric said.

The clock ticking over the fireplace mantle sounded as loud as exploding shotgun shells.

J.S. BAILEY

Esteban spoke up for the first time since Maria had ordered everyone to gather in the living room. "No offense to any of you," he said, "but the guy's dead. Saw it happen with my own eyes."

"Shut up!" Sharon snapped. Her cheeks turned red.

He waved a hand to silence her. "Doesn't matter now, anyway. They obviously know what happened. But Rachel, if he really is a ghost and ran into Jessica, how would he have known who she was?"

"She probably told him her name, and he made the connection since Roman-Dell has to be the least common last name on the planet."

Something made a loud clatter outside. Eric jumped up from the couch and ran to the nearest window then relaxed a bit. "I don't see anything," he said. "Must have been one of the neighbors."

Maria cleared her throat and brushed a stray bit of hair away from her eyes. Some of what Rachel and Eric were saying still didn't make sense. "If this is all true," she said, "why didn't he come after us a long time ago?"

"Easy," Rachel said. "He didn't have a vehicle."

"And now he does?"

"Yeah. Unfortunately for Jessica."

<hr />

Wayne was filling his gas tank at a station along Alexandria Pike when he caught sight of a very familiar Toyota Camry passing by in a long line of traffic. The car was gone before he could get a better look, though he was certain he knew whose it was, because it looked like the driver had red hair. *Sidney.*

Somehow, he found he wasn't surprised.

<hr />

"Two two three Martin Court," Sidney said. "Two two three Martin Court." She had no idea where Martin Court even was, so she started turning down side streets at random. The word "court" made her think of a dead-end street; therefore, it would be unlikely for Esteban's home to be out on the main strip.

Cars lined both sides of the first street she chose. Houses were sandwiched together too close for comfort. The sky was growing darker, so porch lights had come on at some of the homes, illuminating the posted numerals of their addresses. She passed one 223 but did not stop, since she wasn't on the right road.

She sighed. This was going to take a very long time.

~∽∾∿∾∽~

The night was serene. Jessica strolled along the sidewalk, grateful that she didn't have to live in this neck of the woods where the houses were all practically built on top of one another like books competing for space on a crowded shelf. If she ever made it big doing something or another, she could save up enough money to buy one of the fancy estates hidden among the hills outside of Eleanor, and she could have her own library and office and never have to worry about seeing the neighbors' mocking brats flaunting their gift of life in front of her face because there would *be* no neighbors, only books to keep her company until the end of her days.

Where was she, anyway? Oh yeah. Cold Spring. She'd parked her car on another street and had been walking for about five minutes. No need to hurry. She'd get to where she was going soon enough.

Feeling somewhat elated as she imagined her book-filled dream home, she entered the shadows where the light from the two nearest street lamps did not quite reach. A figure stepped out in front of her. A man.

"Hey there," he said, his voice slurred. "Where d'ya think you're going?"

She halted but remained relaxed. No one could hurt her, not even intoxicated creeps.

"Just for a walk," she said in her most jovial voice. "You want to come, too?"

Evidently the discussion was already over, because the man lunged at her. She tried to dodge him by stepping to the side, but he still managed to grab her by the arm and pull her to his chest. His breath was rancid. She nearly gagged.

"Scream," he said, "and I'll slit your throat."

She giggled. "What for? Do you like to rape corpses or something? 'Cause that's just *gross*."

What are you doing? a voice in her head shouted at her. *We have work to get done!*

"But this is funny," she said aloud. "He thinks he's going to hurt me."

The man let out a grunt and forced her to turn right into the hedge-lined yard of an unlit house. He brought her to the porch and placed his free hand on the doorknob when suddenly Jerry's voice cut through the darkness. "I think you're making a terrible mistake."

The man released her, swearing, and whirled around to face the unseen speaker.

As much as she longed to stick around and see what Jerry would do to the guy, instinct told Jessica to run. If the man had acted on his sick desires (whatever they were), she wouldn't have been able to complete the task she had been assigned by the murky presence, whose name was Vindictam. She dashed through the yard, hurtled herself over a low hedge, and ran down the sidewalk until she got a painful stitch in her side. She realized that her cheeks were damp with tears of mirth.

When she slowed to a walk, she felt Jerry return to her. "You shouldn't have left your car so far away," he said. "That could have ended far worse than it did."

She nodded. "Thank you. For stopping him, I mean."

"Anytime."

"I'm glad you're here." But something in the back of her mind told her that she really wasn't glad, that she was making a terrible mistake by allowing him and the other presence to remain with her. She and Jerry had been arguing about something not long ago, but it must not have been over anything too important. Like her earlier argument with Rachel, the details were lost in the fog.

Jerry didn't reply. Maybe scaring the daylights out of the weirdo who'd grabbed her had drained too much of his energy and he needed to reload.

The street she was now on seemed very familiar. The houses here were spaced a little farther apart from one another, kind of like the way they were on Sunset Street in Eleanor. The house numbers that she could see got higher the farther she went. One fifty. One seventy-two. Two hundred. Two thirteen. Two twenty-three.

Light shined through thin drapes in the front window of the latter house. Misshapen shadows glided across the fabric like wraiths.

Anger replaced her joy in an instant. *They* were in that house. The people who had murdered not only a man but her entire childhood and interred both in unholy ground.

The murky presence prodded at her mind like a fist rapping lightly on a door. *Don't allow yourself to be seen.*

She giggled again. This was too weird, like how she knew the presence's name even though no one had told her what it was. Weirder still was the realization that Vindictam had been nearby for days, ever since…

Her lips twisted into a frown. Ever since when? Her memory span only extended back to that afternoon, and though she knew that an entire lifetime had transpired before that, her memories of it lay just beyond her grasp.

Suddenly Jessica was standing on the porch of 223, staring at the front door.

She started to push the doorbell but hesitated. *Don't allow yourself to be seen.* Maybe she was a ghost. Yes, that made sense. She was dead and had been that way for so long that all memories of her life had expired like her flesh.

And what ghost would need to ring a bell in order to be admitted inside a dwelling?

Standing out front like this made her nervous. She felt vulnerable. Exposed. Paying heed to the voice, Jessica slipped into the shadows between 223 and the next house. Her foot caught on something that felt like a watering can, and she stumbled—luckily, she didn't twist her ankle. Though, of course, since she was a ghost she didn't have to worry about breaking any body parts. What was she thinking?

The back yard was much darker than the front. Jessica felt her way along the back wall of the house until she located the rear door. Faint light spilled out from a grid of square panes. She held her face close to the glass and watched as a dark-haired female passed by inside.

She tried the knob. Locked. A curse slipped from her mouth. Breaking a pane to reach for the inner lock would make too much noise, and being heard was just as bad as being seen.

Try it again, the presence urged.

She did. Something clicked, and the knob turned.

Ever so quietly, she crept inside.

~~~

"Our Father, who art in heaven, hallowed by thy name. Thy kingdom come, thy will be done, on earth as it is in heaven…" Wayne kept praying, but it didn't seem to be working. He had been driving around for ages, he didn't know where Esteban lived, and he had no way of calling Sidney to tell her that maybe they should team up and put their heads together.

"Give us this day our daily bread, and forgive us our trespasses as we forgive those who trespass against us…"

His headlights caught a flash of dark green. He slammed on the brakes. To his right, parallel-parked along the curb, was Jessica's Taurus.

He threw the truck into reverse and backed it into an empty place behind the Taurus, his heart hammering at light speed. He climbed out as fast as his legs would allow and peered into the driver's side window of the car. No Jessica.

The house both vehicles were parked in front of was dark. The porch sagged in the middle, and a piece of particleboard had been hammered over a window. Abandoned, by the look of it. The Roman-Dells' Lexus was nowhere to be seen.

A horn honked behind him when he was about to knock on the door just in case the Reyeses really did live here. He turned. Sidney's Camry had stopped in the center of the road. The window rolled down. "Hey!" she shouted. "This isn't the right place!"

He limped over to her car and leaned against the passenger door to take some of the weight off of his legs. "She parked here."

"So? I got the address. It's 223 Martin Court. We're on Brookstone Street."

"Where's Martin Court?"

She shook her head. "Don't know. I've been looking for ages. But we can't be too far off if she ditched her car here."

"What if she hasn't gone to her uncle's house at all?" The thought had crossed his mind a couple of times in the past hour. The fact that Jessica's car was parked in front of this shack only reinforced that idea.

"There's nowhere else she could be. If her car's in this part of town, she's there, plain and simple. Right?"

He glanced back at the abandoned home. "Sure."

"Come on, you can follow me in the truck."

She was right. The only problem was that Rachel had not called to inform him of Jessica's arrival, so she either hadn't shown up yet, or Rachel had been unable to make the call.

Sidney waited until he had started the truck back up before moving forward. He checked to make sure no cars were coming and eased away from the curb. Sidney crawled along at a snail's pace and stopped at an intersection where a road came in from the left. The sign read "Oak Ct." Sidney made the turn without using her signal, and Wayne followed.

They came to a cross street a minute later. Wellington Court. A "No Outlet" sign was posted on the right, which is the way Sidney chose to turn.

He hoped she knew what she was doing.

Wellington Court led them to an Owens Drive, which had to have been a dead-end street too if Wellington Court was one.

They were approaching another street on the right. The headlight beams from Sidney's car illuminated the sign for Martin Court.

Wayne took a deep breath. This was it.

CHAPTER 31

―――❠―――

The presence told Jessica that the woman who had walked past the door was named Maria. A few memories of the woman resurfaced. Maria was the one who had never loved her. The hateful one who had taken Jerry's life. The one who deserved to die.

Jessica paused in the back hall. More memories trickled into her consciousness. This was her uncle's house, and if Jessica remembered correctly, there was a closet right about…there. She found the knob and pulled the closet door open slowly so it wouldn't make a sound.

A babble of voices was conversing in the next room. That was good; they'd be too distracted to hear her if she accidentally banged into something. She stepped over some pairs of boots that were piled in the bottom of the closet and latched the door.

The space was cramped, and the only light she could see came through the crack under the door. The coats hanging above her smelled like mothballs. Hopefully there weren't any spiders shut in with her. Something tickled her arm, and she nearly screamed, but then she realized it was just a strand of her own hair that had fallen out of its ponytail.

Her sinuses began to tickle. Aunt Sharon needed to vacuum up all the dust in here.

Wait a minute. If she were a ghost, she shouldn't be breathing, and therefore she would not have the urge to sneeze. But she had to be a ghost, because she was slowly remembering what it had been like to be alive. Old friends. Family gatherings. A blonde woman in a wedding dress walking up a church aisle toward her. She could even remember dying in front of all those people in the forest. She remembered their hatred and the pain. Then the sudden cessation of feeling as spirit separated from flesh.

She remembered it all. Even the names of those conversing in the other room.

A knocking sound echoed through the house. The voices fell silent. "I'll get it," a man said. It sounded like Eric.

Seconds later, the dull thud of footsteps entered the living room. Rachel said something, and another voice spoke up. "Jessica isn't here?" It was Wayne! How had he known to come here? His presence would complicate things.

"We found her car parked on another street," said yet another voice. Sidney. "We figured she must have walked the rest of the way here."

"Why wouldn't she have parked out front?" asked Esteban. "There's usually enough room."

"She might not have wanted you to know she was coming."

"And what, does she think she's going to get in here without anyone noticing?"

The answer was drowned out by footsteps that passed by Jessica's hiding place. "What are you two doing here?" Maria asked.

"Trying to find your daughter," Wayne said. "She left her car down the street."

"You mean she's outside in the dark somewhere?"

"We don't know. We were hoping she'd be here."

"She hasn't been here at all."

"Then she should be here very soon."

"Wouldn't you have passed her if she were walking here?"

Silence.

"Then where in the world is she?" asked Stephen.

"We don't know!" Sidney said. "Hiding?"

"Why would she be hiding?"

"Haven't any of you been listening? She doesn't want anyone to know she's coming."

"This is ridiculous. You make her sound like a criminal."

Jessica grew restless while she listened. Judging from the sound of things, she would have to wait a very long time for everyone to go to bed so she could get to Maria alone.

In the meantime, though, she could rest. She pulled her hands inside of her sweatshirt sleeves, drew her knees to her chest, and closed her eyes. She was bound to have a long night ahead of her. Even ghosts needed as much sleep as they could get.

<hr />

Wayne considered calling the police. There was no reason for Jessica to have been gone this long. If she had decided to walk all the way from her car to her uncle's house, there was no telling what could have happened to her. Someone could have nabbed her. She could have gotten lost. She could have returned to her car and driven back to Eleanor, in which case she wouldn't truly be missing at all. Besides, it was far too soon to file a missing persons report. Calling the police now would accomplish nothing.

For dinner Sharon Reyes microwaved everyone leftovers from lunch, and they all picked over their food with little appetite. Now everyone was in bed. Sidney was slouched over in a recliner, snoring lightly. Every once in a while she twitched as if being pursued by a phantom in a dream.

Wayne looked out the front window at the deserted street. Empty vehicles lined the road like a frozen funeral procession. Maybe Jessica really had gotten back to her car. She could be sitting on the couch at home watching television, wondering where in the blazes everyone had gone.

That was wishful thinking at its finest. It still wouldn't hurt to check for Jessica's car. It would take him five minutes to drive to the place where she had parked and five minutes to drive back if her car was indeed still there. He could return even sooner if he broke a few speed limits. Nothing wrong with leaving Sidney and the others alone for that length of time.

He removed the truck keys from his pocket and went outside.

~~~

Jessica opened her eyes. She had fallen asleep, and since her cell phone still needed to be recharged, she had no way to determine how long her siesta had lasted unless she snuck out of the closet to find a clock. She didn't know if it was midnight or three in the morning. Either way, she wasn't going to be running into too many people at this time of night.

The sliver of light at the bottom of the door was gone. She listened, hearing nothing but the sounds of her own breathing and the muted hum of vehicles speeding along on some other road. The house itself was quiet—not even the walls or floor creaked.

She rose and felt for the knob. Turned it. Stuck her head out into the hall. The silence continued without interruption, which meant that everyone was sound asleep. Good. Now she could get to Maria without anyone seeing her.

Esteban and Sharon's twins, Tina and Henry, were freshmen at Ohio State University in Columbus. Neither of them had come to the family reunion, so their bedrooms had likely been allotted to the Roman-Dells and Rachel and Eric for the weekend.

She tiptoed out into the kitchen, where the glow of a night-light bulb provided minimal illumination. She set her purse on the table and withdrew a roll of duct tape from the larger compartment where she kept her wallet. She had no memory of purchasing the tape, and the more she strained to recall when and where she acquired it, the more the Presence convinced her that such questions were immaterial. Forget the past. Focus on *now*. Seize the moment, and don't look back.

She put the roll around her wrist like a bracelet and left her purse behind, having no further use for it. What she *did* need were the keys to the Lexus. Maria had probably left her purse around here somewhere unless she'd taken it to the bedroom. She should check for it downstairs first, just in case.

A fraction of light from the kitchen nightlight splayed across two of the living room walls. An inert form lay in one of the chairs. Sidney? Of course. She and Wayne would have no reason to leave until they found her. Wayne must have gone to bed in one of the guest bedrooms, because there was no sign of him here on the first floor.

She let her eyes adjust to the dimness for a few moments. Sidney's purse sat on its side next to the chair. Jessica could swipe Sidney's Camry instead, if that's the vehicle they had brought.

Just to be sure, she went over to the window and parted the drapes. A street lamp shined above the cars outside: a Jeep Cherokee, a Lexus, a Nissan Altima, and yes, the Camry.

Sidney murmured something in her sleep and changed positions.

Jessica reached for the purse. Picked it up.

Sidney remained asleep.

The keys were in an outer pocket. Jessica transferred them to the pocket of her jeans and returned the purse to where she had found it.

She crossed back through the kitchen to the staircase that led to the second floor, where the house's three bedrooms were located. Some of the steps creaked as she climbed. She couldn't help that. She had faith that the Presence would keep everyone asleep for as long as was necessary.

The knob on the first bedroom door did not turn. Locked, from the inside. The occupants must have been paranoid. Poor things. Jessica felt herself grin.

Help me, she prayed.

The knob emitted a soft click. She turned it again and pulled the door open with ease.

Like fish in a barrel.

Darkness cloaked the room so well that she could not see who slept there. However, the exhalations of the pair huddled in the bed did not sound like Maria or Stephen.

She ducked out of the room but left the door ajar in case she was mistaken and needed to return. She continued to the next room where, surprisingly, the door had not been locked. The atmosphere in this room was markedly different than that of the room preceding it. The faint smells of tears and sweat passed through Jessica's sinuses for a moment and were gone almost as soon as she detected them.

She pulled the roll of duct tape off of her wrist and crept closer to the bed with the silence of a feline stalking a rodent. One of the figures on the bed let out a brief high-pitched squeal that made her tense and nearly drop the tape before she realized it was only a half-formed syllable uttered in the obliviousness of slumber. She inhaled deeply, held her breath for a count of three, and exhaled slowly through her nose. Calm. She was calm and would remain that way.

Stephen Roman-Dell was sleeping on the side of the bed closest to the door. She knew it was him, because her eyes had adjusted so well to the dark that for a second she forgot that it was night. One of his hands reached up and scratched at his right sideburn before lowering itself back to the blanket.

She hadn't thought about how difficult it would be to deal with the two of them at once. Stephen was bigger than Jessica and could easily pin her to the ground if he woke up while she was taking care of Maria. She could not permit him to spoil her entire task, because this was the only chance she would ever have to bestow on Maria what the woman deserved. Vindictam told her so.

Jessica's heart began to flutter. She had an idea. A very, very good idea.

~~∽∾∾∾∾∾~~

Jessica's car *was* still in front of the dilapidated house on Brookstone Street. Not good. Wayne executed a perfect three-point turn in the middle of the road and zipped toward 223 Martin Court once more, begging all of the angels and saints to pray with him for Jessica's safety, and begging God to please listen.

~∞∞∞~

Jessica had to immobilize Stephen so he wouldn't try to stop her from extracting Maria from the room. The trick was to do it without awakening the rest of the household.

She tore a strip of tape off the roll. The sound of that alone could have awakened the dead, but neither Roman-Dell stirred.

The floor creaked as she leaned over Stephen's side of the bed. *Please don't wake up.*

She secured the tape over his mouth, tore another piece from the roll, and walked to Maria's side of the bed. *And the same goes for you.*

Now neither of them would be able to speak, though nothing would stop them from screaming wordlessly into the tape.

To execute the next step of the plan, she needed something heavy. The lamp on the bedside table would make too much noise if the bulb or base shattered on impact. A suitcase, perhaps? Perfect.

She lifted a boxy piece of luggage from the floor. It might have weighed ten pounds—probably not enough to kill.

She held it high above her so it would hit her target with maximum force, and smashed the suitcase down on the sleeping man's head.

~∞∞∞~

Maria was jolted awake when something slammed into the bed beside her. She leapt up and stumbled. Her legs caught in the blanket as if it were a snare.

Whumpf. The entire bed shook. In the dimness she could see a figure hefting a large object over her husband's head.

She tried to scream, but her mouth would not open. She slapped her hand to her face and felt something smooth and rectangular where her lips should have been.

Whumpf. Moaning as loudly as she could, she lunged toward the attacker and only succeeded in getting knocked backward by a blow to the head. Stars danced before her eyes, and for a fraction of a second she couldn't remember where she was and wondered if this might be a bad dream.

Cold fingers clamped around her arm suddenly. She was yanked to her feet, and she almost fell again as she was pulled toward the door. "We're going on a little trip," the attacker said.

Maria's blood turned to ice. The voice belonged to Jessica, but the person who had the death grip on her arm had to have been ten times stronger. Maria tried to pry the fingers off of her with her free hand. They wouldn't budge.

The pair started down the stairs when one of the other bedroom doors banged open.

"What's going on?" Esteban.

Rachel's voice joined in. "Who's that?"

"It looked like Jessica and your mom!"

"Mom! Dad! Where are you?"

"Someone stop them!"

"Where's Stephen? Wayne?"

Maria hooked her foot around a chair as Jessica pulled her through the kitchen. She managed to drag it for a few feet until it caught the side of the refrigerator and jolted the unit so hard that some of the cereal boxes sitting on it toppled over. She had to let go or her ankle would have snapped as Jessica dragged her along.

Now they were in the living room heading for the door. A form leapt out of the chair. Sidney. "Holy crap! Hey! Stop!"

Someone upstairs let out a horrific scream.

Jessica acted as if she hadn't heard a thing. She threw open the door, pulled Maria toward a Camry parked outside, and grabbed out a set of keys.

"Jessica!" Esteban was right on their heels. "Let go of her!"

Jessica suddenly put herself between him and Maria, unfortunately without loosening her viselike grip on Maria's arm. Esteban stepped toward her with his arms at his sides. "Jess. Snap out of this. Please."

Jessica brought her fist back and punched him squarely in the nose. He staggered backward, swearing, covering his face with his hands.

She shoved Maria into the car with the strength of a body-builder and dashed around to the driver's side. Maria hastily tried the handle but for some reason couldn't get the door to open. Esteban made a move to assist her, but Jessica was already starting the engine. They tore off down the road so fast that Maria was thrown backward into the upholstery from the force of acceleration.

Tears blurred her vision as houses swept by them. It looked like the mother/daughter bonding that Maria had been putting off for so many years was going to happen at last.

CHAPTER 32

S idney's car squealed past him the moment Wayne turned onto Martin Court, only Sidney wasn't the one driving.

His heart plummeted. He had been a fool to leave, and now it was too late.

Up ahead, people poured out of the Reyes house into the street. Two ran in his direction—Sidney and Eric.

He slammed on the brakes and lowered the window when he pulled up beside them.

Sidney started talking at him before he had the chance to open his mouth. "Where in the blazes were you? She just dragged Maria out of here like she was a rag doll and took off in my car!"

Esteban jogged up to the truck. Blood trickled from his swelling nose. "Stephen's in bad shape. We've got to get him to the hospital."

Wayne's heart sank a few more notches. None of this might have happened if he'd stayed behind like he was supposed to. "Did anyone call an ambulance?"

"Not yet. It just happened a minute ago."

Sidney and Eric clambered into the truck cab, squashing him in tighter than a vacuum-packed hunk of meat.

"Let's get out of here," Sidney said.

Wayne nodded. "Do what you have to do," he said to Esteban. "Just don't call the police."

Esteban gave a humorless laugh. "You think the neighbors haven't heard the commotion out here? This place is going to be crawling with cops in no time."

He prayed that Jessica's uncle was mistaken in his premonitions. "We'll find them," Wayne said, certain there was only one place where the pair could be headed. He lifted a hand in a farewell wave and turned the truck around.

"Do you know where they're going?" Eric asked as they left Martin Court behind. He was wearing plaid pajama pants, a white muscle shirt, and no shoes. Wayne wished the younger man had stayed behind, because he'd be more of a hindrance than help without anything on his feet.

"I think so," he said, focusing all of his attention on the road.

"What are we going to do when we catch them?"

"Get Maria away from Jessica."

"And then?"

Wayne gritted his teeth. Thinking ahead that far wasn't going to help curb his anxiety. "Use your imagination."

"Already did. I didn't like what I imagined."

"Are you going to keep on like this," Wayne said in a controlled tone, "or are you going to be quiet so I can think?"

Eric shifted in his seat. "Sorry. I just wanted to help. I mean, she's my mother-in-law."

"How are you going to help without any shoes on? The ground's going to be a little rough where we're headed."

"Where's that?"

"The graveyard!" Sidney exclaimed. Then her face fell. "Eric, Jessica's probably taking Maria into the woods where Jerry died. You'll cut your feet to ribbons."

Eric swore. "Do we have a flashlight?"

"There's one in the glove box," Wayne said, keeping his eyes on the cars in front of him. He hung a right onto Alexandria Pike, which would meet up with the AA Highway in just a few miles. "Check and see if it works."

Eric did as he was told. "The beam's kind of weak. Maybe we should stop somewhere and get batteries."

Wayne shook his head. "Not enough time." The Camry was little more than a speck on the road ahead of them and was growing smaller by the second.

Sidney craned her neck to see over the sparse traffic. "I think I see them. Dang, she's going fast. I'll kill her if she wrecks my car."

A police cruiser with lights flashing turned out of a parking lot and sped down Alexandria Pike in the direction from which they had just come. That couldn't be good.

"What if they send Jessica to jail?" Sidney asked in a small voice. "Isn't kidnapping a felony?"

"Not to mention assault," said Eric.

"Well," Wayne said as he changed lanes to get around a slow-moving semi, "she could plead not guilty by reason of insanity. She can't know what she's doing, and if she does, there probably isn't a way for her to stop it."

"But she isn't insane," Sidney said. "She's possessed."

"Tell that to a jury, and they'll think *you're* the one who's insane."

"This sucks."

"Tell me about it."

"What if she pleads guilty?"

"Then she might get a lesser sentence."

Sidney's voice thickened from her tears. "Then there's no way this can end well. The only way she won't end up going to jail is if—"

"She dies," Wayne said. "Don't remind me."

Maria considered jumping from the car if they came to a stop. Since the door handle obviously didn't work from the inside, she could try smashing the window with something, reaching her arm through the hole, and opening the door with the outer handle.

Problem was, the only thing she could have used to break the glass was a souvenir baseball bat that Jessica had removed from the passenger floor mat and tucked beside her out of Maria's reach.

She didn't want to think about what Jessica planned on doing with it.

Instead, Maria worked at the edges of the tape on her mouth and managed to peel it off without removing any skin. "Jessica, please—"

"I know what you're thinking," Jessica said, cutting her off. "You want to run away. Go ahead and try it. You won't get very far."

It didn't take a psychic to figure out Maria's intentions, but Jessica's statement still unnerved her. The girl's voice was more frigid than an arctic wasteland, and while the timbre was undoubtedly that of her daughter, her word choice and phrasing belonged to someone else. Someone she had tried to forget long ago.

"I'll have to tie you up, you know," Jessica continued. "I admit this isn't quite like what you did to me, but unlike you, I don't have a network of soulless heathens to turn to for help."

"Where is my daughter?"

Jessica shrugged. "She's here just as much as I am. She sends her regards."

"Why isn't she stopping you?"

The corner of Jessica's mouth turned up in a sardonic smile. "Why should she? She doesn't care anything about you. She begged for your attention. Your approval. Your *love*. And what did you do? You ignored her. Too bad you didn't do the same to me."

"I'm sorry."

"What are you sorry for? Killing me, or the fact that you're about to meet the same end?"

Good question. "You deserved what we did to you."

"I don't deny that."

"But if I could take it all back..."

"Oh, don't get all emotional on me. What's done is done. But if you'd waited, one far greater than you would have taken care of me eventually. You might have forgotten that none of us leave this world alive." They passed beneath a street lamp, and Maria could see that the smile had not left Jessica's face. "Not even Christ could do it. I could have been struck dead in a car accident. Maybe cancer would have done me in. But I'll never know what *would* have happened, thanks to you."

"And thanks to you, my baby girl is gone!"

Jessica snorted. "She's in a more beautiful place than you'll ever see." Jessica's expression changed. "You know I didn't want to do it. I loved children. Did you know that my baby and Sarah would have been the same age? They might have been friends. Maybe they'd have fallen in love, gotten married, and had children of their own by now. We could have been grandparents together, but we'll never know, will we?"

"Your baby?" She wasn't sure what she (he?) was talking about. The Jerry Madison she had known did not have children.

"Yes. The one Abigail robbed from me. You know about it. She was over seven months along when she finally decided that she didn't want it."

Oh. *That* baby.

"It's funny," Jessica was saying, "how people view the death of a fetus and the death of an infant or a toddler or any other child so differently, when it's really all the same thing. A heart stops beating. A brain ceases to function. A soul leaves the body. You'd think that if it's okay to kill a human being inside the womb, then it should be perfectly legal to kill humans who have already been born."

Maria didn't say anything. There was nothing *to* say.

"You might say," Jessica went on, "that I was exercising my right to *choose*."

This had gone too far. "You're sick if you think that what Abigail did and what you did are anything alike! You murdered four children! Destroyed their families! Do you know what happened to them? The Walshes got a divorce. Patrick started drinking and got his license revoked for having too many DUIs. Meredith Scott overdosed on heroin and died in the fall of eighty-six. She was only twenty-nine years old and pregnant with another child at the time. My own father died of a heart attack the next spring because he couldn't handle the stress of it all. You'd better be proud of what you did, because you sure did a lot."

Jessica's voice became solemn. "I told you that I didn't want to do it."

"So you're saying that somebody made you do it?"

She shivered. "Dominoes."

"What?"

"Abigail pushed the first one. And…and…it was the sixth anniversary of the due date. When I did it. When I had to do it."

They were driving down a tree-lined road in the middle of nowhere, the lights of Cold Spring now miles behind them. A sign read, "Iron Springs: 2 mi."

The car turned right onto a road heading south.

Oh no. Oh, no, no, no. Not here. Not this place. She'd vowed never again to come here. Too many memories. Nightmares. Bad. Very bad.

She had to get out of the car if it was the last thing she ever did. She tried the handle a second time. The door remained closed.

Her heart thudded against her rib cage, and her skin was slick with her own sweat.

"Don't be scared, Maria. The pain doesn't last."

But Maria didn't plan on sticking around for the pain. She just nodded. "I'm sure it doesn't."

"The best part is when it stops. When everything stops. *Bliss.*"

A sign in the distance drew nearer. The Camry slowed. This was it.

"Uh…Jerry?" It felt stupid calling her own daughter by that name. "Are you saying there's, well, no heaven? No hell?"

"Oh, there's a hell, all right."

They were driving down a lane. It had been gravel back then, but now it was paved like the road. Shadows danced out of their way as the headlights cut through the darkness.

The parking lot and church came into view.

More memories flooded back to her. She, Stephen, and some others had arrived here early to meet the Zimmermans in the woods. Rich and Joanna had assured them that their domain was so distant from prying neighbors that it was unlikely for them to be caught. They had done other "ceremonies" there before, they said. Neither Zimmerman would elaborate on that last point. Maria had had the sinking feeling that she was selling her soul to some darker power, but if that's what it took to numb the pain of losing Sarah, she was willing to do it.

Her father, Andrés, had been beside himself. Shouting. She feared that someone would hear him. Nobody did.

Jessica put the car in park and killed the engine. She picked up the roll of tape. "Give me your hands."

Maria valued her life better than to do that. She lunged for the baseball bat, grabbed onto the handle, and busted out the window in a single movement. Glass cascaded onto the ground outside. Figuring that the outer handle wouldn't work, either, she simply clambered through the now-empty window frame and tried not to step on any of the shards as she ran.

Jerry was not so smart after all.

Or maybe Maria was the stupid one. She ran toward the exit, but since she had been literally dragged from bed, she wore no shoes. Pebbles and bits of who-knew-what lying on the pavement cut into her feet. Pain forced her to slow her pace.

Jessica let out a startled whoop behind her. Maria knew she should see if her daughter was okay, but it could have been a ruse to make her falter so she could be more easily captured.

A man materialized in the center of the lane. The light from a mercury vapor lamp allowed her to see that he was wearing yellow boxer shorts. Blood dripped from the fatal wounds she had carved into his body. It pooled on the pavement at his feet. Through the blood that streamed from his broken nose, she could tell he was grinning.

She screamed, and the world went dark.

~~∽∾≪∽∽~~

"It's not much farther," Wayne said to his passengers.

Sidney had the shakes. No matter how hard she tried to hold still, her whole body continued to tremble as if she were caught in a nine-point earthquake. To say she was scared would have been an understatement. She was flat-out *terrified*.

They were driving down a tunnel of trees straight into hell itself. Even an agnostic could believe that. Well, maybe she wasn't much of an agnostic anymore. She didn't know what she was. She was just Sidney Miller, age nineteen, part-time student and veteran gas station clerk.

Who really, *really* wanted her mom.

As a child, Marjorie had always made her feel secure. Now Sidney would have to learn to cope with the terrors that life threw at her without anyone's help but her own and possibly that of the God who may or may not exist.

Eric shifted his weight and unintentionally brushed against her. She jumped. She'd have to learn to control her timidity, too.

The truck was slowing down. A sign sat on the side of the road: "Iron Springs United Methodist Church."

They turned.

~~∽∾≪∽∽~~

Jessica was confused. Her thoughts tumbled and turned like images inside a kaleidoscope, always changing before she could fully grasp what she had just seen and heard. She was peeling potatoes in Wayne's kitchen. Arguing with her mother in front of relatives. Picking over lunch. Peeling potatoes again. Eating something from Taco Bell in the car. Arguing with her mother. Arguing with Rachel. Talking to Jerry. A man grabbing her. Hiding in a closet. Driving. With her mother. In a car that wasn't hers.

Something was in her head. Like a splinter that got wedged so far up under a fingernail that she couldn't get it out. It wouldn't leave. Sometimes it let her take partial control of her senses. Memories. It needed her memories to know what to do.

And it wasn't Jerry. He was trapped here, too. He had invited it. Or maybe it had lured him in. It was all so puzzling. The thing was using them. It didn't want them to know which thoughts were their own. It wanted them to think the three of them were one.

Jessica's mouth was moving. She didn't know what it was saying anymore. Words were meaningless sounds that echoed dumbly in her eardrums.

She tried to pray. Her mind drew a blank. What was prayer?

They were in a familiar place. They had all been here before. Brick church. Chain-link fence. Headstones.

Her mouth moved again. The woman with her smashed a window and fled.

Suddenly Jessica was outside. Her thoughts cleared long enough for her to see her mother running back toward the road.

"Mom!" she tried to scream, but something constricted her throat before she could get the whole word out.

A humanlike thing appeared in the lane on the other side of Maria. Yellow shorts. Lots of blood. Must be what Sidney saw in the bedroom. It was Jerry, but it wasn't Jerry, because he was still in her head.

Ahead of her, Maria crumpled in a dead faint.

Jessica's legs were propelled forward. The ghostly image vanished as soon as she reached her mother's side.

Anger flooded her mind. *Murderer.*

A roll of duct tape was in her hands. Maria didn't stir. That simplified things. Jessica bound the woman's wrists and ankles without any trouble.

She paused to scratch an ear. What had she just been thinking about? She couldn't remember anymore. If it was important, she'd remember it later.

But for now, she had work to do.

~∞∞∞~

Jessica had parked the Camry at an odd angle without giving any regard to the painted lines demarcating the parking spaces.

Wayne drew the truck up beside the vacant car, noting that the Camry's passenger window had been busted out and lay in a thousand pieces on the blacktop. He climbed out of the truck and cupped his hand over his ear to try to determine how far ahead of them Jessica and Maria were. He could hear nothing indicating their presence.

Eric stood beside him, shivering. "Now what?"

Wayne nodded toward the graveyard. "We go that way."

Behind him, Sidney swore. "I can't believe I left my bat in the car. Look what they did to my window!"

"Yeah, and I can't believe I took my holy water out of my truck when I got home from the reunion today."

"A bat can kick holy water's butt any day."

He didn't bother replying. They possessed neither bat nor water, so it was irrelevant which was more effective.

Eric set off down the graveyard path at what seemed like a hundred miles an hour. Wayne wondered how the soles of his feet were handling the gravel. Sidney started jogging to keep up but stopped when she seemed to realize they were leaving him in the dust. "Hey, wait up for Wayne."

The younger man paused and glanced back over his shoulder. "Sorry."

Wayne caught up with them in a dozen strides. "We all walk *together*," he said, "seeing as we have only one flashlight."

"So you've been here before?" Eric asked, slowing his pace to match Wayne's but still managing to pull ahead of him by a few feet.

"Yeah, yesterday. Jessica wanted me to go grave digging with her."

"You're kidding."

"Well, not around these graves. The one they stuck our friend in."

"You find anything?"

"Yeah. Jerry." He wove his way through a cluster of knee-high granite headstones when they left the gravel path and almost fell over a smaller marker lying flat on the ground that he didn't see until the last moment. "Part of him, anyway. He was in a garbage bag."

Wayne's chest tightened at the memory of the fleshless skull staring up at them in a silent plea. He'd never thought that seeing a skeleton would have such an effect on him since he'd seen much worse. Hopefully he would never have to look at one again—or any dead person, for that matter. They were too much of a reminder of his own mortality. He had never been punished for what he did to his mother. Dying would likely remedy that.

"What did you do with him?"

His thoughts were whisked back to the present. "Hmm?"

"With Jerry," Eric said. "What did you do with his body?"

"Oh. We left him there. We covered him back up so no one else would find him."

"What was the point of digging him up?"

"Good question."

"Maybe we should be quiet," Sidney said as she stepped over a mossy log. "Jessica might hear us and take her mom somewhere else."

As loud as they had been so far, it didn't matter if they continued to talk or not, because chances were that Jessica had already heard them. "Just keep your eyes peeled."

A hush fell over their little group with a swiftness that made Wayne uneasy the moment they entered the forest. The darkness transformed the forest into a far more alien and sinister place than it had been the day before. It didn't help that the branches closing in around them reminded him of grasping arms reaching out to capture them like bugs in a Venus flytrap. He recoiled and almost screamed when he walked face-first into an invisible silky substance that had to have been a spider web stretched between two branches.

"You all right?" Sidney whispered.

He had stopped to clear the offending web from his skin. "Yeah. I'm fine." But now his hands were shaking, and they wouldn't stop.

"I don't see any lights out here," Eric said. "She can't have come out here without being able to see anything."

A sudden spark lit up the darkness ahead of them and to the left.

"You were saying?" Wayne said. He altered his course to head toward the distant light, feeling yet another spider web brush across his face. Though he'd have preferred to face a firing squad than have an arachnid crawling over his nose, he chose to ignore it. Jessica and Maria needed him, and if something as silly as a spider prevented him from saving their lives, he would never forgive himself.

Up ahead, the light flickered. He had no idea what was causing it. He did have an idea where it would lead.

<hr />

Maria came to but did not open her eyes for fear of what she might see. Through her eyelids came a flickering orange glow. The sudden *pop* of a burning stick made her twitch.

She tried to move but found that her arms were pinned behind her and growing increasingly numb from the unnatural position. Her legs were bound at the knees and ankles but weren't tied to anything else, so she was able to draw them closer to her chest to keep warm.

"How are you feeling?"

Her eyes flew open. Jessica sat Indian-style on the ground a few feet in front of her. Her hands were folded in her lap. The baseball bat lay in the dirt at her right hip.

Maria glanced down at herself. Tape was wound around her middle too many times for her to count. She twisted her neck around and saw that she had been tied to a sapling bare of leaves. The ground she sat on was soft and looked as though it had been recently disturbed.

A small pile of wood burning nearby cast a fluid light over the forest. She must have been out cold for longer than she thought if Jessica had the time to start the blaze.

Maria licked her lips. They were chapped, and she was badly in need of a drink. At least Jessica hadn't put tape over her mouth again. "Do you really expect me to answer that?"

"But I want to *know*."

"You don't need to know."

Jessica laughed in a manner most unlike the daughter Maria barely knew. "I'll find out anyway, won't I?"

"Leave my daughter alone."

"Jessica's fine. I don't have any reason to hurt *her*."

"I don't believe you."

"Then don't."

If Jessica were still inside her head somewhere, maybe she'd be able to hear what was going on and put an end to this. "Jessica, can you hear me? Make him stop!"

Jessica exhaled in a drawn-out sigh. "I find it interesting how someone tried to strangle me that night, and you made them stop. I've wondered about that for years and never was able to figure it out. What was going through your head? Why couldn't you have let me go quickly?"

"I…" Her voice faltered. She had brought the knife with her to Jerry's execution without giving it much thought. When Rich jerked the cord around Jerry's neck, she knew it was wrong. Rich was no part of it. She needed to end it herself and had started in with the knife before she even realized what she was doing. It had both revolted and thrilled her.

And it had ruined her.

"It seemed like a good idea at the time," she said. It was true enough.

This seemed to amuse the spirit residing within her daughter. "Ideas always do, don't they?"

"Are you going to do the same thing to me?"

"I would." Jessica's eyes sparkled. "But I don't have a knife with me. I do have a handy fire. Did you notice all the kindling I stacked behind you?"

Maria squirmed around and saw that yes, there really were a number of sticks piled against the sapling she'd been strapped to.

"Or I could use this," Jessica said, patting the baseball bat. "Only I don't see much beauty in clubbing someone to death with a bat emblazoned with Mr. Red."

Something behind Maria crackled, and heat radiated up her back. The stack of wood had caught fire without anyone lighting it.

Fear surged through her veins. Maria strained against the tape and swung her body from side to side to try to loosen it. Maybe the climbing flames would burn through the tape and free her before it was too late.

Flames licked her fingertips. She jerked her bound hands to the side as far as her bindings would allow. "Let me go! Jessica, do something!"

"It's a painful thing, being completely at another's mercy like this, isn't it? Don't worry, though. I've heard that people being burned alive suffocate from lack of oxygen long before the flames consume them."

The back of her pajama shirt ignited. "Jessica, please! I love you!"

Jessica only laughed. White-hot pain spread across Maria's back.

CHAPTER 33

A fire burned up ahead. All the tree trunks and brambles blocking the view made it difficult to see anything else, but Wayne thought he could see two people illuminated by the realm of firelight—one sitting and one standing.

The sight relieved him, and he uttered a silent prayer of thanks. Jessica and her mother were still alive. Everything would be all right after all.

As they closed in on the pair, another fire sprang to life, and a scream cut through the night air with the sharpness of a razor.

Wayne's breath left his lungs, and his legs froze in mid-stride. "Oh, no."

Eric and Sidney broke into a run. Wayne shook off his sudden paralysis and followed. *God, help us.*

He emerged into the clearing fifteen seconds behind them.

Maria was tied to a tree. Burning. Eric frantically kicked sticks away from the woman while Sidney tried to wrestle a baseball bat out of Jessica's hands.

Wayne would have to ignore Jessica for the time being.

He knelt beside Maria and tried to pat out the flames eating through her shirt. Each time he touched her she whimpered like a wounded animal, and Wayne was afraid he might hurt her worse if he continued in that fashion.

Having removed all the wood from the base of the tree, Eric tugged at the tape that wrapped around Maria's torso and fell backward when the partly burnt bindings broke in his hands.

"I got it!" Sidney shouted. She must have gained possession of the bat.

Though Maria had been freed from the sapling, her shirt was still ablaze. "Get it off me!" she shouted.

Though it embarrassed him profusely, Wayne tugged the shirt off over her head and tossed it aside. He stamped out the remainder of the flames, which was kind of pointless since there was no way she'd ever be wearing the shirt again. It did keep him from having to look at her.

"Here," he heard Eric say. "Put this on."

Maria coughed and murmured something in reply. Sensing it was safe to look, Wayne saw that the woman now wore Eric's undershirt while the latter attempted to undo the tape tying Maria's knees and ankles together.

"Here, let me help." Wayne pulled his truck key out of his pocket and used it to tear at the tape.

"Watch out!"

Wayne lifted his gaze just in time to receive a heavy blow to the side of his jaw. The taste of blood filled his mouth, and it felt like a couple teeth had been knocked loose. He blinked back tears.

Jessica had gotten a hold of the bat again. Wayne held up a hand to block her next blow, which struck his wrist.

Something inside his arm cracked like a snapping twig. Tears sprang into his eyes as pain radiated through his arm and hand. For a moment his eyes crossed, and it looked like there were two Jessicas swinging at him. "Stop," he tried to say, but it came out sounding more like a high-pitched whine. The bat struck his arm again. He tried to swipe the makeshift club from her with his good hand, but she was too quick and stepped to the side.

A sickening sense of déjà vu overtook him. *Mother.*

A red-haired blur flew through the air and barreled into Jessica's side, knocking her into the dirt. "Give...me...the...bat!" Sidney gasped through clenched teeth as she struggled yet again to remove the object from Jessica's grip. "Somebody help me!"

Wayne would have offered his services, but he couldn't speak. His arm had to be broken, and if it wasn't, it would be the greatest miracle since the resurrection. He tried to focus the throbbing of his jaw and wrist into a single point that could be dealt with more easily. *Please let the pain leave long enough for me to help end this.* He took in a deep breath. *Please.*

Suddenly Eric was rushing past him as he came to Sidney's aid. He pinned Jessica's arms to the ground and placed one foot on her chest while Sidney snatched the bat away from her.

"Give it back!" Jessica growled.

Sidney tossed the bat into the fire. "Oopsie." She followed Eric's example and stood on Jessica's ankles.

Even though the pain had barely subsided, Wayne struggled to his feet and stood over Jessica's prone form. She glared at him in an expression of pure loathing that broke something in his heart. He had to remind himself that this *wasn't* really Jessica, that the woman he loved was trapped inside somewhere, unable to set herself free.

"Jerry?" he queried. The act of speaking made his stomach lurch in protest. He spat out a glob of blood and wiped his face on his sleeve.

Jessica blinked. Her expression remained unchanged.

"Get out of her."

"No."

Her icy tone raised goosebumps on his arms. "None of this solves anything."

"It solves everything!"

"And just what is killing Maria going to accomplish? You'll still be dead. Ending her life won't bring you back again."

"That isn't the point." Jessica's eyes narrowed. "You didn't see what she did to me. How much she *loved* it."

"I'm sorry!" Maria yelped from where she sat.

Jessica rolled her eyes. "You hear that? She's sorry. She'll make you think she cares, but really all she's ever cared about is herself."

"That's not true!"

Wayne cut in. "You've got to let it all go. You two are both at fault, okay? How about you both forgive each other and let things be?"

"You're an idiot," Jessica said in a seething voice. "All I ever wanted was a normal life. To be happy. To love my wife, to raise a family. It's all I wanted."

"Maria doesn't have anything to do with your wife."

"Doesn't matter. She ruined me worse than Abigail ever did." Jessica's eyes seemed to blaze with an inner light. "But what does that matter to you? Your life is perfect. You live in your nice little house in a nice town with *two* attractive women—"

"One of whom is my *cousin*," Wayne retorted, his face growing warm.

"And you have a nice *job* and probably never once thought about killing yourself, because you have people who *care* about you—"

"Look—"

Suddenly Jessica leapt up, knocking both Eric and Sidney off of her. She snatched a long stick that was as big around as Wayne's thumb off the fire. Flames spread up the shaft. She held it like a javelin and flexed the muscles in her arm. She aimed it toward Maria.

～～～

The unwanted pair inside her skull let Jessica take the back seat for a while, giving her time to think. She strained with all of her might to take back control of her body. It was as if the part of her brain that directed the movement of her muscles had been disconnected from the rest of her. She tried to speak. Couldn't. Tried to move her legs so she could run. They wouldn't.

She refused to panic. That's what Vindictam would want—to make her lose hope and turn away from the One who would save her. Trouble was, it was becoming harder and harder to believe that God cared. He had let Jerry's baby die. He had let Jerry kill and be killed. He had let Marjorie succumb to cancer. He had let this *thing* overtake her with no apparent qualms.

Maybe she wasn't meant to get through this alive, either.

She could sense that Jerry lingered close by, though she could no longer tell if he was the perpetrator or the victim. He and the Presence were working together despite the fact that Jerry seemed an unwilling participant. Vindictam fed off the man's grudges, toying with his conscience to convince him that killing her mother was the only way to make things right.

Jerry, she thought, *you've got to give me a hand. I can't do this alone.*

Her request went unanswered.

This had to stop.

If she died, would Vindictam leave? Jerry had been dead already but brought it with him anyway, so her demise might accomplish nothing.

She mustered every last bit of will and began to pray as she never had before. Surely God could fulfill this final request, as there was nothing in it for herself. *Father, if it will make Vindictam leave forever and ever, take me. I mean it. Don't let it hurt anyone ever again.*

Long seconds passed. Suddenly her perspective shifted, and she was standing behind a woman holding a burning stick.

She could think and see clearly now. There were two others present whom she hadn't seen before—Sidney and Eric. They cowered beside Maria, gazing up at the stick-wielder in terror. Wayne stood off to one side, panting. Blood had smeared on his chin, and he held his left arm close to his chest as if he were afraid to move it. He lunged at the stick-wielder and pushed her out of Maria's reach with his right hand. She staggered and swiped the stick at his head. He ducked and shouted something at Sidney and Eric.

"Who—" Jessica started to say, but faltered. She saw the woman's face.

It was her own.

A greater fear than she had ever felt coursed through her then. It wasn't supposed to happen like this. If she were dead, she wouldn't be here anymore. She'd be in some glowing state of elation hanging out with her grandparents and Sarah and Marjorie and Baby Madison…

She held her hands out in front of her. They looked solid. She glanced down at her body. Jeans. Worn-out gym shoes. Sweatshirt. She flexed her fingers and toes. All seemed to be in working order, except for the fact that she couldn't feel one blessed thing. Every nerve in her body was numb.

Eric tackled her lookalike, knocking her down and flipping her onto her stomach. He and Wayne knelt on her back while Sidney wrapped duct tape around her wrists and ankles.

Jessica approached them and stared down at her squirming double. "Uh, guys?"

Wayne handed a cell phone over to Sidney. "Call 911. Have them meet us in the parking lot."

Jessica stepped in front of Wayne and waved her hand in front of his face. He didn't even blink. "Hey!" she shouted. "Quit ignoring me! I'm *here*! Not down there!"

He said something to Maria. Sidney was cursing at her phone. "How in the heck is there no reception out here?"

The Jessica lookalike was still raving. "It's all Abigail's fault! I've got to kill her. I want to gouge her eyes out and cut that gloating smile right off her face and make her hurt like she hurt me and our baby!"

"Dude, can you be quiet for one minute?" Sidney snapped, still having issues with her phone.

"I hate her! She needs to die just like Maria and Stephen and Patrick and Amy and Rich and Joanna and all the others who got away with what they did! She's got to be *punished*!"

Sidney gave Jessica's body such a hateful glare that Jessica herself retreated a few steps. "Abigail's already dead, you idiot. She died seventeen years ago." She refocused her attention on her phone. "Good *Lord*, why can't I get any reception?"

Jessica had no clue what Sidney was talking about. Evidently Jerry didn't either, because Jessica's eyebrows knit together in an expression of befuddlement. "How would you know anything about Abigail?"

"She was my mom's cousin. I never knew her, though. Died right before I turned three."

"Sidney, don't," Wayne said. Worry lines stood out sharply on his chalk-white face. He looked as if he had aged a decade.

"She's dead? How did it happen?"

No one said anything. Sidney and Wayne exchanged glances.

"How did she die?" the lookalike repeated in a more demanding tone.

Wayne's eyes glistened behind his glasses. "We don't know if it's her," he said to Sidney. "There's no proof."

"You were the one who was totally convinced just a bit ago," Sidney said. "Remember?"

"But I just...I can't..."

Sidney turned to Jessica's tied-up body. "What was Abigail's maiden name?"

Jessica's blue-gray eyes stared up at her. "It was Thompson. Why won't you tell me how she died?"

Wayne covered his mouth with his hand and shrank back from them, letting out a choked sound like that of someone suffering indescribable despair.

Jessica herself was rendered speechless.

Sidney took a deep breath. "She was beating her son with a fireplace poker. He accidently killed her in self-defense."

The face on Jessica's body went blank. "What son?"

"It wasn't an accident." Wayne's voice was weak.

"Of course it was an accident," Sidney said. "There's no way you'd have *wanted* to—"

The color on Jessica's face deepened to an angry red. "You mean she went and had a child with someone else after what she did to me?" Her body strained even harder against the bindings. "How could she even *consider*—"

Jessica needed to evict the spirit from her flesh before the situation worsened. As much as it horrified her, she knew exactly where this conversation was heading. Jerry would be very, very angry. And he might do something very, very stupid.

"Jerry," she said, praying that he would hear her. "Let it go."

Jerry flicked Jessica's gaze briefly in her direction.

Anticipation hung in the air. Maria and Eric were wide-eyed and silent. Sidney's cheeks flushed. "As far as I know," Wayne said, "my mother was only ever with one man. My father."

Jerry blinked. "But she had an abortion. She took the money out of our account for it."

"They should have given her a refund."

"What for?"

Wayne swallowed. "Because they goofed. Didn't inject enough saline solution into her womb to properly do the job. She was supposed to go back the next day and deliver me dead, but she went into labor in the middle of the night at her parents' house, and they rushed her to the hospital, not knowing at first what she had done. I'd been burned alive for at least twelve hours, and most of my oxygen supply was cut off for that length of time. That's why I'm like this." He tapped on his leg with his good hand. "Her parents convinced her to keep me when I finally got home from the hospital after being held there for a month. They thought that she would learn to love me. And maybe she did, somewhere deep inside where I could never see."

"So you see?" Sidney said, having finally given up on her cell phone. "Your baby never died. He's right here and has been all along."

Jessica's body went slack and rolled onto its side. From her disembodied vantage point, Jessica saw a writhing black mass rise out of her body and dissipate in the air. She thought she could hear a distant inhuman scream fade and then cut short. Vindictam?

Somebody gasped. Jerry's apparition materialized no more than a foot in front of Wayne, gaping. Wayne gaped back at him.

Though she had seen the two together the other night in Wayne's kitchen, Jessica had never really compared them before. Jerry was taller by a good three inches. His face was narrower than Wayne's, and their eyes weren't the same color, so it was no wonder that Jessica had not made a connection. Wayne must have favored his long-dead mother.

Jerry reached out a hand as if wanting to touch Wayne on the cheek but quickly withdrew it. "You," he said. Then, "Oh, God, what have I done?"

Wayne's lower lip trembled. "I'm sorry. She never told me who you were. If I'd known…"

Instead of growing angrier like Jessica had expected, Jerry hung his head in shame and shrank away from the younger man.

Wayne began to look wildly around. "Where did he go? Jerry? Are you still there?"

Jessica could still see Jerry as plain as day, though it was apparent that he was now visible only to her eyes. He faced her. "Please forgive me," he said, taking a step closer to her and bringing his hands together in front of him. "Please, please forgive me."

She didn't know what to say. How could she just forgive a man who had killed four children, including a sister she had never known? "You make it sound so easy."

"Important things never are. But you've got to do it. Please."

"Do you forgive Abigail? For never telling you the truth?"

He didn't answer. His gaze drifted over to Wayne, who was kneeling beside Jessica's body checking for a pulse. "He has her face and eyes," he said. "But not the hair. Hers was golden blonde."

The lips on Jessica's body were turning blue. Eric set to work performing CPR. Jessica couldn't watch, so she turned away. If she were out here, then it was already too late. Eric wouldn't be able to do anything for her.

Sorrow filled her, yet no tears sprang to her eyes, because her physical body lay dead on the ground, unable to weep again.

"It hurts, doesn't it?" Jerry said, sensing her thoughts.

She nodded. Wayne would be inconsolable. And to think that they had joked about getting married that very morning! Only it hadn't been a joke at all. She could see it in the way he wept beside her still form, squeezing her cooling hand as if trying to pull her back from the brink of death.

"Why am I here with you?" she asked.

"As opposed to heaven?"

She nodded again. It was difficult to speak. "Yeah. That."

"You're here for the same reason that I am."

"I never killed anyone."

"God doesn't care what you did, only that you did it."

"But I don't know what I did!"

"Who knows? Maybe it's not what you did but what you didn't do."

She racked her mind in search of an answer to her dilemma. She'd been faithful for her entire life. She'd gone to church and said her prayers. She went to confession once a year and didn't eat meat on Fridays during Lent. She'd even given up microwaveable burritos this past Lent, and that was one of the most painful things she'd ever done. And in the end, it was all for nothing.

But what hadn't she done? She hadn't helped Sidney in her time of need. She hadn't tried to reconcile her relationship with her parents and instead maintained a cold distance from them.

"I guess I really don't deserve heaven," she said.

"Nobody deserves it, Jessica. Not me, not you. But that's the beauty of it all if we do make it there someday. Getting what we don't deserve."

Sidney was sobbing. Maria was saying something to her, but Jessica was hardly listening.

"Have you noticed that it's gone?" Jerry asked.

"What?"

"Think really hard about that for a minute, and you tell me."

Of course—he was talking about the Presence. "I asked God to take me if it would make the thing leave. Too bad he didn't take me very far, huh?"

Jerry's eyes widened. "You did that?"

"Yeah. I tried to make it stop by myself, but it wouldn't leave. This was the only solution I could think of." She paused. "Where did it come from?"

"Where? Who knows? I often wondered the same thing, myself—perhaps they're always out there watching; always looking for an opportunity to be let in. But I can tell you that it was with me from the moment Abigail called to tell me what she'd done. I was weak. And there are forces that love to prey on the weak. They get inside of us. They fester. They make us remember every rotten thing that's ever happened. And they make us *hate*. I could blame *it* for everything I did, but I'm the one who invited it. I'm sorry about your sister and the others. If I could take it all back…"

A sudden whoop of joy went up among those gathered around Jessica's body. "Praise God!" Sidney shouted.

Jessica could feel a breath of wind entering her lungs, and the next thing she knew, she was staring up into her friends' astonished faces. "I'm alive?" she asked, full of wonder. "How…"

"Yes," Wayne said, "you are." He made no move to untie her wrists and ankles and instead watched her with apparent trepidation.

"It's *me* now," she said, feeling her smile stretch into an immense grin. He was probably afraid that her mind was still inhabited by somebody else. "Now get this tape off of me, okay?"

"Tell me something that only Jessica would know."

She rolled her eyes. "Your name means wagon maker in some dead language. I hate to cook. I used to have a giant crush on Harrison Ford. Do you want me to go on?"

Wayne still looked skeptical. "What important thing were we talking about before we left for the family reunion this morning?" he asked.

Her cheeks heated up. "That's easy. Me becoming a housewife in a hypothetical universe."

Wayne surprised her by leaning in and planting a kiss right on her lips in front of everyone. His lips felt so warm against hers, and she felt as though she were floating off the ground. She smiled. *So this is what it's like.* She found that she wouldn't have minded if the two of them stayed like that forever, even though blood was still drying on his face and she was still bound like a prisoner.

"Don't you *ever* die on me again," Wayne said in a scolding tone when he drew back from her, but his eyes were smiling.

She took another breath, relishing the exquisite sensations of living. "But I'll have to someday, won't I?"

"Not if I can help that," he said.

It took Eric and Sidney a minute to peel off the tape, and it felt like a few layers of skin went with it, but Jessica was too happy to care.

"Now come on. Let's help your mother to the truck. She'll need to go to the hospital for those burns."

"What about your arm?" Jessica asked. Wayne still had it hugged to his chest.

"I'm pretty sure you broke it. Eric, do you think you can drive?"

Jessica's brother-in-law nodded. He was naked from the waist up, and her mother was wearing what was probably his under-shirt. "Yep. Give me your keys."

"Wait," Maria said, looking Jessica straight in the eye. Her face was white with fear. "We can't tell anyone what's happened. If someone finds out about what I did..." She closed her eyes. "I could face the death penalty."

"And you could go to prison for kidnapping and assault," Eric said to Jessica.

"Then what are we going to do?"

"I could say I fell and broke my wrist that way," Wayne said. "It's not much of a stretch for me."

"And I could tell them I tripped and fell into the fire at a campout," Maria said. "Could you vouch for me if they ask you? Please?"

They all looked at Jessica. She glanced down at her feet. For the first time in her life, part of her actually cared what happened to her mother. Maria was guilty, no doubt about that. She had murdered a man in cold blood. She *should* be punished for it.

But Maria was her mother. The woman who had birthed her. The only mother she would ever have. If convicted of murder and executed for it, Jessica would have no mother. There would be no chance of getting to know the woman or growing close to her.

She and Maria locked gazes. "I'll do that," she said. "I promise."

Maria gave her a weary smile of gratitude. "Thank you."

"Well," Wayne said, the look of barely-concealed pain return-ing to his eyes, "I suppose we should try to put out this last fire before the whole forest goes up in flames. Sidney, can you do the honors?"

"Sure." Sidney started kicking logs away from each other. Jessica scooped up handfuls of loose dirt and tossed them on the flames to suffocate them.

"How did the fires start, anyway?" Wayne asked. "You could have only been five minutes ahead of us at the most, but when we got here they looked like they'd been burning for an hour or more."

"God only knows," Jessica said, deciding it was better to keep that part to herself. "God only knows."

CHAPTER 34

Jerry watched them leave.

Jessica threw one final look over her shoulder at him and gave a pitying smile. Then she was talking to Wayne, and they were gone.

She had not forgiven him. He didn't blame her.

His mind was clear at last. For the first time in thirty years, no voices preyed on his conscience. If what Jessica said was true, that awful Presence would be gone for good—but that didn't mean that others of its kind wouldn't replace it. They could probably return at any moment and torment him just as they had before.

He sat on the ground by the remains of the larger fire and watched lazy plumes of smoke rise from the dying embers.

If only Jessica would come back. It was too bad that she had been resuscitated. For a minute he had hoped that she would be able to keep him company during his bleak existence. But now he was alone. Again.

He couldn't just keep meddling in Jessica's life. He would have to keep his distance from her so he wouldn't cause additional trouble if another Presence came to afflict him. Jessica and her loved ones didn't need any more trouble. He had given them enough already.

He thought about Abigail. For once, he felt no bitterness toward her, only emptiness.

God, please take me, he prayed. *Do whatever you need to do with me. Just don't leave me here all alone anymore.*

A sudden calm came over him. Nothing moved him onward to bliss or the inferno; he simply remained where he was, sitting unseen on the ground in a Northern Kentucky forest.

But now he had an understanding of what he needed to do.

~∾∾ᢙᢙᢙ∾∾~

St. Elizabeth Healthcare in Fort Thomas saw a glut of emergency room patients that evening. When Jessica, Sidney, and Eric led Wayne and Maria inside, Rachel and Aunt Sharon were already sitting in the waiting room and simultaneously leapt up from their respective chairs in surprise.

"We lied to the cops—"

"Are you okay—"

"What happened—"

"Dad and Uncle Esteban both have broken noses, but they're both going to be all right—"

"The campout didn't turn out so well," Jessica said as loudly as she could. "Mom tripped over a lawn chair and fell right into the bonfire, and Wayne tripped over that same chair and hurt his arm and face trying to help her up."

And when they told that same story to the on-duty staff, nobody batted an eye.

~∾∾ᢙᢙᢙ∾∾~

On Sunday morning after everyone had been patched up and sent home, they gathered in the Reyes house once again, only this time Jessica had no desire to hide in the closet. She sat on the floor next to Wayne, whose left arm was set in a blue cast that already bore six or seven get-well messages. Uncle Esteban and Aunt Sharon shared the couch with Rachel and Eric, Sidney occupied the recliner she had briefly slept in the night before, and Jessica's parents sat in two chairs from the kitchen.

Stephen Roman-Dell's right eye was purple and swollen most of the way shut. In addition to his broken nose, he had sustained a split lip and received three stitches that reminded Jessica of something you'd see on Frankenstein's monster. Maria's burns hadn't been deemed serious enough to be life threatening, so all she had to do was apply ointment a couple times a day. She had gotten off very lucky.

Though it hadn't entirely been her fault, Jessica couldn't stop apologizing. "I'm so sorry I let all this happen," she said. "I had no clue that something could take control of me like that. I'm not even sure how it happened."

"Don't work yourself up over it," her father said, wincing as the movement of speaking stretched the wound on his lip. "At least nobody died."

This statement was followed by what was possibly the most awkward silence Jessica had ever endured. Uncle Esteban coughed a few times but said nothing. Sidney started cracking her knuckles.

"All these years," Maria murmured to no one in particular, "and I never knew his son was right under my nose."

"Let's not talk about that right now," Wayne said, his face turning red. "Or ever."

Stephen shifted in his seat. "I second that."

"So," Jessica said to her parents, "are you still going home today, or are you going to stick around for a while and recuperate?" It was still uncomfortable talking to them like this, especially knowing what they had been involved in. But it would do no harm to practice.

"I already called our employer and told them we're having a family emergency," her mother said. "I said we both need to be off so we can be with our children."

A lump formed in Jessica's throat. *Their children.* "Would you really do that? Be with your children, that is?"

A single tear shined in the corner of her mother's eye. "We want to be able to know our girls better. And our sons-in-law."

"But Wayne and I aren't—"

Wayne butted in suddenly. "Jessica, will you marry me?"

It took her about a tenth of a second to make up her mind, because it felt so right. "Sure," she said. "But don't you have to have a ring in order to propose?"

"Nah," he said, grinning, "I can get you one of those later."

"See?" Maria said. "Wayne will be our son-in-law soon enough."

~~~

One Sunday afternoon in November, Jessica and Wayne returned to the Iron Springs United Methodist Church to go "metal detecting" again. They brought a shovel and a bucket. In the bottom of the bucket, Jessica had carefully concealed a bouquet of yellow and red chrysanthemums.

"Nice out here, isn't it?" Jessica said to dispel the silence. Wayne hadn't said much on the ride over, and he wasn't saying much now. His arm was still in a cast.

He nodded. "Yeah. Pretty."

They trudged through the woods and soon located Jerry's resting place. Jessica pulled the flowers out of the bucket and handed the bouquet over to Wayne. "Here. You do it."

Wayne took the bouquet from her and scanned the ground. Another rainfall had packed the dirt down since they had been here last, but it was still easy to tell that the ground had recently been dug up. "I forget exactly where he was."

Jessica squeezed his hand. His fingers were ice cold. "Does it really matter?"

He sighed. "I suppose not." He limped forward two paces and laid the bouquet down on the damp earth. He made the sign of the cross and bowed his head. "I always wondered," he said. "Mom never told me who my father was. Whenever I asked her, she'd fly into a rage, so I knew better than to pursue the issue. She never did hesitate to tell me how I came into the world, though. Maybe talking about it helped ease her guilt." He straightened and turned to face her. His eyes were red. "Even though Jerry was just as messed up as she was, I still hate the thought of him being out here. Nobody deserves to be buried in pieces like this."

"It's okay," she said. The method of one's burial was meaningless in the grand scheme of it all. The soul—not the flesh—was what counted the most. "At least you know where he is now."

He nodded. "Yeah."

They walked back to the truck. If anyone saw them and asked why they were leaving so soon, they could come up with some kind of excuse. But the parking lot was still empty. Jessica would not have to tell a lie again today.

Stephen had given Jessica the address to the Catholic church in Alexandria. They drove there next in silence.

Jessica picked the other chrysanthemum bouquet off of the floor mat as soon as Wayne killed the engine. Stephen said that the graveyard here was on the other side of the church. An asphalt path led around the side of the massive stone building into a well-kept cemetery. A few other people were strolling around looking at headstones. Since All Saints and All Souls Days had been little more than a week before, many of the other graves sported bouquets of both real and artificial flowers. The sight of the vibrant shades of red, pink, and yellow made Jessica smile. They were signs of hope in a bleak landscape.

"It's in the fourth row back," her father had said to her on the phone that morning. "Third from the left."

Again, his directions were accurate. "Look," Jessica said, angling off the path. "I see it."

They stopped in front of a white headstone that bore an engraving of an angel cradling a young child in its arms. Jessica wiped away a tear. "Sarah Elizabeth Roman-Dell," said the inscription. "March 28, 1980-June 28, 1986."

She lay down the bouquet and burst into tears.

EPILOGUE

———⟨⟨⟨⟩⟩⟩———

I t was cold in the Rodriguezes' basement, but Jessica had dressed appropriately this time, so the chill in the air did little to affect her.

Wayne sat in a chair beside her and kept glancing around him like he thought a be-sheeted specter would come swooping down at him at any moment. It was his first ghost hunt. Jessica had instructed him to ask questions, albeit friendly ones that wouldn't upset a wounded spirit. A voice recorder sat on his shaking knee.

"Hi," he said. "My name is Wayne, and this funny-looking woman sitting with me is Jessica. We want to help you, but if you want us to leave you alone, please let us know, and we'll get out of here and never come back. Deal?"

Jessica smiled. She liked his methods.

She twirled her wedding band around her finger while she listened to him talk to the alleged spirits present in the room. So much had happened since that fateful October. Tragically, Rachel suffered a miscarriage twelve weeks into her pregnancy. After several months of mourning, she and Eric conceived again. They recently found out they were having a baby girl. They planned on naming her Sarah. She was due to be born any day.

And as for Jerry, well, he never really left. Sometimes Jessica saw him when she least expected—standing in line with her at the grocery store, lurking in the kitchen while she figured out how to make dinner without catching the house on fire, and lounging on the end of the couch while she and Wayne watched television in the evenings. He never said anything to her anymore. He'd only give her a wistful smile and nod. He had even showed up at the wedding standing in the front row next to their small wedding party.

That time, he'd smiled and *winked*.

Nobody else seemed to notice him but Wayne. That was okay.

Sidney still lived with them in the little house on Sunset Street. She was planning on renting an apartment to give the newlyweds some space but hadn't yet made up her mind about which complex to move to.

Jessica had noticed that Sidney's First Communion Bible was often out of its shelf and had a bookmark stuffed between its pages. Every time Jessica saw it, the bookmark was closer to the end than it had been before. Neither of them mentioned it to the other. That was okay, too.

The mysterious pain that plagued Jessica eventually faded away. Though she never bothered to get a diagnosis, she knew it had to be from excessive tension. Her body and soul had gone through far too much that week. She prayed she would never have to go through it again.

Jessica finally found a job opening at a local bank four months ago and got hired on as a teller. It was boring work making deposits and withdrawals for people all day, but at least it was something to do. It had also helped her reconstruct The Plan. Now, instead of saving up money for school, she simply put the money into their nest egg account for a rainy day. Maybe someday she would think of something to go to school for. But for the time being, she would just enjoy life and improve her cooking skills so Wayne wouldn't be forced to make his own food every night of the week.

Besides, maybe she and Wayne would have a child, too. Being a mother was bound to be a full-time job in itself.

And speaking of mothers, Jessica had forced herself to spend more time with Maria, and Stephen, too; though at times their conversations grew awkward. She would never be able to look at either of them again without thinking about what Maria did to Jerry.

Little by little, Jessica learned how Rich and Joanna Zimmerman, the so-called Satanists, had become involved in Jerry's murder.

"I knew what they were," Maria had said. "I wanted to report them, but I had no proof other than what someone had told me. But the day that Sarah died, Joanna came over and told me what she'd seen. She said she'd help us out. Her husband was a police officer and would help cover up Jerry's disappearance if anyone came looking for him."

Jessica filled in the rest of the story on her own. She did an Internet search on the couple to see if they still lived nearby but came up with nothing. Were they dead? There was no way to know. It was probably better that way.

In the present, Wayne paused in his speech.

"Bored yet?" she asked him.

He shifted uneasily in the chair. "No."

"Nervous?"

"Maybe."

She laughed. "There's nothing to get worked up about." After all they'd been through, nothing should have been able to scare them ever again.

"I don't want any of them to sneak up on me," he said.

"Boo."

"Ha ha."

Jessica grinned. "We should probably get back on track." To the room's unseen occupants, she said, "We really do want to help you. If you're still here on earth, it means you have another chance. You don't have to suffer forever. God is waiting for you to come home to heaven where you belong."

"What about me?" said an all-too-familiar voice to her left.

Wayne swore. He picked up the flashlight he'd set beside him and shined the beam in the direction of the voice. The beam illuminated a black-clad figure sitting Indian-style on the floor.

Wayne leapt up so quickly that he started to lose his balance and held out a hand to brace himself against the wall.

The scene was so funny that Jessica couldn't help but laugh. "Wayne, cool it," she said. "It's him."

Wayne sank back into the chair, not taking his eyes off of the apparition. "What are you doing here?" he asked.

Jerry made a show of glancing around the unfinished basement. "Not much." He looked at Jessica. "Why is it that you act like you care about others in my position when you never found yourself capable of forgiving me for what I did to your family?"

His accusation startled her. "I didn't?"

"When I asked you that night in the woods, all you said was that I made forgiveness sound easy."

He was right about that. "I had just found out that you killed my sister all because you thought Abigail had killed your baby. Of course I didn't forgive you then."

"Can you forgive me now?"

That's all he wanted? "Of course I forgive you. I decided to do that ages ago." It had taken much prayerful reflection on her part, but eventually she had come to accept that Jerry was just as flawed and in need of forgiveness as any other human being— including herself. *Especially* herself.

It was one of the most difficult things she had ever done.

His eyes widened. "You do? You never said…" He shook his head in wonder and turned to Wayne. "And can you forgive me for not being there? For not tracking Abigail down and saving you?"

Wayne nodded. His knuckles on the hand gripping the flashlight were turning white.

"Say it."

"I—I forgive you. None of that was your fault, though. You didn't know I was alive, so you had no reason to track my mother down."

Jerry shook his head. "I didn't try hard enough."

"You're only human!"

"Unfortunate, isn't it?" He winked and turned back to Jessica. "Please tell your family that I forgive them for what they did to me. I hope that someday they'll be able to do the same."

"I'll let them know." She swallowed a lump in her throat and her eyes began to burn.

Jerry smiled. This time it was one of pure joy; not one tinged with sorrow. "Thank you for coming to that graveyard," he said. "You were the answer to all my prayers. I'll be waiting for you two. But for now, I have two other children to meet." His smile broadened. "Thank you, Jessica. Thank you so much for everything."

He began to fade away.

"Oh, wow," he said, his voice growing faint. Then, "You mean all *three* of you are boys?"

He was gone.

Wayne blinked a few times. His lower lip quivered, and he promptly chomped down on it to keep it from moving.

Jessica wiped her eyes with her hands. "Real men cry, you know," she said. "I've seen you do it lots of times."

"Tell one soul, and I'll dissect you with those stupid chopsticks Sidney puts in her hair."

"You couldn't catch me. Now shall we continue again, or do you think we'll keep getting interrupted by departing spirits?"

"Let's find out." He set down the flashlight and picked up the recorder. "Did you just see that, guys?" he said, addressing the room once more. "That's what we're talking about. We want you to be able to go to heaven just like my—like Jerry did. And trust me, he did some bad stuff. He wanted forgiveness for his sins.

Sure, God forgives us, but other people need to forgive us, too. If you love God, and if you want to be forgiven, just let us know. Pour your heart out and repent. We'll listen."

Jessica started to add her own advice, when suddenly someone far off in the dark began to whimper. She took the flashlight and shined it in all the corners, seeing nothing but a furnace, a water heater, and a washer and dryer.

"Please forgive me," the voice cried, growing closer. She could still see no one. "Please, please forgive me…"

AUTHOR'S NOTE

———◆◇◆———

You know the story. Girl meets boy. Boy turns out to be a supernatural creature. They fall in love against all odds. The end.

I did not want to write that story. The first thing I knew about the novel you just read is that the heroine would *not* fall in love with the supernatural entity, who in this case is a ghost. The rest of the plot came later—much, much later.

I'm a sucker for ghost stories. They're like junk food that never, ever gets old. I've watched *Ghost Hunters* more times than I can count. I've read *The Shining*. I've read *Bag of Bones*. I've read the *Odd Thomas* series and *The Haunting of Hill House*. But it wasn't enough. I wanted to write my own ghost story. So I did.

In the beginning I wanted the "scares" to be the point of the novel, but the plot soon fell flat. I realized it wasn't going to work. So I set the manuscript aside to collect dust.

Months passed. I picked up Dante Alighieri's *The Divine Comedy* for a bit of light reading (joke), and as soon as I began reading *Inferno*, the first book of Dante's work, my breath was taken away.

For those of you who may not know, *Inferno* is the story of a man's journey through hell. He is led by Virgil, his spirit guide, and they encounter many other spirits along the way. Virtually all of the spirits in hell are full of remorse for their sins and have come to accept their punishment because they know they deserved it.

Wow, I thought. *Maybe Jerry could be remorseful of his sins! Maybe he is in search of redemption!*

The idea wouldn't leave my head. I started writing again.

As I wrote, I unintentionally brought out my own inner demons to join in the fun—doubt, grudges, and so on. There have been times in my life when "bad" things have happened to me, and I got so hung up on them that I couldn't move forward. I was stuck in the past, just like Jerry was "stuck" in our own world far from heaven. My anger consumed me. I couldn't forgive those who had done me wrong. It felt good at first to hold a grudge against them, but after years I realized that I had to let it all go or I was never going to heal.

In the end, *Rage's Echo* was never about ghosts. It was never about trying to make contact with the dead. (I would advise against communicating with spirits in real life. *Rage's Echo* is, after all, a work of fiction.) What it came down to was learning to let go of our grudges. We need to forgive those who hurt us, as I was finally able to do through the grace of God. Jesus even did it while dying on the cross—"And Jesus said, 'Father, forgive them, for they know not what they do'" (Luke 23:34, American Standard Version).

Jesus expects for us to follow His example. It *isn't* easy, not by any means. But, with His grace, it can be done; and your soul shall be healed.

Peace and blessings to you all,
—J.S. Bailey, April 2013